Edward Jewitt Robinson

Tales and Poems of South India

From the Tamil

Edward Jewitt Robinson

Tales and Poems of South India
From the Tamil

ISBN/EAN: 9783744642187

Printed in Europe, USA, Canada, Australia, Japan

Cover: Foto ©Andreas Hilbeck / pixelio.de

More available books at **www.hansebooks.com**

TALES AND POEMS

OF

SOUTH INDIA.

From the Tamil.

BY

EDWARD JEWITT ROBINSON.

As certain also of your own poets have said.'—Acts xvii. 28.
One of themselves, even a prophet of their own, said.'—Titus i. 12.

LONDON:

T. WOOLMER, 2, CASTLE STREET, CITY ROAD, E.C.

AND 66, PATERNOSTER ROW, E.C.

1885.

PREFACE.

———o———

In this volume is presented, with much diffidence, an improved and enlarged edition of *Tamil Wisdom*, which was published in 1873. A returned missionary thinks it not impossible thus to serve indirectly the great cause which he may seem to have deserted, and at the same time assist young English gentlemen entering the employment of the Government in India. The youthful evangelist, magistrate, or politician will welcome any revelation of the mental condition and habits of the people whom he is called to benefit. The following tales and poems are not merely entertaining; they are of serious importance, because always in the thoughts and on the lips of the natives of South India and North Ceylon.

Readers who may be surprised to meet with not a little sacred truth in the heathen writings here unfolded, will remember that wisdom, like the sun, has travelled from the East. A comparison of Tamil sayings with the precepts and proverbs of Holy Writ would tend to show that the fountain of the water of life has supplied the world, in streams coloured by the ages and countries through which they have flowed.

It is interesting to find in Tamil a few of the fables commonly ascribed to Æsop. To those acquainted with the treasures which the language contains, it may seem strange that *Panjatanthirakkathay, Stories of Five Devices,* has not been drawn upon for this anthology. The work in its Tamil form is so considerable as to merit separate attention ; but it is supposed to be of Sanscrit origin. It appears to have been the source whence Bidpai or Pilpai derived his fables. For centuries it has been translated, more or less closely and fully, not only into all the Indian and other Eastern languages, but into most of the tongues of Christendom. Perhaps it is better known to Europeans in the selection from it entitled, *Hitopadēsa, Good Doctrine.*

The tales of India are originally concise. How capable they are of amplification and adornment may be seen in Miss Frere's *Old Deccan Days,* "Alfred Crowquill's" *Gooroo Simple,* and articles in periodical literature. The stories translated in the present volume are without mixture or dilution.

The writer gladly acknowledges his indebtedness to the following works :—

The Cural. By Mr. Ellis. Madras.

The Cural. By the Rev. W. H. Drew. Madras, 1840 and 1852.

Latin Translation of the Kural. By Dr. Graul. Leipzig, 1865.

Atthi-soodi. By the Rev. J. Sugden, B.A. Bangalore, 1848.

The Nithi - neri - vilaccam. By H. Stokes, Esq. Madras, 1830.

The Folk-Songs of Southern India By Charles E. Gover. London and Madras, 1872.

If the Rev. John Kilner had not commended the author for returning to what he was pleased to call his first love, this task might not have been completed. The writer is therefore grateful to his old friend, whom he had the honour to welcome to Jaffna, and further thanks him for a timely copy of Graul's *Valluvar*.

CONTENTS.

—o—

TALES AND POEMS OF SOUTH INDIA.

TALES AND POEMS OF SOUTH INDIA.

LANGUAGE AND LITERATURE.

TAMIL, the most fertile and extensive bough of the Dravidian branch of the Turanian tree of language, covering fifteen millions of people, subjects of the British Crown, is to be respected as having been the adopted or familiar tongue of such men as Beschi, Ziegenbalg, Schwartz, and Percival. It was the first of the languages of India acquired by missionaries; and probably Europeans have spoken and written more in it than in any other Eastern language.

As its name signifies, it is a *sweet* speech. The oldest extant treatise on Tamil was composed by a sage called Agastya, who is therefore regarded as its founder, and is honoured as a god. The parent language of Southern India, it had existed in perfection long before Sanscrit mingled in its stream. The Tamils call Sanscrit *Vada-morlyi*, the northern speech, supposing it to have originated in the north, and their own language *Ten-morlyi*, the southern speech, because Pothiya-malay, the mountain in which Agastya lived and is fabled still to reside, is in the south of India. A sufficient reason for the name is that, in fact, Tamil

A

is the southern language, used in the territories which embraced the Chera, Chola, and Pandiya kingdoms, which form now the southern section of the Madras Presidency. It has also been for centuries, in its overflow, the vernacular of the northern half of the island of Ceylon.

Cities conversed in it ages before the Christian era, and, as might be inferred from its beauty and finish, it possesses an ancient and honoured literature. A native scholar, Mr. Simon Casie Chitty, records in his *Tamil Plutarch* the names of one hundred and ninety-six authors. The traditions respecting them are inextricably blended with fiction, and many of their compositions are irrecoverably lost; but they have bequeathed writings of a character to invite close examination and reward persevering research.

The title of what may be called the first edition of this work, *Tamil Wisdom,* is withdrawn in admiration of Professor Williams' *Hindu Wisdom,* published afterwards. When a minister said with some severity, " I know what the wisdom is that cometh from above, but am doubtful as to the source of this Tamil wisdom," the writer mentally took refuge in the introduction to " this little volume of heathen morals and learning," which was kindly written for him by the late Rev. Elijah Hoole, D.D. Adverting chiefly to the *Cural,* Dr. Hoole, who had himself virtually advised us to attempt its translation, observed, " Some of the sayings which are here rendered into English are probably as old as the earliest writings of the Old Testament." We may regard Valluvar, Cumara-guruparan, Saravanapperumalayer and others as Tamil Solomons,

Ezras, or Tuppers, who collected and arranged the "proverbial philosophy" of primitive times. Dr. Hoole continued, "There are very few historical records in the Tamil language. Fables and moral sayings in verse, having a strong hold on the memory, have been preserved through the revolutions of four thousand years, while history has perished. Perhaps if we had the songs and sayings of our ancestors of four thousand years ago, they would be equally interesting."

The literature of the Telugu language, spoken of also, subordinately to Sanscrit, as the northern tongue, the second greatest branch of the Dravidian or, as it has likewise been named, Tamilian family of speech, extending over the north-east section of the Madras Presidency, is believed to consist chiefly of translations from the Sanscrit; but Tamil literature is mostly original.

There are two orders of Tamil classics : *Ilakkanam*, philology and the art of composition, or grammar; and *Ilakkiyam*, correctly executed works, mythological, epic, and didactic. The most esteemed of the moral writings are those which, like the *Cural*, obtained the approval of the celebrated Madura College, of which more will be said on a succeeding page. A great difference exists between *Sen-Tamil*, correct or polished Tamil, which is also sometimes named *Ariya-Tamil*, difficult or profound Tamil, and *Codun-Tamil*, which, less refined and concise, is yet beautifully regular and complete. Another distinction is *Mut-Tamil*, that is, the three kinds of Tamil, namely, *Iyat-Tamil*, plain or prose; *Isait-Tamil*, high or poetic; and *Nādagat-Tamil*, theatrical or dramatic Tamil. The *Cural, Mūthuray,*

Agaval, and *Nīthi-neri-vilaccam* are in the poetic dialect, in which all the most ancient Tamil books extant, on whatever subject, are composed in various metres.

"The reader," said Dr. Hoole, "will acknowledge that God 'left not Himself without witness' among the Tamil people. 'There is a spirit in man, and the inspiration of the Almighty giveth them understanding.' The maxims and morals of the ancients, preserved in the traditions of the people, prevented society from falling into entire barbarism, and in principle, at the least, anticipated the Christian rule which now prevails to the great advantage of all classes of the natives of India." He was nevertheless compelled to remark that the volume "affords an additional illustration of the truth of the apostle's words, that the 'world by wisdom knew not God.'"

The samples of Eastern wit and story now offered to the public may be taken as a hint of much service of the sort remaining to be done by English residents in India. They will also show the superiority of the Hindus in civilisation, thought, and culture to the inhabitants of other heathen lands, and the delicacy and difficulty of the evangelist's work in the Tamil country. Let the missionary call the Tamils to a virtuous life, and they reply that their own moral maxims are as good as his, and, in view of the conduct of some Europeans on their shores and in their towns, not less effective. They need more than to be pointed to the remaining flowers of the pristine paradise, and amused by eclectic ethical teaching; it is necessary that consistent Christians should preach to them the Gospel of the atoning Son of God.

A discreet and godly missionary touches hearts and kindles hopes when, depending on divine grace, he cries, " God so loved the world, that He gave His only-begotten Son, that whosoever believeth in Him should not perish, but have everlasting life." It is well that a certain class of estimable evangelists should restrict themselves to proclaiming naked Christian truth with simplicity and zeal, and not affect a knowledge of Hindu literature and doctrine; but it would be a pity if there were no experienced missionaries acquainted with the writings of which the people are proud, and respecting which the remark is frequently encountered, not only from native lips and pens, that they are comparable with the Decalogue, the Book of Proverbs, and the Sermon on the Mount.

It matters little how soon hopelessly unaccomplished missionaries make way for successors; but it is most desirable that men versed in the language and literature of the country should remain in it as many years as possible. Directors and managers would do better to bear with the eccentricities and severe correspondence of veteran agents, than hastily change them for new servants who have everything to learn. It is painful to see men of standing, whose attainments have cost the Churches a little, imperiously recalled from spheres in which they were doing important service, and put to home work which is foreign to them, while persons ignorant of the alphabet of their labours are sent to attempt the impossibility of occupying their places. A similar sacrifice is need-lessly removing agents from districts of which they have acquired the language, to stations of a strange tongue.

The following story illustrates the importance of being at home in a language. A Tamil in the southern country, distressed for want of subsistence, reflected, "If I go to the northern country, I shall live." In the way as he went forth, he came one night to a rest-house belonging to a village in the Telugu country, and stopped there. A man of the northern country, distressed for food and other things, reasoned, "If I go and do service in the Tamil country, I shall make a living." Taking a lance in his hand, he begged in every place, and supported himself till he arrived that night at the same rest-house, and lay down. When the northerner rose in the morning, and took his lance, saying, "I must go to the south," it was caught in the hollow hanging ear-lobe of the Tamil who had come from the south. The southerner took hold of the lance, and the northerner pulled it, one crying out in Tamil and the other in Telugu about the imperilled and troublesome ear; and, as neither knew the language of the other, there was a pretty quarrel. At length a person who knew both the northern speech and Tamil explained to them both, and stopped the dispute. The two therefore came to the conclusion that without a knowledge of the common dialect of a country it was a mistake to say, "We will go to that country, and get a living;" and each returned to his own land. Therefore, remarks the Hindu moralist, it is useful to all to learn the speech of every country.[1]

A conscientious young missionary in the Tamil

---

[1] *Kathâmanjari.* From this and *Kathâsinthâmani* are taken such stories and fables in this volume as are not derived from the memoirs of the poets.

country deserves sympathy. The hot climate, un-congenial school engagements, and the demands of an English pulpit, from which, with tyrannous kindness, the older resident apostles retire, rejoicing in the new light, are oppressive and exhausting to him. The mastery of the language, which ought to be his chief aim, is the forced work of languid intervals. And perhaps he is shy, and unwilling to open his mouth till he can speak correctly. The poor young man lashes himself with the motto, *Errando discitur*, but continues to get on faster with the eye than the tongue, and is tempted to believe it as easy to do harm as to learn by publicly blundering.

It is not so great a wonder that Bishop Heber forbade the missionaries under his jurisdiction to preach in the open air. Think of a foreigner coming to an English city, getting up a discourse in a fashion with the assistance of a hired teacher, carrying the thunderbolt in the pocket of his memory to the market-place, and there with bad accent loudly stammering, "What a fine boy am I!" Not so courteous as Hindus, yet, habitually tolerant of street tomfoolery, we might bear with the zealot, especially if he would only refrain from writing to his native country of England yielding to his miraculous eloquence. Every Italian in Great Britain is not a Gavazzi, every Swiss among us is not a John Fletcher, every Frenchman is not a Waddington, every Hindu visiting our shore is not a Chunder Sen; and not every Englishman receives the gift of tongues on landing in India.

It is no disparagement to missionary preachers to say that we laugh at the recollection of some of their

Tamil discourses.   There are excellent persons who
find idiom as difficult to acquire as pronunciation.
Do not Frenchmen make mistakes when they come to
England ?   We have heard of one who, having learnt
from his dictionary that the phrase, " I do not care a
fig," expressed a sneer, wanting fruit at table, said,
" I will take one sneer ; " of another who, enraged at
a postmaster for not having found out how to deliver
his letters, threatened with clenched fist, " I will blow
your nose ; " and of another who, seeking a barber,
inquired on the pavement, " Where shall I go to be
saved ? " and was directed first to a chapel, and then
to a savings bank.   Do not Englishmen trip in Wales ?
A medical gentleman told us that, airing his Welsh,
when he intended to say to a patient, " Put out your
tongue," what he did say, as they afterwards told him,
was, " Turn the sheep into the field."   Do not Britons
blunder when they visit France ?   " I am done " is a
good saying for a Scotchman at the end of his dinner ;
but the continental waiter did not think Dr. Guthrie,
king of preachers, at his last gasp when he said the
same thing in French.

Missionaries are equally liable to err.   A studious
and careful brother claimed the aid of the orb of day
to expel ants from a biscuit, commanding, " Put it in
the sun ; " and his servant looked upwards, wondering
how to pitch the biscuit into the heavenly furnace.
Another, who had no doubt that he knew the Tamil
for *rat*, holding up a specimen of that animal by the
tail, exclaimed, " Behold my father ! "   Another, when,
in defiance of Hindu principle and prejudice, he
astonished certain guests with a huge dish of mutton,

shouted to his horrified vegetarian servant, "It is not enough," only meaning, in Yorkshire idiom, that it was not well cooked. We fear that it is a little too common for curious natives, through interpreters, to ask evangelists of fast but swollen tongue, "What is the use of talking to us in your language, which we do not understand? Tell us in our own what you have been saying." Judson, the apostle of Burmah, still shrank from preaching to the Burmese when he had been studying their language for four years.

These remarks are seriously made to indicate that it is not only for preaching exercises that Tamil should be acquired by European officers of the missionary army, but to aid them in training native soldiers, controlling and using the press, performing episcopal and pastoral duties, and rendering services to literature which are helpful in the long run towards the conversion of nations.

The good words of India, when transferred to English pages, have the advantage of separation from the worst of the bad company in which they are discovered in native writings. Dr. Graul was bold in translating the third part of the *Cural* into even the Latin language. If moral maxims could themselves do good, their useful power is lost in evil associations. Not only side by side with the wise sayings of the East, but interwoven with the language of many of them, are indelicate statements and outrageous sentiments. The ethical rules of the Tamils are hung, darkened with foul devices, about the cars and temples of idolatry, and spoken from altars which obey no moral inspiration. The evangelist finds it a difficult task to take the jewels from the mire, and attach them to the atoning and cleansing cross. He has to train his converts to combat the errors of Hinduism, while respecting whatever truths are in it, as the Christians of the early centuries, upholding the universal moral law, found it necessary to sweep away the mythological abominations by which it was trammelled and obscured.

L ONG before the Christian era, the Tamil people were driven into the south of India, and many of them passed over the straits into the island of Ceylon. The intruding Brahmanists laboured to deprive them of their scriptures and religion, and to introduce the mythology and idol-worship of which we hear so much in descriptions of Hindustan. The people enjoyed the long stories from Sanscrit sources recited and acted for their entertainment, but kept alive their own literature and faith, not by organized means of formal education, but by quiet transcription and constant repetition, and in immortal proverbs. The living of many among the invaders depended upon their success in substituting their fables and follies for the ancient faith and practices of the population. When they found that they could not eradicate, they did their utmost to adapt, pervert, interpolate, and mutilate the indigenous writings. A comparison of old and later copies of Tamil standards shows the extent to which they proceeded. Some of the modern editions are like mixtures of water and oil. Books in present circulation are disfigured by inconsistencies which betray the torturing treatment they have undergone. The Mohammedans, when they poured into the country, were less delicate than even the Brahmans. They made no attempt to alter or modify, but only strove to snatch, tear up, and burn.

Neither Brahmans nor Moormen, in all the centuries of fraud and violence, fear and change, have been able wholly to deprive the Tamils of their sacred treasures. The arrival of the English in the distracted country, in the ruling providence of God, arrested the processes of absorption and dissipation, making it safe to bring to light the oldest and therefore purest copies of native literature, and possible, if not to recover all the sentences suppressed and erased, yet to mark and separate much of the foreign and adverse. The Mohammedans are merchants and bankers, and the Brahmans high in social position and influence; but they are a minority of the population, and the authority of England has paralysed their power to corrupt, distort, and destroy. The inhabitants still possess some of the ancient standards, though lamentably soiled and disfigured; and the old religion lingers in their hearts and minds.

So much has been said of the idolatry of the Tamils that many are surprised to be told that in their hearts they are a God-fearing people. The wise men who moulded the nation were wont, in language which has been carried in the mind generation after generation, to protest, almost like Hebrew prophets or Christian apostles, against the encroachments and practices of idol worship. In *Evidence from Hinduism itself*, a Jaffna tract prepared by a native mudeliar, the number is astonishing of testimonies produced against idolatry from ancient Tamil authorities. The following quotations from such authorities in English works

remind us of the second commandment. " Anxiety of
mind cannot be removed, except from those who are
united to the feet of him who is without likeness."[1]
So said Valluvar. Almost as early a sage, Sivavakyer,
wrote :—

> " When once I knew the Lord,
>   What were to me the host
> Of pagan deities,
>   Some fixed in temple shrines,
> Or carried in the crowd,
>   Some made of unbaked clay,
> And some burnt hard with fire ?
>   With all the lying tales
> That fill the sacred books,[2]
>   They've vanished from my mind.

> " Of two stones on the hill,
>   The first you take and carve,
> Into an idol make ;
>   You rub with sandal ash,
> Adorn with brilliant flowers,
>   And worship it as God.
> The next serves for a road ;
>   You tread it under foot.
> In neither can our God
>   Take pleasure or delight.

> " How many flowers I gave
>   At famous temple shrines !

---

[1] *Cural*, i. 7. Drew.   [2] Of the Brahmanists.

How many mantras said !
   Oft washed the idol's head !
And still with weary feet
   Encircled Siva's shrines !
But now at last I know
   Where dwells the King of gods,
And never will salute
   A temple made with hands."[1]

Another rendering of the last lines is: " This I
have left off, for the wise, who know the true God,
the Lord of heavenly beings, believe not the idol of the
temples, apparent to the eyes, to be God, nor lift up
to it their hands."[2] About the tenth century of the
Christian era, Pattanattu thus continues the protest :—

" My God is not a chiselled stone,
   Or lime, so bright and white.
Nor is He cleaned with tamarind,
   Like images of bronze. . . .
   . . . Can the Deity
Descend to images of stone,
   Or copper dark and red ?

  .   .   .   .   .   .

Alas ! how long did I adore
The chiselled stone, and serve
An image made of lime, or brass
That's cleaned with tamarind !

" Men cannot know from whence they came,
   Else they would never call the sun
   Or moon their god. They would not bow

---

[1] *Folk-Songs*, by Charles E. Gover.   [2] Ellis.

To idols made of clay, or mud
Baked in the fire.   No image made
Of stone or wood, no linga stump
Built up of earth and made by hand,
Could ever seem divine to one
Who knew he came from God.

. . . . . .

How mad are ye who offer praise
To carven stones ! as if such things
Could fitly image God most high !
Can He be but a dirty stone ?

. . . . . .

Who teach that copper, stones or wood
Are gods, and also those who follow them,
Shall never reach the blessed home,
But perish in the seven dark hells."

Patirakiriyar, who flourished in the same age, sings:—
" Oh, when will mankind learn to use aright
    The carved stones, the clay baked hard with fire,
The burnished copper shining in the light,
    And not to worship them as gods require ? "

A dramatic Tamil song contains these words :—
            " Poor fools
Must bow to idols.   They cannot discern
The higher things.   As when some weakly man,
Who cannot walk a mile, is urged to pace
Such distance as he can, so fools adore
An image. . . .
No stone can image God.   To bow to it
Is not to worship."[1]

                    [1] Gover.

It is not contended that many Tamils exclusively worship the living and true God. One might as well affirm that clouds never obscure the noonday sun, as that inferior and imaginary deities are not honoured in Southern India. It is as certain that the people, with not too many exceptions, invoke the idols which some of their best books denounce, as it is that the dominant Brahmanists, before the days of printing, introduced the names of those false gods into the Tamil writings. There is little use in apologizing for the idol-worship of a race claiming or seeming to be essentially monotheistic; but are such Gentiles more inconsistent than Christians who adore relics, wafers, crosses, paintings, images, and saints? Is the truth more mixed with falsehood in their authoritative writings than Christianity is travestied in the clever Tamil pages presented to them as scriptural and orthodox by Jesuit propagandists? The fact remains that there are thoughtful men among them who look up to the Supreme Being, by whatever name they call him—Siva, Vishnu, or God. It would be difficult to find more correct and forcible representations of the Eternal One than are contained in many passages of their standard poems. His unity, spirituality, omniscience, omnipresence, almightiness, providence, justice, and mercy are clearly brought to view; and, as in sentences already quoted, He is declared to be the source of good, and the refuge and salvation of the soul.

The first of Tamil sages, Agastya, who seems to have tried to blend the many-faced system crowding in from the north with the monotheism of the south, thus taught the unity and perfections of the Divine Being : " I salute the great Teacher, the Bestower of divine happiness and supreme bliss, the image of perfect wisdom, who is removed from all griefs, who is represented by the sky, who is denoted by the Truth and other names; the One, eternal, stainless, stable, and omniscient; the Incomprehensible, who knoweth neither passion, partiality, nor folly; the God who is embodied goodness." [1]

" There is a Supreme Being, who is the sun which shines with unreflected light without setting, who is infinite, free from infirmity, not subject to birth, who is everywhere and at all times, who is all, and the Creator of all, and who is the final beatitude itself." [2]

" In all worlds, the eternal God is Chief." [3]

" There is but One in all the world, none else.
That One is God, the Lord of all that is ;
He never had beginning, never hath an end." [4]

In the following lines there is no allusion to the divisions of Christians. They were written before Europeans had made themselves known in India. " There is but one God ; there is but one Veda ; there is but one way of imitation by the good spiritual Guide ; there is but one kind of bliss which He grants ; and there is but one caste amongst mankind upon the earth. They who hold the contrary, by asserting that there are four Vedas, and six sects, and many gods, will surely enter the fiery hell." [5]

[1] Ashtakam.
[2] Alavanthar, in Nyanavinmaganeathay.
[3] Valluvar, i. 1.   Ellis.   [4] Sivavakyer. Gover.
[5] Conganar, in Nyanam.

"Into the bosom of the one great sea
Flow streams that come from hills on every side.
Their names are various as their springs.
And thus in every land do men bow down
To one great God, though known by many names.

. . . .

What though the six religions loudly shout
That each alone is true, all else are false ?
Yet when in each the wise man worships God,
The great Almighty One receives the prayer." [1]

"He hath no end, nor had beginning. He
Is one, inseparate. To Him alone
Should mortals offer praise and prayer.

. . . .

The wise man saith
That God, the omniscient Essence, fills all space
And time. He cannot die or end. In Him
All things exist. There is no God but He.
If thou wouldst worship in the noblest way,
Bring flowers in thy hand. Their names are these :
Contentment, justice, wisdom. Offer them
To that great Essence ; then thou servest God."

"If thou wouldst worship Him,
Lift up thy heart ; in spirit serve thy God.

. . . .

For God hath neither form nor earthly frame,—
A spirit only." [2]

"Our God an ocean is, infinity ;
No eye can see the end. He has no bound.

[1] Pattanattu. Gover.   [2] Translations by Gover.

He who would see and know Him must repress
The waves of his own heart, must be at peace.
His sole desire is God.   His every sense
Must turn to that great One, and clasp but Him.

· · · · · · · ·

He hath no shape,
Nor dwelleth only in some single thing.   ·
This Infinite surpasseth all our thoughts." [1]

He is " pure knowledge " and a " sea of virtue."
" Whose eightfold attributes," by which are probably
intended independence, holiness, wisdom, intelligence,
immateriality, mercy, power, and happiness, " pervade
the world." [2]   " The expanded ether, water, earth, fire,
and air, these Thou art not, but without form art
hidden among them ; I rejoice that I have seen Thee
now with the eye of the mind." [3]   " Thou art in the
heavens, Thou art above the mountains, Thou dwellest
in the ocean, Thou revolvest in the earth ; but among
all these, though everywhere present, Thou art everywhere hid.   Thou art among other worlds, among
systems beyond the reach of thought; and Thou
sportest also in my soul.   Wilt Thou ever thus remain
concealed without manifesting Thy form ? " [4]

Some of the preceding sentences will have brought
to mind well-known words of the New Testament.
The following will recall familiar passages of Scripture
respecting the love of God and love to Him.   " The
ignorant think that God and Love are different.   None

[1] Sivavakyer. Gover.   [2] Valluvar, i. 2, 8, 9.   Ellis.
[3] Tiruvasagam.   Ellis.
[4] Tiru-vay-morlyi.   Ellis.   Compare Nithi-neri-vilaccam, vv.
94, 95, 98.

knows that God and Love are the same. Did all men know that God and Love are the same, they would dwell together in peace, considering Love as God. To those of soft hearts, whose minds are melted by divine love, although their flesh be cut off, their bones used as fuel, and their moisture dried up by wasting in the golden flame, and to those only, it is not forbidden to approach the God who is the golden jewel of my soul."[1] "The Eternal Being, whom none can fully know, removeth darkness from the understanding of those who are steadfast in their love towards Him, and dwelleth in their enlightened minds. Who, therefore, can comprehend the greatness of divine love?" "When God, the cause of all, who, even when wholly embraced, eludeth the grasp, cometh and is taken in the net of the good deeds of sinless piety, where is the utility of letters, of science, of the brightest acts of devotion, or of contemplative wisdom? Unspeakable is the greatness of divine love, which nothing can destroy." "Thou, whom all the Scriptures, by which sin is dispelled, declare to be without form, taking on Thee a form, and entering into this world, searchest for those who rejoice in love, and, having tried their hearts, conferrest happiness upon them. Where, oh where, are they who know the greatness of those who feel divine love in its purity?" "They who conceal nothing they do, who do nothing that ought to be concealed, who, when the universe is shaken, are unmoved, who speak nothing but truth, who open not their eyes to the faults of others, but to consume them to ashes, who are ignorant of deceit, who have no

[1] Tirumular, in Manthiram. Chitty, Ellis.

thoughts, either of friend or foe, but such as proceed from benevolence, may truly be said to be adorned by the love they bear to His feet who is the manifestation of goodness." "O God! I intreat that the high aspiration of my soul may be accomplished. On this only I think: this is the only thing I require. That on which I thus think, is that love of Thy sacred feet may melt and soften my heart; and I desire, fervently desire, that it may never diminish, but for ever increase."

" O Almighty, it is Thee I ever desire!
O Instructor, it is Thee I ever desire!
O Eternal, it is Thee I ever desire!
O Immaculate, it is Thee I ever desire!
O Most Holy, it is Thee I ever desire!
O Enlightener, it is Thee I ever desire!
By all means and at all times I desire
To be filled with the boundless love of the feet
    of our God!" [1]

A scriptural expression in frequent use among Christians, denoting reverence, worship, affection, and obedience, is *being at the feet of God.* The old Tamil authorities use the same language when treating of the soul's refuge from the sea of sin. They employ another significant Christian phrase, *knowing the Lord.* There seem to have been those who not only believed in the one God, but, we may not irrationally conclude, were the happy subjects of His absolving, assuring, and regenerating grace. It is true that they had not heard of Jesus Christ as we have heard of Him; for

[1] Perunthirattu and Gurunthirattu. Ellis.

they lived in the time of the patriarchs. But who shall say that they were not, like the Hebrews, inheritors of divine truth? Who shall say that they were not, like the worthies of Israel, enlightened and sanctified by the Angel-Jehovah, the anointed Prophet, Priest, and King to be revealed to men in the fulness of time? As in some extracts preceding, so in the following sentences from Tamil writers of different periods, an ear familiar with the language of Christian fellowship may distinguish the voice of those who hate sin and love God:—

" O Father of the energy which supports the earth and heaven, I perceive Thee by meditation, and dance with delight. . . . Bow, O my soul, at His resplendent feet by which the miseries of the world are removed. He removeth the impurity of the mind, and causeth the flower of purity again to blow. . . . He, who is my Life, hath no superiors."[1] "O Lord, O my Father, even mine, who am the slave of those who love Thee, Thou art the light of truth which pervadeth my body and my soul, which melteth my heart, and dispelleth the darkness of falsehood. . . . Thou art unqualified happiness: what more can they require who are united to Thee? Thou art the full weight, without diminution. Thou art unadulterated nectar. Thou art a hill of unextinguishable, eternal light. Thou comest in the words and in the sense of the Scriptures, and art for ever fixed in my mind. Like undammed water, Thou flowest into my thoughts. O Lord, Thou hast taken Thy abode within me! what more can I ask?"[2] "In my heart I place the feet,

[1] Tirn-vay-morlyi. Ellis.   [2] Tirn-vasagam. Ellis.

the golden feet of God. If He be mine, what can I
need ? . . . See yon fool.   Beneath his arm he
bears the sacred roll. . . . The truth should fill
his heart, but 'tis beneath his arm.   To him who
knows, the sun is high: to this, 'tis starless night. . . .
If knowledge be not thine, thou art as one in deep
mid-stream, a stream so wide that both the banks are
hidden from thine eyes." [1]

" When may my thoughts be fixed alone on Him,
   Who is Himself all sweetness, made all things,
Whom all the Vedas sought, though seeing dim,
   Who saveth him that to His mercy clings ?

" When will my God attract to Him my soul,
   And keep it ever near, beneath His care,
Just as a magnet draws, as to a goal,
   Unto itself the weighty iron bar ?

" When will that God who hath no earthly shape,
   Of all the end, and yet who maketh all,
Whose clear pervading eye nought can escape,
   Accept my service, all my soul enthrall ? " [2]

         " I have learned of Him,
And find no single thing in all the world
To show how great His glory.   Words must fail
To tell the joy, the bliss I have in Him :
Yet when I try no man believes my speech.
   O God, I once knew nought of what Thou art,

---

[1] Pattanattu. Gover. Compare *Cural*, chap. i., on the praise
of God.
  [2] Patirakiriyar. Gover.

And wandered far astray.   But when Thy light
Pierced through my dark, I woke to know my God.
O Lord, I long for Thee alone.   I long
For none but Thee to dwell within my soul.
When Thou didst make me, Thou didst know my all.
But I knew not of Thee.   'Twas not till light
From Thee gave me to understand of Thee
That I could know.   But now, where'er I sit,
Or walk, or stand, Thou art for ever near.
Can I forget Thee ?   Thou art mine; and I
Am only Thine.   E'en with these eyes I see
And with my heart perceive, that Thou art come
To me as lightning from the lowering sky.

If thy poor heart but choose the better part,
And in this path doth worship only God,
His heart will stoop to thine, will take thy heart
And make it His.   One heart shall serve for both.
When thy poor mind has always God within,
The Highest One will surely dwell with Thee,—
Will rob thee of thy sins.   As with his tool
The artisan will shave or cut clean off
Each roughness from the wood, so will He make
Thee free from sin, and altogether pure.

To lay her eggs the turtle swimmeth far
To reach the sandy shore.   She buries them,
And swimmeth back again.   Yet doth her mind
Adhere to them.   When young ones break their shell,
They feel the tie.   It draws them as a rope
Along their mother's path.   At last they meet.
Just so hath God placed us.   We wander here
While He is far above.   Yet in His mind
We ever stay.   The tie doth reach to earth

From highest heaven.   If we but follow it,
We cannot fail to reach and live with Him.
   Some think to find their God upon the hills,
And climb with weary feet.   So some declare
He is beyond the sea.   They sail afar
To find Him out.   Oh, ignorant and fools !
'Tis pride that prompts your work.   His sacred feet
Are in your heart.   If there you seek, your soul
Will find the Being that alone is real.
   Not for a single moment has my God
Forgotten helpless me.   Oh, only God !
My King, and King of kings ! I could not live
One moment without Thee.   One mercy more
Bestow, that praise may dwell upon my tongue." [1]

The *Song of the Seven*, contained in this volume,
illustrates the essence of Tamil faith in regard to
Divine Providence.   The seventy-fourth verse of *Nithi-neri-vilaccam* resembles the statement of Holy Scripture, that " whom the Lord loveth He chasteneth, and
scourgeth every son whom He receiveth."   From the
evident fact that retribution is not entirely in the
present world, have been developed the unhappy
notions of destiny and metempsychosis which, as will be
apparent in the following pages, pervade the works of
Tamil authors.   Yet, as well as against idolatry and
false ideas of the nature of God, some of the Tamil
sages have protested against doctrines which deepen
the darkness of futurity.   They seem to have believed,
in the first instance, that final retribution would take
place at death, and to have been slow to allow either

[1] Sivavakyer.   Gover.

the Buddhist prospect of absorption and annihilation, or the Brahmanist theory of transmigration. The vigilance and fierceness of their priest-ridden and purana-burdened oppressors from the north made them careful not to object too zealously; but the following passage indicates what they really thought: " As milk once drawn cannot again enter the udder, nor butter churned be recombined with milk; as sound cannot be produced from a broken conch, nor the life be restored to its body; as a decayed leaf and a fallen flower cannot be reunited to the parent tree : so a man once dead is subject to no future birth."[1]

Not only the Tamils, but the smaller branches of the same race, the Canarese, Badagas, Coorgs, Malayalas and Telugus, as shown in Mr. Gover's *Folk Songs*, are opposed, in their poems and proverbs, to the idolatries and fables of Brahmanism ; and in every section of the great southern family a morality is enjoined like that taught by our Lord Jesus Christ.

If the Tamils have correct views of God in their standard writings, if they are directed by their sages to worship and serve Him only, and if obedience to the moral law is their idea of the way to everlasting blessedness, it may be asked why they should be disturbed by missionaries ? There are certainly those among them who seem to fear and love God, and whose virtuous life is a reproach to many nominal Christians ; but it has come to pass that the crafty priests from the north have proved too many and strong for the common people. The cloudy network of idolatry obscures their view of the Eternal Father,

[1] Sivavakyer. Ellis.

whom they cannot altogether forget, and whom, according to their sects, they invoke by different appellations. The prospect of a dreary succession of retributive and corrective births hides heaven out of their sight. The work of meditating upon the Divine Being is seen by them, not more in departure from idol-shrines than in the filthy pride of beggarly asceticism. Providence and judgment are veiled by a fatalism that fetters hope and paralyses resolution. God, and the inferior divinities that choke the way to His footstool, are regarded as angry, inharmonious, and vindictive powers, to be dreaded, appeased, and flattered. There is no native conception of universal atonement by voluntary vicarious sacrifice. Ubiquity becomes identity. The doctrine of God's presence with and in all things has changed into pantheism. It is no wonder that, in great part, an air of disappointment, depression, and despondency rests upon the nation. The Gospel is what they require, to enable them to uncover the old foundation, and rebuild the temple of Jehovah.

The fact that there is common ground upon which Christians can meet Tamilians is a cause for joy. It is possible to conciliate them by pointing out in what respects their ancient books correspond with our inspired writings. We may ask them if they ought not to agree with what they know to be right in the teaching of their authorities, remind them what that teaching is, and show them that if they concur therein with their own standards, they are so far in harmony with our prophets and apostles. So we shall engage their attention and secure their sympathy, and may lead them to respect the courage with which we prevent our path being darkened by fables and blocked up by idols, and to imitate the simple and direct faith with which we go to God the Father. They will learn their need of our Lord Jesus Christ, and be allured to His redeeming cross, to the throne of ready and abounding mercy for His sake, to the company and guidance of His Holy Spirit, to the resplendent gate and blissful mansions of His Father's house.

How great the pity that such a people have been oppressed, ensnared, and perverted! The ancient river, purer the farther it is traced back, has been polluted by violent tributaries, and almost turned from its course. What a responsibility to English Christians to have had the Tamils and kindred races brought under our influence! If we had not sent them a few teachers, how must we have been troubled in conscience! What a joy that the chord of brotherhood has been touched, and that we have so far won their confidence and attachment that in thousands they have accepted the message of reconciliation and restoration we conveyed to them from God! In no part of our Eastern Empire has the Gospel triumphed more than in South India and North Ceylon. Yet there are millions of Tamils to whom we have yet to proclaim "the grace of the Lord Jesus Christ, and the love of God, and the communion of the Holy Ghost."

The following tales show that the natives are not blind to the follies of idolatry and the vanities of schism, and that they can satirize selfishness, hypocrisy, and imposture.

TALES OF SUPERSTITION, CREDULITY, AND IMPOSTURE.

1. *The Chirping of a Lizard.*

A BELIEVER in signs had climbed a tree halfway, when he heard a lizard speak. He knew from the chirp that he must stop, and remained in that situation a long time, neither ascending nor descending. At last he came down no better than when he left the ground.

2. *A Naked Idol.*

An inhabitant got his living by the use of ten ploughs. The authorities exacted money from him in proportion; and he sold his ploughs and crops to pay his fine. Afterwards the collector came on account of the arrears of produce due. Not wishing to see him, he ran off, with only a modest strip of cloth tied about him. In the way, seeing another officer approaching, he was alarmed, and entered a Jaina temple on the spot. Observing that the idol was entirely nude, he said, "Father, I have driven ten ploughs, and go with this strip of cloth. How many have you employed and lost? For you are destitute even of this covering." And he wept as he saluted the image.

3. *Blind Religion.*

Several persons, blind from birth, met in one place.

They said to an elephant-driver that they wanted to see an elephant. He stopped one, and told them to look at it. " Good," said they ; and one blind man felt the foot, another the trunk, a third the ear, a fourth the tail. When they had accomplished their examination, they began to speak to one another of the nature of the elephant. He who had felt the foot said, " The elephant is like a mortar for pounding rice." He who had handled the trunk said, " It is like a pestle for beating grain." He who had examined the ear said, " It is like a winnow for sifting corn." He who had laid hold of the tail said, " It is like a broom." Thus answering one another, they quarrelled till they parted. So sectaries, biassed by their respective systems, dispute about the nature of God, which the mind cannot reach.

The same illustration occurs in the higher dialect, and Mr. Gover translates it from Pattanattu in poetic form :—

" Six blind men once described an elephant
That stood before them all. One felt the back.
The second noticed pendent ears. The third
Could only find the tail. The beauteous tusks
Absorbed the admiration of the fourth.
While, of the other two, one grasped the trunk,
The last sought for small things, and found
Four thick and clumsy feet. From what each
    learned,
He drew the beast. Six monsters stood revealed.
Just so the six religions learned of God,
And tell their wondrous tales. Our God is One."

4. *Rival Shrines.*

Tiru-vanaykka, the sacred place of Siva, and Sirangam, the sacred place of Vishnu, are very near each other. Therefore the votaries of Vishnu at Sirangam are angry against Tiru-vanaykka. Though such is the case, a worshipper of Vishnu went daily to Sambukesvaram (Tiru-vanaykka) and performed restraint of his senses. When, according to custom, he went one day, a crow mounted upon the wall of Tiru-vanaykka, and whetted its beak upon it. Seeing that, he said, " Oho, a Vishnu-ite crow of Sirangam is thus beating and rejecting the wall of Anaykka. So I do mischief in gathering alms in this village." Such is the foolish difference of religious sectaries from one another.

5. *The Nose a Sacrifice.*

In a certain country a man without a nose, who could not bear being laughed at by many that saw him, devised within himself a method of relief, and put it into execution. Every time the offence happened, he lifted up his eyes to heaven, and said, " Lord of the world, I meditate on thee, salute thee, worship thee. Give thy sacred hand to a wretch lying down pained in this sinful world. With what shall I compare the splendour of thy holy body ? " While he thus spoke, his eyes filled with tears, and his frame trembled. Afterwards, looking on the people standing round, and affecting to pity them, he said, " O people, behold ! See the god standing ! Alas ! why do you loiter vainly ? " Some, believing him, fell at his feet, and said, " Sir, you must make the god known to our eyes also." The noseless man answered, " Would you see the god distinctly ? You would see if, like me, you were without your noses." So they cut off their noses, and discovered that he had cheated them. There was no god visible. Fearing that people with noses would laugh at them also, they said, " The god is well manifest to our eyes. At a small loss, what great profit we have gained ! what bliss is ours ! " Believing this, all the people in that country cut off their noses in a few days. It is thus that one of a false religion tries to draw others into it.

6. *Hobgoblins.*

An inhabitant, to make a plough, went to cut down a tamarind tree that had stood for a long time in the country, and aimed a stroke at its foot. Some demons who had dwelt in it many days, descending, said, " Sir, why do you cut this ? " He answered, " I want a plough to prepare the ground for oil-seed." They replied, " Every year, whatever oil you want, we will bring and present it to you. You must please not to cut this tree." He consented to the good luck, and went a hundred times a year to receive the oil. Meanwhile a casual demon, calling on those that stayed there, asked, " What are you so troubled about ? " They said, " What are we going to say ? It is wandering continually, and stealing oil for a citizen who lives in this town, that we are tired of." The new demon, hearing this, said, " Will you be afraid of a little man ? Behold, I will kill him." It went, and took its station, without the man's knowing, on the fence of his cow-fold. He was engaged in branding cattle, and, meaning to brand a beast lately procured in the country, the name of which was New Demon (Puthuppey), he said, "Bind New Demon; I must brand it." The new demon, fearing that himself was intended, leaped down, and, falling at the man's foot, said, "Do not brand me." Seizing the hobgoblin, he demanded, "Where do you come from? Say quickly." It said, "The demons in this country told me of your coming to ask them for oil-seed or oil for so many days." He insisted, "You also bring oil with them from this day." "Very well," it answered, and then complainingly informed the local demons. They were displeased, and said, "What! is this the kindness with which you help us? You have taken a medicine, and fallen asleep." Thenceforward they accepted the new fairy as a partner with them in the work of collecting oil.

7. *Envious Prayer.*

A poor Brahman, from the desire of obtaining happiness for himself, sat on the upper side of a tank, and, looking at the god, did penance. Another Brahman, seeing that, went to the lower side, and did penance also. After a few days had passed in this way, the god came to one of them, and asked, "What do you want?" He said, "Whatever he doing penance on that side asks of you, let that be mine in double measure." Afterwards the god, going to the other, asked, "What do you wish?" He said, "What has he on that side prayed for?" He replied, "He begs

c

a double portion of what you ask." With the envy which says, "Shall greater happiness come to him than me?" he replied, "O god, destroy one of my eyes." "Good," said the god, laughing. Consequently, directly one eye was lost to this one, both eyes were lost to the other. An envious person thinks another's loss his happiness, and will not see his own.

8. *A Tradesman making Atonement.*

A merchant threw a weight at a cat that came into his shop, and it was its fate to die. Fearing it was a great sin, the shopkeeper addressed an augur who came to his house next day, and said, "Swamy, if any one should kill a cat, what penance must he do for that?" The augur said, "He must make an image of gold like a cat, and present it as an offering." "But if he be not rich enough for that?" "Then he must make it of silver." "But if he have not power to that extent?" "He must make it of copper." "If he be so poor that he cannot do even that?" "He must make it of sugar." "But if he have not the means of doing that?" The augur said, "He must get a little sugar, and make the figure, however small, and bestow the gift." Hearing that, the merchant rushed up into the interior of his house, took sugar the size of an areca-nut, made it into the similitude of a cat, and three times caused the augur to affirm that, if he gave it with betel-leaf into the hand of a Brahman, the sin of destroying the cat would be gone. Afterwards, in a state of drowsiness, he took the sugar, and put it in his own mouth. The augur inquired, "O merchant, may you do thus?" "Sir," he answered, "the swamy

is not angry with me. Whatever the sin of killing
the cat, and whatever the crime of eating the sugar,
let it be."

9. *Begging a Boon.*

A Comatti[1] who was always poor, and had been
born blind, and was without a wife, did penance for a
long time towards a certain god. That god, thinking,
" This man is a Comatti, and I must therefore bargain
with him beforehand how many blessings he shall
ask," spoke thus: " O Comatti, I am much pleased
with your devotion. However much you want, ask
only one gift. If you ask more, I will not bestow."
" I was expecting to receive many gifts," the Comatti
reflected, " and he has spoken thus ! What shall I do
in this case ? " Beholding the god, he prayed, saying,
" Lord, I ask according to your sacred will. If you
will do me only this one favour, it is enough. That I
may die, let me see with my eyes my grandson's
grandson dwelling in a seven-storeyed house, and
eating milk and rice out of a golden dish." He asked
thus, to obtain riches, posterity, old age, a palace,
sight, and other gifts. The divinity was much pleased
with his shrewdness, and graciously granted his request.

10. *A Jackal's Breakfast.*

A jackal that had obtained no meat for two or three
days of rain and wind, impelled by hunger, went
abroad. In the way it went, under a banian-tree,
were a pair of sandals which a few days before a wood-

---

[1] The Comattis are a caste of traffickers.

seller had forgotten and left, completely wet and soaked with the rain. Looking at them with a desire to eat, the jackal thought, " Whereabouts here is the owner of these sandals ? " and said, " Sir, I will give you a fanam if you will graciously bestow one of these to appease my hunger." Then an invisible divinity said, " Good, I give on that condition." The jackal, directly it heard that, gladly ate one sandal. When hunger was subdued, saying, " If I stand here, he will come for the fanam," it ran very swiftly to a great distance, entered a thicket, and hid itself. The god, standing there like a man, said, " Where is the fanam ? " The startled jackal ran again, and was beaten by thorns, stones, trees, bushes, till its eyes and feet were so wounded that the blood flowed apace ; and, losing strength and spirit, it lay in the shadow of a bush for concealment. The never-leaving god, standing there, said, " Where is the fanam ? " The jackal asked, " What fanam ? " The god said, " That in exchange for the sandal ? " The jackal said, " It was all right. Was that jackal blind and lame ? " " No." " But I am ; be off," answered the jackal. The god vanished, wondering at the artful trick.

11. *Destroying Life.*

A sannyasi, who would not destroy any life, went upon the bank of a lake. Seeing a fisherman catching fish in the pond, he said, " Alas ! when will you ascend the shore ? "[1] He answered, " Sir, if you will fill my basket, I will mount the bank."

---

[1] Of heavenly bliss.

12. *Love of Money.*

A sannyasi who was without lust of money, going along the road in the country, saw a hid treasure, and fearing ran away. Two sannyasis, coming with their servant from the opposite direction, looking on him, said, " Why are you running ? " He answered, " I saw yonder that which destroys a person, and ran fearing." Afterwards they, thinking that he spoke of money as that which destroys a person, and that he was wanting in intellect, went to the spot, took up the money, and carried it off. Their servant, thinking that if he killed them he would possess himself of the money, mixed poison with the rice he was cooking for them, and set it ready. The two sannyasis, supposing that the servant would perhaps want to share with them, when they were bathing in the tank, plunged him in the water, and left him drowned. Afterwards, eating the rice he had cooked, they died themselves, confirming the phrase, " that which destroys a person."

13. *Carrying a Mountain.*

A man, seeing a person of distinction, said, " If you will supply me with good food for six months, I will afterwards carry a great mountain." He gave him good food accordingly. Afterwards, calling him to a mountain, he said, " Bear this." The man answered, " You all lift it, and place it upon my head, and I carry it."

14. *Swallowing the Ocean.*

A cunning man went to a great king. On seeing

him, the king demanded, "Whence do you come? What are you skilled in? What do you want?" He said, "I come from Casi, and can drink all the water in the sea at once. If you are wishful to behold that wonder, you must give a thousand pagodas for the expenses of the sacred rites I must perform with a view to it." The king, from his eager desire to witness such a feat, gave him three thousand five hundred rupees. Afterwards, on the day when he promised to drink up the sea, the king went with the people of the city to the seashore, and said to the cunning man, "Sir, drink up the sea." He answered, "If you will effectually stop the mouths of all the rivers falling into it, so that no water may come but what is in the sea now, lo! in an instant I drink it: is this a great thing to me?" The king, when he heard that, unable to say anything, was speechless.

15. *This Burden of Wood.*

A wood-seller of sixty years, still making his living by selling wood, was breaking and binding wood one day in a forest. Thinking of the troubles he endured, and grieving in his mind, he said, "Alas! alas! when will my days come to an end? Ema-tutha (Messenger of Death), is it not right to fetch me?" As he spoke, a person who owned the name of Ema-tuthan, walking that way, came opposite him, and said, "Why, wood-seller, have you called me?" Then he said, "Sir, do not be angry. I called you to lift up this burden of wood."

16. *A departed Man's Ghost.*

Vengadaretti, an inhabitant of a certain town, said to his wife, "I must go four years to Tiruppathi." One day, having made his premises secure, he went. When he had gone, a calf in the backyard upset a fire-pan by the side of a heap of straw. The straw caught fire, and the calf perished. Without knowing either of its death or of Vengadaretti's having gone to Tiruppathi, the townsfolk coming, said, "Vengadaretti has been burned in the fire made by the kindling of the straw." When they examined the ashes, there was a bone of the calf. Concluding that it was Vengadaretti's bone, they sprinkled milk and such-like things, and divested the wife of her bridal ornament. Ten days after she was thus declared a widow, at the time of placing the lamp at the garden-entrance to the house, a girl saw him coming with his head shaven in the Tiruppathi style, and his forehead bearing the Vaishnava mark, and with his staff on his shoulder. Her hands trembled, her body shook, and she screamed, and cried out a long time, "Vengadaretti who died is come as a devil." Hearing that word, they who came and saw felt their tongues dry and their bodies parched, covered their eyes in fear, fell on the ground as dust with dust, and fainted away. Vengadaretti thought, "All who see me are afraid of me as an evil demon. The exorcising priest in Cali's temple will not be alarmed. If I let him know that I have been to Tiruppathi, and come back, he will tell all, and dissipate their fear." So thinking, he stood in the threshold of the temple. When the priest went to set the lamp, he thought, "If Vengadaretti's devil come here, what then?" He saw him standing at the temple-entrance, and was frightened and taken ill, fell down and died. Vengadaretti went into the town, and knocked at the door of house after house, calling out, "Townspeople, open the door. My name is Vengadaretti. I have been to Tiruppathi. See my staff. Look at my bald head. Behold the mark on my forehead." All were frightened, and did not sleep the whole night, supposing the devil to be knocking at the door of house after house. When day broke, seeing him, they recognised him, dismissed their fear, and welcomed him to the town.

17. *The Gates Ajar.*

A heron, resting on the shore of a pond, looked on a swan that came there, and said, "Your feet and beak and eyes are very red. Who are you? Whence do you come?" The swan said, "I am a swan, and come from the celestial world." The heron asked, "Where do you dwell there? What sort of a place is it?" The swan answered, "I dwell in a great lake, the water of which is very sweet and clear. It has the name Manasam, and is adorned with golden lotus-flowers, a shore made of gems, and trees of paradise." The heron, with desire, said, "Good! are there snails in it." The swan replied, "Snails are not in it." The heron responded, "What is a lake without snails? Go." Mean persons think that good which is pleasant to them, even though it should be out of place. Or they think the place defective which is without the food they crave.

THE OUTCAST CHILDREN.

THE narratives in this volume are compiled from accounts that differ in some particulars. The reader is left to distinguish in them the probable from the improbable. Veracious Hindu biographers and historians are unknown.

A part of Southern India, fertilized by branches of the river Cavery, is called Chola-nadu. Somewhere in that favoured country a Brahman's house was filled with rejoicing on occasion of the birth of a boy, whom his delighted father named Pagavan. The blossoms of happiness are too often blighted. There is bitterness in the sweetest cup. In a few days the good man appeared before his wife with a sorrowful face, announcing, as a revelation of the horoscope, that their handsome child would some day marry a low-caste girl. What could be done to avert, if possible, a calamity so dire? He would go on pilgrimage to the Ganges. Thither he went.

The pensive woman, waiting many years without welcoming her husband's return, found her highest pleasure in watching over her beautiful boy, and securing to him the best education. Clever and studious, the youth well repaid her kindness. When fifteen years old, he was revered by all as learned in the Veda. At this period he obtained from his mother an answer to a question with which he had often troubled her, "Why did my father leave you?" Greatly grieved to discover the reason, he determined to follow his pious parent, and at once set out as a pilgrim to Casi (Benares).

When in a rest-house on the way he had concluded his morning devotions, and was preparing himself some food, a simple girl was curious enough to appear in his presence. An encumbrance to her parents, who were going on pilgrimage, she had been left by them on the roadside; and a kind-hearted Brahman had taken her and brought her up as his own daughter; but Pagavan saw that she was of inferior birth. "What low-caste thing are you, presuming to come here?" exclaimed the resolute and circumspect young gentleman; and in his anger he threw, some say the wooden spoon with which he was cooking, others a stone, at the innocent damsel. Wounded on the head, she ran crying to Melur, the adjoining village, in which dwelt her foster-father Nithiyayan.

The choleric pilgrim, having quickly bathed and eaten, resumed his journey. On his return, in a year or so, from his vain search for his father, he ventured to stop at the same choultry as before. The maiden chanced again to visit the place; but time had altered and improved her appearance, and Pagavan did not recognise her. She was now beautiful as Lakshmi, and under the powerful protection of the God of Love. Nithiyayan, who owned the rest-house, perceiving that the traveller's affections were captivated, and wishing to do the best he could for his adopted daughter, said to him, "Marry my child, and abide with us." He replied, pointing to a jar of water which he had brought on his shoulder from the Ganges, " I will do so when I have presented this offering at Ramesuram (Ramisseram)."

As soon as possible the young Brahman was back again, where he had left his heart and treasure, at Melur. Nithiyayan's relatives were assembled for the wedding. On the fifth day of the feast, the time having come for the bridegroom to pour oil on the head of his bride, arranging her soft hair for the purpose, he discovered a scar. Memory was awake in a moment, suggesting terrible fears and doubts. He asked, " Are you not Athy-al ? " that is, " the girl I first met with ? " Not waiting for a verbal answer, but certified by her silence, he ran away.

Known ever after by the name Pagavan thus gave her, Athy, by her reputed father's advice, followed the fugitive. It was a toilsome pursuit ; but love was swift, and hope was strong. She found him at length resting in a shed in a low-caste village, and said to him pitifully, " God having united us, is it kind or right to forsake me in this way ? " After a minute's consideration, he replied, " Woman, if you love me, agree to what I propose. You may accompany me on condition that, whenever a child is born, you abandon it then and there." The terms were hard to accept ; but she could not give up Pagavan, especially after such a chase. So she went with him as his wife.

Three sons and four daughters appeared in succession, in the rest-house, in the grove, or on the mountain side, as they travelled. On the birth of each the heart of the mother contended with the conscience of the wife. Pagavan, no doubt, reasoned severely on fate and providence; but Mr. Gover errs in attributing to him the wise and consoling words which helped the troubled woman to keep her vow. On the birth of every child, Athy, with her foot rooted to the ground, exclaimed in agony, " Oh, who will take care of my babe ? " Each wonderful infant assured her that he who had provided for herself would watch over her offspring. The pious sayings, of which a translation follows, are known, not as those of Pagavan, but as the " Song of the Seven."

The names of the children were Uppay, Ouvay, Uruvay, Vally, Athigaman, Valluvar, and Cabilar. They are not always mentioned in the above order, which assigns priority to the girls. Ouvay is frequently represented as the firstborn, Cabilar as the fifth, and Valluvar as the youngest child. In Mr. Gover's list Valluvar speaks the saying here attributed to Ouvay, Ouvay that ascribed to Athigaman, and Athigaman that belonging to Valluvar; but the seven stanzas are generally connected with the names respectively as now presented in the order in which they were read on the classical Tamil page.

It is impossible to say who were the real sages whom these appellations cover, or when and by whom they were brought together as members of one family, and placed side by side in the monumental vault of fabulous narration. It is not likely that the seven stanzas were composed by one author, or in one age; but from what sources they are collected none can tell. Perhaps they were first associated because all on the same subject, providence or fate.

Like the separate sayings of the song, many passages

in the works published and accepted as those of Valluvar, Ouvay, and Cabilar were probably composed at different times by poets of other names. Of sentences mingled and arranged beyond the possibility of distinction and separation, it is believed that not a few were launched centuries before the Christian era.

In introducing translations from their reputed works, accounts will be given of the three chief celebrities last named. It will suffice to record here a summary of what is credited by the people concerning the other four wonderful foundlings.

Uppay was born in a choultry at Uttu-cadu, a place of fountains, as the name indicates. Taken possession of by a washerman, she grew from the mire of low-caste into a flower of eminent beauty and worth. She became a distinguished poetess, and wrote a treatise on ethics. After her death she was deified, under the title of Mariyammay, one of the names of the not very amiable goddess to whom offerings are made for the prevention or removal of small-pox.

Uruvay saw the light in a shed at Caveripatnam, and was taken and reared by a family of Sanars, toddy-dealers, a very low class of people. She became a distinguished dancer and poetess, and is worshipped as a mischievous goddess, representative of Cali, at Tiruvalangadu.

Vally, left on the slope of Mount Vel, was found and adopted by basket-makers, another extremely low caste. She gained such a reputation for piety and wisdom that, after her decease, she was worshipped as Vallyammay, a form of Parvati.

Abandoned in a grove at Caruvur, Athigaman was

brought up by a king of the Chera country, became an accomplished archer, grew learned in the wisdom of Menu, and rose to rank and affluence. He was a bountiful patron of bards, and in his own writings presented to the world " the nectar of the poets."

Mr. Gover gives the following as an alternative address from the lips of Cabilar to his distressed mother, rather, as he represents, from the mouth of stern Pagavan to his suffering wife. To any reader who has not seen the *Folk Songs of Southern India*, it will be interesting as a specimen of the flowing style of the translations in that admirable work.

" Though God cannot be seen, He knoweth all
    Our many needs.   He feedeth every day
The frog that on the forest rock doth crawl,
    And from our birth till now hath found a way
To give us day by day our daily food.
If thus it pleaseth Him to do us good,
Will not the future bring such plenitude ? "

THE SONG OF THE SEVEN.

Uppay.

Shall Nari's lord[1] the rain command,
    And dew, to feed the thorny trees
Which in the dismal forest stand,
    Where eye of mortal never sees,
And not my daily food supply,
But leave his votary to die ?

    [1] Parvati's husband, Siva.

Ouvay.

Why, mother, snatch me from the ground ?
   Of living things am I not one ?
Preserving life wherever found,
   Is there a God, or is there none ?
To fate with faith surrender me :
Whatever is to be will be.

Uruvay.

The lively chick that breaks the shell
   May guardian grace and power attest,
And nourish'd infancy dispel
   The doubts that tear thy troubled breast.
In Aran's [1] name of truth and power
Find firmness for the evil hour.

Vally.

Whose head the serpent's gleams adorn,
   Who dances at the Veda's end,
Who cherish'd me when yet unborn,
   Will Peruman [2] not still befriend ?
The future's written in the past :
His providence must ever last.

Athigaman.

Be strong in heart.   Is Siva dead ?
   According to his gracious will,

[1] Siva.   [2] Siva.

He wrote my doom within my head ;[1]
And will he not my fate fulfil ?
If famine come, not thine the care ;
The burden is for him to bear.

Valluvar.

On whom ovarian life depends,
    The rock-encompass'd frog who feeds,
The true one pitifully sends
    Whate'er thy helpless offspring needs.
O make his sovereign care thy choice,
And weep not, mother, but rejoice.

Cabilar.

My all since I began to be,
    How shall he now refuse to keep ?
Can he evade himself, or me ?
    Or can his eye be seal'd in sleep ?
Or can dismay his mind confound,
Like thine in love and trouble drowned ?

---

[1] The marks of the cranial sutures are supposed to be inscriptions upon the skull of the fortune of its owner.

THE DIVINE PARIAH.

IT has already been said that the names of the legendary children of Pagavan and Athy are not necessarily those of the respective authors of the stanzas in the *Song of the Seven*. Hindu poets have not been wont to connect their names with their writings; and their commentators have not always been careful to preserve or able to ascertain them. The name of the illustrious Tamil who composed the *Cural* has hence been lost. He has been called Tiru-Valluvar, till that descriptive title has come to be universally used as his real name. *Tiru* means *holy, reverend, divine;* and *Valluvar* is the appellation by which a priest or sage of the Pariah tribe is known. The history of Tiru-Valluvar, like that of his alleged brothers and sisters, only more abundantly, is buried in the adornments of fabulous tradition. He is even regarded as having been an incarnation of Siva. We can only repeat what is written and believed concerning the divine Pariah.

Our first sight of him is in a grove of Ilupay trees at Mayilapur (Mylapoor), afterwards called by the Portuguese, and now known by Europeans as St. Thomé, near Madras. He lay exposed, a newborn babe, subsisting on the honey that dropped from the flowers of the trees. Contiguous to the grove was a temple sacred to Siva. Thither came the wife of a

D

Velalan of high rank, paying offerings and worship with a view to being blessed with a son. Parvati, the god's consort, took pity on her, and said, "Adopt this divine infant." Undeniably an out-caste, yet he was a proper child. The goddess called him Tiru-Valluvar. Carrying him home, the delighted lady gave him into her husband's hands. He received the babe with a thrill of pleasure ; and they carefully nursed him from day to day, till their relatives and neighbours said contemptuously, "They bring up any child, they do not know whose." Ashamed and intimidated, they hung up a swinging cot in an adjacent cowshed, and therein laid the precious infant, appointing a Pariah family to protect and tend him.

The boy throve very well. When five years old, seeing how his father and mother, as he fondly called them, were scorned by their kindred on his account, he looked on them, and said, "There is no need that I should cause you affliction. I will be off to another place. Do not trouble about me." They answered, "Let it not be so. Can you speak thus ? We thought you a great one, come to put an end to our childlessness." The divinity in him replied, "You have only to think of me at any time, and I am with you, to render you whatever aid." Then he departed, and rested near the village in the shadow of a palmyra-tree, the least likely of trees to afford shelter. Observing that the shadow of the crowning leaves of the tall thin tree never left its foot at any hour of the day, the people burst into exclamations of astonishment and praise. "This child," cried they, "is either a sage or a god." He turned to them, and humbly answered,

" What worth or glory is there here? There is nothing in me. Go away."

He thought it well to leave the too wonderful palmyra-tree, and repaired to a mountain where Tiru-Mular, Pogar, and other renowned men dwelt. Observing him join them in their religious rites, Tiru-Mular said to him, " O Valluvar, in old time, when I was favoured to dwell in Siva's paradise, you were there. Have you become incarnate, and approached us, to bless the inhabitants of the world with prosperity and joy? Are you about to teach them concerning virtue, wealth, and pleasure in the sweet language?" Thus flattered and encouraged, he gladly made himself one of those who pursued their studies and devotions in that quiet place; and soon he was learned in all the sacred writings which the wise men prized.

Valluvar was approaching manhood, when a demon began to ravage the surrounding country, destroying crops, and killing men and beasts. A Velalan, named Markasagayan, who lived at Caveri-pakam, and owned a thousand yoke of cattle, promised great riches, a house and land, and every requisite to any one who should subdue the monster. None being able to claim the reward, he consulted the great personages of the mountain. "Apply to Tiru-Valluvar," they said. He did so, with worship; and the young sage, spreading ashes on his hand, and writing thereon the five sacred letters, repeating over them mantras, and scattering them in the air, destroyed the malignant depredator, and saved the people's property and lives.

That was a happy day for our hero. Seeing his superhuman greatness, the Velalan, in addition to the

estate and untold money, offered him in marriage his
only daughter Vasugy. Impressed with the necessity
of illustrating the virtues of the domestic life, the
young man responded, " She shall be my wife if she
will take from me sand and return it in the shape of
boiled rice."   The maiden modestly accepted the
challenge, cooked the stony grains, and produced the
required food. Valluvar enjoyed the wonderful meal,
and the wedding soon took place with the usual
ceremonies.

He went with his wife to his native town, Mayilapur,
and there built himself a house. Whatever the amount
of property received by him from his father-in-law, he
determined to earn his living. His choice of occupation may show to what caste he belonged. In these
days a weaver would not be permitted to have a
Velalan's daughter in marriage. The aim of all the
perversions and inventions of the story seems to be to
make him better than a man of mean birth. Saying,
" The business of weaving is without sin," he purchased
thread of a merchant named Elelasingan, and lived,
like others, on the profits of the loom.

In proof of his right to teach, he continued to work
wonders. Of some of his miracles, Elelasingan was
the subject or a witness. One day, when Valluvar
called at his house for some thread, the good merchant
worshipped him, saying, " Swamy, take me from the sea
of desire, and make me ascend the shore." To test his
worth, and the faith of a few other disciples, he led
them into the jungle, and there caused to rise before
them a spreading flood. They opened their eyes, and
stood trembling, except Elelasingan, who followed him

as he walked on; and as the master and his worthy disciple approached, the water shrank away. He afterwards told him to climb to the top of a high tree; and when he had done so, he said, "Lift your feet from the branch you are standing on, and let go the branch you have hold of." Elelasingan obeyed, and received no hurt. Valluvar therefore took him into confidence, instructed him in wisdom, and endued him with a will proof against the strongest charms. Then they returned to their homes.

The occupant of the throne mockingly advised Elelasingan to apply to his guru for the gift of children. He did so, and Valluvar answered, "Siva will favour you." The merchant and his wife, going as usual to visit the cow they daily worshipped, found Siva himself as a babe lying and crying at the beast's side. The happy woman took and showed it to Valluvar, by whom it was named Arlyakananthar. Her husband reported the event to the king, who unbelievingly replied, "If the child has come to you from the swamy, let it also come to me." It was in a moment in the raja's lap, and the queen was joyfully nursing it before long.

A ship belonging to Elelasingan ran aground, and he informed the king. His Majesty answered, "What can I do? tell your priest." Valluvar fastened a rope to the vessel, and many sailors pulled at it in vain till they were exhausted. He then touched the ship with his holy hand, and ordered them to try again; and it was immediately in deep water.

There came a time of drought and dearth, when many people perished because they could buy no corn.

Valluvar said to Elelasingan, "While the famine lasts, sell the paddy (rice in the husk), which you have bought and stored, for the price you gave for it, but always give a quantity over." He did so, and for seven years the rice remained undiminished. His wealth grew to a mountain. On rain falling at length, Valluvar said, "Sell at the same price, but now give short measure in the same proportion." He obeyed, and before the next day's sunset all the store was gone. Then the divine man commanded, "Melt together the money you have got by selling the paddy, and throw it into the sea." So he did, and a great fish swallowed it. A few days after, the fish was caught, and the fisherman found in it what looked like a black old stone. This they gave to Elelasingan. Believing it to be what it seemed, he put it into the water to stand upon when bathing. The blackness gradually wore away, and at last the mass shone. Discovering his name miraculously cut in it, he exclaimed, "The guru's grace!" and knew it to be the treasure he had thrown away.

Arlyakananthar, the son given miraculously to Elelasingan, having become an illustrious personage, waited, with other learned men, on Tiru-Valluvar, and said, "Write an ethical treatise for the world's good." Collecting the essence of the Vedas, he accordingly composed, in thirteen hundred and thirty distichs, a work on the three subjects, virtue, wealth, and pleasure. His enraptured friends advised, "O divine man, go with it, and triumph over the college of the doctors!"

The didactic poems in highest repute in Southern India are those called College Works (Sanga-cheyyurl),

in the belief that, at different times, they obtained the
sanction of the Great College (Maha-sangam). That
celebrated seat of learning is thus described by Mr
Simon Casie Chitty :—

" The inducements held out to poets, and the
rewards bestowed on them, by the long line of
Pandiya kings who graced the throne of Madura from
the ninth century before to the fourteenth century
after Christ, were most liberal, and might have done
honour even to the court of Augustus. These kings
had three different *Sangams,* or colleges, established
in their capital at three different periods, for the pro-
motion of literature, more or less corresponding in
character with the Royal Academy of Sciences founded
by Louis XIV. at Paris ; and made it a rule that
every literary production should be submitted to their
Senatus Academicus before it was allowed to circulate
in the country, for the purpose of preserving the
purity and integrity of the language. It may be well
imagined how favourably these *Sangams* operated on
the talent and genius of the nation. From every part
of Southern India poets crowded into the *Sanga-
mandapam,* or college-hall, to recite their compositions ;
and the successful candidate, besides winning the
smiles of royalty, was rewarded with something more
enduring and substantial. Neither were the kings
of Chera and Chola backward in patronizing poets, for
they had a certain number of them always attached to
their courts. There can be no doubt that an infinite
number of works in the different departments of science
and literature was composed during this brilliant age ;
but in the early part of the fourteenth century, when

the Mohammedan hordes poured into Southern India,
and Prakrama-Pandiyan was led away captive to Delhi,
the Tamils had to deplore the loss of almost all their
literature; for those ruthless fanatics, amongst other
outrages, ransacked all the libraries in the country, and
committed to the flames 'all that genius had reared
for ages.' "[1]

Madura being 292 miles distant from Mayilapur,
it is not surprising that Valluvar left his wife at home
when he set out for the Great College. He was to
have the company of his learned sister, however, of
whom an account will be given on a succeeding page.
Approaching Idaykarlyi, he met Ouvay and Idaykadan,
an accomplished and ambitious poet of the day. When
he told them the object of his journey, Idaykadan said,
" Siva has cursed the college, saying, ' Let it be destroyed
by the middle and the lowest.' It may therefore be
defeated by me and you. Let us go along with you."

Having reached Madura, and walked round the
magnificent temple, they entered the presence of Siva
and his consort Parvati. Before the god, and in the
hearing of the Pandiya king and his ministers, chiefs,
and people, among whom were many famous persons,
Valluvar submitted the three divisions of divine
couplets which he had prepared. The assembly of
professors were alarmed at his ability; but joy rose in
the breasts of others, who heaped praises on the new
poet. He had yet to pass the ordeal of severe
examination; and Idaykadan, Ouvay, and others encouraged him to humble the proud doctors of the
college, who sat as kings of the sweet tongue on the

[1] *The Tamil Plutarch.*

bench of poets by the tank covered with the golden
lotus, and had detected hundreds of errors in the
compositions of the most skilful, and even dared to
say to Siva, on his appearing to favour an author,
" Though you show us your frontal eye, a fault is a
fault," so incurring the malediction spoken of by
Idaykadan, and who deemed themselves more learned
than Agastya. Coming before them, the Pariah poet,
like a tiger entering a flock of sheep, or a kite pounc-
ing on a group of serpents, or a lion fighting a herd
of elephants, or fire devouring a bamboo forest, easily
answered them in high Tamil, not without merry
satire, and baffled all their cunning questions.

The learned assembly had one hope left of being
able to avoid the acceptance of a work from a low-
born author. They said, " We have yet a doubt on
our minds, O Pariah, whether we can receive the
Cural you have sung. The bench on which we sit
will make room for a treatise in pure Tamil. Let that
sign be given, and we shall all consent." Tiru-Valluvar
confidently laid his poem on the bench in the midst of
them, and it immediately contracted to the size of the
precious book, causing the immaculate professors to
fall one after another into the lotus pond. The
exulting spectators applauded ; and the forty-nine
discomfited doctors, scrambling out of the water,
exceedingly mortified, yet felt themselves bound in
honour each to pronounce a stanza in praise of the
Cural of the wonderful Pariah.

The forty-nine impromptu verses, it is pretended,
have been preserved. There is a collection of stanzas
in honour of Tiru-Valluvar, attributed to the professors

of the Madura College, each with its reputed author's name affixed. Some of the names are those of distinguished men, but others would have been unknown without the traditional list. The following are specimens of the poetic acknowledgments : —

" The moon full of Kalei (the whole of her face being illuminated) pleases the external eyes, in like manner as the *Cural* full of Kalei (knowledge) pleases the intellectual eyes ; but nevertheless she cannot be compared to Valluvar's production, for she is neither spotless, nor does she retain her form and splendour unchanged like it."—*Akarakani-Natshumanar.*

" The gods have known the taste of ambrosia by having partaken of it ; but men will know it when they imbibe the milk issuing from the three teats (parts) of the *Cural.*"—*Alangkudi-Vanganar.*

" Who but Valluvar is able to separate, according to their order, all the things blended together in the Vedas, and impart them to the world in a condensed form and with due amplification ? "—*Arisitkirlyar.*

" Valluvar's *Cural* is short in words, but extensive in sense, even as in a drop of water on the blade of the millet might be seen reflected the image of the tall palmyra-tree."—*Cabilar.*

" Of the six sects, one will condemn the system of the other ; but none of them will condemn the system propounded by Valluvar in his *Cural:* it has the merit of harmonizing the opinions of them all, so that each sect would admit it to be its own."—*Caladar.*

" He who studies the two-lined verses in the three divisions of Valluvar's *Cural*, will obtain the four things (virtue, wealth, pleasure, and eternal happiness) ;

for they contain the substance of the five Vedas (including the Mahabharat), and the six systems of the six sects."—*Calattur-Kirlyar.*

" It is no other than Ayan (Brahma) himself, seated on the beautiful lotus-flower, who, assuming the form of Valluvar, has given to the world the truths of the Vedas, that they may shine without being mixed up with falsehood."—*Carikananar.*

" The short distichs which the learned poet Valluvar has composed, in order that we may know the ancient right way, are sweet to the mind to meditate on, sweet to the ear to hear, and sweet to the mouth to repeat ; and they, moreover, form a sovereign medicine to promote good and prevent evil actions."—*Cavuniyanar.*

" The Brahmans preserve the four Vedas orally, and never commit them to writing, because if read by all they would be less valued ; but the *Cural* of Valluvar, though committed to writing, and read by all, would nevertheless not lose its value."—*Cothamanar.*

" As the *Cural* of Valluvar causes the lotus-flower of the heart to expand, and dispels from it the darkness which cannot otherwise be dispelled, it may well be compared to the hot-rayed sun, which causes the lotus-flower of the tank to expand, and dispels the darkness from the face of the earth."—*Culapathiyar.*

" The *Cural* which has proceeded from the mouth of Valluvar, the king of poets, will never lose its beauty by the lapse of time : it will be always in its bloom, shedding honey like the flower of the tree in Indra's paradise."—*Irayanar.*

" What is the use of works of great length, when the short work of Valluvar alone is enough to edify the world ? It contains all things, and there is nothing which it does not contain."—*Madura-Tamil-Nayaganar.*

" Valluvar is in reality a god ; and if any shall say that he is a mere mortal, not only will the learned reject his saying, but take him for an ignorant man."— *Mamulanar.*

" The beauty of Valluvar's *Cural* is, that it not only illustrates the abstruse doctrines of the Vedas, but is itself a Veda, easy to be studied, and having the effect of melting the hearts of the righteous who study it."— *Mangudi-Maruthanar.*

" All are relieved of their headache by smelling the sindil-salt, and sliced dry ginger mixed with honey ; but Sattanar (a fellow-professor) was relieved of his headache (brought on by his habit of striking his head with his stylus when he found a fault in an author) by hearing the three parts of the *Cural* recited."— *Maruttuvan-Tamotharanar.*

" It is no wonder if those who have bathed in the water of a tank abounding with lotus-flowers will not desire to bathe in any other water ; but it is a wonder indeed if they who have read Valluvar's work will desire to read any other work."—*Nagan-Devanar.*

" They say that Siva is the patron of North Madura; but this poet, who pours out instruction in honeyed words with a parental solicitude, is the patron of South Madura abounding with water."—*Nalkur-Velviyar.*

" Valluvar has lighted a lamp for dispelling the darkness from the hearts of those who live in the world ; having virtue for its bowl, wealth for its wick, pleasure for its oil, the fire of expression for its flame, and the short stanza for its stand."—*Napalattanar.*

"Mal (Vishnu) in his *Cural* (or dwarfish incarnation) measured the whole earth with his two expanded feet; but Valluvar has measured the thoughts of all mankind with his (stanza of) two short feet."—*Paranar.*

"It is said that the *Cural* (meaning Vishnu in his incarnation as a dwarf) produced by Casypa in times of yore measured the earth; but the *Cural* now produced by Valluvar has measured both the earth and the heaven."—*Ponmudiyar.*

"To call any one a poet upon this earth besides the divine Valluvar would be like calling both the evening illumined by the moon, and the evening shrouded in darkness, a fine evening."—*Sengkundurkirlyar.*

"By the *Cural*, the production of the divine Valluvar, the world has been enabled to distinguish truth from falsehood, which were hitherto confounded together."— *Tenikudikiranar.*

"The great poet's work comprises everything, or, if there be anything which it does not comprise, he alone knows it."—*Todittalay-Virlyuttandinar.*

"The four-faced (Brahma), disguising himself as Valluvar, has imparted the truths of the four Vedas in the three parts of the *Cural*, which is therefore to be adored by the head, praised by the mouth, pondered by the mind, and heard by the ears."— *Ukiraperuvarlyuthiyar.*

"They who have not studied the *Cural* of the divine Valluvar are incapable of good actions: neither their tongues have expressed what is sweet in language, nor their minds understood what is sublime in sense."— *Urayur-Muthukutanar.*

"Water springs forth when the earth is dug, and

milk when the child sucks the mother's breast, but knowledge when the poets study Valluvar's *Cural.*"— *Uruttirasanmar.*

" It is difficult to say whether the Sanscrit or the Tamil is the best. They are perhaps on a par, since the Sanscrit possesses the Veda, and the Tamil the *Cural* composed by the divine Valluvar."— *Vanakanshattanar.*

Idaykadan, the friend who had accompanied Valluvar to Madura, to be present when he should submit the *Cural* to the college bench, though not himself one of the professors, could not be silent. Having heard the forty-nine, he thus gave his opinion : " The *Cural* contains much in a little compass. Such is the ingenuity of its author, that he has compressed within its narrow limits all the branches of knowledge, as if he had hollowed a mustard seed, and enclosed all the waters of the seven seas in it." Hearing this comparison, Ouvay remarked to him that it would have been more appropriate to liken her brother's *Cural* to an atom, which is even smaller than a mustard seed."[1]

The captivated college, enraptured king, and others, while congratulating Valluvar, suggested, " If Agastya also accept the work, it will be well." That was a difficult sign to secure ; for, however remote the age in which Valluvar flourished, being subsequent to the creation of the Madura College, it must have been after the day in which the oldest of Tamil writers moulded the language. Agastya had lived in a mountain called Pothiyamalay, in the south of India, as far north, however, as Madura was west from Mayilapur. " By

[1] *Tamil Plutarch.*

Sanscrit and Tamil writers the wildernesses of India are described as filled by the hermitages of recluses. When Rama, for example, banished by the intrigues of his mother-in-law from Ayodhya, the capital of his father's dominions, retires to the forest, he reaches, immediately on crossing to the southern bank of the Ganges, the hermitage of Baradwaja, and, successively, of Sarabhanga, Suticshna, and Agastya. These are described as extensive bowers, situated in chosen spots in the midst of deserts or forests, watered by perennial springs, and adorned by fruit-trees and flowering shrubs. They are sometimes inhabited by a single recluse; sometimes by a pair, a man and his wife, for a woman was allowed thus to devote herself as a Vanaprasthi in company with her husband; sometimes by a society of devotees and Brahmans under the direction of a superior, employed in the study of the Veda and Sastras, and in the performance of sacred rites." [1] It is said that the poet obtained grace to visit Pothiyamalay, and occasioning great delight, was praised there in many songs. An appeal to Agastya, it may be concluded, meant an appeal to a sangam founded by him or to his honour, and pronouncing judgments in his name.

The above commendations of Valluvar are sustained by the opinions of later and more sober critics. "It is difficult," says Mr. Simon Casie Chitty, an accomplished native of Ceylon, "to judge from the tenor of his *Cural* to what sect he belonged; for he has entirely avoided in the work everything that savours of sectarianism, in order to harmonize the suffrages of all the sects. The Jainas, however, claim him to belong

[1] Ellis.

to their sect, from his having used, in one of his distichs in praise of God, the epithet *Andanan*, which is applicable to *Arukan*, the object of their worship." This is a slender foundation for their claim, the said word not being their monopoly. "The primary dogma of this sect is that every act, whether good or evil, is necessarily followed by an appropriate retribution. Deafness, dumbness, and the like, therefore, are not natural defects to be commiserated, but the effects of crimes to be reprobated."[1] They believe in the eternity of the material universe as it now exists, and that seclusion from the world, for either sex, is necessary to the divine life. That Valluvar was not a member of their denomination appears in his statement that "Indra is a proof of the strength of a man who has subdued his five senses," the allusion being to the fulfilment of a curse pronounced on the king of heaven by Gautaman. The Jainas do not believe ascetics capable of possessing or exerting such malignant power, and would therefore make the Divine Pariah mean that Indra was a witness, not as a sufferer, but as an infallible observer. The probability is that the poet himself had no faith in the story, but only uses it as an illustration.

It may be satisfactory to inquire in what estimation the *Cural* is held by competent Europeans. The Rev. Elijah Hoole says, "The *Cural* of Tiru-Valluvar is a poetic work on morals, of great merit as a literary performance. . . . The author commences his book with an acknowledgment of God, in a style which, in the production of a heathen, we cannot but greatly

[1] Ellis.

admire; and throughout the whole he evinces a singular degree of freedom from many of the strong prejudices of the Hindus, although he frequently illustrates his positions by allusions to the mythology and doctrines of the superstition of his country."[1]

"Called the first of works, from which, whether for thought or language, there is no appeal," says the Rev. W. H. Drew, "the *Cural* has a strong claim upon our attention, as a part of the literature of the country, and as a work of intrinsic excellence. The author, passing over what is peculiar to particular classes of society, and introducing such ideas only as are common to all, has avoided the uninteresting details of observances found in Menu and the other Shastras, and thus in general maintains a dignified style, though it must be acknowledged that he sometimes descends to puerilities."[2]

The Rev. Peter Percival gives extracts from the work of Tiru-Valluvar, which, he says, "will be read with pleasure, as affording proof of the existence of the loftiest sentiments, the purest moral rules, and equal power of conception and expression. Nothing certainly in the whole compass of human language can equal the force and terseness of the sententious distichs in which the author conveys the lessons of wisdom he utters."[3]

Mr. Charles E. Gover describes the poem from his point of view that "men like Tiru-Valluvar and Sivavakyar used their tongues and pens in favour of Deism and against the ceremonial Polytheism of the

---

[1] *Personal Narrative.*   [2] The *Cural* of Tiru-Valluvar.
[3] *The Land of the Veda.*

Brahmans." He says, " It will seem strange to a Western reader that the *Cural* of Tiru-Valluvar should be the most venerated and popular book south of the Godavery. To those who know the *Iliad*, the *Æneid*, the *Divine Comedy, Paradise Lost*, and the *Nibelungen Lied* as the epics of great nations, it seems incredible that thirty millions of people should cling to a series of moral essays as their typical and honoured book. There is no doubt of the fact that the *Cural* is as essentially the literary treasure, the poetic mouthpiece, the highest type of verbal and moral excellence among the Tamil people, as ever Homer was among the Greeks. We can only explain it by the principle that the whole aspect of the Dravidian mind is turned towards moral duty. May we not imagine that it was this moral tendency of the masses which prepared the way for, and maintained the existence of, Buddhism ? The Brahmans frequently explain the tone of Tiru-Valluvar, Sivavakyar, Cabilar, Ouvay, and the other early Dravidian poets, by asserting that they were Jains. There is no proof of this; but it can hardly be doubted that both Buddhism and Jainism reflected the same popular tendency that we see in the early poets. The Brahmans extirpated Buddhism in India by fire, sword, and relentless persecution. They could not touch the *fons et origo* from which the rival religion derived its life. By careful avoidance of theological discussion, Tiru-Valluvar saved his work from the flood that destroyed every avowed obstacle in its grievous course. The Brahmans could find no ground for persecution. No priest can openly condemn the poet who called upon wives to love their husbands, upon men to be truthful, benevolent, and peaceful, who enjoined mildness and wisdom on those who governed, and justice, obedience, and willing aid on those who were ruled. The *Cural* says no word against a priest, commands faithful service towards God, paints the happiness of a peaceful home. Few persons out of the Madras Presidency can have any idea of the reverence and love that surrounds the *Cural*. Its sentences are counted as binding as the Ten Commandments on the Jews. Its very language has become the test of literary excellence. It is no exaggeration to say that it is as important in Tamil literature, as influential on the Tamil mind, as Dante's great work on the language and thought of Italy." [1]

Mr. Gover may be right in saying that Valluvar uses no word against a priest. He certainly does not directly oppose the sacerdotal orders; but in such a work silence is significant. Brahmans are not necessarily priests: they are rather the patrons and employers of priests. A title of Brahmans is *Anthanar*; and the poet insinuates that they do not deserve to be so called. The epithet, beautiful or cool-minded, belongs to the self-controlled and unworldly. " The virtuous are truly called Anthanar; because in their conduct towards all creatures they are clothed in kindness." The whole work amounts to a protest against religious pretence, imposition, and oppression. There is even a vein of satire in it against the gods of the Brahmans.[2]

The *Cural* consists of one hundred and thirty-three chapters, each containing ten couplets. They are

---

[1] *The Folk Songs of Southern India.*   [2] *E.g., Cural,* cviii. 3.

arranged in three parts, thirty-eight chapters on Virtue, seventy on Wealth, twenty-five on Pleasure.

There is a limit to the praiseworthiness of the poem in its moral aspects. It would be impossible to present the concluding part in an English dress. Mr. Gover says: "Even the great and good Tiru-Valluvar has written in praise of lust. Let us pity rather than blame." "The third part," says Mr. Drew, "could not be read with impunity by the purest mind, nor translated into any European language without exposing the translator of it to infamy." It may be true that the Tamil turn of thought is ethical. It is as likely, alas! that the degeneracy of the *Cural* towards its close accounts in part for its popularity.

This poem is the only composition of any magnitude attributed to the Divine Pariah. Visiting places in returning from Madura, which he had not called at on his way thither, he recited it to delighted hundreds. As he approached Mayilapur, his fellow-townsmen, with Elelasingan at their head, met him with joyful excitement, and conducted him in triumph to his dwelling. Warmly welcomed by Vasugy, he resumed his exemplary life of homely virtue.

In the *Garland of Advice for Women*, translated in the present volume, young ladies are instructed to perform domestic duties as did the wife of Valluvar. It is therefore important to ascertain how tradition depicts her conduct. We have seen that, before her marriage, rather than not do what she was bid, she metamorphosed a handful of earth into a dish of cooked rice. She was not less obedient afterwards. A notable personage, presenting himself one day at

Valluvar's house, said, "Swamy, graciously inform your servant which is better, a married life or the life of a lonely hermit." Many days he waited vainly for a verbal answer. The philosopher had his own ways of settling questions. During his visitor's sojourn, he called Vasugy. when she was in the act of drawing water from the well; she left the vessel suspended half-way, and hastened to her husband. One morning, when she was serving up cold rice boiled the. day before, he exclaimed, "This is burning me:" she ran for a fan and cooled him. On another occasion, at bright noon-day, when Valluvar was engaged in his occupation as a weaver, his shuttle missed and dropped to the ground, where it could be distinctly seen; he directed his wife to fetch a light, and she brought it. Witnessing these and like occurrences, the visitor concluded, "If such a wife can be had, it is wise to marry; if not, the monastic state were better." Without a syllable having fallen from the lips of the weaver-sage in reply to his question, he went away enlightened.

At length the darkest of shadows fell on Valluvar. Vasugy, at the point of death, was looking inquiringly into his face. Not in the habit of using more words than necessary, he curtly but affectionately demanded, "What?" "I wish to know," said she, "why, on the day you married me, you directed me always to bring a needle to you, and a vessel of water, when serving you with rice?" He answered, "In order that, if a sacred grain should fall, I might pick it up with the needle and wash it in the water." No rice having ever fallen from her careful husband's hand, she knew not till now the reason of a command which she had ever obeyed, but of which it would have been unseemly before to request an explanation. Receiving the information, she contentedly went to heaven. The lamenting poet buried her body in a sitting posture, the attitude of meditation and devotion. The loss of such a wife was a most sorrowful bereavement. Lying sleepless and agitated the night after her decease, he extemporarily complained,—

"Dost thou depart, who didst prepare
My savoury food with skilful care,
On whom alone of womankind
In ceaseless love I fix'd my mind,
Who from my door hast never stirred,
And never hast transgress'd my word,
Whose palms so softly chafed my feet,
Till charm'd I lay in slumbers sweet,
Who tendedst me with wakeful eyes,
The last to sleep, the first to rise?
Now weary night denies repose:
Can sleep again my eyelids close?"

The Divine Pariah survived his wife for many years and continued to perform glorious deeds, favouring and helping to the utmost Elclasingan and his other disciples. At last he summoned his friend to him, and graciously directed him thus: "The region of completeness is near me. When I am perfected, tie my body with cords, and draw it outside the town, and throw and leave it among the bushes." Seeing him to be like one whose penance and meditations were consummated, Elelasingan was preparing to place

him in a golden coffin and deposit him in a worthy
grave. Whereupon Valluvar awoke from the sem-
blance of death, looked at him, and benignly remonstrated, "Dear man, do not transgress my word;" and
then he immediately became perfect. Elelasingan,
having done according to his express desire, observed
that the crows and other animals which devoured
his flesh became beautiful as gold; and therefore,
greatly wondering, he built a temple, and instituted
worship, on the spot where the poet's corpse had lain.

CURAL.

FIRST PART.—OF VIRTUE.

I.—*The Praise of God.*

1 Eternal God all things precedes,
   As Alpha all the letters leads.
2 The learning's vain that does not fall
   At his good feet who knoweth all.
3 His feet their flowers of thought among
   Who joy to feel, shall flourish long.
4 Who hold his feet who neither knows
   To long nor loathe, avoid all woes.
5 God's praise who tell, are free from right
   And wrong, the twins of dreaming night.
6 They prosper evermore who keep
   His law in whom the senses sleep.
7 His feet, whose likeness none can find,
   Alone can ease the anxious mind.

8 Who swims the sea of vice is he
Who clasps the feet of Virtue's sea.

9 Like palsied sense, no head's complete
That bows not at Perfection's feet.

10 The sea of births, of all who swim,
They only pass who cleave to him.

II.—*The Blessing of Rain.*

1 The genial rain ambrosia call:
The world but lasts while rain shall fall.

2 'Tis rain begets the food we eat:
The precious rain is drink and meat.

3 Let clouds their visits stay, and dearth
Distresses all the sea-girt earth.

4 Unless the fruitful shower descend,
The ploughman's sacred toil must end.

5 Destruction it may sometimes pour,
But only rain can life restore.

6 No grassy blade its head will rear,
If from the cloud no drop appear.

7 The ocean's wealth will waste away,
Except the cloud its stores repay.[1]

8 The earth, beneath a barren sky,
Would offerings for the gods deny.

9 Were heaven forgetful, men below
Nor rites could pay, nor alms bestow.

10 Since without water, without rain
Life's duties were essay'd in vain.

[1] This is not a mere allusion to the formation of clouds by evaporation from the sea. "The belief is that pearls are produced by the pearl-oyster drinking in the drops of rain ; and that these and other precious stones cannot be formed, nor fish spawn, without rain."—DREW.

III.—*The Merit of Ascetics.*

1 No merit can be named so high
  As theirs who sense and self deny.
2 As soon you'll count the dead as tell
  How much ascetics all excel.
3 No lustre can with theirs compare
  Who know the right and virtue wear.
4 With hook[1] of firmness to restrain
  The senses five, is heaven to gain.
5 Indra himself has cause to say
  How great the power ascetics sway.[2]
6 The small the paths of ease pursue :
  The great attempt what's hard to do.
7 They grasp the world, the bounds who tell
  Of taste, sight, hearing, touch, and smell.
8 Full-worded men, by what they say,
  Their greatness to the world display.
9 Their wrath, who've climb'd the mount of good,
  Though transient, cannot be withstood.
10 With even kindness clothed towards all,
  The beautiful[3] the virtuous call.

IV.—*The Power of Virtue.*

1 From virtue heavenly riches flow :
  What greater good can mortals know ?

[1] As the hook guides elephants, to which the five senses are compared.

[2] An allusion to the dreadful curse pronounced against the King of Heaven by Gautaman, in consequence of a discovered intrigue.

[3] *Anthanar*, a title of Brahmans: as much as to say, the virtuous man is the real Brahman.

2 O'ertaking it is joy and gain;
  Forsaking it is loss and pain.

3 To practise virtue be your strife,
  Your ceaseless rule and aim of life.

4 In purity of mind 'tis found,
  Not selfish show and swelling sound.

5 Four ills to quit does virtue teach,
  Ill-will, lust, anger, bitter speech.

6 Your friend without delay if made,
  'Twill be in death your deathless aid.

7 Needless are words: its worth is seen
  Outside and in a palankeen.[1]

8 Like stones are days in virtue spent,
  Which other trying births prevent.

9 'Tis only virtue leads to praise;
  Its paths alone are pleasant ways.

10 Vice is whate'er 'tis meet to shun,
  And virtue that which should be done.

V.—*Married Life.*

1 The worthy householder is he
  Who duly aids the orders three.[2]

2 His help the poor and pious share,
  And dying strangers are his care.

3 By him the fivefold rule's obeyed,
  The dead, God, guests, kin, self to aid.

[1] The lack of virtue in a former birth makes one man a bearer of the palankeen, whilst its reward to another who practised it is that he rides in the palankeen.

[2] The three other orders, his own, that of the householder, being the second of four. The first is that of the student (Bramachari), the third that of the married hermit (Vanaprastan), the fourth that of the lonely anchorite (Sanniyasi).

4 Who dares no wrong, and food bestows,
His house is strong, and stronger grows.

5 In heart and hope the home excels,
Where love with virtue sweetly dwells.

6 Who turns from such a life to be
A monk austere, what profits he ?

7 Of all who work for bliss, the great
Is he who fills the married state.

8 He helps ascetics in their line,
And thus his merits doubly shine.

9 Marriage is virtue, though the same
Is hermit-life when free from blame.

10 On earth domestic bliss who prove,
In heaven among the gods shall move.

VI.—*The Worth of a Wife.*

1 Help meet is she who fits the house,
But spending what her lot allows.

2 The greatness of the married state
The wife is, or it is not great.

3 What is there not, when she excels ?
Where she is useless nothing dwells.

4 On what may more esteem be placed
Than faithful woman firmly chaste ?

5 Her husband who as God adores,
Says, " Let it rain," and down it pours.

6 The true wife keeps herself from blame,
Her husband cares for, gilds his name.

7 Of what avail are prisons barr'd ?
Their chastity is women's guard.

8 The wife whose husband is her pride
Shall flourish where the gods reside.

9 Not his the lion's gait, but shame,
Whose spouse is careless of her fame.
10 A perfect wife is full delight,
And children good are jewels bright.

VII.—*The Wealth of Sons.*

1 The world no higher good supplies
Than children virtuous and wise.
2 With sinless sons their hearts to cheer,
Men face the future without fear.
3 They call them wealth, for only they
The rites that buy them heaven can pay.
4 The rice is all ambrosial made
In which their tiny hands have played.
5 Their touch imparts a blissful thrill;
Their notes the soul with sweetness fill.
6 Whose little ones ne'er prattled near
May say, "The lute delights the ear."
7 A father's blessing is to enthrone
Amid the circling wise his son.
8 With yearning pride his bosom swells
Because his boy himself excels.
9 The mother, hearing of his worth,
Rejoices more than at his birth.
10 He loves his sire who wakes the strain,
"What penance such a son could gain?"

VIII.—*Loving-kindness.*

1 What bolt imprisons love? the tear
Of sympathy avows the dear.
2 Their own the loving nothing call;
But they who love not grasp at all.

3 In love and virtue were the worth
   That won the matchless human birth.
4 By love desire is waked, and hence
   Springs friendship's boundless excellence.
5 The joys of home and paradise
   In love and virtue have their rise.
6 Love is not virtue's friend alone :
   By vice its kindliness is known.
7 God's justice, as the solar blaze
   Shrivels the worm, the loveless slays.
8 The homes for love that find no room,
   Like wither'd trees in deserts bloom.
9 The heart the labouring limbs must move,
   Or vain the outward life will prove.
10 The soul of love must live within,
   Or bodies are but bone and skin.

IX.—*Hospitality.*

1 Of keeping house with saving pain
   The end is guests to entertain.
2 To wish them absent is not good,
   Although you eat ambrosial food.
3 The hospitable day by day
   In trouble shall not waste away.
4 Prosperity[1] will gladly rest
   Where smiles salute the needy guest.
5 Need seed in that man's field be sown
   Whose guest's repast precedes his own ?
6 Guest after guest who waits to see,
   A welcome guest in heaven shall be.

[1] Seyyarl, the Red Goddess, a name of Lakshmi.

7 The good thus gain'd can no one count :
The worth relieved is its amount.

8 Who none have succour'd shall lament,
" We've scraped and saved, and all is spent."

9 The man of means, who will not feed
A worthy guest, is poor indeed.

10 As fades the anitcham[1] when smelt,
Averted looks by guests are felt.

X.—*Sweet Speech.*

1 From lips of love without deceit,
In season spoken, words are sweet.

2 Bright smiles and pleasant tones dispense
More joys than dumb beneficence.

3 The heart of virtue lights the face,
And speaks in sparkling words of grace.

4 The woe of want they need not fear
Whose words with joy enrich the ear.

5 He is adorn'd, and only he,
Who speaks with sweet humility.

6 His sins decrease, his virtue grows,
Whose useful speech with sweetness flows.

7 The courteous word and kindly deed
To righteousness and merit lead.

8 Pleasures from cheerful speech and true
In this world and the next ensue.

9 How can he utter words that sting,
Who sees what sweets from sweet words spring?

10 With sweet words near, who harsh words try,
Eat fruit that's sour when ripe is nigh.

[1] A fabulous flower, which dies when only smelled, without being touched.

XI.—*Gratitude.*

1 For nothing had, assistance given
   In worth surpasses earth and heaven.
2 Favours bestow'd in time of need,
   Though little, yet the world exceed.
3 What's right, not what the gain will be,
   Who weighs, his gift outweighs the sea.
4 A help as seed of millet small,
   Who know it count a palm-tree tall.
5 The worth of those to whom 'tis shown
   The favour measures, not its own.
6 While they are blameless, cling to those
   Whose friendship was your staff in woes.
7 Through sevenfold births, in memory dear
   Remains the friend who wiped the tear.
8 Forgetting goodness is not good ;
   And over wrongs 'tis wrong to brood.
9 Who injure now, but once were kind,
   For former favours favour find.
10 Who slay all virtues death may fly,
   But benefits who kill must die.

XII.—*Equity.*

1 High virtue fitting justice shows
   Alike to strangers, friends, and foes.
2 The just man's store secure remains,
   And happy children reap his gains.
3 Though strongly lured, without delay
   From lawless profit turn away.
4 Who just and who unjust have been
   In their posterity is seen.

5 Since gain and loss from causes rise,
  An even mind adorns the wise.

6 " I perish," let him think, whose mind
  From justice turns, to sin inclined.

7 Who dwells in honest poverty
  Is wealthy still, the world can see.

8 The wise to neither side incline,
  But deck'd with balanced justice shine.

9 Justice, from more than words of sin,
  Is free from crooked thoughts within.

10 For others' right a trader fair
  As well as for his own will care.

XIII.—*Self-Control.*

1 Self-rule's the path with gods to dwell,
  Its want the way to darkest hell.

2 No gains with self-restraint compare :
  This truest treasure keep with care.

3 In self-control who knowledge see,
  And practise it, shall famous be.

4 Not stirring from their proper state,
  They'll rise above the mountain great.

5 Though good in all, the rich possess
  The highest wealth in humbleness.

6 One birth keep in the senses five,
  Like tortoise, through the seven to thrive.

7 If nothing else, your tongue restrain :
  Unguarded words bring ill and pain.

8 One sinful word, its power so strong,
  Turns good to bad, and right to wrong.

9 A burn by fire may find a cure,
   But wounds from burning tongues endure.
10 Their steps will virtue watch to bless
   Who anger curb and self suppress.

XIV.—*Good Behaviour.*

1 Care less for life than how you live :
   Behaviour good will greatness give.
2 In many ways though you excel,
   This aid in all be guarded well.
3 Good birth in conduct good is seen ;
   Mean manners make the birth that's mean.
4 Reading recalls forgotten lore,
   But sin-slain birth is found no more.
5 For wealth in vain as envy sighs,
   To greatness badness cannot rise.
6 In duty's practice onwards press,
   And shun their sorrow who transgress.
7 High honour from good conduct grows,
   But vile disgrace from evil flows.
8 Behaviour good is virtue's seed,
   But endless griefs from bad proceed.
9 They ne'er forget, by rule who walk,
   To keep their tongues from baneful talk.
10 The world's respect who fail to earn,
   Though much they know, have much to learn

XV.—*Against Impurity.*

1 The blind to right and rights alone
   Desire whom others fondly own.

F

2 Outside the law, no fool's so great
As stands outside his neighbour's gate.

3 They're viler than the dead who aim
To whelm confiding friends in shame.

4 No boasted qualities suffice
To compensate for schemes of vice.

5 The guilt thought lightly of will stay :
Its mark will never fade away.

6 Hatred, sin, fear, disgrace, these four
Attend intriguers evermore.

7 On him its blessings virtue showers
Who covets not his neighbour's bowers.

8 The dignified themselves deny :
The virtuous avert the eye.

9 To none but men of moral worth
Comes good in all the sea-girt earth.

10 No sin surpasses theirs who pine
Another's home to undermine.

XVI.—*Patience.*

1 As earth its diggers bears, to bear
The slanderous is virtue rare.

2 'Tis greatness not to punish ill :
Forgetting it is greater still.

3 He's poorest who the poor repels :
Who suffers fools in strength excels.

4 He greatness reaches and retains
Who patience practises with pains.

5 In no esteem the hasty hold :
The patient prize as hidden gold.

6 Resentment pleases for a day :
The praise of patience lasts for aye.

7 From harming hurtful foes refrain :
  'Twere pity to increase their pain.
8 The proud who no restraints respect
  Are by the calmly patient checked.
9 Ascetics are than they less pure
  Who meekly haughty words endure.
10. They're good and brave who fast with care,
  But nobler who reproaches bear.

XVII.—*Against Envy.*

1 Esteem'd like good behaviour be
  A character from envy free.
2 There can no excellence be won
  Above the power of envying none.
3 Who envy where their greeting's due,
  Nor virtue seek, nor wealth pursue.
4 Commit through envy nothing wrong,
  For woes the ways of evil throng.
5 When foes their arts in vain employ,
  Envy suffices to destroy.
6 Who envies gifts that others get,
  For kindred, clothes, and food shall fret.
7 From envy Seyyarl [1] turns her face,
  And leaves her sister [2] in her place.
8 First stripped of wealth, the envious leap
  At death into the burning deep.
9 Envy enrich'd, or goodness brought
  To poverty, were theme for thought !
10 The envious never great were seen :
  The free from envy never mean.

[1] Lakshmi, Si-devi, the goddess of prosperity.
[2] Tavvay, elder sister, namely, Mu-devi, the goddess of adversity.

XVIII.—*Against Covetousness.*

1 A greedy wretch the guilt assumes,
  And all his house to ruin dooms.
2 Who blush at deeds deserving blame
  Refrain from gainful sin with shame.
3 For better bliss to come who long
  Will do for transient joy no wrong.
4 The free from sin and sense's chain,
  However poor, content remain.
5 Is learning any plea at all
  For stupid guilt that preys on all ?
6 Their path to grace shall end in pain
  Who evil measures hatch for gain.
7 The fruit of covetousness shun :
  In all the crop there's glory none.
8 Wealth's permanence in this is known,—
  Not coveting what others own.
9 To bless the virtuous fortune flies,
  And help the unrepining wise.
10 Contentment's greatness conquers all ;
  But reckless misers ruined fall.

XIX.—*Against Backbiting.*

1 For even one who greatly strays,
  " He does not backbite " is some praise.
2 Who present smile, and absent curse,
  Than virtue's open foes are worse.
3 'Twere better, virtue says, to die,
  Than live to backbite and to lie.

4 Though to one's face your mind you say,
Yet speak with caution when away.

5 Who loves to backbite makes it clear
His praise of virtue's insincere.

6 His failings will be search'd and shown,
Who makes another's failings known.

7 By merry words your friends are tied:
Who speak not gaily friends divide.

8 What will they not to strangers do,
Who bring their friends' defects to view?

9 The world's mere charity their weight
Supports, who of the absent prate.

10 If they, as others' faults, their own
Could see, what evil would be known?

XX.—*Against unprofitable Conversation.*

1 With useless words who many grieve
Deserved contempt from all receive.

2 Vain talk that many ears offends
Is worse than evil done to friends.

3 The babbler's hasty lips proclaim
That " good-for-nothing " is his name.

4 Excessive words which none approve,
From virtue lead, from right remove.

5 If silly things good people say,
Their reputation flies away.

6 As human chaff, not men, they're known
Whose worth in weightless words is shown.

7 Talk nonsense, if it be your choice;
But wisdom regulates the voice.

8 The wise who good themselves would gain
From words that do no good refrain.

9 No useless words, their words who weigh,
   E'en in forgetfulness will say.
10 To purpose speak, whenever heard,
   And never breathe a pointless word.

XXI.—*Fear of Sin.*

1 Not sinners fear the pride of sin,
   But they who virtue's honours win.
2 Dread wickedness as fire you dread;
   Sin leads to sin, as flames are spread.
3 The chief of all the wise are those
   Who do no evil to their foes.
4 His ruin virtue plots who plans
   In thoughtless thought another man's.
5 Who sinning makes " I'm poor " his plea,
   In consequence shall poorer be.
6 No ill let him to others do,
   Who'd have no ill himself pursue.
7 Men spite of other foes may live,
   But sin its deadly blow will give.
8 Destruction, as their shadow true,
   The heels of sinners will pursue.
9 Let none who loves himself at all
   Do any sin, however small.
10 Know ye, he's from destruction freed,
   Who turns not to an evil deed.

XXII.—*Benevolence.*

1 The kind seek nothing back again :
   What get the clouds for giving rain ?
2 The aim of toil, of wealth the end,
   Is want to help, and worth befriend.

3 'Tis hard in either world to find
  A greater good than being kind.
4 He lives whose life's in kindness led ;
  Another reckon with the dead.
5 The wealth expended by the wise
  Is like the tank the town supplies.
6 Who freely of their plenty give,
  Like fruit-trees in a city live.
7 Like plants of healing virtue sure,
  Diseases and distress they cure.
8 From blessing, though their wealth decrease,
  Their sense of duty will not cease.
9 The good man's poverty and grief
  Is wanting power to give relief.
10 Of loss by kindness ne'er complain,
  But sell yourself such loss to gain.

XXIII.—*Almsgiving.*

1 They give who give to helpless need,
  Not they whose gifts to getting lead.
2 A good way call'd, still begging's bad :
  To give is good, were heaven not had.
3 Not pleading, " I am nothing worth,"
  But giving, argues noble birth.
4 The beggar's call for charity
  Displeases till his smile we see.
5 Higher's the power which hunger cures
  Than that of penance which endures.
6 Drive from the poor their gnawing pains,
  If room you seek to hoard your gains.
7 Who's wont with food to freely part
  Is safe from hunger's burning smart.

   8 Do they who, hard eyed, save to waste,
      Not guess what joys the generous taste ?
   9 More pleasure is in begging known
      Than eating selfishly alone.
10 Joyless as death is nought; yet this,
      If charity must cease, is bliss.

XXIV.—*Reputation.*

1 They gather fame who freely give,
  And profit most of all that live.
2 Of one alms-deed the world will raise
  Its common voice in lasting praise.
3 'Gainst ruin proof there's nothing known
  Save towering fame that stands alone.
4 From praising gods the god-world turns
  To praise the man who praises earns.
5 The famous flourish in decay,
  And none in dying live but they.
6 If praise may not this life adorn,
  'Twere better never to be born.
7 'Tis strange that such as all deride,
  Their censors, not themselves will chide.
8 All own it shame to end their days   ·
  And leave no progeny of praise.
9 The land turns sterile that upbears
  A body which no glory wears.
10 They live who are exempt from blame:
    The life of life is faultless fame.

XXV.—*Graciousness.*

1 The rich in goods may yet be base:
  The really rich are rich in grace.

2 Men many paths may try, but find
The heavenward help is being kind.

3 The kind in heart shall never go
Within the world that's black with woe.

4 Whose care for others' life is shown
Need dread no damage to their own.

5 The wind-blown world wide witness bears
That sorrow the kind-hearted spares.

6 In heartless wickedness who stray
In previous births have missed their way.

7 This world's the rich man's happy place :
The better world's for men of grace.

8 To wealth in time the poor may grow :
The heartless no advance can know.

9 The truth when idiots clearly see,
The hard in heart may virtuous be.

10 About to drive the weak along,
Suppose thyself before the strong.

XXVI.—*Abstinence from Flesh.*

1 What graciousness by those is shown,
Who feed with others' flesh their own ?

2 Neglected property departs :
Who feast on flesh neglect their hearts.

3 Who lifts a weapon is as good
As they who take to flesh as food.

4 If merciless it is to kill,
To eat what's slaughter'd must be ill.

5 Not eating flesh is life : on those
Who eat it hell its mouth shall close.

6 Were flesh for food not bought and slain,
Then none would offer it for gain.

7 Not meat in flesh, but, all unclean,
  Another body's wound is seen.
8 Whose minds from fleshly lusts are freed
  Refuse on lifeless flesh to feed.
9 To let one life unhurt remain
  Exceeds a thousand victims slain.
10 All life with palm-join'd hands will praise
  The man who eats not flesh, nor slays.

XXVII.—*Austerity.*

1 The way is, never to complain,
  But bear, without inflicting pain.
2 Ascetics born are saints sincere :
  In vain are hypocrites austere.
3 Is it true penitents to aid,
  That others pious rules evade ?
4 In penance lies the power they crave,
  Who'd ruin foes, or friends who'd save.
5 Men practise penitence in this,
  To make secure the next world's bliss.
6 Ascetics duty's guerdon gain :
  Desires delusive others chain.
7 By fire of pain the constant shine
  As bright as gold which flames refine.
8 He worship wins from every soul
  Who o'er his own acquires control.
9 By strength which strict devotions give,
  O'er Cuttam's[1] gulf men leap, and live.
10 Why most are poor, and wealthy few,
  Is that no more themselves subdue.

[1] Death.

XXVIII.—*Simulation.*

1 Unconquer'd elements [1] of sense
  Deride the hypocrite's pretence.

2 By show, though high as heaven, is brought
  No good to those who sin in thought.

3 Such fortitude the cow displays,
  That wears a tiger's skin to graze.

4 As bird-catchers in thickets lurk,
  False saints their veil'd intentions work.

5 Who vainly boast, " Desire we've slain,"
  "Done what? done what?" shall cry with pain.

6 None live so cruel-eyed as they,
  The saint with sinful heart who play.

7 Like berry red[2] to outward view,
  Its apex black's their inward hue.

8 Too many bathe, with crafty pride,
  Their moral filth to keep and hide.

9 Acts speak : the crooked lute that charms
  Is straight ; the straightest arrow harms.

10 The world's ideal asks no care
  For shaven head or flowing hair.[3]

---

[1] The five elements within the body, viz., earth, water, fire, wind, and ether.

[2] Cundi or cundimani, the black-pointed red seed of a shrub.

[3] Of Saiva ascetics, the Pandarams, who marry, shave their heads, and the Tambirans, who are celibates, wear their hair long and tangled. The saints of the Jainas polled or clipped their hair, so that they looked like Negroes. Ellis quotes the following : " If it be thought eternal felicity can be obtained by wearing long and matted hair, by bathing in water, lying on the ground, and emaciating the body, then may the bears that bathe in the lakes and wander in the forests also obtain felicity."—*Sinthamani.* "To

XXIX.—*Fraudlessness.*

1 Let him who would reproachless be
From fraud preserve his conscience free.

2 Say never,—for the thought is sin,—
By craft another's wealth we'll win.

3 Wealth made by fraud shall bounds o'erflow,
And vanish while it seems to grow.

4 What fruit the fraudulent obtain
Is never-dying grief and pain.

5 Nor know nor love they what is kind,
Who watch to cheat an absent mind.

6 They cannot walk as rules require
Who're led by covetous desire.

7 With fraud's black art are none imbued,
Who'd earn a name for rectitude.

8 Dwells virtue in the good man's breast:
Defrauders are by guile possessed.

9 They perish in their lawless deeds,
Whose knowledge never fraud exceeds.

10 Thieves cannot their own bodies trust:
The world of gods stand by the just.

XXX.—*Veracity.*

1 If " What is truth ? " the question be,
'Tis speech from taint of malice free.

wear tangled hair, to poll, or shave the head, to be clothed in
garments dyed yellow or coloured by ochre, to abstain from
flesh meats, to observe fasts and vigils, to swallow only the wind
or dry leaves from the earth, to sleep on the bare ground or on
stones ; these painful inflictions appertain to those who have not
attained to the true love of Him who is the manifestation of
love."—*Perunthirattu.*

2 E'en falsehood may for truth suffice,
 When good it does that's free from vice.
3 Their conscience turns to quenchless flame,
 Who consciously a falsehood frame.
4 Untruth from life and heart expel,
 And in the minds of all you dwell.
5 In words of truth from heart sincere,
 There's more than gifts from hands austere.
6 A name for truth all praise exceeds;
 And truth to every virtue leads.
7 Though other virtues he have none,
 The truthful man is safe in one.
8 As water makes the body clean,
 The mind in truth is spotless seen.
9 It is not every lamp gives light;
 To wise men only truth is bright.
10 Of all that's truth-like to our view,
 No good surpasses what is true.

XXXI.—*Refraining from Anger.*

1 Restrain the anger that would tell:
 What means it harmless wrath to quell?
2 The wrath is bad that has no force;
 Than that which hurts there's nothing worse.
3 Tow'rds none be anger borne in mind:
 It genders sins of every kind.
4 What enemy's so arm'd with ills
 As wrath which joy and laughter kills?
5 To keep thyself, keep it away:
 Unguarded anger thee will slay.
6 The raft of counsel wrath destroys,
 A fatal fire to friendly joys.

7 For service like the hand 'tis found
That dares to smite the solid ground.
8 'Tis well from anger to refrain,
Though as from touch of fire in pain.
9 His wishes all fulfill'd shall be,
Who keeps his heart from anger free.
10 Before the wrathful die they're dead :
From death ere death the meek have fled.

XXXII.—*Not doing Evil.*

1 Though wealth and honour should ensue,
No evil will the spotless do.
2 They will not seek revenge on foes
Whose bitterness has wrought their woes.
3 Revenging even causeless hate
Will permanent remorse create.
4 To punish wrong don't sharply blame,
But put with kindly deeds to shame.
5 Our neighbours as ourselves from pain
Unless it keep, is knowledge gain ?
6 Let none another man expose
To ills whose bitterness he knows.
7 Not purposely will honour true
The slightest act of meanness do.
8 Why should you wound another's heart
With what has made your own to smart ?
9 The ill that's in the morning done
Returns itself ere sets the sun.
10 All pains to those who hurt are sure :
No pain they give who'd none endure.

XXXIII.—*Not Killing.*

1 The course of virtue's not to kill :
  To slay's the source of every ill.
2 'Tis highest virtue food to share,
  And life in all its forms to spare.
3 The one chief good is not to slay :
  The next is nothing false to say.
4 What way is right ?   'Tis that alone
  Where care to take no life is shown.
5 Of saints who fear in births to stay,
  The chief is he who fears to slay.
6 Life-eating Cuttu[1] spares the breath
  Of him who nothing puts to death.
7 No one of pleasant life deprive,
  Even to keep thyself alive.
8 Though great the gain of sacrifice,
  'Tis all too small to lure the wise.[2]
9 In their esteem, who meanness know,
  The men who life destroy are low.
10 The poor in bodies sick and sore
  Have lives dismiss'd in births before.

XXXIV.—*Unstableness.*

1 The shallow notion cast away
  That things which are unstable stay.

---

[1] Death.
[2] Destroying life in sacrifice procures at best the happiness of being numbered or of dwelling with the subordinate deities in their paradise ; but ascetics aim through meditation at infinitely superior bliss, absorption into God.

2 Wealth's like a crowd of dancers, slow
To get together, quick to go.

3 Though wealth, which lasts not, you procure,
Yet toil for treasures that endure.

4 Life looks the day all fresh and fair,
Time's cutting falchion 'tis that's bare.

5 Ere hiccough quell the tongue, proceed
To practise every virtuous deed.

6 The sum of this world's greatness weigh,—
Here yesterday, not here to-day.

7 Men cannot call a moment theirs,
Yet give their minds to countless cares.

8 As chipp'd the bird the egg, and flew,
So souls are to their bodies true.

9 Resembles death a slumber deep,
And birth's like waking out of sleep.

10 In bodies souls for shelter stay,
Because their home is far away.

XXXV.—*Renunciation.*

1 Whatever one forsakes, 'tis plain
There's that the less to waken pain.

2 Renouncing present wishes, learn
To stifle many more in turn.

3 Whate'er thou hast desired avoid:
The senses five must be destroyed.

4 'Tis penitence all things to lack:
Possession brings corruption back.

5 The body is too much to bear:
To cut off births, shun added care.

6 Let pride that says " I," " Mine," be slain,
The world above the gods[1] to gain.

7 From clinging to desires they cease,
Whom sorrows from their grasp release.

8 Who all relinquish, bliss obtain :
Still snared, the rest confused remain.

9 Desires rejecting, births preclude ;
Else yet behold vicissitude.

10 Wish thou His wish[2] who wishes nought :
The wish to cease to wish be sought.

XXXVI.—*Knowing Truth.*

1 The error brings ignoble birth
That deems illusions things of worth.

2 The final pleasure, free from night,
Is theirs of pure and cloudless sight.

3 The free from doubt, whose minds are clear,
Have heav'n than earth itself more near.

4 From five-fold knowledge can accrue
No good, until we know the True.

5 To know is what is true to find
In everything of every kind.

6 Who here the Truth distinctly learn,
Enter the path whence none return.

7 No other birth to fear has he
Who can in thought the Essence see.

8 Discern the Right, and glory know :
Their births to ignorance men owe.

---

[1] Not Suvarkam (Svarga), the paradise of Indra and other popular deities, but Motsham (Mocsha), the heaven of final liberation and bliss.

[2] God's will.

9 From passions in thy Refuge cease,
And clinging pain shall thee release.
10 The names extinct, the woes expire
Of folly, anger, and desire.

XXXVII.—*Cutting off Desire.*

1 Desire's to all the common seed
Whence births incessantly proceed.
2 From births wish freedom, wishing ought:
Wish nought to wish, and have thy thought.
3 In this world as in that no state
Like freedom from desire is great.
4 To nothing crave is purity:
Crave truth, and it will come to thee.
5 The free from birth are only they
Who wholly put desire away.
6 'Tis virtue its approach to dread;
For by desire are men misled.
7 Cut off its work, and be thy choice
In deeds immortal to rejoice.
8 Desire extinct, no sorrow pains:
Grief comes on grief where it remains.
9 Desire, the grief of griefs, destroy,
And even here is steadfast joy.
10 Desire insatiate cast behind,
The state immutable to find.

XXXVIII.—*Fatality.*

1 We active ply, as Fate commands,
Or empty lazily our hands.
2 The fate to lose in folly shows;
The fate to have in wisdom grows.

3 Whate'er thy course of study deep,
  Thy wits their native limit keep.
4 Two natures in the world obtain :
  Some wealth and others knowledge gain.
5 In getting rich, things change their mood :
  Good things turn bad, and evil good.
6 'Gainst fate can nought be made thy own,
  Nor what is thine be from thee thrown.
7 Who millions heap, enjoy but what
  The great Disposer doth allot.
8 The destitute desire will quit,
  But not till Destiny permit.
9 Who good in time of good perceive,
  In evil time why should they grieve ?
10 What power surpasses Fate ? 'Tis still
  The foremost, purpose what we will.

SECOND PART.——OF WEALTH.

XXXIX.—*The Greatness of a King.*

1 A lion among monarchs boasts
  Wealth, forces, fort, friends, servants, coasts.
2 Four features mark his kingly mind :
  He's brave, judicious, firm, and kind.
3 In governing the earth, he's seen
  Unsleeping, learned, and serene.
4 Still resolutely great and strong,
  He will not swerve from right to wrong.
5 He shows his power to get, and hoard,
  And keep, or portion what is stored.

6 Approach'd with ease, in language bland,
   He causes all to praise his land.
7 So sweetly helps he, and defends,
   That as he speaks the world commends.
8 For conduct just, and guardian strength,
   Men see in him a god at length.
9 'Neath his umbrella all would stay,
   Whose ear e'en bitter words can weigh.
10 Paternal, bounteous, mild, upright,
   He is to other kings a light.

XL.—*Learning.*

1 Precise and true let learning be ;
   And with it let the life agree.
2 These two, according to the wise,
   Numbers and letters, are men's eyes.
3 Eyes have the learned in their head,
   The ignorant two wounds instead.
4 The learned all with joy receive,
   And think of fondly when they leave.
5 As on the rich poor beggars wait,
   To men untaught the wise are great.
6 As men dig deep, the water flows ;
   And as they learn, their knowledge shows.
7 All lands and towns are learning's own ;
   Why then till death its absence moan ?
8 The learning in one birth men gain,
   A pleasure will through seven remain.
9 Who feel and see the joys it pours
   Would fain increase their learning's stores.
10 Man's chief and lasting wealth behold
   In learning, not in gems and gold.

XLI.—*Lack of Learning.*

1 Untaught who learning's throng address,
On squareless board play games of chess.
2 A dunce's words the heart elate,
As breastless women captivate.
3 Great goodness men unread display,
While nought before the wise they say.
4 Though much they know that's just and clear,
Their voice the learned will not hear.
5 Their fancied competence is dumb,
When 'mid the learned crowd they come.
6 Waste land exists, and so do they :
That said, there is no more to say.
7 Who do not learning's treasures know
Are earthen puppets, paint and show.
8 Riches for fools more griefs create
Than poverty can cause the great.
9 By learned men, though low in caste,
Are high-born ignorants surpassed.
10 With those who learning's splendours wear
The rest as beasts with men compare.

XLII.—*Hearing.*

1 Ear-wealth is wealth of wealth confessed,
Of treasures all the first and best.
2 Of food whene'er the ear's in want,
Then let the belly's meat be scant.
3 Like gods on sacrifices fed
Are men whose ears enjoy their bread.

4 E'en the untaught should hear and heed,
  To have a staff in time of need.
5 The words the upright speak are found
  A staff of help on slippery ground.
6 If little the instruction heard,
  Abundant is the good conferred.
7 Though wrong, not foolish things they say,
  Who listen well, and nicely weigh.
8 Whate'er into the ears be poured,
  They're deaf, unless with hearing bored.
9 For such as have not heard with care,
  To own a modest mouth is rare.
10 Who taste by mouth, not ear, may die:
   What can their living signify?

XLIII.—*The Possession of Wisdom.*

1 Wisdom's a weapon to defend,
  A citadel no foes can rend.
2 It checks when wayward sense rebels,
  From evil frees, to good impels.
3 It sees, from whomsoever heard,
  What truth's contained in every word.
4 It speaks in terms that sense convey,
  And sees what others subtly say.
5 True friendship to the world it shows,
  Not opening like the flower to close.
6 It marks the way the world pursues,
  Content itself the same to choose.
7 Who wisdom have, know what will be:
  Who want it, no event foresee.
8 Blind folly into danger runs,
  But wisdom what is fearful shuns.

9 No dire affliction can surprise
The prescient, self-guarded wise.

10 Who've wisdom, all things have: who've not,
Whate'er they own, have nothing got.

XLIV.—*Guarding against Faults.*

1 The greatest are the self-subdued,
Nor proud, nor passionate, nor lewd.

2 Base greed, mean grandeur, pleasures low,
Are faults a king should never show.

3 Sins but a millet-stalk in size
To conscience tall as palm-trees rise.

4 With serious caution vice avoid,
A foe whose captives are destroyed.

5 His home's like straw before the flame,
Who does not guard himself from blame.

6 What further faults, their own who quit,
And others' see, can kings commit?

7 The niggard's wealth will waste and end,
Who does not what he ought expend.

8 Of faults not one, but worst apart,
Esteem a greedy griping heart.

9 On no account thyself admire,
Nor praise of useless acts desire.

10 Thy ruling wish from knowledge veil,
And counsels of thy foes shall fail.

XLV.—*Obtaining the Help of the Great.*

1 The ponder'd friendship seek and prize
Of moral men maturely wise.

2 Such mates prefer as have the skill
To overcome and hinder ill.

3 Of hard things 'tis the hardest known
 To make and keep the great thy own.
4 No power excels the power to make
 Thy betters thine for thine own sake.
5 A king should look about to see
 Who round him as his eyes shall be.
6 Fit friends to choose the way who knows
 Of last resource deprives his foes.
7 Who can destroy a prince, whom bold
 His faithful ministers may scold ?
8 With none to chide, a guardless chief,
 Though none would hurt him, comes to grief.
9 No gain is where's no stock in trade,
 No standing without prop of aid.
10 'Tis ten times worse to lose the good
 Than to offend the multitude.

XLVI.—*Avoiding the Society of the Small.*

1 The great the little-minded fear,
 And only small ones hold them dear.
2 As water changes with the soil,
 Associates make the man or spoil.
3 Perception's proper to the mind,
 But company decides the kind.
4 By company are features wrought
 That seem the inward work of thought.
5 In mind and act is chasteness sure,
 When friendship's influence is pure.
6 Pure minds produce a goodly breed :
 Pure friendship prospers every deed.
7 The good in mind to wealth attain :
 The well-allied all praises gain.

8 The wise, however good in mind,
Good company a succour find.
9 Goodness of mind wins future bliss :
Good company helps even this.
10 No help good company exceeds ;
While every woe from bad proceeds.

XLVII.—*Acting with Forethought.*

1 Ere taking action, ascertain
The outlay, yield, and gradual gain.
2 Nought's hard to men, of friends well tried
Who counsel seek, and then decide.
3 The wise exhaust not all their store
In doubtful work, to make it more.
4 They who disgraceful errors fear
Begin no course not fully clear.
5 Who unprepared to battle goes
Into a garden leads his foes.
6 Unfitting conduct ruin brings :
So does not doing fitting things.
7 Think, then resolve : 'tis credit none
To say, " Let's think," when work's begun.
8 Toil without ponder'd plan and cost,
Though many stand to save, is lost.
9 The temper know of every one,
Or doing well may be ill done.
10 At acts which none can censure aim :
The world accepts not things of blame.

XLVIII.—*Knowing the Strength.*

1 The deed, till weigh'd its strength, thy own,
Thy foe's, and that allied, postpone.

2 No hindrance their assault who learn
  What they can do and how, will turn.

3 Many their force unknown have tried,
  And found defeat in feeble pride.

4 Self-ignorance, with self-applause,
  Molesting neighbours, ruin draws.

5 The load though peacock's feathers make,
  If in excess, the wheel 'twill break.

6 Who climbs the branch's length must close
  His life, if farther on he goes.

7 To keep his goods the way he sees
  Whose income shapes his charities.

8 No harm is in an income strait,
  If but the outflow be not great.

9 His life, his means who does not know,
  Will fade from view, whate'er its show.

10 Away his sum of greatness speeds
   Whose bounty his effects exceeds.

XLIX.—*Knowing the Time.*

1 Kings need occasions foes to slay :
  The crow defeats the owl by day.

2 A cord that ties success unmoved
  Is opportunity improved.

3 What's hard to him, with means exact,
  Who knows the proper time to act ?

4 The world thy aim, thou shalt succeed,
  If wise in season, place, and deed.

5 Who patient keep the time in view,
  Shall without fail the earth subdue.

6 Restrains himself the man of might,
  As butting rams step back in fight.

7 The wise quench anger's outward fire,
   And watch their time with inward ire.
8 If thou shouldst see, salute thy foe,
   Till when his head may be brought low.
9 When comes the fitting moment rare,
   What's hard to do do then and there.
10 The time for stillness, heron-like,
   Observe, and seize the time to strike.

L.—*Knowing the Place.*

1 Till found the place where siege to lay,
   No action take, no scorn display.
2 With heart and power for war, 'tis well
   To own a guarded citadel.
3 The cautious weak, the field who know,
   Are strong to overcome their foe.
4 His sanguine hope thy foe will lose,
   Who sees thee local knowledge use.
5 The crocodile 'gainst all prevails
   In water deep: on land it fails.
6 Sea-going ships can't sail on shore,
   Nor strong-wheel'd cars the sea run o'er.
7 Who thoughtful finds fit place for deeds
   No help but fearless courage needs.
8 A little force, where it can fight,
   Destroys a cumbrous army's might.
9 'Tis risk in their own land to fall
   On men, their forts and strength though small.
10 A fox an elephant can beat,
   Fearless, war-faced, with swamp-sunk feet.

LI.—*Choosing with Discernment.*

1 Choose none but men of virtue clear,
  Who hold not wealth, joy, life too dear.
2 Choose those well-born, of spotless name,
  From wounds of sin who shrink with shame.
3 Though learnèd they and stainless be,
  Few tried are found from error free.
4 To judge of men, with even care
  Their virtues and their faults compare.
5 By touchstone of his deeds is seen
  If any man is great or mean.
6 Elect not those who friends have none :
  Who feel no ties, no crimes will shun.
7 On fondness leaning, dunces choose,
  And folly in all forms ensues.
8 Choose men unknown, and ceaseless woe
  Posterity to thee shall owe.
9 Make no unthoughtful choice, and then
  Fit service find thy chosen men.
10 Unending sorrow is the cost
  Of confidence misplaced or lost.

LII.—*Ordering with Discernment.*

1 Use men who right and wrong discern,
  And who to good by nature turn ;
2 Whose measures revenues augment,
  Swell wealth, and obstacles prevent.
3 Trust him in whom 'tis plain to see
  Love, wit, decision, charity.

4 Official life makes many stray,
  Though tried in every careful way.
5 Wise, patient men with power invest,
  Not those whom fondness deems the best.
6 Look out the agent and the deed;
  And at the time for both proceed.
7 " This man can thus this work achieve,"
  Convinced, to him the business leave.
8 His fitness for the duty scan,
  And then employ the proper man.
9 Think loyal agents not thy friends,
  And favourable fortune ends.
10 Let kings their servants daily view :
  The world's not crooked while they're true.

LIII.—*Embracing Relatives*

1 Though all a man's possessions go,
  His kindred still the old love show.
2 This blooms, long as it shall endure,   .
  With plenteous riches ever sure.
3 Wastes friendless wealth, as from a tank
  Runs water o'er a levell'd bank.
4 In bringing relatives around
  The gain of getting wealth is found.
5 Thy words be sweet, thy giving free,
  And circling kindred shalt thou see.
6 Large givers, temper who subdue,
  Can count most friends, the great world through.
7 Crows hide not what they eat, but call :
  To men thus minded treasures fall.
8 Live many near the king, who sees
  Not all alike, but worth's degrees.

9 Such friends as left return to stay,
When discord's cause is done away.

10 To welcome them the king should try,
And aim their hopes to satisfy.

LIV.—*Non-Forgetfulness.*

1 Excessive joy's unmindfulness
Is worse than anger in excess.

2 As want at last the wit decays,
Forgetful dulness murders praise.

3 Philosophy all says the same,
That inattention fails of fame.

4 As men afraid no fortress find,
They gain no good who never mind.

5 Who is not on his guard before
Will afterwards his fault deplore.

6 'Tis excellence beyond compare
To think of all with ceaseless care.

7 With mindful hope the work pursue,
And nothing is too hard to do.

8 Thy course through the seven births to end,
Scorn not, but do what men commend.

9 When joy deludes, their fate recall
Whose scorn of virtue caused their fall.

10 Thy mind apply, with ease to get
The thing on which thy mind is set.

LV.—*Just Government.*

1 Tries justice all, and favours none,
Affirms the law, and sees it done.

2 Subjects right rule beholding thrive,
As showers the watchful world revive.

3 The scriptures of the holy [1] stand,
   And virtue, on the king's command.
4 His royal feet who rules with grace,
   Shall all the world with love embrace.
5 Full rains and harvests join to bless
   The country ruled in righteousness.
6 His rigid sceptre conquest brings,
   And not the lance the monarch flings.
7 Earth's safety on the king depends,
   And steady justice him defends.
8 Not apt to search, judge, act, a king
   Deep ruin on himself will bring.
9 His people's guard, with fostering will,
   His work, not fault, 's to punish ill.
10 Manslayers must from men be torn,
   As weeds are pluck'd from growing corn.

LVI.—*Crooked Government.*

1 Worse than a murderer is he
   Who rules with lawless tyranny.
2 Requests from those who sceptred stand
   Are like a robber's arm'd demand.
3 Daily a king's domains decay,
   Who deals not justice day by day.
4 If thoughtless he his powers abuse,
   Both stores and subjects will he lose.
5 Are not the tears he makes to flow
   A file to wear his treasure low ?
6 Justice gives permanence to praise ;
   No light round kings without it stays.

[1] *Anthanar*, the beautiful and merciful, a title claimed by Brahmans, iii. 10.

7 A graceless sway occasions pain,
As when the earth's athirst for rain.
8 They prove, 'neath sceptred wrong who groan,
To want is sweeter than to own.
9 A king perverse disturbs the sky,
Makes dry times wet, and rainy dry.
10 If guardians guard not, cows give less,
And idle priests forget to bless.[1]

LVII.—*Not making Afraid.*

1 Who probes, to check an evil thing,
And chastens duly, is a king.
2 Severe, yet, if he'd flourish long,
He must with mildness punish wrong.
3 His certain ruin's swift and near,
Whose cruel sceptre causes fear.
4 When men their chief a tyrant call,
Their bitter speech preludes his fall.
5 Fiends' looks upon his wealth have been,
Who's hard to see, and sour when seen.[2]
6 His wealth continues not, but flies,
Who's kind in neither tongue nor eyes.
7 Reproofs and penalties profuse,
Like files, the power to strike reduce.
8 A heedless ruler's fortune fails,
'Gainst those he trusts who hotly rails.

[1] Literally, men of six occupations forget their book. The six duties of priests are reading and learning, teaching, sacrificing, ordering things offered, bestowing alms, and receiving.

[2] What a demon has looked upon, and aided to procure, is of no use.

9 The time of war the prince appals
  Who's rear'd no fort, and soon he falls.
10 The greatest burdens earth supports
  Are cruel aud uncultured courts.

LVIII.—*Benign Looks.*

1 The conscious world's existence lies
  In beauteous grace of kindly eyes.
2 While churls like weights earth's patience tire,
  Benignant looks its march inspire.
3 What's sound till tuned to song it rise ?
  What, wanting kindness, are the eyes ?
4 What use, without benignant grace,
  Are eyes, but that they're in the face ?
5 The eyes kind looks as jewels wear :
  Without them they're but wounds that stare.
6 Like earth-fix'd knot-eyed trees they grow
  Whose eyes no pleasant glances throw.
7 Kind looks the living orbs reveal :
  They're sure to smile whose eyes are real.
8 Who, not neglecting their affairs,
  Can yet look kind, this world is theirs.
9 In patience bland, the highest vein
  Still bears with those whose forte's to pain.
10 They'll drink the poison they see poured,
  Who would for mildness be adored.

LIX.—*Employing Spies.*

1 A king should count these two his eyes
  A praise-deserving code, and spies.

H

2 His office 'tis to quickly learn
  All haps that daily all concern.

3 The use of spies who does not see
  Can never win the victory.

4 He spies, who watches all he knows,
  As agents, relatives, and foes.

5 Uncow'd, in unsuspicious guise,
  Who their own counsel keep are spies.

6 They'll play the monk, their quest pursue,
  And faint not, whatsoe'er men do.

7 They're skilful to search secrets out,
  And fact detect beyond a doubt.

8 Not on report of one rely,
  But test it by another spy.

9 Use spies apart, and credit three,
  Each strange to each, when they agree.

10 To spies no open favour deal:
   That were thy secret to reveal.

LX.—*The Possession of Energy.*

1 Proprietors by vigour stand:
  Without it, have they what's in hand?

2 Mere wealth of goods will slip away,
  But property of mind will stay.

3 "We've lost our store," not they complain
  Who magnanimity retain.

4 Wealth asks the way the man to find
  Of steadfast energy of mind.

5 The water's depth's the lily's length:
  The height of man's his mental strength.

6 All thought on greatness fix, and, though
  'Twere thrust from thee, it cannot go.

7 Like elephants when arrows shower,
   The great are firm in ruin's hour.

8 The pride that says, " The world we've blessed,"
   None reach but men of mind possessed.

9 Huge sharp-tusk'd elephants will quail
   When tigers quick and bold assail.

10 Who own no mental force, not good
    As trees, are only man-shaped wood.

LXI.—*Freedom from Idleness.*

1 Let sloth's foul dimness round it close,
   And out the light ancestral goes.

2 Who wish their house a house to be,
   Must live from idle follies free.

3 The end of silly drones is base ;
   But first they kill their native race.

4 To effort dead, they're more to blame,
   Because they bring their kin to shame.

5 Delay, oblivion, sloth, and sleep
   Are jewels[1] the self-doom'd will keep.

6 Earth's wealth were to the idle vain :
   Small good can they from greatness gain.

7 Lovers of sloth, of honour shorn,
   Hear words of censure and of scorn.

8 Let sloth a noble house invade,
   And bondmen to their foes they're made.

9 When one from sloth's oppression breaks,
   The tyrant vice his house forsakes.

10 A king not tied by sloth may mete
    All regions with his godlike feet.

---

[1] The word also means *vessel, ship.*

LXII.—*The Possession of Manly Resolution.*

1 Say not, " 'Tis hard : " he does, who tries :
In strenuous effort greatness lies.
2 Mind work begun, to finish it :
The world quits those their work who quit.
3 With hearty industry the pride
And praise of bounteousness reside.
4 When sloth in giving takes delight,
The coward[1] sword in hand will fight.
5 Who covets toil, not joys, away
Wipes griefs of friends, their prop and stay.
6 'Tis effort wealth accumulates :
Its want to want opens the gates.
7 Dark Mugadi[2] with sloth will be ;
The Lotus-throned with industry.
8 Misfortune is a fault in none :
The fault is nothing learnt or done.
9 Fate disallows, may people say ;
Yet labours of the body pay.
10 Toilers, still sanguine, ever bold,
The back of baffled fate behold.

LXIII.—*Not Succumbing under Adversity.*

1 'Tis best to laugh when cares annoy,
And tickle trouble into joy.
2 The wise divert their minds in thought,
And flood-like sorrows turn to nought.

[1] Androgynus.
[2] The goddess of adversity, elder sister of Tamarayināl, the Dweller on the Lotus, namely, Lakshmi. See XVII. 7.

3 Thy grief itself compel to grieve,
  Who will not grief in grief receive.
4 All troubles troubling, onwards go,
  As through deep mud the buffalo.
5 Sorrows pass sorrowful away,
  When thick they press, but can't dismay.
6 "We want," will they lament with tears,
  "We have," who never say with fears?
7 The high count not affliction woe:
  The body's evil's butt, they know.
8 As natural who evil see,
  And wish not joy, from grief are free.
9 For joy to joys who do not run,
  In sorrows suffer sorrow none.
10 The glory that his foes would gain
  Is his who pleasure finds in pain.

LXIV.—*The Office of a Minister.*

1 A premier's greatness is to heed
  Resource, occasion, method, deed.
2 He's firm of eye, the people's fence,
  For culture famed, and diligence.
3 His power divides men, keeps them friends,
  Or when they're separate re-blends.
4 He sifts affairs, the truth to find,
  And acts and speaks with single mind.
5 Replete with virtue, apt in speech,
  He's ready daily, skill'd to teach.
6 What stands his subtlest wit before,
  His native genius joined with lore?
7 To do as law directs he aims,
  And meet the world's peculiar claims.

8 He dares the king himself oppose,
Who knowledge scouts, and nothing knows.
9 In him, if he should harbour hate,
Close-gather'd foes in millions[1] wait.
10 Though well-consider'd be their act,
They gain no end, who have no tact.

LXV.—*The Power of Language.*

1 Tongue-good's a good 'tis well to own:
Such good in no good else is known.
2 The tongue can wealth or ruin reach:
Shun therefore impotence of speech.
3 The eloquent bind hearers fast,
And hold the listless chained at last.
4 Fit words for seasons understood
Surpass all virtue and all good.
5 Speak what thou reason hast to know
No adverse speech can overthrow.
6 Men like to hear the purely great
Who're able others' words to rate.
7 'Tis hard to match a speaker clear,
Unfaltering, and free from fear.
8 An able, sweet-voiced statesman found,
And swiftly lists the world around.
9 They much would say, who've skill to tell
In faultless language few things well.
10 Like bunch of scentless flowers are they,
Who cannot what they've learnt convey.

[1] Seventy kodis = 700 millions.

LXVI.—*Innocence of Action.*

1 By help some profit is acquired ;
  By action all that is desired.
2 The tempting action aye refuse,
  Whence neither praise nor good accrues.
3 Aspiring souls must acts avoid
  By which a bright repute's destroyed.
4 The fearless wise, oppress'd with grief,
  Do nothing shameful for relief.
5 Do nought thou wouldst regret with sighs :
  Once done, 'tis well if not done twice.
6 Thy mother's hunger see, and still
  Shun acts the wise denounce as ill.
7 Privation by the wise endured
  Is more than wealth by guilt procured.
8 To those who dare forbidden things
  Success affliction with it brings.
9 All gain from tears thou'lt weep away :
  Good deeds, though fruitless now, will pay.
10 Unholy gain, like water poured
  In vase of clay unburnt, is stored !

LXVII.—*Strength in Action.*

1 The strength to act may be defined
  Exclusively as strength of mind.
2 This twofold maxim guides the wise,
  Shun checks, but face them when they rise.
3 Its issue will fit force display :
  Woe comes to work exposed midway.
4 In words can all devise with ease :
  'Tis hard to do things as we please.

5 Who glory win their power evince
  By profits which they bring the prince.
6 The end on which the mind is set
  They reach, who strength to reach it get.
7 Despise no form ; what thou dost see
  The pivot of the wheel may be.
8 The mind made up what may be done,
  Be sloth subdued, and work begun.
9 Though pain oppose, with soul intent
  Do what is sweet in the event.
10 The world wants none, however strong,
  But those for strength to act who long.

LXVIII.—*Manner of Action.*

1 For counsel consultation's had :
  The course made clear, inaction's bad.
2 In slow affairs there's time to sleep :
  Awake in business urgent keep.
3 Prompt steps, when feasible, are good ;
  But look till all is understood.
4 What's left in work or war, the same
  As smouldering fire, may burst to flame.
5 Proceed when thought can darkness chase
  Concerning stores, means, time, act, place.
6 The labour and obstructions view,
  And profit great, and then pursue.
7 Obtain the mind of persons skilled,
  That what's resolved may be fulfilled.
8 Another elephant snares one :
  So deeds by previous deeds are done.
9 There's more in making friends of foes
  Than doing good to friends one knows.

10 The small who fear for their estate
Make up by worshipping the great.

LXIX.—*Embassy.*

1 They're legates true who love their friends,
Well-born, with traits a king commends.
2 Their prince they love, their minds have stored,
And speak with ease on things explored.
3 In law amid the wise they're strong,
Their words prevail the brave among.
4 The man for embassies who's fit
Is learned, comely, full of wit.
5 Concise in speech, harsh words he leaves,
Talks merrily, and good achieves.
6 No eyes he fears, and understands
The winsome words the hour demands.
7 He knows his calling, times can trace,
And speaks with mindfulness of place.
8 He's moral, helpful, clear in view,
And in his way of statement true.
9 To kings, in words that never fail,
With valiant eyes, he tells his tale.
10 If death upon himself he bring,
He'll swell the greatness of his king.

LXX.—*Walk with Kings.*

1 Wait on a king inflamed with ire,
Nor far nor near, as at a fire.
2 Want not whate'er the prince would gain,
His useful favour to retain.
3 Thyself to guard, excesses shun :
Where kings suspect, there's comfort none.

4 Nor whisper to another nigh,
  Nor laugh, in presence of the high.
5 Keep secret things thou hear'st them say,
  In sudden words they do not weigh.
6 Their mood discern, the moment seize,
  And talk the willing ear to please.
7 To genial words while they attend,
  Yet never speak without an end.
8 As kin and juniors rate them not,
  But honour their resplendent lot.
9 The firmly wise do nothing base,
  Relying on a monarch's grace.
10 Presumptuous friendship ruin brings,
  That ventures on improper things.

LXXI.—*Discerning Thought.*

1 Who thought unspoken notes, his worth
  Adorns the changeless sea-girt earth.
2 Esteem as God the knowing man,
  Able the soul to surely scan.
3 For him with any member part,
  Whose mind can read another's heart.
4 All else are limbs the man before
  Who thoughts unutter'd can explore.
5 'Mong members what avails his eye,
  Who cannot thought by thought descry?
6 As mirrors picture objects near,
  Heart-workings in the face appear.
7 Can more be known than from the face,
  Which heat betrays, or gladsome grace?
8 To mark the countenance will do
  For such as pierce the surface through.

9 Hatred or friendship eyes will tell
  To those conversant with their spell.
10 Their rule who say they scrutinize
  Thou'lt find is nothing but the eyes.

LXXII.—*Knowing the Assembly.*

1 The pure, with care, who've words in force,
  With those they know may hold discourse.
2 The good, with thought, who know the walk
  Of words, in fitting place may talk.
3 In conclave strange, who'd speak at length,
  Nor know the way, nor have the strength.
4 Be brilliant before the bright:
  As clouds, before the dull be white.
5 The self-restraint all good outweighs,
  Which nothing before elders says.
6 Like such as in the highway slip,
  Are they before the sage who trip.
7 Who faultless speech can recognise,
  To them with splendour shine the wise.
8 Before the learned language flows,
  Like water where the corn-crop grows.
9 When noble ears thou canst beguile,
  Forgetful speak not to the vile.
10 Who waste their words on grades below,
  Into the mire ambrosia throw.

LXXIII.—*Not Fearing the Assembly.*

1 Their friends the wise, with words in force,
  The pure without a slip discourse.
2 Who 'mid the taught are learned called
  Produce their learning unappalled.

3 Who'd meet the foe and die abound;
   But few to face the sage are found.
4 As wise before the wise to shine,
   Acquire what wisdom's over thine.
5 In college dauntless to contend,
   Be learning's lengths thy studious end.
6 Is theirs the sword, who dare not look ?
   Who dread the wise, is theirs the book ?
7 His science, of the wise afraid,
   Is like the coward's[1] polish'd blade.
8 Useless, though much they've learnt, are they
   Who 'mong the good no good things say.
9 The conclave of the good who fear,
   Though wise, yet arrant fools appear.
10 The field of lore who silent dread,
   Although they live, are like the dead.

LXXIV.—*Country.*

1 Where dwell the good and rich, and where
   The fields ne'er fail, the country's there.
2 'Tis where great treasures aptly lure,
   And woes are rare, and harvests sure;
3 Where ills are borne if they invade,
   And royal dues are duly paid;
4 Where pleasantly the order flows,
   From famine free, disease and foes;
5 Where crowds are none, nor schisms work,
   Nor traitorous assassins lurk.
6 Let that of lands be named the chief,
   Where wealth is proof 'gainst tides of grief.

[1] Androgynus.

7 Its members rain and wells are called,
  Mountains and rivers, cities walled.
8 Health, wealth, corn, joy, security,
  In these the country's jewels see.
9 Its plenteous fruit obtrudes unsought :
  Were search required, the land were nought.
10 Though all the rest a land contain,
  Without a king belov'd 'tis vain.

LXXV.—*Fortress.*

1 The fort is prized by men of deeds,
  And those whose fear a fastness needs.
2 Therein are gem-like water found,
  Mount, shady grove, and open ground.
3 Height, breadth, and strength its bounds possess,
  And 'tis not easy of access.
4 Though large the place, not hard to hold,
  It awes and tames assailants bold.
5 Impregnable, with food supplied,
  Its occupants with ease abide.
6 It comprehends all goods and arms,
  And warriors prompt to meet alarms.
7 It yields to neither circling foe,
  Direct assault, nor mine below.
8 Though long the hostile force assail,
  Its strong defenders still prevail.
9 Its aspect fills its foes with shame ;
  Its prowess gets a glorious name.
10 But fortresses, however grand,
  Are nought unless by heroes manned.

LXXVI.—*The Way of Wealth.*

1 No wealth is affluence indeed,
  But what enriches those in need.
2 All scoff at men of poor estate,
  And laud the opulent as great.
3 From any region darkness goes,
  Where wealth its lasting lustre throws.
4 Wealth fairly got, and wisely used,
  Is virtue wrought, and joy diffused.
5 If love and kindness do not bring,
  Hug not, but riches from thee fling.
6 Unsought possessions, spoils of foes,
  And tolls a monarch's wealth compose.
7 The nurse is wealth, in whose embrace
  Love's offspring thrives, benignant grace.
8 Handwork is like the sumptuous height,
  Whence elephants are watch'd in fight.
9 Get wealth : no blade succeeds so well
  The haughtiness of foes to quell.
10 He who accruing substance sees,
  Attains the other two[1] with ease.

LXXVII.—*The Greatness of an Army.*

1 Full-member'd, dauntless, conquering,
  His army's dearest to a king.
2 Though sad and few, still brave and bold,
  There's nothing like an army old.
3 A host of rats may sea-like roar :
  The serpent breathes, and they're no more.

[1] That is, virtue and pleasure.

4 Nor crush'd nor driven, its famous name
  The army keeps, with wonted flame.

5 If Cuttu[1] come, its ranks 'twill close,
  With force the angry god to oppose.

6 'Tis safe while courage it displays,
  With honour, loyalty, and praise.

7 The way to bear attacks it knows,
  And turn the battle on its foes.

8 Nor strong to stand, nor fit t' assail,
  'Twill then with proper wiles prevail.

9 Not base, exempt from fears that stay,
  And free from want, it wins the day.

10 With steady men though it abound,
   Yet, lacking leaders, vain 'tis found.

LXXVIII.—*Military Pride.*

1 Many who've stood my chief t' oppose
  Now stand in stone :[2] desist, ye foes.

2 With hitting hares compared, 'tis bliss
  To aim at elephants and miss.

3 In fight no foe the warrior spares,
  But after for the humbled cares.

4 At elephants the lance he'll fling,
  And laugh to draw the darts that sting.

5 Is it no detriment, dost think,
  When arrows fly, if heroes wink ?

6 Let days among days lost be placed,
  To which no glorious wounds are traced.

7 For circling praise, not life, who care,
  A foot-ring's their delight to wear.

---

[1] Death.   [2] The allusion is to stone monuments in memory of the slain in battle.

8 The king may check, but in the strife
Their fear's for glory, not for life.
9 Who'll censure, should they not prevail,
The men who'd rather die than fail?
10 'Tis then a soldier fitly dies
When for him stream his chieftain's eyes.

LXXIX.—*Friendship.*

1 What's hard as friendship to secure?
'Gainst mischief what defence so sure?
2 Serene, like waxing moon it shines;
Unwise, like waning moon declines.
3 Its happiness, when pure and true,
Like learning's joy, is always new.
4 Not vain amusement is its aim,
But checking faults with faithful blame.
5 On converse it does not depend:
The mind congenial makes the friend.
6 It more than smiles of face creates:
With laughter it the heart elates.
7 From ruin's course it points the road,
And helps to bear misfortune's load.
8 'Tis quick distresses to allay
As hand the falling robe to stay.
9 Its stately throne if thou wouldst see,
Admire its firm stability.
10 The love that boasts may not be much,
" They're such to us, to them we're such."

LXXX.—*Judgment in contracting Friendship.*

1 Than thoughtless friendship nothing's worse:
Such compacts none can well reverse.

2 Received ere search'd and search'd, a friend
Gives mortal trouble in the end.

3 To choose one, first his temper, race,
Connections pure, and failings trace.

4 Be friends with him, though great the price,
Who's nobly born, and shrinks from vice.

5 Who wrong denounce with melting tone,
And right set forth,—choose such alone.

6 In bane there's good, since to provide
Full help's the rule for those allied.

7 Do not to part from fools complain,
But count their commerce lost a gain.

8 Nor ponder hurtful thoughts, nor know
The friends who'd weakness work in woe.

9 In death 'twould burn thy mind to think
They let thee in misfortune sink.

10 The spotless as thy friends embrace,
And something give to quit the base.

LXXXI.—*Old Acquaintance.*

1 What's old acquaintance ?   Mindfulness
No friendly duty to suppress.

2 Attention's friendship's excellence,
Its salt, which wise men must dispense.

3 What good's in lengthen'd friendship known
To those who friendly acts disown ?

4 Familiar courtesies unsought
Should fit as if desired be thought.

5 Not foolish deem a painful deed,
But kind,.from friends if it proceed.

6 In friendship's bounds, though loss ensue,
Consistent friends continue true.

7 Old friends from love their love retain
   For even those who work them bane.
8 The day will still to them belong
   Who'll hear no ill, though friends do wrong.
9 Such worthies all the world would own
   As leave not friends they long have known.
10 Ill-wishers are to those inclined
   Who claims of ancient friendship mind.

LXXXII.—*Friendship with the Wicked.*

1 Though bad men's thirst for thee seem sore,
   Their friendship's better less than more.
2 What good's in friendship, lost or held,
   By wealth attracted, want repelled ?
3 The friend who weighs what he receives
   Resembles prostitutes and thieves.
4 Friends like unbroken restive steeds
   In fight, a lonely life exceeds.
5 Their wretched friendship's best not won,
   Who leave their guardian deeds undone.
6 Wise foes, ten million times above
   Fond fools esteem, with all their love.
7 Than laughter-making friends, from foes
   More good ten times ten millions flows.
8 Without a word the friend discard
   Who makes an easy service hard.
9 If but in dreams, bitter's the tie
   Of friends whose deeds their words belie.
10 Keep clear, though in thy house they smile,
   From friends who out of doors revile.

LXXXIII.—*False Friendship.*

1 Friends close, not join'd, if chance they see,
Will anvils for thy bruising be.
2 Fickle, like woman's heart, are friends
Who want the love that each pretends.
3 The mean may with good learning fill
Their minds, but cannot learn good-will.
4 Dread men with bitter hearts of guile
Who falsely with sweet faces smile.
5 Not join'd in soul, speak as they may,
'Tis wrong to rest in aught they say.
6 Though like good words of friends, the word
Of foes is known as soon as heard.
7 Trust not their lip-obeisance low :
Mischief is meant when bends the bow.
8 Hands join'd in worship may enclose
A weapon : doubt the tears of foes.
9 Make laugh, and with embracing kill
Such acting friends as scorn thee still.
10 When foes are friendly, friendship chase
Out of thy heart into thy face.

LXXXIV.—*Folly.*

1 Embracing loss, dismissing gain,
Is peerless folly's special vein.
2 Folly supreme is his who leads
A lawless life of lustful deeds.
3 No shame, no aim, no love, no care,
These marks a finish'd fool declare.
4 No fool surpasses such as learn,
Know, teach, and yet good manners spurn.

5 Fools sink in this life to the hell
  In which for seven to come they'll dwell.

6 The fool who knows not how, but dares,
  Besides defeat, himself ensnares.

7 Strangers, when fools get rich, are fed,
  While their own kindred pine for bread.

8 If fools on substance lay their hand,
  Like men confused with wine they stand.

9 Theirs is the sweetest friendship known:
  They're parted from without a groan.

10 Like carpet trod by unwash'd feet,
   Their entrance is where wise men meet.

LXXXV.—*Deficient Knowledge.*

1 No knowledge is worst want of all:
  Other defects the world counts small.

2 The ignorant with glee may give;
  But only to receive they live.

3 With sorrow they themselves torment
  More than their haters could invent.

4 What's ignorance? The pride that cries,
  " We are the knowing and the wise."

5 Meddlers with knowledge not attained
  Bring doubt on what they've really gained.

6 Impell'd its errors to reveal,
  Can little wit its shame conceal?

7 When dunces publish secrets rare,
  They trouble for themselves prepare.

8 Do not what's bid, and look for pain
  Long as this life shall yet remain.

9 Who show the sightless, sightless go:
  The sightless see the way they know.

10 They who the world's beliefs disown
 As demons in the earth are known.

LXXXVI.—*Hatred.*

1 'Tis hatred, with contagious smart,
 All lives infests, and keeps apart.

2 Provoked with aim to separate,
 Best not indulge resentful hate.

3 This woful sickness put away,
 And praise unstinted thine shall stay.

4 Where dies the chief of troubles, spite,
 There's born superlative delight.

5 Who'll humble those who, while they live,
 To rising hate no entrance give ?

6 His joys, ere long to cease, abate,
 Who says 'tis sweet to cherish hate.

7 Whose learning's with sour hate combined,
 To truth with glory link'd is blind.

8 Suppressing hatred gain secures :
 Fomenting it distress insures.

9 Unseen is hate, when gains accrue ;
 In times adverse, 'tis most in view.

10 From hatred flow all bitter things ;
 From laughing love proud goodness springs.

LXXXVII.—*Success in War.*

1 Refrain from combat with the strong :
 For battle with the feeble long.

2 How, wanting love, allies, and might,
 Shall any put his foes to flight ?

3 The covetous, unskill'd, afraid,
 And friendless easy prey are made.

4 The choleric and base a foe
  Can anywhere or day o'erthrow.
5 Who'll neither seek nor do the right,
  Nor shun the wrong, 's his foes' delight.
6 His enmity, who's blind with ire,
  And sunk in lust, is their desire.
7 A price his enmity deserves,
  Who starts, and from engagements swerves.
8 His vices please his foes, for they
  Are what have driven his friends away.
9 Ne'er cease the pride and joy of those
  Who find untrain'd and trembling foes.
10 The facile strife who leaves undone
  'Gainst men unskilful, praise has none.

LXXXVIII.—*Knowing how to oppose.*

1 It is not fitting, e'en in sport,
  The monster enmity to court.
2 Their hate who plough with bows tight-strung
  Prefer to theirs whose plough's the tongue.
3 Less than a madman's sense he shows,
  Alone who rouses many foes.
4 The world's support's the ruler's grace
  Whose walk makes hate to love give place.
5 Of foemen two, no helper nigh,
  Make one a friend and sweet ally.
6 Of likes and dislikes heedless be
  In seasons of extremity.
7 To none with plaints thy pain be shown,
  Nor make to foes thy weakness known.
8 Known means for self-protection use,
  That foes their confidence may lose.

9　The tender thorn with ease we tear :
　　Grown hard it rends the hands that dare.
10　They do no more than breathe who fail
　　To make their adversaries quail.

LXXXIX.—*Secret Enmity.*

1　As shade and water harm may do,
　　E'en relatives can prove untrue.
2　No need the sword-like foe to fear,
　　But him who's like a kinsman dear.
3　The secret foe, in evil day,
　　·Wounds deep, as potters cut the clay.
4　Incited by the skulking foe,
　　Kindred themselves work ample woe.
5　If hate in kindred's aspect rise,
　　In death's it trouble multiplies.
6　Should enmity the join'd divide,
　　Apart till death will they abide,
7　Though like an inlaid casket one,
　　A family's by strife undone.
8　As gold the rubbing file will wear,
　　Will secret hate a home impair.
9　'Tis ruin sure, though small it be
　　As piece of seed of sesame.
10　With serpent in a hut as well
　　As with the loveless 'twere to dwell.

XC.—*Not offending the Great.*

1　Not mocking power the potent wield
　　Is self-protection's surest shield.
2　The great in all thy walk revere,
　　Or they become thy life-long fear.

3 If death thou covet, disobey
The powers that when they like can slay.

4 The weak who trouble men of might
So Cuttam[1] with the hand invite.

5 Where can they stay, and whither turn,
Who make the ruler's anger burn ?

6 Thou might'st escape the raging fire,
But not the great inflamed with ire.

7 Abounding joy and goods are vain,
If men of excellence complain.

8 The seeming firm lose home and all,
Who treat the mountain-like[2] as small.

9 Kings fall, and in the blaze expire,
When sages flash with anger's fire.

10 Full substance fails before the frown
Of mighty men of full renown.

XCI.—*Going the Way of Women.*

1 Wife-worship from great profit leads,
And hinders from alluring deeds.

·2 Their course, whose dames are all their aim,
From deep disgrace proceeds to shame.

3 Debased before the good are they,
Unmanly who their wives obey.

4 None praise his acts, who dreads his wife,
Regardless of the coming life.

5 Who fear their wives have daily fear
Of doing good to good men near.

---

[1] Death.

[2] A title of men of saintly eminence, *Arunthavar*, those who do rare penance, unshaken as the hills.

6 They're little, though they live like gods,
   Who dread their arms as bamboo rods.
7 Be modest woman's name preferred
   To manhood walking by her word.
8 No friend they help, no good obtain,
   Who step as sweet-faced wives ordain.
9 No blessing they acquire or share,
   No feat achieve, who serve the fair.
10 Not in uxorious folly caught
   Are such as own the wealth of thought.

XCII.—*Women who transgress.*

1 The bracelet-wearing speak, for gain,
   Not love, sweet words producing pain.
2 Ponder their aim in what they say,
   And shrink from those who profit weigh.
3 Shun venal falsehood in the gloom,
   As 'twere a corpse inside a tomb.
4 Who search in good for gain disdain
   Low good of those whose good's their gain.
5 The great in good of knowledge flee
   Base good of those whose good is free.
6 'Tis sign of worth to shun their arms
   Who worthless sport their outward charms.
7 Their heart's depraved, for arms who care
   Of those whose heart is otherwhere.
8 The ignorant of truth are they
   Whom artful women lead astray.
9 Of hell, wherein the basest sink,
   A courtesan's the miry brink.
10 Close friends of those whom fortune flies
   Are fickle women, wine, and dice.

XCIII.—*Not drinking Wine.*[1]

1 Not fear'd for their remaining days,
  Who thirst for wine surrender praise.
2 Leave it to those who do not prize
  The good opinion of the wise.
3 How vile in sages' view must be
  What even mothers mourn to see !
4 Sweet modesty averts her face
  From those whom faults of wine disgrace.
5 They pay a price to lose their sense,
  And purchase manual impotence.
6 They drink but poison in the wine,
  And sleeping like the dead recline.
7 They spy for corners where to quaff,
  And make the prying townsfolk laugh.
8 Cease saying, " Wine's to me unknown ; "
  The bosom's secret soon is shown.
9 Like seeking with a torch the sunk
  In water, 'tis to teach the drunk.
10 In drunkards can't the sober see
  What wine's effect on them would be ?

XCIV.—*Gaming.*

1 Though on a player triumph wait,
  He's like a fish that bolts the bait.
2 Have they one course of good to choose,
  Who, one game got, a hundred lose ?
3 Of luck in play they ceaseless cry,
  While stores and dues together fly.

---

[1] Toddy, fermented juice of the palm.

4 Much meanness acting, losing fame,
No want's like theirs who keenly game.
5 The die, the hell, the throw who sought
With glee, are people brought to nought.
6 Their mouth unfill'd, their future void,
By play, the ogress, they're destroyed.
7 Who time in gaming-places spend,
Their ancient wealth and honour end.
8 Play leads to lies, makes riches go,
Of grace deprives, and gathers woe.
9 It aims at gain without success,
Wealth missing, food, praise, knowledge, dress.
10 When gamesters fail, they'd play again ;
So life's more loved for every pain.

XCV.—*Medicine.*

1 Of sufferings three[1] which doctors count,
Too much or little is the fount.
2 On what he can digest who feeds,
No medicine his body needs.
3 The way to make the system last
Is due restraint in each repast.
4 With nought indulge the appetite
But what thou know'st is safe and right.
5 No hindrances their lives afflict,
Themselves in eating who restrict.
6 As joy with temperance remains,
Excess begets abiding pains.
7 They're victims of unmeasured ill,
Who ignorant their maws o'erfill.

---

[1] Namely, wind, bile, and phlegm.

8 Inquire the pain, its cause, its cure,
To make remedial action sure.

9 Skill'd leeches note the sick man's state,
Symptoms, the time, then operate.

10 The patient, healer, med'cine-store,
And treatment,—physic's parts are four.

XCVI.—*Nobility.*

1 Uprightness and pure shame adorn
No natures but the gentle-born.

2 Good manners, truth, and modesty
Are signs of real nobility.

3 They show good birth, with laughing eyes,
Who give, speak sweetly, none despise.

4 Though millions ten of wealth they gain,
Their virtues unabridged remain.

5 Be their condition overthrown,
Their ancient worth is still their own.

6 They'll practise no deceit, who say,
" Our stainless birth prescribes our way."

7 Like spots upon the shining moon,
Their failings are distinguish'd soon.

8 Their noble birth would doubted be,
If lack of love the world should see.

9 By growth what's in the ground is shown ;
By language lineage is known.

10 Be modest, if on good intent :
For rank, tow'rds all be reverent.

XCVII.—*Honour.*

1 Though nothing else could grandeur gain,
From unbecoming acts refrain.

2 Who true esteem with praise desire
Do nothing mean, though men admire.

3 The prosperous need lowly be :
The low have need of dignity.

4 When men from eminence come down,
They're like hair falling from the crown.

5 The mountain-like to meanness fall,
Whose deeds, though crimson-bright,[1] are small.

6 To serve thy scorners gets no praise,
And cannot to the god-world raise.

7 Better to die in poor estate,
Than at their heels for life to wait.

8 While lives the flesh, what cure is known
For native greatness overthrown ?

9 As deer[2] won't live when hair they lose,
Not shame but death the noble choose.

10 The world adoring spreads their fame
Who'll not survive to suffer shame.

XCVIII.—*Greatness.*

1 They've light, whose minds are high and bright ;
Who live low-minded, shame and night.

2 In birth though all men start the same,
Their doings get them various fame.

3 The low, though high, continue low ;
The high, though low, their stature show.

4 When greatness walks, like matron pure,
With self-restraint, its course is sure.

5 Rare deeds, in paths by them pursued,
They do, who are with worth endued.

---

[1] Brilliant as the red seeds of the *cundi*, a medicinal plant.
XXVIII. 7, XC. 8.   [2] *Cavarimā*, a sort of deer.

6 Of converse with the great, the small
Have in their hearts no thought at all.

7 When base men opulence possess,
Their evil deeds are in excess.

8 While greatness always pays respect,
By .meanness self is praised and decked.

9 Its measure greatness never tells :
To boast its vastness meanness swells.

10 The great in mind defects conceal ;
The small with loudness faults reveal.

XCIX.—*Full Manliness.*

1 All goodness may be call'd their own,
Who give full strength to duties known.

2 Heart-good is that which rules the best :
No good's so good of all the rest.

3 Perfection's pillars five we name,
Politeness, favour, truth, love, shame.

4 As penance takes not life away,
Perfection no repute will slay.

5 Humility is valour's might,
And puts the baffled foe to flight.

6 Perfection's touchstone wouldst thou know ?
'Tis helping those who're fallen low.

7 What certain profit canst thou find,
If not to those who hurt thee kind ?

8 Where virtue's utmost power is won,
Disgrace in indigence there's none.

9 For men through changing times the same,
Perfection's shore's the proper name.

10 Were excellence to fail the great,
The world would cease to bear its weight.

C.—*Possession of Good Manners.*

1 With ease in ways polite they walk
   Who're free with all that come to talk.
2 A loving mind and perfect birth
   Produce a life of moral worth.
3 Man's shape, not in his members find,
   But in a meek and patient mind.
4 The world the useful soul commends
   Who charity with justice blends.
5 Even in play, contempt is hard :
   In hate, the wise their manners guard.
6 Good-manner'd men are strength to all :
   Without them to the dust we fall.
7 Not rasping files are the ill-bred,
   But saws of senseless wood instead.
8 Coarse conduct's base tow'rd even those
   Who, never friendly, act as foes.
9 For such as yield no pleasant light,
   The earth by day is dark as night.
10 Much riches ill behaviour mars,
   As good milk turns in faulty jars.

CI.—*Useless Wealth.*

1 He's dead, whose goods lie unemployed,
   Much wealth who's saved, but none enjoyed.
2 Low birth the niggard folly wins,
   Which says, " From money all begins."
3 For stores, not praise, who lust, their birth
   Is but a burden to the earth.
4 What thought has he about his heirs,
   For whom unfear'd no person cares ?

5 They're nought, ten millions though they hoard,
Who nought enjoy, and nought afford.

6 Great wealth's a pain to those who live
Inclined to neither use nor give.

7 Like comely dame grown singly old,
Are they who never yield their gold.

8 Unsought they keep their useless load,
Like pois'nous tree in village road.

9 Loveless, to virtue blind, self-slain,
For strangers their bright stores remain.

10 Praise-winning wealth, in transient straits,
Is like an emptied cloud that waits.

CII.—*Possession of Modesty.*

1 Shrinking from sin is proper shame:
It decks the bright-faced, honest dame.

2 All living creatures eat and own;
But shame belongs to man alone.

3 All lives to their own bodies tend;
But holy shame's perfection's end.

4 This grace the great must decorate,
Or painful is their grand estate.

5 Their own, as others' faults, who blame,
In them resides transcendent shame.

6 The high, who'd make the world their care,
The guardian shield of shame must bear.

7 Not shame for life the modest pay,
But life for shame's sake cast away.

8 Shameless where others shamed would be,
Such may with shame their virtue see.

9 Who strays, his race in ruin burns,
And shamelessness all good o'erturns.

10 Men shameless-minded only go,
 As string-pull'd puppets action show.

CIII.—*The Way to establish a Family.*

1 Beyond what says of work begun,
 " I'll not desist," there's greatness none.
2 Full knowledge, with firm exercise,
 Will cause a family to rise.
3 Fortune, with garment girt, obeys
 A man resolv'd his house to raise.
4 Success the enterprise attends,
 And without thought he gains his ends.
5 The world will kinship with him claim,
 Who keeps his house from harm and blame.
6 They demonstrate their manly worth
 Who lift the race that gave them birth.
7 Like strong-eyed heroes in the fight,
 They bear the burden with their might.
8 Not seasons the householder guide :
 There's ruin in delay and pride.
9 Is not his frame for pains an urn,
 Who trouble from his home will turn ?
10 A house, when dashing woes appal,
 With no good man to help, must fall.

CIV.—*Tillage.*

1 The plough is chief, if hard to use :
 Its lead the world, though turn'd, must choose.
2 Since ploughers are of all the stay,
 The linch-pin of the world are they.
3 They live, the plough for life who steer :
 All others worship in the rear.

4 Umbrellas many 'neath their own
  They see, whose corn's shade wide is thrown.
5 Not begging, by their hands who live,
  Nought hiding, they to beggars give.
6 Should tillers fold their hands, no stay
  Have they " Desire we've left" who say.
7 Without manure the fertile field,
  Though dried and shrunk, will produce yield.
8 Yet, plough'd, the land should be refreshed:
  When clean'd, not water, watching's best.
9 Unless the master stir about,
  His fields, like women, sulk and pout.
10 The woman earth laughs such to see
  As idly say, " Nothing have we."

CV.—*Poverty.*

1 Than want what can more bitter be ?
  Nothing but deeper poverty.
2 It brings no happiness in this,
  And for the world to come no bliss.
3 Its vain desires to ruin chase
  Ancient nobility and grace.
4 'Twill high-born victims so confuse,
  That language low and mean they'll use.
5 Along with this prolific pest
  Are many woes made manifest.
6 Though good things poor men know and say,
  Their eloquence is thrown away.
7 The destitute, whom virtue flies,
  Are strangers in their mothers' eyes.
8 The killing want of yesterday,—
  To-day, too, comes it not to slay ?

9 Some means to sleep 'mid fire may be :
There's next to none in poverty.
10 Till hungry men their life despise,
They're death to others' salt and rice.

CVI.—*Begging.*

1 Discerning who should give, apply :
The fault is his, if he deny.
2 Unless it be but troublesome,
With pleasure will the suing come.
3 'Twill even with some beauty show
To open hearts that duty know.
4 Petitioning like giving seems
To those who're kind even in dreams.
5 The world contains such friends in need :
The needy therefore stand and plead.
6 Men free from ill of greed to see,
Dispels all ills of poverty.
7 Without abuse who gifts impart,
With gladness fill the poor man's heart.
8 But for the poor, like puppet-show
The frigid world would come and go.
9 To bless the poor were none inclined,
Where'd be the praise that givers find ?
10 The needy never should wax hot :
Full witness is their evil lot.

CVII.—*Fear of Begging.*

1 Men who, like eyes, bestow with mirth
Non-begging deem ten millions worth.
2 Who framed the world may tramp, if he
Ordain'd that men should beggars be.

3 No hardness equals theirs who say,
    "We'll beg the woe of want away."
4 Not all the world accommodates
    The fulness that can't beg in straits.
5 Though thin as water, there's no meat
    As that which labour gives so sweet.
6 Though water for a cow one ask,
    To beg's the tongue's most shameful task.
7 To any one if you apply,
    Yet, beggars, pass the niggard by.
8 When begging's helpless boat is tossed
    On greed's rock-shore, 'tis split and lost.
9 The heart at thought of suppliants flows,
    But dead at thought of misers goes.
10 Where'll hide the hoarder's life, I pray?
    In words the beggar's goes away,

CVIII.—*Villainy.*

1 Like human beings are the mean :
    So close a likeness we've not seen.
2 Than those who virtue know more blest,
    No anxious sorrows wound their breast.
3 They're like the gods, for even they
    Desires achieve without delay.
4 When others caught in wrong they see,
    They boast of greater villainy.
5 They no restraint but fear respect :
    Else scarcely would their lusts be checked.
6 They publish, like a beaten drum,
    What secrets to their knowledge come.
7 Their hand they open but to those
    The fist to smite their cheek who close.

8 A word for aid the high subdues :
The low like sugar-cane we bruise.

9 Let them but see their food and dress,
And others' faults they surely guess.

10 For what except, from doom to flit,
To sell themselves, are villains fit ?

ALTHOUGH, as might be expected, the list of Tamil sages is not adorned by many female names, yet four learned women have handed valued writings down to the present day.

Sudicodutta Naychinar, a foundling brought up by a Vaishnava devotee, consecrated to the service of her foster-father's god, composed the works entitled *Tiruppavay* and *Tirumorlyi*.

Punithavati, a merchant's daughter early married, was deserted by her husband, who took another wife. As he withstood all advances made with a view to reconciliation, she assumed the habit of an ascetic, and repaired to the Imaus, where she died. Among other productions, she left the *Atputhattiruvanthathi*, a poem in high repute with the Saiva sect.

Sanpagavadivi was the daughter of one of the hand-maids of a Chōla rajah. Captivated by her precocious genius, King Carical adopted her, while yet a child, into the royal family, and gave her a splendid man-sion and an imposing retinue. The fame of her maturing charms attracted numerous suitors; but she resolved not to marry any one who could not vanquish her in poetical conflict, and exulted in remaining single till her twenty-fifth year. Then she was proved to be not invincible. The professors of Madura, whom she had characterized as a senate of dunces, were unable to endure her scorn any longer; and their doughty president Narkira put on the disguise of a wood-seller, and himself encountered the beautiful boaster. The combatants assailed each other with poetic enigmas, all of them preserved; and after a severe and protracted struggle, the head of the university led captive the discomfited damsel.

Ouvay, the fourth excellent lady, is the queen of female sages. Indeed, among Tamil writers she is second to none but the author of the *Cural.* She is a distinguished proof that the garden of knowledge was not always forbidden ground to the women of Southern India, and that they formerly enjoyed more social liberty than in the present day. It must of course be remembered that she was of low caste on her mother's side; but it is doubtful, from the traditions respecting her character and conduct, and from the writings in which she speaks to successive generations, whether she was a temple-woman. Hindus get over the difficulty by referring to the divinity in her. The fire of genius, watched by the eye of restraint, and fed with the oil of perseverance, was the real deity in possession.

It is greatly to be lamented that the biography of Ouvay or Ouvayār is not less absurd and varnished than that of Tiru-Valluvar. A new-born babe, she was discovered by a minstrel in a choultry near Urayūr. As she grew up, she fared very well among the Pānars, a class, now nearly extinct, of musicians and singers, whose office was to wait upon kings and pronounce their praises; and she became proficient in their arts and accomplishments. She is supposed to have been an incarnation of Sarasvati, Brahma's consort, who, as the goddess of music, poetry, and learning, knew with whom to choose her habitation. From her fifty-sixth maxim in *Attisūdi*, it would seem that she worshipped Perumal (Vishnu) as the Supreme Deity. Wherever she went, her lips breathed piety and wisdom, and her hand wrote moral verses and proverbs. She was a benefactress to all who needed her blessings, and was welcomed and honoured by people of every caste. It is said that she wrought miracles, healing diseases, creating circumstances, converting base things into gold, and mixing the medicine of immortality.

Descriptive titles and surnames are peculiàr to no age or country. Many a Hebrew appellation brings a picture to the mind. Among ourselves Armstrong, Greathead, Scattergood, Shakespeare, Sheepshanks, and the like, are familiar names. England has had her Black Prince and Iron Duke, and France her Little Corporal; and we have heard much lately of The Grand Old Man. In like manner, the people of India confer telling titles. A grim British general was called by them The Devil's Brother. Of three missionary colleagues in North Ceylon, one was commonly spoken of as The Tall, the next as The Short, and the oldest, who was comparatively a little gentleman, as, in an honourable sense, The Great Padre. The Tamil poets not having been accustomed to affix their names to their writings, several of them are known by only their acquired titles. One, for example, is called Ashdavathani, from the retentiveness of his memory, and another Curlyangayar, from his crippled hand, injured by a red-hot iron which he had been compelled to seize when on trial by ordeal; and the real name of the Divine Pariah has long been forgotten.

Ouvay means The Elderly Lady. She was also called Curlyuccupadi, or She who sang for a Meal, a title for which she was indebted to the vanity of a dancing-girl, Silambi of Ambal, and the churlishness of the poet Cambar, who bought many meals for one song. Silambi had offered the versifier five hundred pons[1] for a metrical inscription in her praise. That being only half the price he took for a stanza of the sort, he inscribed with charcoal but half a verse on the wall of her dwelling, and craftily departed. Fortunately Ouvay called presently; and for merely a dish of rice, she removed the girl's perplexity, and defeated the selfish rhymester's object. He had written—

Of rivers the best is Cāvery, and Chōla all kings
surpasses,
Of lands his are the richest, and the comeliest
of lasses—

Ouvay completed the inscription by adding—

Is Silambi of Ambal, and no silambu's[2] so sweet
As the golden one soft tinkling upon her lotus-feet.

Ouvay once honoured with a visit the island of Ceylon, where it rains twice a year, each time for a succession of days, and never rains but it pours. Caught in the torrent, she took shelter in the dwelling of two women of low caste; and Angavay and Sangavay treated her so kindly that she rewarded them with the

---

[1] A coin, valued at 3s. 6d. sterling.   [2] A foot ornament.

promise, "I will cause you to be given in marriage to the divine king of Tirucovalūr." Remembering her word, she waited upon the rajah, and commended to him her friends. His majesty replied, "If Chēran, Chōlan, and Pandiyan give me these women in marriage, I will receive them forthwith." He thought he had required an impossibility ; but the poetess, accepting the condition, addressed the following invocation to the elephant-headed god of wisdom and enterprise, and of marriage rites,—

O son of him[1] who joys to wear
A tiger's skin, and made thee bear
The elephant's huge head, appear,
Reveal thy fragrant presence here,
And swiftly by my fingers write,
And make this leaf the kings invite.
Thou double-tusk'd one, heed my will,
Thou single-handed, show thy skill,
Or she who breathes this pious verse
Will vex thee with her venom'd curse.

Pillayar readily vouchsafed his aid; and she inscribed the charmed invitation on an ola (palmyra-leaf), folded it up, and despatched it, by the god of the winds, to the three kings. When they had read it, they proceeded without delay to a marriage-saloon called into existence for the occasion by the marvellous woman ; and on their arrival they thus addressed her, "Mother, here is a piece of palmyra-wood: if you make it become a tree, put forth leaves, and bear young fruit, and will present to each of us a specimen of its ripe produce,

[1] Siva.

we will do as you desire." Consenting to a condition
which they thought could never be fulfilled, she lifted
up her voice, and sang,—

> Before the palace-like saloon,
> Umbrellas silvery as the moon
> The bridegroom's royal friends reveal,
> Who're come with holy oil to seal
> Their happy fate whose sheltering roof
> Render'd the stranger tempest-proof.
> They first insist, my claims to show,
> This lifeless wood be made to grow.
> So let the shell-white sprout be seen,
> Unfold its leaves of deepening green,
> And form its fruit, till ripe there fall
> For each his black and ruddy ball.

Her incantation ended, the astonished kings witnessed the fulfilment of their hard request. Each held
in his hand a round specimen of the red-tinged fruit.
There was no escape. Ouvay had complied with their
requirement, and they, trembling with awe, hastened
to comply with hers. Chēran, Chōlan, and Pandiyan
gave the two women away in marriage to the divine
king of Tirucovalūr, according to his own decision.

When Ouvay accompanied Valluvar to the Madura
College, she was not to be put to shame by the
assembled sages. In spite of the maxim, if then in
vogue, "Talking by gesture is improper for women,"
she asked the professors to explain, if they could,
certain signs she made. Not satisfied with their
answers, she thus gave her dumb actions a voice,—

Bestowing alms, in virtue live.
Though but a pinch of rice, yet give
Before you eat your own.
The five great sins will pass away,
When power you get to know and say
That God is One alone.

The moral philosophy of India is based upon the four questions, What is virtue, wealth, pleasure, heavenly bliss? Tiru-Valluvar, in his *Cural*, considered only the first, second, and third. If the judgment of Todittalay-Virlyuttandinār, one of the Madura professors, was correct, the fourth was not unapproached by the poet, but anticipated in his discussion of the other three. Ouvay, however, on learning the construction of the work, thought her brother liable to censure; and, in her opinion, it was an easy task to solve the questions. It had taken him thirteen hundred and thirty couplets to answer three of them: she settled all the four in one impromptu stanza, which may be thus rendered,—

Virtue's giving without halt.
Wealth is getting without fault.
Pleasure is the mutual flame
Of two who burn with tastes the same.
Giving, getting, loving nought,
Gathering all the power of thought,
Losing self in the abyss,
Searching God, is heavenly bliss.

Ouvay knew how to acknowledge merit, and to rebuke pretence. As she chanced one day to be sitting on the ground with her feet outstretched, in a street of Urayūr, the Chōla king Culōtunga came along, with Ottaycūtar, one of his poets, and Pugarlyēnthi, who was also a poet, but of the Pandiya court. As the monarch went by, the old lady withdrew one of her feet; and as the Madura poet passed, she retracted the other. To Ottaycūtar, who came last, she must surely pay some equal mark of respect. On the contrary, as if he were nobody, she made haste to stretch out both her legs again. The offended courtier desired an explanation. She said to him, "I drew back one foot for the king, because he wears the crown, and both feet for Pugarlyēnthi, because he is a great poet; but I have not pulled up either of my feet for you, as you are nothing but a dunce. If you are as able as Pugarlyēnthi, prove it by improvising a verse in which, while you praise the Chōla country and its king, the word *mathi* shall occur three times." The said word, signifying *the moon* and *wit*, only coming twice in his laboured stanza, she asked with concern, "Where is thy other wit?" He was so ashamed, that he could give no answer. She then applied to Pugarlyēnthi, only politely suggesting that he should substitute the Pandiya kingdom; and Ottaycūtar was outdone by the more ready poet of Madura. She applauded him, and tried him with another word, in the use of which he was equally successful.

Like other reputable women, Ouvay was slightly inconsistent. She declared in favour of marriage. The third line of her *Conday-vēnthan* is quoted by a modern Tamil poet in the following verse, which serves to show the esteem in which she is held:

" Ye dispute vainly among yourselves, O sages, when ye say that among the four established orders of life this or that is to be preferred, and deceive yourselves: our revered mother, who was herself a manifestation of virtue, has said, ' No virtue is more excellent than the virtue of domestic life.' "[1] This virtue, nevertheless, which the Divine Pariah studiously exemplified, the Revered Mother did not manifest. It may have been her misfortune, not her fault or choice, that she remained single. In the present day it is a disgrace to be an old maid in India; but they who think so never impute any blame to Ouvay.

Europeans are tempted to see evidence of her having been a proud and peevish old maid in the eighty-fourth maxim of her Attisūdi, " Do not associate with children." Perhaps its offensiveness will be reduced if we dare to suppose that it was not intended for everybody. The good lady may have been thus recommending such as had risen into youth to seek the presence and follow the counsel and example of their elders and betters, rather than content themselves exclusively with the friendship of those who were not so old and thoughtful as themselves. Solomon says that " foolishness is bound in the heart of a child." Or people inclined to be too inquisitive about their neighbours may have been advised by Ouvay's words not to take advantage of the innocent communicativeness of little children. Or the line may be a caution against too early entering upon married life.

She could speak severely, and even disparagingly, of her sex. " Do not listen to the words of women," is

[1] Cited by Ellis.

the sixty-second maxim in her Attisūdi. It is not
necessary, however, to suppose the advice to be intended
absolutely. The reference may be to such women as
Solomon warns against. " A foolish woman is clamor-
ous ; she is simple, and knoweth nothing." " The
strange woman flattereth with her words." " The mouth
of strange women is a deep pit."[1] Ouvay's heart could
be wounded when others spoke against women, and she
could come effectively to their rescue. Upon some
lords of creation whom she heard aspersing their
character, she turned with the impromptu,—

> All women are good if let alone,
>   They are spoilt by those who rule them;
> And by men might a little sense be shown,
>   But the women so befool them.

Tradition says that Ouvay reached the age of two
hundred and forty years, and then voluntarily retired
from earth. As her final engagement before passing
away, she selected the worship of the wise and
powerful god whom she had once threatened to curse.
The object of her devotion found it necessary to demand
why she, who had never offered worship in a slovenly
manner before, now went through it hurriedly. Men-
tioning the names of two sages, she answered, " Swamy,
they are going to Kailasam, and desire my company."
" I will get you there before them," said benignant
Pillayar ; " only finish your ceremonies in your usual
style." The believing woman did so ; and with his
gentle trunk the elephant-headed deity lifted her to
Siva's heaven, where her two friends, on their arrival,

See *Mūthuray*, verses 22, 27 ; *Conday-vēnthan*, lines 41,
42, 80.

were amazed to find her already. A plainer account records that, according to the custom of the times, she made the great journey to the Imaus (*mahāprasthānagamana*), and died there.

The compositions attributed to the Elderly Lady have received unmeasured commendation. Mr. S. C. Chitty thinks that she "was more keen and clever than even her brother."[1] Father Beschi pronounces her " moral sentences worthy of Seneca himself."[2] The Rev. Peter Percival regards her works as "of great beauty and value, replete with lessons of wisdom," and is of opinion that they "have never been surpassed for sententious brevity, and generally are equally distinguished by purity of principle."[3] Another critic says, "She sang like Sappho, yet not of love, but of virtue."[4]

Thirteen books are ascribed to her,—*Nigandu*, a dictionary of materia medica; *Panthananthathi*, a panegyric on Panthan, a wealthy merchant of Caveripatnam; *Nyana-Cural*, a treatise on metaphysics; and the ten following on ethics and religion, *Tarisana-pattu, Arunthamirlmalay, Nanmarnicovay, Nannutcovay, Asathicovay, Calviyorlyuccam, Nalvarlyi, Condayvēnthan, Attisūdi*, and *Mūthuray.*

The most important are the five named last, of which three are translated in the following pages. Like all the rest, these are composed in the high language; and some of the sentences they contain are ambiguous even to educated natives. They are often

---

[1] *Tamil Plutarch.*
[2] Introduction to Shen-Tamil Grammar.
[3] *Land of the Veda.*　　　　　　　　[4] *Calcutta Review.*

above the comprehension of little children. The experience of every missionary agrees with that of the Rev. James Hough. " A short time before I left Madras, I went into one of the native schools, and requested the teacher to let me see what the boys were reading. He showed me some olas, on which were written the sayings of Ouvay. I desired him to explain them to me ; when he took up another ola, which contained the interpretation, and began to read. I stopped him, saying that I wished him to tell me from his own mind what he supposed to be the sense of the proverbs, or even of the written interpretation. Upon this, he looked in my face, and confessed, with a smile, that he understood neither the one nor the other. Such is the ignorance of most of the native schoolmasters ; and it is evident that their scholars can derive no moral benefit whatever from repeating sentences, however sound the morality they contain, unless they are made to comprehend their meaning and application."[1]

Yet Ouvay's works seem to have been originally prepared chiefly for the young ; and certain it is that they are among the first, as well as best, put into the hands and heads of the people of Southern India. Commentaries, as intimated above, are attached to them ; and the living teacher, when not so incompetent as the schoolmaster referred to is represented to have been, offers his own explanations. There is no doubt that native schoolmasters are sometimes idle machines in the processes of education ; but they are not always so ignorant as they appear to be, being occasionally

[1] Reply to the Abbé Dubois.

either in a state of suppressed agitation, or politely resolved not to be unnecessarily inconvenienced. The Hindu system of instruction stores the memory with picked and packed words, leaving the fruit of them, if not nipped by fate, to develope gradually under the maturing influences of thought and time, and be gathered by the judgment in after days.

There is not a purer composition among the standards of India than Ouvay's *Mūthuray* (Old-saying), or *Thirty Aphorisms*, frequently called also, from the first words of the dedication, *Vakkundam.* It is especially interesting to the author of the present volume as the first Tamil poem with which he became acquainted, and as the foundation of this little work. A stanza in English verse was submitted at the break-fast-table, morning after morning, to the Rev. Peter Percival, whose commendation was sufficient encouragement to perseverance. He kindly applied for a copy of the translation a few years afterwards ; and it was a flattering surprise to find it printed in his *Land of the Veda.* The generous reader will not see un-pardonable vanity in the transcription here of some of the words with which it was introduced by Mr. Percival. "I have been obligingly favoured by my friend, the Rev. E. J. Robinson, with the following poetic versions of the Hindu matron's thirty aphorisms. They are very beautiful, and will be read with equal pleasure and regret, when it is known that the English versifier is not now in circumstances at once to benefit the Hindus by his labours, and his countrymen by continued examples from an ancient literature that, in some of its moral features, suffers nought from comparison with the best ethical writings ever brought to light."

Missionaries have admitted the *Mūthuray* into their schools, and themselves given editions of it to their pupils and to the world. It is included, for instance, in the *Fifth Instructor*, published and used in North Ceylon; but in this edition, besides the substitution of another dedication or introduction, the arrangement of the stanzas is entirely changed. There is an omission of the twenty-seventh, without compensation; and for the third, seventh, eighteenth, twenty-second, twenty-third, and twenty-ninth, there are introduced verses from other sources, two of them from Ouvay's *Nalvarlyi.* It may be urged that perhaps the missionaries arranged their edition from conflicting ola copies before the press in the service of native editors had fixed the order of the verses. Otherwise, how could they shut out the eighteenth, twenty-second, twenty-third, and twenty-seventh, while retaining the fifth, nineteenth, and twentieth?

Is it moral, even on moral grounds, to take such liberties with honoured writings? The practice invites charges of presumption, fraud, and imposition. If the anxiety to withhold pernicious aliment may be commended, let the impossibility of withholding it in this way be considered. Omitted verses are easily and invariably supplied, even in Christian schools, from original copies belonging to pupils or to the native teacher. When the padre comes in sight, the forbidden olas are hidden within the desk, under the mat, or in the folded garment. Deceit thus begets deceit, and leads to a closer acquaintance with objectionable passages. Nothing is gained for the truth by endeavours to make pagan writers shine in other than pagan colours.

Have not the missionaries taken needless and inconsistent trouble in editing and printing books of this description for the purposes of education? A time may come when such volumes may be handled with advantage in their seminaries, as the works of old European heathens are now used in Christian colleges; but at present, important as it is to recognise and honour truth in whatever associations found, and desirable as it seems to conciliate the people by paying all possible respect to their treasured literature, the propriety is seriously questionable of using the productions of ancient native authors, steeped with heathenism as the best of them are, as class-books in missionary institutions. The works of Ouvay herself, some of them the most excellent of Tamil writings, repeated by the lips of generation after generation in Southern India and North Ceylon, suffice to show the necessity of essentially and originally Christian books in the vernacular languages being provided for evangelistic institutions in our Eastern empire. The thought is mournful that in mission seminaries, for more than half a century, along with her lessons of profound wisdom, she has been left to teach the children to believe, like their fathers, in a blind fate, in a succession of dependent births, in the servile subordination of her sex, and in idolatry. Granted that her sayings are wonderfully correct and moral for a Gentile writer, they are not pure and true enough for Christian teaching. Difficult as many, particularly young people, find it to understand some of her sentences, and to appreciate their literary excellence, yet the paganism dwelling in her writings reveals itself to babes. Let the missionary Church be content for a season to place such books where the Indian Government thinks it wise to deposit even the Holy Bible, on the shelf, in sight and within reach, and neither on the torturing wheel nor in any shape on the day's programme.

After Ouvay's *Thirty Aphorisms,* follows a translation of her *Attisūdi.* This title is taken from the first words of the dedication of the work to Ganapathi (Pilleyar). The sentences being arranged in the order of their initial letters, like the lines or stanzas of twelve of the Hebrew poems in the sacred volume, some have called this the *Golden Alphabet* of the Tamils. Only one hundred and eight letters are thus honoured in the *Attisūdi;* whereas the Tamil letters and their combinations, exclusive of the Grandonic or Sanscrit characters used in association with them, amount to two hundred and forty-seven.

The fifty-sixth line of the *Attisūdi* brings an illustration of the difficulty which conscientious missionaries and others encounter when editing Tamil classics. Careful to retain the initial letter in its rank, they refuse the divinity which it introduces into the golden alphabet. Instead of "Serve Tirumāl (Vishnu)," the Rev. J. Sugden prints, "Serve the Lord." The Madras Tract and Book Society change the sentence to "Praise the Divine Name." Another Christian editor substitutes "Serve the Triune God." Tamils who do not accept Vishnu as supreme, find themselves tempted to take the same liberty. A worshipper of Siva altered this maxim of Ouvay to, "Do not frighten any one."

A translation is next given of the *Conday-venthan*, the production which puts a commendation of matrimony into the mouth of the singular old lady. It takes its title from the opening word of the brief invocation. As in the *Attisūdi* and other collections of moral sentences, the arrangement is alphabetical. Yet not so many letters are honoured as in the former golden alphabet, while one is admitted which that work passes over. It may be observed that the *Attisūdi* is hortatory and imperative, the *Conday-venthan* indicative and aphoristic.

MŪTHURAY.

Who statedly with floral gifts attend,
Before the trunk-faced red one's[1] footstool bend,
  And pious homage reverently pay,
Shall from the goddess lotus-throned[2] acquire
Wit, eloquence, and all that they desire,
  And never sink in bodily decay.

---

1 If suffering worth to acts of kindness move,
  Dismiss the fear your bounty may not prove
    A source at last of profit and delight:
  The water furnish'd to its early root
  In sweeter draughts from future plenteous fruit
    The cocoa's crown will gratefully requite.[3]

---

[1] Pilleyar, Ganapathi, Ganēsha.   [2] Lakshmi.
[3] The young cocoa-nut tree needs copious and frequent watering. The fluid of its fresh fruit is a pleasant drink.

2 The benefits which the deserving gain
  Like sculptures in eternal rock remain ;
    Of virtue's tribute charity is sure :
  But vain are favours to the worthless shown,
  Who debts and duties evermore disown;
    Like words on water written they endure.

3 In vain attractively the garden blooms
  When senseless grief the live-long day englooms ;
    In vain the mateless maid her beauty wears ;
  And youth when needy is a tiresome stage ;
  And wealth is misery in helpless age,
    A bitter mockery of peevish cares.

4 To love, though loved, the callous base ne'er learn ;
  But love for love the good and wise return ;
    Their greatness through calamities remains ;
  A purer whiteness as the sea-shell shows
  When fiercely the containing furnace glows ;
    As seething milk its flavour still retains.

5 Although in foliage richly dress'd they rise,
  In figure faultless, and mature in size,
    As trees no fruit except in season bear,
  In any project sooner to succeed,
  And gain the end before the time decreed,
    Nor wealth avails, nor toil, nor wakeful care.

6 Not softly yielding as the building towers,
    Not bending gently when the load o'erpowers,
    The stony column will asunder fly :[1]

  [1] Frangas, non flectes.

So they who scorn their honour to survive
Against o'erwhelming adversaries strive,
    Refusing homage when they muster nigh.

7 The depth and surface of the pool decide
The growth and limit of the lily's pride :
    So erudition is on study based ;
So riches show accumulated worth
By penance purchased in a previous birth;
    So character from son to sire is traced.

8 Happy the eyes that on the pious rest,
The ears that hear their useful words are bless'd,
    And bless'd the lips that all their virtues tell ;
More happy they their character who wear,
Their friendship gain, their reputation share,
    Their sacred paths frequent, and with them dwell.

9 The very sight of wicked men is ill,
Their graceless words the ear with evil fill,
    The lips with risk their attributes portray,
And 'tis the height of self-inflicted wrong
To mingle with their sin-infectious throng,
    Attend their cursed steps, and with them stay.

10 The water turn'd to where the rice-crop grows
Refreshes kindly, as it thither flows,
    The common grass that by its channel lies ;
In every age the genial rains that fall
To cheer the good are shared alike by all,
    And virtue's revenue the world supplies.

11 To instruments the great their glory owe ;
    The lofty are supported by the low ;
      Without assistance rank and skill were vain :
    What brings us good 'tis sinful to despise ;
    The rice denuded unproductive dies,
      The husk we spurn preserves the living grain.

12 The scentless *taly* flower in bulk excels,
    The little *magul* 'tis that sweetly smells :
      In seeming meanness may be hidden worth :
    The spacious sea, with all its vauntful roar,
    E'en for ablution fits not,[1] while ashore
      The humble spring with nectar gushes forth.

13 The branching trees that in the jungle grow
    No excellence like cultured palms can show :
      Appearing proudly with the learned, he
    Who, lacking skill to scan the proffer'd verse,
    Or seize the sense of what the rest rehearse,
      Is disconcerted, stands a jungle tree.

14 As when the clumsy turkey, having seen
    The forest peacock step with graceful mien,
      Struck with the beauty of his gorgeous train,
    And thinking one of kindred plume he spied,
    His feathers spread with pomp of strutting pride,
      Poetic skill unlearned coxcombs feign.

---

[1] English blue-jackets will drive off canoes, and make room for their own boat, by naughtily dipping a hand in the sea, and dashing water on the shoulders of the native sailors in their way. The saline deposit spoils the look of their brown skin.

15 Who aid the ingrate in their yearning zeal,
   Like him who dared the poison'd tiger heal,
     But bless the brutal to become their prey :
   Like vase that falls upon a granite block,
   Or freighted bark that greets a sunken rock,
     Their blind beneficence is thrown away.

16 The noble in distress are still esteemed ;
   The mean of wealth bereft are worthless deemed ;
     The former like a cup of gold are found
   That fractured its intrinsic worth retains ;
   The latter like an earthen bowl, that gains
     Contempt when strewed in fragments on the
       ground.

17 Insult not over those in self-conceit
   Whose self-restraint may end in your defeat,
     Though void they seem of wisdom, tact, and
       strength :
   If smaller fish may dart securely by,
   The heron watches with unerring eye
     The proper victim that appears at length.

18 No friends are they who heartlessly forsake,
   As water-fowl the sun-exhausted lake,
     Their old associates in their time of need :   .
   As lilies wither when the pond gets dry,
   And, where they flourish'd, parch'd and prostrate lie,
     Who share our troubles are our friends indeed.

19 Say, fretful spirit, whether shall ensue
   The visionary good we fondly view,
     Or every just award decreed by fate ?

From Indra's tree, for fruits of blessing known,
Who gilded nuts of poison pluck, atone
    For deeds that stained their pre-existent state.

20 Because in ocean dipp'd, not four times more
The measure holds than it could hold before.
    What futile hopes our silly sex employ !
Though wealth be gained, and homely sweets
    abound,
No greater happiness is therefore found,
    Since fate has fixed the limits of our joy.

21 'Tis not in blood that kindred always lies,
From birth connections that true friendships rise :
    Congenital disease may mortal prove :
A distant mountain may the medicine yield
By which alone a sickness can be healed ;
    A stranger may desponding care remove.

22 The dwelling with a frugal mistress blessed,
Though all things lacking, is of all possessed,
    For peace, content, and cleanliness are there ;
The house not suited with a thrifty wife,
Or cursed with one intent on angry strife,
    Though plenty reign, is like the tiger's lair.

23 The good and learned to their sort repair,
As seeks the swan the placid water where
    The beauteous lotus breathes its fragrance round ;
But like the crow, by carrion instinct led,
That scents the corpse, and lives upon the dead,
    The base and ignorant with fools are found.

24 By hasty wrath disjoined, the meaner kind,
   Like broken stone, are never more combined ;
     Remingled soon are some divided hearts,
   Like fractured gold by fusion blent again ;
   No longer sunder'd do the good remain
     Than water that the pointed arrow parts.

25 While, conscious of his fatal power to harm,
   The guilty cobra hides in just alarm,
     The guileless water-snake abroad appears :
   Deceitful workers, shunning public view,
   In secret their perfidious schemes renew,
     While innocence at large no danger fears.

26 Though servile hosts the king's behests obey,
   The grave philosopher bears ampler sway ;
     While homage meets the sage wherever known,
   And every step extends his spotless fame,
   The monarch's title is an empty name
     Beyond the narrow realms that prop his throne.

27 To fools the words of the resentful wise,
   To vicious souls the virtue they despise,
     As plantains to the stalk from which they
       sprung,[1]
   Are terrible as Yama's fatal name ;
   But better still this suits the tyrant dame,
     They know, who fear and feel her clamorous
     tongue.

[1] Having yielded one bunch of fruit, the leading trunk of the plantain or banana-tree perishes, making room for the stalks, in different stages of development, rising from the root. In gardens the old stem, having served its turn, is immediately cut down.

28 Attrition, in its merciless delay,
   May wear the precious sandal-wood away,
       But leaves its grateful fragrance all behind :
   So, though calamities their coffers drain,
   Triumphant o'er misfortune, kings retain
       Their royal fortitude of heart and mind.

29 With Lakshmi come, and vanish when she flies,
   The pleasures that from constant friendships rise,
       Resources keeping pace with high desire,
   The pride of beauty, dignity of birth,
   And all things loved and coveted on earth :
       Then toil for wealth, and prize what you acquire.

30 Till by the ringing axe in ruin laid,
   As trees afford a cool refreshing shade
       To mortals shrinking from the scorching heat,
   The sons of knowledge, till they cease to live,
   As far as can be, good for evil give,
       And acts of kindness to their foes repeat.

ATTISŪDI.

The chance of doing good desire.
Extinguish anger's kindling fire.
The means at your command confess.
Be no one hindered who would bless.
Of riches do not idly brag.
Let zeal and courage never flag.
Figures and letters claim esteem.
All shameless begging shameful deem.
Give alms, then eat with gratitude.
Be customs pleasantly pursued.

10

No idle pause in learning seek.
A word of envy never speak.
Make not the price of corn to rise.
Let candid lips report your eyes.
Consort like letters in array.
Bathe you with oil on Saturday.[1]
Your speech with pleasing words be filled.
Do not too large a dwelling build.
When friends you find, be found a friend.
With fond regard your parents tend.   20
Remember every kindly deed.
In seed-time sow the precious seed.
Live not by tilling stolen ground.
Be all your practice comely found.
Who sport with snakes, with danger jest.
Upon a bed of cotton rest.
Disdain to breathe a word of guile.
No graceless deeds your name defile.

[1] In this weekly ceremony, the head is first smeared with oil and other substances, and water is afterwards affused. The atmosphere of a school deteriorates as Saturday approaches. A Tamil stanza says: "If you bathe on Sunday, death will seize you; if on Monday, you cannot gain the favour of God; if on Tuesday," the day assigned to the widow, "you will fall sick; if on Thursday, sorrow will oppress you; if on holy Friday," kept as sacred to Lakshmi and Parvati by many women, "you will lose your property. Avoid all these, and, anointing, bathe on Wednesday and Saturday." Women clean the house on Friday. *Garland,* line 92. Saturday is a somewhat sacred day. A worshipper of Vishnu expressed to the writer his regret that Christians had so declined that, in the face of their own *shastras,* they had ceased to observe the seventh day as the day of rest and worship. But for this change, he remarked, they would have had common ground on which to stand with seriously disposed Hindus.

Let learning be in youth your choice.
Forget not virtue's form and voice. 30
In early morn drive sleep away.
Say nothing cruel all the day.
To fasting due attention give.
By proper living teach to live.
For baseness give no cause to chide.
Good tempers never lay aside.
United with your friend remain.
Avoid inflicting wrong or pain.
They learn the most, the most who try.
Your trade be free to own and ply. 40
Nor steal, nor wish to take away.
Refrain from every sinful play.
In ways of justice keep your feet.
Be found where saints and sages meet.
In speech be open and sincere.
To what is excellent adhere.
To stir up anger nothing say.
With gamesters have no wish to play.
In all you do correctness show.
Go where you know you ought to go. 50
Your steps from fault-detecting stay.
Say plainly what you have to say.
Get not the wandering idler's name.
Acquire the well-known worthy's fame.
Let priests your cheerful presents view.
To Perumal[1] pay service due.
From sin desist, and evil chase.
To care and trouble give no place.

---

[1] Vishnu.

Consider well ere you essay.
Blaspheme not God, but keep His way.   60
Live with your countrymen agreed.
The words of women do not heed.
The things of eld be kept in view.
No doubtful, novel course pursue.
Hold fast the good until the end.
Perform such acts as all commend.
Where you were born, contented stay.
You should not in the water play.
Be dainties from your palate spurned.
Let many sciences be learned.   70
The rice-field diligently tend.
Be righteousness your way and end.
From fatal evils stand afar.
With no low words your language mar.
By no excess disease induce.
Bespatter none with foul abuse.
Contract no friendship with a snake.
With wicked lips no mischief make.
By patiént toil at greatness aim.
In all your living live for fame.   80
First till the ground, then eat your rice.
Consult your betters for advice.
Let ignorance be put away.
With children neither join nor stay.
Retain what you possess, and thrive.
Nor stir to angry strife, nor strive.
Preserve your mind from trouble free.
Yield nothing to an enemy.
Your words be but the few you need.
Do not immoderately feed.   90

From where contention rages run.
Perverse and stubborn people shun.
Live with your wife in homely cheer.
When wise men speak incline your ear.
Avoid the doors where harlots dwell.
Correctly told be all you tell.
Throw every sinful lust aside.
Boast not your parts with angry pride.
In strife be not your word the first.
In knowledge covet to be versed.   **100**
Be heaven your first and final aim.
Acquire the good man's fragrant name.
Live happily among your own.
Be sharp in neither word nor tone.
Ill wishes must not lead astray.
Awake and rise at break of day. ·
All intercourse with foes refuse.
Say nothing based on partial views.

CONDAY-VĒNTHAN.

Our parents first of all the gods are known.
 From temple worship matchless good accrues.
True virtue lives in married life alone.
 What niggards heap the wicked get and use.
In little eating female beauty lies.
 His country's foe both branch and root decays.
Figures and letters are a pair of eyes.
 Our children's balm-like fondness age delays.
Your duty do, though with a beggar's fare.
 One master serving, in one district stay. **10**
Good life in priests surpasses sounding prayer.
 The slanderer's substance quickly melts away.

M

In seeking land and treasure spend your days.
    The wife who heeds her lord's commands is chaste.
In being watch'd consists the sex's praise.[1]
    Objects of vain pursuit forget with haste.
Speak modestly, though by inferiors heard.
    The man who looks at faults no kindred own.
Though sharp your arrow, use no braggart word.
    All hurtful things are better let alone.   20
The firm their lost estate shall repossess.
    The rich are poor when wisdom's wealth appears.
The monarch's smile brings succour to distress.
    Slander is wind to fire in willing ears.
The heartless railer all men hate and shun.
    No loving children bless the debauchee.
The pride of parents is a learnèd son.
    True penance theirs, engross'd who Siva[2] see.
In husbandry is trod the path of gain.
    The worth of kindred is their being nigh.   30
Gambling and brawling lead to grief and pain.
    Forgotten penance makes good fortune fly.
Sleep not till night, although confined and still.
    Before you dine give alms, however small.
Of good and joy the rich can have their fill.
    To vagrant beggary the idle fall.
No word excels a father's sage decree.
    If not a mother's, no advice is wise.
In search of wealth, e'en cross the fearful sea.
    From quenchless anger endless quarrels rise. 40
A stubborn wife's a firebrand in the breast.
    She's death who gives the winds your faults to
      show.

---

[1] *Cural*, vi. 57.   [2] *Attisūdi*, line 56.

God's wrath aroused, in vain men do their best.
Who spend, yet nothing get, to ruin go.
Beneath a roof in *Tay* and *Masi*[1] sleep.
The freeman's plough procures the sweetest food.
From friends themselves your want a secret keep.
Who lack good company, in sorrow brood.
No ills invade a neighbour-loving land.
By every word you calmly speak abide.   50
Your dwelling fix where wells are at command.
The smallest matters thoughtfully decide.
The laws you know consistently observe.
No mask to others hides from self one's mind.
They fast in vain, from rules who idly swerve.
Though poor your hearer, let your speech be kind.
By diligence the mean may mighty grow.
He does not fast who hungrily devours.
The springing blades the coming crop foreshow.
Take food, though rice and milk, at proper
    hours.   60
'Tis virtue from another's home to stay.
Reserve your equal strength the load to bear.
Eat not of flesh, nor steal, nor dare to slay.
The base the garb of virtue cannot wear.
Who gain the highest state, nor hate nor love.
Simplicity is woman's jewel bright.
The earth bears longest those who gently move.
All kinds of evil banish out of sight.
The ploughman's honest meal is food indeed.
With guests your meat, however costly, share. 70
Where rain is wanted, there is every need.
The welcome showers succeed the lightning's glare.

[1] January and February, the dewy season.

The ship without a pilot makes no head.
At eve the fruit of morning's acts you reap.
There's nectar found in what the ancients said.
Who softly lie enjoy the sweetest sleep.
What wealth the plough produces will remain.
In silence wisdom has its end and proof.
Their efforts who disdain advice are vain.
From black-eyed women[1] go and keep aloof.   80
Be all excess e'en by the king eschewed.
No showers descending, feeless Brahmans smart.
Good manners hospitality include.
A hero's friendship pierces like a dart.
The poor who scorn to beg deserve respect.
The strength of wealth in perseverance lies.
The incorrupt deceitful thoughts reject.
Let but the king be angry, succour flies.
Go worship God in every fane on earth.
Choose places fit wherein to close your eyes.   90
The lagging student gains nor lore nor worth.

[1] Courtesans blacken their eyelids.

THIS brother of Ouvay and Valluvar was born in a rest-house at Tiruvārūr (Trivalore), in the cloud-blessed Chōla country. There his parents, Pagavan and Athy, left him to Providence.

It was the grief of Pāppayan, a Brahman of the place, that he had no child. Walking in the direction of the choultry, he saw the pretty babe, and was as delighted as a poor man would be on finding in a lonely spot a vessel of gold. He gently took up the little stranger, and carried him home; and his wife received him kindly. In the face of the world Pāppayan named him Cabilar, and brought him up as his own son. The boy grew in wisdom, and was remarkable for good conduct.

When Cabilar had reached the age of seven, the time for investment with the sacred cord, all the Brahmans in the town were invited to join in the appropriate ceremonies. They met accordingly, but with one voice refused to assist, on the ground that the candidate was not born in their caste. Pāppayan was overwhelmed with disappointment; but his lamentations were soon interrupted. The boy himself, divinely favoured, appeared in the assembly, and maintained his right, composing and chanting the poem of which a translation is given. He argued, " It is nothing to say that caste comes by birth, it is won by deeds." Unable to gainsay his remonstrance, the astonished Brahmans now, with as much delight as his foster-father, initiated him into the privileges of their order. The poem is called Cabilar's *Agaval*, the word *agaval* being the name of the metre in which it is composed.

Mr. Gover gives what he entitles *The Brotherhood of Man*, as a song derived from Cabilar's *Agaval*, and modified by popular use. The following stanza of it, the seventh, will suffice as a specimen :—

> " O Brahmans, list to me !
> In all this blessed land
> There is but one great caste,
> One tribe and brotherhood.
> One God doth dwell above,
> And He hath made us one
> In birth and frame and tongue."

No further memorials or traditions of Cabilar's life are known. It has already been stated that he is believed to have been one of the authorities who gave judgment on his brother Valluvar's great poem, when acceptance was obtained for it at Madura. The inference is obvious that, in the progress of time, he gained a seat as one of the forty-nine professors in the Pandiya College. The decision which he pronounced on the occasion referred to may be translated as follows :—

> The *Cural*, of fair lands, O King,
> Where tutor'd birds in houses sing

Till lull'd by women's sweeter song,
Though short in words, in sense is long,
On millet blade as dew-drop small
Reflected shows the palm-tree tall.

The Brahmans appear to have done their utmost to eradicate or neutralize the evidence contained in the ancient Tamil writings that their system was an intrusion in Southern India. Whatever their success in destroying or mutilating and perverting works of which they did not approve, the history and poems of Cabilar and others, as now accepted, continue to be a protest against their teaching and tyranny, and especially their present law, that connection with women of inferior station is fatal to caste. In old time, even where Brahmanism was dominant, the husband's excellence was imputed to the wife. Menu wrote : "Whatever be the qualities of the man with whom a woman is united by lawful marriage, such qualities even she assumes, like a river united with the sea. Acshamala, a woman of the lowest birth, being thus united to Vasishtha, and Sarangi being united to Mandapala, were entitled to very high honour. These, and other females of low birth, have attained eminence in this world by the respective good qualities of their lords."

The Tamil poet Pattira-Kiriyār, who is supposed to have flourished in the tenth century, dared to ask, "Oh, when will the time come that men shall live together without any distinction of caste, according to the doctrine promulgated in the beginning by Cabilar?" This passage shows the antiquity of Cabilar's *Agaval.*

Cabilar may be alone in having made caste the special object of attack, but he is not alone in objecting to the northern yoke. In spite of Brahman editors, the questions of Sivavakyar survive: "What, O wretch, is caste? Is not water an accumulation of fluid particles? Are not the five elements and the five senses one? Are not the several ornaments for the neck, the breast, and the feet equally gold? What, then, is the peculiar quality supposed to result from difference in caste?" And Valluvar's thirtieth distich remains, intimating that the real caste is character. "The virtuous are truly called *Anthanar*, because in their conduct towards all creatures they are clothed in kindness." The name *Anthanar*, the beautiful, the cool-minded, a title of God, is assumed by the Brahmans, who are not always virtuous.

The ancient remonstrance against the impositions of the invading, conquering, and oppressive North continues to be echoed in the popular songs of Southern India. Mr. Gover gives striking illustrations, not only from the Tamil language, but also from the Telugu and Canarese, of the fact that the people who speak these tongues are not blind to the evils and absurdities of caste.

The hold of caste, still strong in South India and North Ceylon, yet is relaxed throughout the whole Tamil region in comparison of its power in other provinces. Missionaries have found help in the poem of Cabilar, and such passages from other Tamil authorities as have been quoted; and the history of the Seven Outcasts, and the works of Cabilar, Valluvar, and Sivavakyar, whatever the follies which they contain, will continue to be a refuge and an armoury on the side of education, social improvement, and religious reformation. The Pariah shall be elevated, and the Brahman born again. As in other countries, so in India, "God hath chosen the foolish things of the world to confound the wise; and God hath chosen the weak things of the world to confound the things which are mighty; and base things of the world, and things which are despised, hath God chosen, yea, and things which are not, to bring to nought things that are: that no flesh should glory in His presence."

AGAVAL.

Of the world, Nanmuga's[1] grand creation,
With its secret laws, an explanation,
   And its glories, who can render?
O ye sages, did the male sex first,
Or the female, into being burst,
   Or the things of neuter gender?

Does the day or star precedence claim?
From the other which derived its name?
   Which is older, good or ill?
Which must higher, wealth or lore, be rated?
Was the spacious ancient earth created,
   Or a work that knew no will?

Are the births and castes you fondly own
The event of nature's growth alone,
   Or a scheme designed and finished?

[1] The Four-faced, Brahma.

Who will live till fate shall fairly call ?
Who will prematurely victims fall,
   Their appointed time diminished ?

Will infectious evil ever die ?
Why and where do all the senses fly
   When the man that own'd them's dead ?
Do ascetics some new form obtain,
Or acquire a human birth again ?
   Is the soul or body fed ?

With a ready mouth and tongue I come,
As a drum-stick this, and that a drum :
   Ye good people all attend.
But a hundred years our life can number ;
And of these we fifty lose in slumber,
   And in childhood five expend.

Then of thrice five more by youth bereft,
From the hundred we've but thirty left :
   And now joy, now grief is rife.
What is wealth ? a river overflowing :
What is youth ? its crumbling bank ; and growing
   Like a tree thereon is life.

So of only one pursuit be heedful ;
And from doing well, the one thing needful,
   Not a moment dare to borrow.
This first concern demands to-day,
Nor admits another hour's delay :
   Ye are fools who claim to-morrow.

For you cannot tell what luck is near,
If to-morrow Yama will appear,
  Or another day you'll gain.
Every moment Cuttuvan[1] expect,
When he comes all worship who'll reject,
  And your richest gifts disdain.

You may argue, but you'll be denied;
With your kin he'll not be satisfied;
  All alike in death must share:
He will neither from the good man turn,
Nor the needy, nor the wicked spurn,
  Nor the man of money spare.

Not a moment will the Fierce-eyed stay;
And the body he'll not bear away,
  With the soul alone content.
For a spirit fled, O men bereaved,
Or a carcase dead, are ye so grieved?
  Or for what do ye lament?

Do you say ye mourn the spirit's flight?
As it ne'er before appeared in sight,
  So to-day it is not seen.
Do you say the body stirs your grief,
While you watch it still, though like a thief,
  When itself has rifled been?

Lo! you strip it; hands and feet you tie;
From the kindled pile the flame mounts high;
  Only ashes now remain.

  [1] Death, Yama.

You have laved, and to your kindred go.
Does complacence or regret o'erflow,
   That you mingle tears again ?

With repeated mantras and good cheer,
Will your children keep you lingering here,
   O ye Brahmans, when ye die ?
To return were suppliant ghosts e'er known,
And with hands outstretch'd keen hunger own,
   And their cravings satisfy ?

While the Hunas, Ottyas, Singhalese,
And the Mlechas, Yavanas, Chinese,
   And the Chonakas,[1] and others,
Have no Brahmans throughout all their borders,
You have ranged in four exclusive orders
   Whom creation meant for brothers.

It is conduct marks the high and low.
The consorted cow and buffalo
   Were a wonder to be seen.
Do your castes thus mutually repel ?
Is their union so impossible ?
   Has it never fruitful been ?

Wheresoe'er whatever seed is sown,
It will there produce its kind alone.
   Let a Brahman's progeny,

---

[1] The Chinese and Singhalese excepted, these names are now used to signify Mohammedans, Infidels, and Barbarians. It seems impossible to determine exactly their ancient application. Probably the Arabians were called Chonakas. The Greeks were Yavanas. The Hunas, Ottyas, and Mlechas occupied countries bordering on Hindustan.

Though a Puliah[1] mother gives them birth,
Be accepted by the lords of earth
  As their equals in degree.

As the cow and buffalo between,
Who have ever such a difference seen
  Among men of divers classes?
In the life men lead, the limbs they wear,
In their bodies, in their form and air,
  And in mind, no rank surpasses.

When a Puliah with a Brahman's mouth
For the north forsakes his native south,
  He is there a Brahman deemed:
When a Brahman from the north betrays
In the south a Puliah's crooked ways,
  But a Puliah he's esteemed.

In the mire as crimson lilies grow,
Vasishta,[2] Brahma's son, we owe
  To a lowly concubine.
A Chandály[3] to Vasishta gave
Sattyanáda by a Puliah slave,
  Who prolong'd the famous line.

To Parásara her son, the birth
Of Vyása[4] seal'd a fish-girl's worth.
  And because all basely born,—

---

[1] The ancestors of the Puliahs are said to have been circumcised slaves of the Mohammedans. They were probably an aboriginal tribe of Southern India.   [2] One of the seven great sages.

[3] A Pariah woman, by name Arundhati.

[4] Compiler of the Vedas. His mother was a Valaya, net-maker, sea-coast villager.

In the Vedas versed, for learning famed,
With the very first of sages named,—
  Are they aught of glory shorn ?

I am Cabilar, whom Athy bore
Unto Pagavan, in Caruvore,[1]
  She a Puliah, he the sage ;
And I'll tell you how we all have fared ;
For by seven of us is proudly shared
  The unequal parentage.

In a place where streams and springs abound,
With a lowly washer Uppay found
  All the fostering care she needed.
Nor could Uruvay of aught complain,
Though its juice they from the palm-tree drain
  Who her wants have kindly heeded.

With musicians Ouvay found a home.
On the mountain-side, with those who roam
  In the woods, was Vally bred.
Among Pariahs Valluvar appeared.
In a grove Athigamān was reared,
  Where the bees on flowers fed.

Gentle Brahmans I am bound to bless,
Who these richly-watered lands possess,
  For their never-failing care.
Does the rain keep clear of men low-born ?
Do the breezes in their progress scorn ?
  Does the earth disdain to bear ?

---

[1] Trivalore, according to the previous account, which named
Caruvore as the birthplace of Athigaman.

Does the sun refuse them light and heat ?
Does the jungle yield what mean men eat,
   While the fields support the high ?
All alike may wealth or want inherit ;
All alike may earn devotion's merit ;
   And we all alike must die.

There is but one race o'er all the earth ;
Men are one in death, and one in birth ;
   And the God they serve is One.
Who the sayings of old time revere,
And in virtue firmly persevere,
   Are inferior to none.

Who relieve the suppliant day by day,
Who abhor to lie or steal or slay,
   Who the fleshly fire subdue,
And who blandly speak, contemn your scorn.
O ye fools, let graces rank adorn,
   Or no good does thence accrue.

THE YOUNG DIVINE TEACHER.

O F the Vēlalā caste, the author of the following poem, Cumara-Guru-Para-Thēsigar, was born at Striviguntam, in Tinnevelly, in the former part of the seventeenth century, during the reign of Tiru-Malanāyacar, king of Madura. As became dwellers in Southern India, his parents taught him to fear God under the name of Siva. The descendants of the family which he adorned reside in his native town, bearing the title of *Cavirāyar* or bards, " and enjoying," says Mr. Stokes, in the preface to his translation, " some small endowments for services performed in the pagoda at that place."

It is a custom to give children the names of deities, and therefore not less likely that Cumara-guruparan received his name in infancy than that he acquired it by his piety and learning in after life. A title of the god Supramanyar, it signifies *The young divine teacher*, and is suitable for a poet whose inspiration came to him in his early days. It is believed that, to appearance, his faculties developed slowly till he was five years old, and then, like Valluvar's and Cabilar's, suddenly burst into full bloom. He is said to have been unable to speak till he reached that age, when, as if to express accumulated thought, his lips became those of a sage, and he composed his first poem, *Calivenpa*, in honour of Supramanyar, the divinity of a temple in Tiru-chendūr.

While yet a child, he also wrote *Pillayttamil,* a poem in praise of Mīnākshi-amman, the goddess of a pagoda at Madura, and recited it with commendation before the king.

"He soon afterwards," says Mr. Simon Casie Chitty, "entered the Matam at Dharmapuram, and after studying there the Saiva system of philosophy, and improving his knowledge of the Tamil and Sanscrit languages and poetry, assumed the habit of an ascetic; and the heads of the Matam, being convinced of his deep learning, invested him with the title of Tambirān (Principal or President). He then repaired to Benares, and presided over a Matam in that city until his death, which occurred in the prime of his manhood. Besides his two juvenile productions, he was also the author of twelve others, of which the last one, entitled *Nīthi-Neri-Vilaccam,* consisting of one hundred and two stanzas on moral subjects, is considered the best." He was never married, but a Vālipa-sanniyāsi—a recluse from his youth.

The metrical rendering now offered of *Nīthi-Neri-Vilaccam,* the *Light of the Way of Uprightness,* is based upon a translation in prose by H. Stokes, Esq., of the Civil Service, published at Madras in 1830. In this work the translator says, Cumara-guruparan "has given the result of his reflections on a variety of subjects, appearing to have followed the usual method of Tamil moralists in treating of the four great objects of human desire — virtue, riches, enjoyment, and final beatitude. He seldom touches upon the peculiaritise of Indian mythology: when any such do occur, they appear to be introduced rather for the purpose of

N

poetical embellishment than as articles of his creed. His language is remarkable for its purity and elegance, and admits but few words from the Sanscrit. His manner of expression is very forcible, but is sometimes a little obscure. His style abounds much in antithesis, a figure to the use of which the didactic poetry of the Tamils, like that of the Hebrews, is favourable."

NITHI-NERI-VILACCAM.

1 O friends, why not the court of God adore,
  When youth's a bubble by the zephyrs chased,
When wealth's a billow rolling full on shore,
  And when the body is itself effaced
  Like letters vainly on the water traced ?

2 Our fleeting life no surer succour knows
  Than what in never-failing learning stands,
Which virtue, wealth, enjoyment, heaven bestows,
  A good report both far and near commands,
  And on the troubled waits with helping hands.

3 By learning ignorance is fought and slain,
  And wider knowledge permanently won ;
It leads to pleasure, if it starts with pain ;
  But ways of sin, O richly-jewell'd one,
  Soon end in pain, in pleasure though begun.

4 From learning's fruitful bosom chaste there springs
  The filial treasure of refreshing song ;
The affluence of eloquence it brings,
  A title clear to sit the wise among,
  And power to brighten the resplendent throng.

5 With learning must discretion be allied—
   Or let it not to show its store be bold;
And time and place require a fluent tide
   Of fitting words the treasure to unfold;
   And then it is a fragrant flower of gold.

6 The learning quaking where the learned meet,
   The prate of fearless fools before the wise,
The wealth that dares, ere giving alms, to eat,
   And merits that from poverty arise,
   Than to possess, 'tis better to despise.

7 Though Wisdom's goddess[1] in his face reside,
   Yet Tamil bards him of the flower[2] excel:
While empty creatures of his breath have died,
   The offspring of their tongues no foes can quell,
   They ever live their origin to tell.

8 A sorer evil than a faithless wife
   With guilty neighbour seen in open day,
Is palsied learning shrinking from the strife,
   When called its hoarded treasures to display;
   For not like her can it be put away.

9 Who fail the learning they have scraped to hold,
   Yet to some novel study bend their mind,
Are men who cast away their gathered gold,
   And sift the dust, superior wealth to find,
   At more aspiring, leaving all behind.

[1] Calaymagal, the daughter of learning, namely, Saratshuvathi (Saraswati), the goddess of learning, music, and poetry, the wife of Brahma, said to reside on his tongue.

[2] Malaravan, that is, Brahma, who resides on a lotus or Tamara-flower.

10 With every virtue though he be adorned,
     If base his wife, the husband all despise.
   So learning link'd with poverty is scorned,
     Whatever its amount: in people's eyes
     'Tis but a little millet-seed in size.

11 His walk though lowly, and his words though sweet,
     Seldom or harshly is the poor addressed:
   Whate'er the rich man says, beneath his feet
     They crouch, as to the wisest and the best:
     With folly is the sea-girt world possessed.

12 All court the rich, and do the things they bid,
     Although their sordid avarice they rate:
   Who in a previous birth no penance did
     On those who were devout submissive wait:
     'Tis not from ignorance, but rigid fate.

13 Learning is ornament enough alone;
     Philosophy suffices for the wise;
   The jewel set with every precious stone
     No other needs to sate discerning eyes;
     To render beauty beautiful who tries?

14 So wise are none, that all to them is plain:
     " We've learnt the whole," exulting dare not say:
   The blacksmith's sledge assails the rock in vain;
     The ceaseless dropping wears the stone away,
     O thou with massive ear-rings richly gay.

15 Mark those who learning less than thine possess,
     With secret joy that thou such wealth canst
       show:

Then look at men whose wisdom's in excess,
 And with this thought let self-complacence go,
. " What's all I've learnt compared with what
 they know ? "

16 A double wealth they own, it may be said,
 Who with much learning ample means command,
If with humility they bow their head,
 As do the poor who reverently stand,
 Beseeching alms of them with open hand.

17 The truly noble stoop with deeper grace,
 When persons of an abject class are nigh,
Who, void of manners, overstep their place :
 The heavy scale, when we the balance try,
 Sinks lower, as the light one rises high.

18 The fair behaviour of the most precise,
 Who things forbidden shun, and rules obey,
Is changed by boasting to a course of vice.
 " We've never turn'd aside from virtue's way,
 But conquer'd sense," 'tis damning pride to say.

19 Like pouring water to support a flame,
 Is praising self that others may admire.
Is not self-disesteem the lure to fame ?
 And do not they felicity acquire,
 Who make not happiness their sole desire ?

20 Who great distinction to themselves would draw,
 One mode of penance never must forego,

In others not to indicate a flaw,
But all their better qualities to show,
And speak with deference to high and low.

21 This only force is in their vacant speech
Who do not follow what they've learnt and taught,
That, if not plainly ask'd how they can teach
What they observe not, the reproving thought
Is indirectly to expression brought.

22 To such as covet it, who yield for gain
The knowledge which themselves has never led,
Another proper benefit obtain,
The services of him who rules the dead,[1]
And power to face the future without dread.

23 The ceaseless noise of boors, o'erstepping fate,
As if philosophy could be their law,
Who in the hall of learning boldly prate,
But tells us not to let their guise o'erawe,
As birds and beasts are scared by shapes of straw.

24 The charms of learning mindful scholars prove,
Not those the smiles of vain pretence who wear.
With perfect beauty let a woman move,
At which e'en Tāccanangu[2] might despair,
None but the manly can possess the fair.

25 Who'd knowledge hook in ears that can't receive,
And disrespect for wasted labour earn,

---

[1] The king of those who dwell in the southern region, that is, of the dead—Yama, death.
[2] Lakshmi, the goddess of beauty and prosperity.

May blame themselves ; for wherefore should they
  grieve
That dunces fail their merits to discern,
Whose nature they, all learned, had to learn ?

26 The great attend not at the royal court,
  And others find no joy in waiting there.
While cats may through the secret bowers sport,
  The elephant, whose hollow hand could tear
  The post up, stands outside with patient air.

27 To well-born wives their husbands are divine ;
  Divine their parents children meekly call ;
The good see Godhead in their teachers shine ;
  And, dazzled by his leaf-like jewels, all
  Before the king as god in worship fall.

28 Does power, derived from former excellence,
  With eyes that speak, and ears that can observe,
Avail, unless it o'er the world dispense
  Benignant grace ?   Do mighty weapons serve
  In hands that hold them without manly nerve ?

29 To him who slays his subjects to secure
  A revenue, it were as wise a thought
To cut the milch cow's udder milk t' insure :
  We've seen to kings a tide of treasure brought,
  · Their people's welfare as their own who've sought.

30 Who will not patient till to-morrow stay
  For this day's dues, nor counts the minutes since

The needy came for help to stand and pray,
    And grinds his teeth at those who would con-
        vince,
    Is neither kingly freebooter nor prince.

31 Who all his selfish faculties applies
        To deck himself, anoint, attire and feed,
    And will not open either ears or eyes
        To those who earnestly for succour plead,
        Is now a corpse before his breath is freed.

32 Aware that getting proof of crime is hard,
        Not even trusting to the practised spy,
    His shoulder gold-adorned his only guard,
        A monarch's part is private search to try,
        And ne'er be deaf to a complaining cry.

33 A prince's wisdom tests what men declare,
        Detecting all the labour of deceit.
    Who, standing opposite a crow, will swear
        'Tis white, what falsehood will they not repeat?
        E'en matricide some call a noble feat.

34 Though threat'ning ruin visibly assail,
        Have dullards wit the danger to discern?
    Although their heavy-breathing mouths inhale
        The fumes of furious flames that round them
            burn,
        To neither side will slumb'ring rock-snakes turn.

35 Old friends dismissing, taking foes for new,
        Suspecting all around, however good,

Refusing counsel from the tried and true,
Despising spies, and changing oft in mood,
As signs of ruin must be understood.

36 While men of worth outside for audience stay,
They who in mean delights themselves abase,
With Ilayāl[1] though now they madly play,
Shall soon, when to her sister she gives place,
The pleasure know of Mūttāl's[2] close embrace.

37 The generous, with verdant grace arrayed,
Their glance the bud, their smile the flower
fresh-blown,
Their truth of speech the fair young fruit displayed,
Their charity the same to ripeness grown,—
The calpa-tree[3] is seen in such alone.

38 If from its ball of rice some grains should fall,
The easy elephant will take no heed:
Ten million emmets, on the ground that crawl,
Will by the treasure plentifully feed,
And keep their swarming progeny from need.

39 From him whose angry silver-shining spear
Can slay the beasts that make the country fly,
No royal bounty is so proudly dear,
No mount of treasure lessening the sky,
As kindly favour beaming in his eye.

[1] The goddess of prosperity, Lakshmi.
[2] The goddess of adversity, Lakshmi's elder sister.
[3] The tree in Indra's heaven.

40 When subjects succour need, no selfish aim
    Will make the brave their worthless bodies
      spare.
  The better body of untarnish'd fame
    They guard and nourish with exclusive care,
    Howe'er the tott'ring fleshly body fare.

41 Let any save, who can, their darling life,
    To courage dead, their name no longer pure,
  When satisfied they do escape the strife,
    And make themselves of added moments sure,—
    Though brief the respite shame and fear secure.

42 Chaste widows wearing ornaments no more,
    True saints the senses five who mortify,
  And heroes dauntless on the field of gore,
    Try not from cruel Marali[1] to fly,
    Though crown'd with flowers of conquest he
      draw nigh.

43 The ignorant will heave a heavy sigh,
    Whose sores pollute the air for miles around,
  That, though alive with worms, they have to die:
    But such as have the body's value found
    Will lay the burden promptly on the ground.

44 The warlike king's the pattern of the world;
    Where he commends, it equal praise bestows;
  Where he reviles, its scoffs are likewise hurled:
    Does not the boat the same, that dancing goes
    The easy way the ruling current flows?

              [1] Yama.

45 The keeper who the elephant assails,
　　When moisture down its frantic forehead flows,
　Nor fears its fury, but, till he prevails,
　　Asserts his will with ear-inflaming blows,
　　The office of the palace-premier shows.

46 Do not thy wishes out of season tell,
　　Thinking the king beneath thy hand to find;
　But fitting times and tempers study well.
　　He's won with ease when in an even mind,
　　But hard to please when hot with rage and blind.

47 What sympathies have kings in anger's hour?
　　They cannot then by claims of years be won;
　In vain affection tries its luring power;
　　The closest ties of kindred are undone;
　　In none they neighbours see, and friends in none.

48 Say not in scorn, " What profit have we seen
　　In long attendance at the royal gate ? "
　The many weary days that intervene
　　Will reach the hand that shall improve thy state,
　　And lift thee in thy turn a courtier great.

49 It is not wrong the cordial to drop
　　Into the lips of men as they expire.
　There may be much their enterprise to stop,
　　Who aim at good; yet should they never tire:
　　Events that seem impossible transpire.

50 The thought that labour cannot baffle fate
　　No plea for easy idleness conveys.

None are so foolish that, to illustrate
Predestination's force, a light they'll place
Unshelter'd in the wind's determin'd face.

51 That there's a power which destiny's surmounts,
    If perseverance all its aid bestow,
The pious child, whose feat the world recounts,
    That ate the germ of fate lest it should grow,
    And drank the life of Death,[1] does clearly show.

52 Of time and place when study has been made,
    And root and fruit are properly conceived;
When plans of action have been fully weighed,
    And means available due thought received,
    An undertaking may be well achieved.

53 Whose eyes are on a project firmly set,
    Shrink not from pain, nor look at danger near,
Nor sleep, nor mind what harm they do or get,
    Nor hind'ring circumstance regard with fear,
    And in the sight of scoffers persevere.

54 They greatly err who fail a guard to keep
    'Gainst little foes on whom contempt they pour:
Let but a frog into the water leap
    Whose surface showed the elephant before,
    And then the mighty shadow's seen no more.

55 Ten million open enemies appear,
    And bring no terror to the gallant mind;

[1] Marali. The reference is to a story in the *Scanda-Purānam*, of one doomed to die at the end of sixteen years, who prolonged his life by extraordinary devotion.

But one insidious foe is cause for fear.
 The saints whose word the universe can bind,
 Against desire the need of watching find.

56 From outward friends make haste to turn away,
  When facts their poisonous enmity reveal,
 Nor much attention to their pleading pay.
  Who use the knife a cruel sore to heal
  Do not the wound, before 'tis cured, conceal.

57 Already is their day of judgment passed,
  Who, false to friendship, ill returns devise,
 And stand maliciously opposed at last.
  If Naduvan[1] a while forgetful lies,
  Against such traitors, when he wakes, he'll rise.

58 That all the good the reprobate receive
  Is wholly evil, their black hearts are sure;
 But all that's done to them they good believe
  Whose minds are stainless and their conscience
   pure,
  Although unmeasured evil they endure.

59 The kind speak sweetly every word they use;
  But bitter are the sweetest things they say,
 Whose evil temper no pretence subdues:
  Though borax burns, it drives your pain away;
  Though arsenic cools to shivering, 'tis to slay.

60 Who in the way of righteousness would walk,
  Nor false, nor slanderous, nor harsh, nor vain,

[1] Yama.

From fourfold blame must ever keep their talk,
    And watchfully the senses five restrain,
The heart protecting from whatever stain.

61 To those who've firmly virtue's path pursued,
    Though poor, in vain are ways of vice revealed.
By hunger's fierce extremity subdued,
    The spotted red-eyed tiger will not yield
    To eat the crop that spreads the verdant field.

62 The wealth by selling rights of birth obtained,
    The might for which the good of truth is lost,
The ease by negligence of penance gained,
    The food that does the ties of friendship cost,
    Are far away by tempted virtue tossed.

63 Their boasted wealth who seized the chance they
      knew,
    With wrath the comfort of the poor effaced,
And by deceit their substance from them drew,
    Like woman's swelling bosom grown, shall haste
    Ere long to lessen like her slender waist.

64 The more he gets, who is the more in need,
    A satisfying portion vainly hails:
The furious fire that with devouring speed
    O'er all that comes within its reach prevails
    Must die away itself when fuel fails.

65 Before their gate shall wealth for welcome lie,
    Who keep the limits of their lot and line,

With all their might to do their duty try,
Nor from distress to vice themselves resign,
And never for their neighbour's substance pine.

66 The wealth that spends in gifts profuse its life
    May with a lavish courtesan compare ;
That which is prudent, with a virtuous wife ;
    That of the miserly, which none can share,
    With useless charms unjewell'd widows wear.

67 His want is better than the niggard's store,
    To help his neighbour who himself denies ;
It keeps him from the scoffs that people pour
    Upon the covetous, whom all despise
    As selfish, pitiless, and lacking eyes.

68 A lower need than wanting means to give
    Is theirs whom fate of kindly words has shorn.
How but in cruel silence can they live
    Whose tongues, as by a smith, are pierced and
        torn,
    And lock'd their mouths, for sins ere they were
        born ?

69 They who neglect the power of speech to employ,
    Whose talent of impressive words is clear,
The force of their deserving deeds destroy.
    With swiftness should their substance disappear,
    What reason have the eloquent to fear?

70 When little effort will large profit earn,
    Should any hindrances their steps retard

Who from the path of facile folly turn,
And follow that of righteousness, though hard,
Pursuing wisdom with a fixed regard ?

71 Politeness false, engaging things to do
For which ability is not possessed,
Is like his tenderness of mercy who,
Averse with words to wound another's breast,
Cuts off his head to set his heart at rest.

72 To reap for nothing wrought a crop of sound,
With proud pretence the ear how many stun !
How few, in feign'd forgetfulness, are found
The praises of a worthy act to shun,
As if by some one else it had been done !

73 Like him that, but to watch the quivering frame,
Deals causeless on the face a fatal blow,
They who, not meaning ill, but making game,
Laughter promote with scandals as they flow,
Arouse a shuddering dread where'er they go.

74 Who say, " A God there is," God will not spare,
But reprimand, if they to evil veer ;
Who say, " There is no God," less safely fare :
Do any but his hopeful children dear
A father's patient admonitions hear ?

75 If wealth by evil-doing any gain,
Its sinful source they never can conceal :
Things evil, evil are, and must remain.
The wild cow's soothing tongue may pleasant feel,
Yet only licks, its victim's life to steal.

76 Who, erring slightly, still with heartfelt shame
        Lament the force of their unhappy fate,
    No more than others merit only blame
        Who, daily showing virtue's outward gait,
        Secure the praises of the good and great.

77 'Tis virtue's opposite, but, were it right
        To be unto a neighbour's hurt inclined,
    And did it even yield a short delight,
        No joy, but torment, does the sinner find
        In guilt that shakes the body and the mind.

78 So long as business is not set aside,
        Nor learning checked, nor conduct turned to bad,
    Nor household substance greatly minified,
        There is propriety in being glad
        With those in tender branch-like beauty clad.

79 They fearless kill, in falsehood know no shame,
        For reputation wholly cease to care,
    Rob every way, in sin are blind to blame,—
        What is there infamous they will not dare,
        Who're fallen low in lust's delusive snare ?

80 With wife at home who Tiru's[1] self excels,
        Some will not rest with what is pure and meet,
    But basely turn to where their neighbour dwells,
        As, from its mouth rejecting fodder sweet,
        An evil beast takes bitter food to eat.

81 In chasteness robed, and crown'd with love his wife,
        With modesty anointed, wearing meek

                    [1] Lakshmi.
                         O

The jewels of a blameless heart and life,
With wealth of fruitfulness her praise to speak,
What more by penance can a husband seek ?

82 Their husband handsome, bright with youthful
grace,
With power of song to sway the public voice,
The eyes of maidens charming with his face,
And making with his speech the ear rejoice,—
On others still will women fix their choice.

83 Their beauty who, with golden bracelets graced,
Put out to interest, their bread to win,
Are better far than is a spouse unchaste :
They harass not their husband by their sin,
Their neighbours, and themselves, and all their
kin.

84 What feature in false women can we find,
Above their native folly to prevail ?
To duty, lineage, and fitness blind,
In shame and modesty they wholly fail.
'Tis fruit of sin that they are born so frail.

85 Who scout their charms, their names forbid the
tongue,
Nor eye and breast with lawless look excite,
Nor feast the ear with music and with song,
Nor aught commend that is not meet and right,
Such men successfully the senses fight.

86 Aware that feasting colours beauty's charms,
And captive to the sweets of slumber leads,

He is a hero that no foe disarms
Who, idiot in taste, but scantly feeds,
Not craving more than conquer'd nature needs.

87 Though kind at heart, yet to a sinful state
The holy turn not back, their bones though bare.
Should they, whose works a better house create,
Their fleshly tent corrupt and yielding spare,
And not with speed to their long home repair?

88 Superior delights they cast away,
Who give themselves to sensual desire.
Shall they in true enjoyment's sea who play,
And in celestial bliss to bathe aspire,
Be lured to sink in earthly pleasure's mire?

89 Their foes, to those who're chaste, do what they may,
Uplift their hands in reverence unfeigned.
Do what they will, no people homage pay
To hypocrites by acts immoral stained;
By profligates themselves they are disdained.

90 Will ever the unthrifty reap success
Who day and night in restless hurry moil,
For ever watering the wilderness,
And, when they're shown a surer way of toil,
With instant trembling helplessness recoil?

91 Could we the bound of life afar behold,
Fate might allow the careless slumb'ring plea,
"We're young, and can be pious when we're old;"
But penance would by none neglected be
Who could the limit of their lifetime see.

92 The hopeful good which men begin to do
  Is turned to evil by malignant fate ;
As travellers a proper road pursue
  Till led astray, when dark it grows and late,
  By thieves who for their coming watch and wait.

93 Devotion's cloak they wear with wisdom's mien,
  Who outwardly the sinful world reject ;
Whereas a garment does the body screen,
  Whatever senses it may leave unchecked ;
  Not ev'n the body does their cloak protect.

94 O fools, who practise falsehood day by day,
  Think not, "We've cheated all," with inward glee:
'Tis wisdom, trembling every limb, to say,
  " Is there not One who, wheresoe'er we be,
  Is present, all deceitfulness to see ? "

95 The shame of secret sin's by God revealed,
  As if by beat of drum He spread it wide :
Putrescent flesh may be from sight concealed,
  But any cov'ring carefully applied
  Will fail its scent from the remote to hide.

96 A way to rise is by the feeble found,
  But mighty men are shatter'd, when they fall :
Loos'd from their places, light things touch the
    ground
  Without a crash, and are not hurt at all ;
  Things heavy are reduced to fragments small.

97 We should not of their tuneless deeds complain,
  And blame the high as others we despise :

Are they who flesh by eating flesh sustain
Like those who slay a cow in sacrifice,
And guard the sacred fire, and read the skies ?

98 The masters who, whate'er our lot or need,
Direct us as our various states demand,
All things to all men, other guides exceed,
And ever foremost in distinction stand,
As everywhere their Master is at hand.

99 Who know the truth desire not lies to catch,
But, learning more, their senses keep subdued;
To caution's door-post they the door attach
Of modesty, resolved all sin t' exclude,
And lock it with the bolt of rectitude.

100 A virtuous wife's largess, a son first-born,
Is joy to those who learning's shore attain ;
Such bliss do they, the world who leave with scorn,
In contemplating what is true obtain ;
All pleasure past compared with this is pain.

101 The learned, who in self-restraint proceed,
Who cease from evil, only good obey,
Contented live, from works by merits freed,
And all their mind on life's one object stay,
Pursue felicity's unending way.

102 Their vision who, beyond mistake and doubt,
Have measured all that reason did reveal,
Who sleep with dreamless eye to things without,
And only look within on what is real,
Is perfect, final, and eternal weal.

TAMIL WOMEN.

THE birth of a daughter is a disappointment in the south, as in other parts of India. The chief element of distress with the Tamils is the prospect of care and expense in connection with marriage. There are also anxieties, in the case of a first-born child, with reference to the other world, arising from the belief that only sons can minister to the interests of departed progenitors.

The history of Ouvay would imply that it was the custom in old time to educate girls. Yet the saying is attributed to her that ignorance is the ornament of women.[1] In later centuries there has been no general education of females. At the time when Christians entered the country, the few girls sent to native schools were those intended to serve in temples, and no system prevailed of private literary instruction. The power to read and write was considered dangerous for women to possess. The successes of missionary teachers have wonderfully modified this opinion; and now, where formerly presents and promises were necessary to secure even a low-caste girl as a pupil, girls of all classes are presented as candidates for education.

The little book next translated, the *Garland of Advice for Women*, is a proof that in late years the Tamil people have not been wholly indifferent to the

[1] *Conday-vēnthan*, line 66.

education of their daughters. Umāpathi, a title of Siva, is the name of the author. The work appears to be of modern composition, and may have originated in a purpose to counteract the teaching of Christians. It is a purely Gentile production, commending Ouvay's maxims to observance, and the example of Valluvar's wife to imitation.[1] Evidently it was not intended for children in training for temple service, since it inculcates the duties of domestic life.

It may be that its sentences have reached the minds of girls through the ear chiefly, by dint of sing-song repetition; but that they have acquired them there is proof abundant. A native friend of the writer spoke to him with admiration of a child who, when a case of frailty was being discussed in a village assembly, had suddenly settled the question, to his astonishment and that of all present, by quoting from the *Garland* a precept which we should think un-becoming in the mouth of a little maiden.

The *Garland of Advice for Women* is another golden alphabet. At the end of every line in the original is a word equivalent to "My girl" or "My dear." It does not countenance too much knowledge, but echoes Ouvay's praise of ignorance and simplicity in women.

The condition of the Tamil woman is worse than it would have been but for the resistless invasions of Brahmanists and Mohammedans from the north. She is always a minor, chained by the law of Menu, which says, "Her father protects her in infancy, her husband in youth, and her son in old age: no woman ever possesses independence."

[1] *Garland*, lines 12 and 86.

A flower in the *Garland* of Umāpathi is filial piety. We are reminded of the fifth commandment, "Honour thy father and thy mother," and of Shakespeare's line, "To you your father should be as a god."[1] The daughter is instructed to make her parents happy, and to follow her mother's example.[2] Children must regard their parents as their sagest advisers and first gods. "Devotion to their father and mother is the appropriate devotion of children; there is no other."[3]

But the *Garland* contemplates the girl's early burial in married life, for which she cannot be too soon prepared. It is a description of a good wife, and may be compared with a golden alphabet on the same subject, in "the words of King Lemuel, the prophecy that his mother taught him."

The wife must not forget to worship God, and to fast in season. "It is prescribed to a virtuous and chaste matron, as the first of domestic duties, not to exceed the words of her husband, and to perform the duties of religion by serving the gods, worshipping them, and scattering flowers before them."[4]

Whom, under God, is she required to love and honour after marriage? In place of the mother appears the mother-in-law; and here perhaps the *Garland* presses most heavily on the young wife's brow. If any one arrests her homage on its way to God, it is not her husband's mother, but himself. She is taught to fear him beyond the Christian requirement, "Let the wife see that she reverence her

---

[1] *Mids. N. Dream.* [2] *Attisūdi*, line 20.
[3] *Casi-candam; Conday-vēnthan*, lines 1, 37, 38; *Nīthi-neri-vilaccam*, verse 27. [4] *Casi-candam.*

husband." He is enthroned by her as a divinity along
with her parents. Not only must she regard him as
the owner of all she has, and obey him, please him,
and supply his wants, but pay him the honour due to
a god.[1] She is careful not to pronounce his sacred
name. "Yesterday and to-day busy with the cate-
chists," wrote Mr. Rhenius in his Journal. "In the
Dohnavūr district, a woman of the new people has a
husband whose name is Pākianāden. *Pākiam* means
happiness, and it occurs in the catechism where our
first parents are spoken of as happy in Paradise.
When learning the catechism, she stopped at that word
pākiam, and would not pronounce it except after a
deal of trouble with her; and all this because it is
her husband's name!" Pious and careful wives
"worship in an innocent way their respected father
and mother-in-law, and fulfil towards them all the
duties of affection. Firmly believing that to tell
their husband's name would bring him to an untimely
end, they pronounce it not even in a dream."[2] "The
terrestrial deities and the mighty clouds obey the
sure words of those chaste matrons who devote themselves to their husbands as to gods. To them, therefore, the male sex is by no means equal."[3] Sāndilei
said, "I daily reverence my father and mother-in-law,
and I diligently execute all that they command, and
to the gods, to ancestors and to guests, I humbly
perform every prescribed duty. Regarding my husband
as a divinity, I fulfil faithfully all my duties, and
perform every necessary service to him; I ascertain

---

[1] *Cural*, vi. 55, 58 ; *Nīthi-neri-vilaccam*, verse 27.
[2] *Bāradam*.   [3] *Scandam*.

carefully those things that are pleasant to his taste, and, having procured them, I prepare food accordingly, and affectionately serve it to him." Sācuntalā asked, " Is it a proof of wisdom to do evil to a feeble woman, who considers her husband as her god, her joy, her strength, her beauty, as everything ? " " Formerly a Brahman had two wives, the elder of whom, without consulting her husband, performed various charitable acts, while the younger, employed solely in his service, discharged all her duties conformably with his directions. When the three, according to their destiny, quitted their old bodies, and had obtained a blissful state in heaven, the god, the dispenser of justice (Brahmā) approached, and thus addressed them : ' O thou, the elder wife, as thou didst not act by the command of thy husband, what benefit could result from thy acts ? Depart, for thou art not worthy to remain with him.' Thus saying, he expelled her from heaven, while he permitted the husband to remain, with the wife who had never disobeyed his voice. Then the Great One, who is without stain, beholding the other troubled in mind and overwhelmed by confusion, spoke thus : ' Come forth, O woman, return again to the earth, and, assuming a growing body, bestow thy affections, with all thy mind, on thy husband, and, considering him as thy god, administer to him in every service with perfect goodwill : so shalt thou hereafter attain to a high station in heaven.' So saying, he departed."[1]

A good wife does not forget, but carries out such advice as the *Garland* offers. When she asks direc-

[1] *Bāradam.*

tions, it is with the intention to follow them. Like the spouse of Valluvar, she specially guides herself by the words of her husband.

Her aim is to excel in household duties. She begins the day early, spends it wakefully, and prevents darkness with lamp-light. She provides suitable and sufficient food, cooks it with care, and is economical. She is clean in person and dress, and keeps the dwelling clean.[1]

She does not make herself awkward by look or manner, and considers it wrong to express herself by signs. She commands her eyes and tongue. She speaks carefully, gently, humbly, and truly, and never uses low or slanderous words. And she teaches her children to say no evil.

Her movements are decorous and quiet, and she restrains herself in regard to appetite and pleasure. She is of a contented, patient, sincere, charitable, and forgiving disposition, refrains from strife and adventure, and maintains a pleasant temper. As to her household, so to visitors and neighbours, her conduct is irreproachable. She sympathizes with the needy and suffering, and does her part in the supreme duties of beneficence and hospitality.

The wife does not lose self-respect. It is as much her pleasure as her duty to wear in her husband's presence jewels and other ornaments, which are unbecoming when he is away, and are forbidden to the widow. Her ruling motive is the blessedness, for herself and her house, of a good and honourable name.[2]

She does not go abroad without cause. Yet she

---

[1] *Attisûdi*, line 16. [2] *Cural*, xxiv.

has considerable freedom. Ouvay's history shows that Tamil women enjoyed their liberty in former days. The glory described in the saying attributed to her, "In being watched consists the sex's praise,"[1] was certainly not her own. There is indignation in Valluvar's protest, "What avails the guard of a prison ? The chief guard of woman is her chastity." No one is more competent than Mr. Ellis as a witness on this subject. "In Southern India," he says, "the conduct of women is much less restrained than in the northern provinces. Their persons are not concealed, and they are allowed to partake of the business and amusements of their male relations. Those whose circumstances compel them to personal labour may be seen crowding the public wells and reservoirs; and it is thought no disparagement, even for those of higher station, to bathe in the open tanks, where they display admirable address in avoiding any indelicate exposure of their persons. At religious festivals, marriages, processions, and other public shows and ceremonies, the number of women of all ranks frequently exceeds that of the men; though immoderate indulgence in this respect is not deemed consistent with strict propriety and that self-denying reserve which the Indian moralist regards as the crown of female excellence. This liberty the women of the south do not abuse. The immuring of women in harems, though the custom has always prevailed as an appanage of their dignity among the princes of India, has probably, when practised by Hindus of inferior rank, proceeded partly from imitation and partly from apprehension of their

[1] *Conday-vēnthan*, line 15.

Mohammedan conquerors. The Tamil writers afford but few traces of this usage."

A part of the house is assigned to the female members of a Tamil family ; but it is not such a prison of slavish seclusion as the zenana of Northern India. However desirable, it is not absolutely necessary that English ladies should invade the inner apartments of Tamil dwellings. School work, if slow, is sure to reach the native women. If there had been more haste, there might have been less speed. Women born in the country, educated in missionary schools, and some of them Christians in spirit and habit as well as training and name, are available and occasionally employed as private teachers. But the old fears and prejudices are vanishing. Girls of good families go to select schools, and there is no great difficulty in gathering together for education those of inferior grade. There are already many veiled forms among the worshippers in Christian sanctuaries. And women unveiled frequent bazaars for the purchase and sale of goods for domestic use.

It is customary among the Tamils, as in some Christian countries, to speak with contempt of women. Even Ouvay says, " Do not listen to the words of your wife."[1] Other voices are : " What good quality is there compatible with the folly of frail women ? "[2] " The man who acts not according to his own opinion, but according to that of his wife, cannot discharge the necessary duties connected with this world or the world to come."[3] " One may trust deadly poison, a

---

[1] *Attisūdi*, line 62.   [2] *Nīthi-neri-vilaccam*, verses 84, 82.
[3] *Cural*.

river, a hurricane, the beautifully large fierce elephant, the tiger come for prey, the angels of death, a thief, a savage, a murderer ; but if one trusts a draped woman, without doubt he must wander about in the streets as a beggar." "The eyes and minds of women will still follow strangers." "They are void of the feelings of honour, regardless of the pride of birth, their minds are ever vacant, and they have a thousand varying wills."[1]

It does not follow that women are never asked their opinion, never relied upon, never respected, never influential. The *Garland* confesses the contrary;[2] and they may laugh at their despisers who can point to Ouvay and other examples of female wisdom and excellence. An English woman is not much more than a Tamil woman the heart and spirit of her home; and as often as in other countries, the wife in Southern India is better than her contemptuous lord.

It may be asked if the *Garland of Advice* is accepted and worn by those for whom it is intended. The impression of the writer is that there are not more virtuous women in any land ; but he prefers to adduce a competent witness. Mr. Ellis says : " The women of Southern India are uniformly chaste and temperate by nature. Gentle and timid as they are, usually shrinking from observation and exertion, they are nevertheless ardent in their attachments ; and this disposition, directed by education, acquires a force which nothing can shake, and enables them, when actuated by motives of duty or honour, to display an energy beyond their sex, and a courage which no

[1] *Nĭthi-sinthāmani.*   [2] Lines 68, 73.

terrors can daunt. Devoted in body and mind to their domestic and conjugal duties, they are affectionate and attentive wives, anxious and tender mothers, and, not infrequently, sage and prudent friends. In fact, they possess, in a considerable degree, the qualities which are stated to constitute the perfection of the female character."

GARLAND OF ADVICE FOR WOMEN.

Hear advice, my lass, and heed it.
Share your rice with those who need it.
Find no joy in others' sadness.
Live to give your parents gladness.
Let not guile within you labour.
Earn the praise of every neighbour.
Why should anything distress you ?
Give the needy cause to bless you.
Tortoise-like restrain the senses.
Virtue gives a house pretences.   10
Beauty's woman's wealth, not science.
Ouvay's precepts claim compliance.
Shine in every household duty.
Tending well is wifehood's beauty.
Worship your good man each morning.
Shrink from fraud, though poor, with scorning.
Fame with pleasant words be gaining.
Gentle dames are uncomplaining.
Bickering suits not loyal spouses.
Err not, entering others' houses.   20
When you ask for counsel, take it.
Owning aught, your husband's make it.

Flowers in tufted hair are pleasing.
Cow-like shame at home is teasing.
Ribald words are seemly never.
What's a head-wife, if not clever ?
Telling lies is sure to hurt you.
Sweet is firm domestic virtue.
Void of virtue, earth were charmless.
Who will blame you, if you're harmless ?   30
Game and strife misfortunes gender.
Right to all impartial render.
Friends, when true, are never distant.
Talk by gesture's inconsistent.
Do as wisdom's lips advise you.
Go astray, and all despise you.
Brag not, bravely self-reliant.
Let your master find you pliant.
Water to the parch'd deny not.
Slumbering after sunrise lie not.   40
Sin is virtue's paths not keeping.
Let not mid-day see you sleeping.
Cuttu[1]-like's calumniating.
Think of God when meditating.
Wasting's losing all your getting.
Why should women e'er be fretting ?
Food enough provide, and spread it.
Be your caste's delight and credit.
Mark your mother's steps, pursuing.
Hell's not purchased by well-doing.   50
By your husband's words be guided.
Truth who speak, are not derided.

[1] A name of Yama.

Never Nili's[1] name inherit.
All you hear 's not void of merit.
Boast not, though you have a hundred.
Falseness from your heart be sundered.
Virtue 'll ever be befriended.
Store no malice when offended.
Haughty dark words be unspoken.
Fasts must not too soon be broken.　　　　60
Roe-like leaping brings repenting.
Hunger's face behold, relenting.
Bad's the fruit of sinful walking.
Children cure of evil talking.
Health is cleanly, wash your linen.
Virtue's sure of praises winning.
Flower-like live, a fragrant treasure.
From the sex come power and pleasure.
Artless women wear the graces.
Softly move with ordered paces.　　　　70
Early bathe you, saffron using
Loving strife is credit losing.
Honest matrons awe the ocean.
Glory crowns a wife's devotion.
Reverence your husband's mother.
Proud provoking tempers smother.
Fish-eyed looks at strangers take not.
Sullen nasal murmurs make not.
Workers have no sleeping corner.
Gentle lips provoke no scorner.　　　　80
Aim on earth at praises winning.
Madly seek not joy in sinning.

[1] A title of Cali; hence a common name for a malicious woman.

Nothing say to your undoing.
Fraudful deeds are fraught with ruin.
Teeth like jasmine-buds display you.
Valluvar's wife's pattern sway you.
Look for evil, if you quarrel.
Though in sport, say nought immoral.
Set the lamp, ere dark your dwelling.
Aim in cooking at excelling.   90
Helping neighbours, help them truly.
Clean the house each Friday duly.
Fast by scripture regulation.
Gain the country's commendation.
Willing walk above correction.
Proverbs point you to perfection.
In the way of good progressing.
Get and gain by every blessing.

STORIES OF MARRIED LIFE.

1. *Jungle and Garden.*

A king, on a hunting expedition, observed how independent of doctors and nurses was a hunter's wife who came under his notice. On his return he commanded that his queen should not be many days in retirement, waited upon by physicians and servants. The indignant lady sent for the workmen of the pleasure-garden in which his majesty took delight, and directed them, saying, "From to-day draw no water for the shrubs and creeping plants and trees, apply to them no manure, do not bind up the weeds; let no such attentions as these be given to the garden." Two days after, when the king went with his attendants to walk in the garden, he was angry at seeing it all lying in a faded condition, and asked the gardeners, " Why are things thus ? " They answered, " Swamy, it is the queen's command." He went to her apartments directly, and demanded, " Woman, why have you given orders that no water shall be drawn for my flower-garden ? " She replied, " Listen, heap of cleverness. Who pay so much attention to bushes and trees of the jungle as to draw water for them and cultivate them ? Therefore I ordered that these also should be allowed to grow in that way." Hearing that, the king was ashamed, and rose and went to his quarters, and issued instructions to the physicians and the rest to wait upon the queen after the ancient custom. She also directed the gardeners to draw water as usual. It is needful to conduct ourselves with due regard to degrees of difference.

2. *Domestic Harmony.*

Two friends, going to a certain country, rested on the way in the entrance of a Brahman's house. They observed that the husband and wife in that dwelling were very harmonious. One of them wondered, and, looking at the other, said, " See how united they are : their love will never alter." The hearer made a bet, saying, " See if I do not change it." Afterwards he began to talk in the manner of a wise man. Meanwhile the woman and her husband treated each other with loving courtesy. The seeming sage taught each of them, without the other knowing. Addressing the Brahman lady, he lamented, saying, " Madam, you are a most excellent consort. Alas! that to such as you one should be the husband who was a basket-maker in a former birth." "How can I know that?" she said. He answered, "In the night, when he is sleeping, kick his foot, and you will see." She agreed to do so. Afterwards, looking on the Brahman, he said, "You are a very worthy gentleman. Alas! alas! that one who was a dog in a previous birth is now your wife. I am sorry for this." "How may I know it?" said he. He replied, "Be like one sleeping in the night, but keep awake. She will kick your foot. See." "Be it so," he said. So in the middle of the night the wife kicked her husband's foot. He beat her, saying, "Off, you dog!" She struck him, crying, "Away, you basket-maker!" Thus the two quarrelled and fell out. He who wrought the mischief, showing it to his friend, rejoiced, and departed with him.

3. *A Feast of Cakes.*

A poor Brahman had been longing many days to eat a vadey-cake. One day, by great exertion, he obtained meal, oil, and spice, and put them in the hand of his wife, saying, "Bake these in a hundred vadey-cakes, and give them me quickly." She herself ate every cake while it was hot, except one, which she brought and placed before her husband. He asked, "Where, my dear, are the other ninety and nine cakes?" "I have eaten them myself," she said. He replied, "How, my girl, have you eaten so many?" "In this way, see," she answered; and taking that one cake, dipped it in salt, and put it into her mouth. The Brahman was disappointed.

4. *An Attentive Hearer.*

When a man in the market-street was reciting the *Rāmāyanam,* a herdsman's wife, thinking wisdom would come to her dull husband, sent him, saying, " Hear the Rāmāyanam, and come back." He went accordingly, and stood stooping, leaning his chin upon his staff. Among those present, a rogue mounted upon his back. The herdsman bore the burden till the recitation was over, and then went to his house. His wife, seeing him, said, " How did you enjoy the *Rāmāyanam ?* " He answered, " O dear, my lass, it was too much of a load for one person even for a moment." Having listened to his explanation, she was pained at his stupidity.

5. *Worse than a Demon.*

In a certain country a Brahman was accustomed to collect alms, and give them into the hand of his wife. She was wont to cook and place his food, and to beat him one stroke every day with the handle of her broom. He thought, " She is a bad one : how many days am I beaten by her hand ! " So thinking, he said to her, " I am going for ten days into a neighbouring village." She inquired, " If you go, whom do I beat with the broomstick ? " He answered, " There is the fig-tree I have trained,—beat that." Directly her husband was gone as he said, setting the food which she had prepared for him, she struck that tree with the broom-handle. The stroke fell on a fairy who had dwelt in it for a long time. "She is a greater hobgoblin than I," said the sufferer, and ran away. Doing so, it saw that Brahman, and said, "I am aching in my body from the beating of one day. How many days have you been beaten? I will do you the favour to free you from her persecution. Do you ask how? I will seize the wife of the king of this country. Whoever else may come, and whatever enchantments they use, I shall not go away; but if you come, I will go and leave." So saying, it took possession of the queen. When the king looked into the affair, and called for many exorcists, that Brahman went like a magician, and said, "Go out of the king's wife." The goblin left, saying, "I go: hereafter, if you come to the place where I am, I will kill you." The king sent for the Brahman who had dismissed the demon, and bestowed on him the riches he desired. The goblin went and seized the wife of the king's minister. His majesty, made aware of it, sent that Brahman. When the Brahman arrived, the goblin demanded in anger, "Why have you come?" and was going to kill him. He answered, "My wife has come bearing her broomstick. I came to apprise you of that." It asked, "How near has she come?" He replied, "Behold, she has come into the street." On hearing that, it was frightened, and ran away.

6. *Do as I say.*

A silly servant-man was in the habit of beating his wife every day. She reflected, "I must bring good sense to this foolish man, who without cause beats me when I have not committed the slightest fault." One day, according to custom, he struck her. She asked, "Why do you beat me so?" He answered, "Because you do nothing I say." She rejoined, "Hereafter I will do according as you say; and when I do so, you must not beat and revile me, but treat me kindly." She persuaded him to make oath that so he would behave. Afterwards one day he called out, "Adi, adi,[1] where are you going?" She came running, and struck him with a stick. He asked, "Why have you done that, adi?" Hitting him once more, she replied, "I have done as you said." Another day, when she was putting rice into her husband's bowl, he said, "Adi, umi[2] on the head." She beat him once, and spat upon his head. On a subsequent day he said, "Vay[3] this money in the house." She reviled, saying, "O money of a foolish fellow! O money of a stupid man! O money of an idiot!" Afterwards, considering and understanding all these things, he was ashamed, ceased from anger, heard and walked according to her gentle counsel, and became a good man. Thus a person destitute of understanding is made inferior to women.

7. *Renewal of Youth.*

A king kept a parrot. One day it flew, with birds of its feather, to the celestial world, and brought thence

---

[1] A word by which wives are addressed, but which also means *strike*.

[2] *Scum*, or imperative *spit:* either, "There is scum on the top," or, "Hit me on the head."

[3] Either imperative *place* or *abuse*.

the stone of a fruit that was there, and gave it into the hand of the king. Afterwards, looking on the king, it said, "If you set this, and let it grow, age will go from those who eat it, and youth will come to them." "Indeed?" said the king, rejoicing, and caused the nut to be set in his pleasure-garden. It germinated, and in a few years blossomed, and became ripe with fruit. Then the king directed that a fruit of it should be cut off and brought to him; and he gave it by way of experiment to an old man. But a kite had previously pierced that fruit with poison brought from a snake. Therefore the aged man immediately lost his senses, fell down, and died. The king, seeing that, was frightened, and saying, "Did not this bird mean to kill us?" seized it in his anger, whirled it round, dashed it on the earth, and killed it. Thenceforth in that country the tree had given to it the name of poison-tree. While that was the case, a washerman, taking the part of his wife, struck his mother, who was an old woman. Abhorring her child, and purposing to die, the aged dame went to the poison-tree in the garden, and plucked and ate some of its fruit. Immediately she stood a very beautiful woman, apparently sixteen years of age. She published the wonder; and the king, receiving the news, sent for her, and saw her. He afterwards caused the fruit to be given to some old persons, witnessed its effect to be as represented, and, having discovered its astonishing nature, exclaimed, "Alas! I slew the wonderful parrot that gave me this marvellous possession. What place is there for such a traitor? Where shall he go?" So saying, he stabbed himself with his own sword and expired. Thus easily comes destruction to those who do anything unadvisedly.

8. *Which has died will be known at Sunrise.*

A man had living with him his mother and his mother-in-law. His wife thought she could do as she liked if there were only her own mother, but not while her mother-in-law was with them. Without revealing this, she said in conversation with her husband, "Your mother is always making a disturbance with mine." He said, "What can we do in the matter?" She answered, "Kill my mother." He replied, "I will not kill: you kill my mother." She responded, "Is this really your meaning?" He thought in his mind, "I shall know her cruelty," and said, "Certainly it is." She rejoined, "When she is sleeping to-night, I will take up and bring the grind-stone, and throw it on her head and slay her." "Well, do so," he said. When she got up in the middle of the night, raised the wick in the lamp, and went and saw, her mother and mother-in-law lay in one house. She looked at them, tied a straw rope to the foot of her mother-in-law, put out the lamp, and went to fetch the grinding-stone. Her husband, who, as if asleep, yet saw these things, got up quickly, undid the knot of straw, tied it to the foot of her mother, pushed his own mother a little on one side, and left them. She brought the heavy slab, saw the sign of the twisted straw, struck the stone on the sleeper's head, and came away. Then she tapped her husband, to awake him, saying in a joyful tone, "I have killed your mother." He said, "Which is dead we shall know at daylight." So this came to be a proverbial saying.

9. *A Woman's Advice.*

A learned man went to a king, and carried away as a reward a gem of the greatest value. A servant-woman in the king's palace knew of it, and talking with her husband, insisted on his snatching the precious stone, and bringing it home. So he came into the jungle road, stopped Kavirāyan, and menacingly said, "Give the gem, give it." The learned man quickly put it in his mouth, and swallowed it, and said, "What gem?" The husband of the servant said, "You have just swallowed it; hawk it up." A hunter, hearing the two thus quarrelling, came running, and said, "Both of you bring up the gem you have swallowed. If you do not, I will kill you both." Then the servant's husband, being a considerate person, thought within himself, "Alas! it has chanced that, through my hearkening to the advice of a woman, this learned man also will lose his life. I must deliver him, anyhow." He said, "Sir hunter, we were pretending, and only in sport. There is no swallowing of a precious stone. If you had a weapon, and were to open and search my body, and find it there, then he also has swallowed. If you do not trust me, yet let him alone." The hunter, having torn open and inspected the stomach of him who so suggested, as there was no gem in it, took no notice of the poet, and went off. Though enemies, yet clever men will do a favour.

CHILDREN.

THE first inspection of a school of Tamil children is very interesting. Their black hair is not woolly, their eyes are not set awry, their noses are not flat and broad, their lips are not thick and protruded, the shape of their heads and faces is that of English children. Their looks are full of meaning, blushes show warmly even in their dark cheeks, smiles light up their features, their voices are musical, and they are good-tempered and polite. They are also sharp and clever. Many an experiment has proved that they can run an equal race in learning with European boys or girls. They are only inferior in the playground.

All these children are precious in the sight of their fathers and mothers. We are perhaps too apt to say that there is no word in foreign languages answering to the English word *home*, and that in no country are the ties of family affection so strong as in England. The seventh chapter or section of the *Cural* shows the power of domestic attachment among the Tamil people; but Valluvar is not alone in singing the praises of children. Passages have been culled from the rich pages of Mr. Ellis, and will presently be found strung together in metrical English, in proof that this is a favourite theme with the Tamil poets.

The ancient Hebrews did not long for offspring

more ardently than do the people of India. As the seventieth couplet of the *Cural* intimates, penance is wrought to procure good children. Vows are entered into, offerings made, pilgrimages performed, and various bodily sufferings endured, to persuade the gods to bestow this blessing. " The wise say that it is comparatively easy to obtain the ambrosia of the gods produced from the ocean and the earth it surrounds, and elephants with eyes of fire foremost in war, and heaps of sparkling jewels, but difficult to beget virtuous children."[1] " To procure a crowned elephant with a perforated trunk and an elongated face, much gold, many jewels, is easy; but for mothers to bear children who become prosperous by their own virtue, is of all things in this earth surrounded by the deep waters the most difficult."[2] " From the desire of obtaining one child, men continually make great sacrifices, and engage in a course of austere devotion, according to the strictest rules prescribed; and it is granted unto them."[3] " That family, resembling the all-producing carpaca tree, the master of which is the trunk, the branches the wife by whom domestic virtue is maintained, the bunches of flowers children, and the well-informed among them the honey on those flowers, is deemed pleasant by all."[4] " By every possible means should a father make his children walk in the right path; for thus the image he hath made becometh to him as a god."[5]

The following extract is from a rendering by Mr. Gover of a wedding-song of the kindred Coorg people:—

[1] *Negarltham.*   [2] *Chuthamani.*   [3] *Bāradam.*
[4] *Chuthamani.*   [5] *Parlyamorlyi.*

" With precious stones my chests are rife,
A useless heap when I've no wife.
And all my toil is toil in vain
Unless a child the house contain.
For, no ! there is no joy on earth
Without a wife or children's mirth.
The tank that never gathers rain
Was surely dug and built in vain.
Of little use is garden fair,
Unless the flowers flourish there.
For who would like to eat cold rice,
Unless some curds should make it nice ?
So every house should have a son,
And little children in each room."

It is painful to remember that when Tamil poets
sing in praise of children, they are thinking chiefly, if
not only, of boys.   We are as proud of our daughters
as of our sons ; but the people of India made up their
minds ages ago, and have not changed their opinion,
that boys are the more desirable.   The reasons for
this belief, as already stated, are that girls are expected
to cost more than boys, and that it is supposed a son
can do what a daughter cannot for a deceased father.
If a man die without leaving a son, it is thought that
his forefathers pursue him with vengeance because the
race is extinct.   For want of food in the shape of
daily sacrifices, the household gods turn thin and pale,
and wander about cursing the dead man.   The name
for son, *puttiran*, means one who, by continuing the
daily offerings, draws forth from *put*, or keeps his
father from descending into *put*, a sort of hell or place

of punishment for men who have no boys.[1] Hence the importance of adopting a son, when one is not born in the house. Daily, monthly, and yearly ceremonies must be attended to, or the departed cannot rest in peace.

It will be seen why, in districts where infants were put to death, females chiefly were destroyed. The Tamils were never guilty of systematic infanticide.

English boys often try to play the man when very green in age. The Tamil youth, sooner mature naturally and legally, might put on airs, but continues humble and docile. He has a share in the family estate from his birth. Even degradation from caste would not deprive him of his claim to maintenance. At sixteen he attains majority, and becomes his father's equal and partner in the eye of law. Still he treats him with reverence and confidence, and leaves the management of the property in his hands. The rule of the country is—

> For five years to a son
>   As to a prince behave ;
> While ten years more shall run,
>   Command him as a slave ;
> Then when his fifteenth year shall end,
> Let him be treated as a friend.[2]

Tamil sages recommend early training and study. " Learn in youth."[3] " What benefit is there in children who are neither learned nor virtuous ? Of what use is the feeding of a buffalo that never gives milk ? "[4]

---

[1] Ellis.
[2] *Nīthi-saram.*
[3] *Attisūdi,* line 29.
[4] *Panjatanthirakkathay.*

There are Tamils who, with all their fancies about angry ghosts and hungry gods, would rather not have even a son than have a wicked one. "It is better to endure the grief of being childless than to have begotten a son who, scorning the right path, acts contrary to the customs of his tribe; rather than the whole family should be involved in distress, they should at once reject him, and clear themselves from guilt."[1]

Thus is explained what we consider the cruelty of Hindu parents to their children who join the Christian Church. When a boy gets to be sixteen, and the law allows him to think for himself, he may wish to declare his faith in Jesus Christ. Should he seek holy baptism, he is often bitterly persecuted by his friends, and sometimes in danger of his life; and the responsible missionaries are perplexed by their success.

The father's pride is wounded when his son turns Christian. The mother's heart is torn. The Tamil woman trains her children conscientiously. Alas! she trains them in idolatry. The writer cannot forget having seen her, at the festival, lift her naked little one above the heads of the crowd, telling it to look towards the image in the car, and join its tiny hands in adoration. With all her intellectual error and prejudice, there is the strictest virtue in her example, and considerable wisdom in her teaching. "A highly cultivated Hindu, who was in the habit of speaking of his father and mother in terms of great veneration, said that on one occasion, as a boy, he was travelling by palanquin with his mother, and on the way mani-

[1] *Cāsi-candam.*

fested some impatience at the slowness of their progress, and objurgated the bearers in somewhat harsh
terms. When they put down the palanquin opposite
the portico of a temple dedicated to Ganēsha, to
permit their drinking water at a well close by, she
expressed her sorrow that he had used such language
to those who were so usefully engaged in promoting
their comfort by bearing him on their shoulders, and
told him to get out of the palanquin, and join his
hands, and ask forgiveness at the shrine of Ganēsha."[1]

Whatever the Tamil woman's subordination, she is
not a cipher in the house. Where the patriarch
rules, the matron moulds. Children especially love
and obey their mothers.[2] The following Tamil proverbs indicate the mother's influence. "The child is
like its mother, as the cloth is like the yarn." "If
the mother leap seven feet, the daughter will leap
eight." "The mother is an areca-nut, the daughter a
grove of areca-nut trees." "Knowing the mother,
marry the daughter."

Make Christians of the women of India, and the
whole country will turn to Christ. At present, in
most places, they are the greatest hindrance to the
conversion of their more educated children. They
undo at home the work of the missionaries in the
schools. Many a boy has been prevented by his
weeping mother alone from giving himself to the faith
and service of Jesus Christ.

No woman of any race is more loving and devoted
to her children than the Hindu mother. She lives for

[1] Percival's *Land of the Veda.*
[2] *Conday-vēnthan*, line 38. *Garland*, line 49.

them. When they die, she sits on the ground, and wails in strains like the following. *Amma* (*mamma*), in the third line, means "mother." *Amma* and *abba* (*papa*) are the natural cries of infants in all countries, the first words spoken in all languages. The seventh line refers to the sutures of the skull, which are believed to be inscriptions of the individual's fortune:—

Where is he gone who in my bosom lay ? Alas ! my
    child ! my child !
My golden idol who has snatched away ? Alas ! my
    child ! my child !
" Amma ! Amma !" was all his pretty cry. Alas ! my
    child ! my child !
A face so lovely never filled my eye. Alas ! my
    child ! my child !
He played around me like a spinning toy. Alas ! my
    child ! my child !
The master proudly caught his darling boy. Alas !
    my child ! my child !
Within his head was writ a royal doom. Alas ! my
    child ! my child !
The envious eyes that killed him—fire consume !
    Alas ! my child ! my child !
Remain, or let thy mother with thee go. Alas ! my
    child ! my child !
Return, or leave me not to mourn below. Alas ! my
    child ! my child !

PARENTAL FONDNESS.

The garden with no bunching blossoms bless'd,
   Sweet promises of fruit to cluster soon,
The pond with no fresh lilies on its breast,
   The night unbrighten'd by the crescent moon,
Such is the house which, empty and forlorn,
Can never sing, "To us a child is born!"

As by a single kindled lamp produced,
   And placed upon a stand in dead of night,
The chains of darkness suddenly are loosed,
   And the freed dwelling fill'd with quickening light,
So does a son his father's heart illume,
And all th' horizon round relieve from gloom.[1]

Who has no babes to climb into his arms,
   And with their playfulness his heart rejoice,
Or run with tears from infantile alarms,
   And clinging melt him with their prattling voice,
As sweet as juice from ripen'd fruit that flows,—
So poor a man no true enjoyment knows.[2]

As knowledge void of meekness, flowers of smell,
   A lotus-cover'd pool beyond access,
A town without reserves in tank and well,
   Mere beauty unadorn'd with beauty's dress,
Poetic talent without learning, pain
Of love-lorn youth, so childless wealth is vain.[3]

[1] *Chuthāmani.*   [2] *Bāradam.*   [3] *Valeiyapadi.*

A plenteous feast may guests in number please,
    But if no tottering little ones intrude,
With tiny hands outstretch'd the dainties seize,
    Distend their careless mouths with blended food,
And scatter bits and crumbs on every side,
Their lives are fruitless who the feast provide.[1]

Whatever his accumulated gain,
    Although his wife, by sacrifices won,
The pride and beauty of his house remain,
    Be his religious duties strictly done,
Though opulence its pomp around him show,
The childless man is lowest of the low.[2]

A monarch's elevation he may gain,
    Behold the sea-clad earth before him bend,
May Indra's peerless majesty attain,
    And all the lesser gods in power transcend,
Yet has he nothing worth possessing won,
And does not live, who cannot boast a son.[3]

Whatever means of pleasure they possess,
    They still are destitute of true delight
Who have no red-lipp'd children to caress,
    In prattle musical, in beauty bright
The treasure craving of parental joy,
In acts of penitence yourselves employ.[4]

The hunger quenching by whose restless fire
    The manes else would be consumed with woe,

[1] *Purananuru.*   [2] *Bāradam.*
[3] *Bramottura-candam.*   [4] *Cāsi-candam.*

Performing all the rites the gods require,
 And helping worthy men on earth below,
One son begotten richer blessing brings
Than from a hundred sacrifices springs.[1]

The curses of your household gods to shun,
 To save ancestral ghosts from vengeful pains
Because in you their ruin'd race is run,
 Enter the course which ancient writ ordains,
And rest not till the happiness you earn
Of having loving children in your turn.[2]

Not power from acts of charity that springs,
 Nor merit that repeated fasts procure,
Nor virtue purchased by burnt-offerings,
 Makes future bliss to anxious mortals sure;
Of happiness, excepting through a son,
The present world and world to come have none.[3]

SARAVANAP-PERUMAL-AYER.

In various parts of India there are native stars of
magnitude in character and learning. Such gentlemen
are the giants of Hinduism, who defy the servants of
the God of Israel. With their scholarship they help,
and by their zeal hinder the evangelist. A man of
this excellent sort was Saravanap-Perumal-ayer, in the
beginning of the present century. He assisted studious
Europeans, and published several Tamil works, including an edition of Valluvar's *Cural.*

---

[1] *Bāradam.*   [2] *Scandam.*   [3] *Bāradam.*

He at least edited *Pāla-pōtham*, a book for boys, drawn from the wells of the Tamil classics. It is a specimen of the training given to the children of India, and of the thoughts common to the sages. Translating it again after an interval of many years, the writer has almost lost sight of his English surroundings now and then, and returned in mind to the good Brahman who recommended it as a capital Tamil book for a beginner. It was a manuscript copy which Cartigesayer lent, and the rendering is from a careful transcription. Some ascribe the work to Ouvay.

INSTRUCTION FOR CHILDREN.

I.—*Lessons of one Idea.*

1.

Children, learn your lessons well. If you study, you will possess knowledge. If you have knowledge, you will acquire skill to make money. If you get money, you will obtain food, raiment, jewels, and other things as you may need them. If, moreover, you practise virtue, charity, kindness, and every sort of good behaviour, you will live prosperously, so that all will praise you.

2.

Children, knowledge is better than wealth.

How is that, sir ?

Thieves can take away riches; but none can deprive you of knowledge. Besides, if you spend money, it will decrease; but learning will grow, the more you impart it to others. Know that so it is.

3.

Children, according to your study, your knowledge will increase.

How is that, sir?

The deeper you dig into the sandy ground, the springing water will come in greater abundance. Know that so it is.

4.

Children, if one tell others what he has learned, his knowledge will be brighter: if he keep it to himself, it will bring contempt.

How is that, sir?

When a well is used, its water is purer; when left, it becomes corrupt and offensive. Know that so it is.

5.

Children, if the impure and mean join the pure and great, they will become pure.

How is that, sir?

If the water of an unclean stream flow into the clean water of a large lake, it will be cleansed. Know that so it is.

6.

Children, if one is rich, all will approach him; if he become poor, none will join him.

How is that, sir?

If there is water in a tank, the heron and other creatures will frequent it; if it get empty, not one of them will come near. Know that so it is.

7.

Children, if a good-natured person lose his wealth, and become poor, all will esteem him more than before.

How is that, sir ?

If a large precious stone, by being ground and polished, lose its weight and size, all will prize it more highly. Know that so it is.

8.

Children, if a man of weight associate with a worthless person, he also will become base.

How is that, sir ?

If a heavy stone - pillar join with a light raft, it will itself become light, and float on the water. Know that so it is.

9.

Children, if one who has acquired wealth lay it up, neither enjoying it himself nor bestowing it on others, strangers will take possession of it.

How is that, sir ?

Hunters will drive away the bee that hoards honey in its nest, without eating it, or giving it to others, and appropriate the honey. Know that so it is.

10.

Children, if a man of superior spirit be treated courteously, he will come to the assembly ; if not, he will remain at home alone.

How is that, sir ?

If the fragrant flower of the talay come out in bloom, it will mount to some one's head ; if not, it will stay on its shrub. Know that so it is.

11.

Children, if in business the help of a bad man be

necessary, there must be as little friendship with him as possible; if the intimacy be too great, he will cause grief.

How is that, sir?

To areca-nut and betel-leaf a little lime only must be added; if there be too much, it will burn the mouth. Know that so it is.

12.

Children, though a wicked man prosper greatly, do not associate with him: if you associate with him, you will get no good, but harm.

How is that, sir?

If you go near a snake because it has a ruby, it will not give you the ruby, but only bite you. Know that so it is.

13.

Children, if something is wanted from one who will not give it you, it must be got through his friend.

How is that, sir?

They who would milk the cow can do so, when they bring its calf near it. Know that so it is.

II.—*Lessons of two Ideas.*

14.

Children, it is necessary to acquire learning in youth. After mature age, the mind will be occupied with domestic cares. Though you should study then, knowledge will not fix itself in the understanding.

How is that, sir?

In cloth which has not been soiled, a colour will

take hold easily; in stained cloth, the dye will not take well. Know that so it is.

15.

Children, although the learned be like others in figure, they have honour in this world, while the others are undistinguished.

How is that, sir?

The heron and the swan resemble each other in form; but the swan is regarded as superior because it can separate the milk mixed with water, and the heron as inferior from its inability to do so. Know that so it is.

16.

Children, although a man of acquirements be not good-looking, yet all wish for him. A man without accomplishments may be very handsome, but none care for him.

How is that, sir?

The fragrant root of the ilāmitcham is not pretty, but all desire it. None want the scentless flower of the lemon-tree, though very beautiful. Know that so it is.

17.

Children, a clever man, though poor, commands esteem: a simpleton, though rich, gets none.

How is that, sir?

The eye, which perceives and understands, is without ornaments; but it is most precious. The hand, which does not see and know, may be adorned with rings, bracelets, and other jewels, but is not so excellent. Know that so it is.

18.

Children, if you join the good, you also will be good : if you join the bad, you also will be bad.

How is that, sir ?

When the rain-drops fall on good ground, there will be good water : when they fall on salt ground, the water will be brackish.   Know that so it is.

19.

Children, if you speak kindly to everybody, you will be respected ; if harshly, you will be disliked.

How is that, sir ?

Because the parrot speaks sweetly to all, they give it milk and fruit, take it in the hand, and kiss it : because the voice of the crow is unpleasant to men, they throw stones at it, and drive it away.   Know that so it is.

20.

Children, if you are humble towards the great, it will be to your profit; if you resist them, you will suffer.

How is that, sir ?

The rush, bending its head to the torrent, will lift it again, and flourish ; the tree, not bending its head, but standing against it, will be carried away by the flood.   Know that so it is.

21.

Children, though a man of evil disposition be born of a high caste, none will confide in him ; though a good-tempered man be born of a low caste, all will accept him.

How is that, sir?

Because the flower of the sweet-juiced sugar-cane is without fragrance, none care for it; because the flower of the poisonous oleander has a delicious smell, all desire it. Know that so it is.

22.

Children, superior persons wish to perform superior actions; inferior people rejoice in inferior deeds.

How is that, sir?

When a lion hungers, he will eat the choice flesh of an elephant; but a dog is glad to bite a stinking bone. Know that so it is.

23.

Children, when you are rich, since wealth elevates, you should be deferential to all; but when you are poor, because poverty depresses, you must be without servility.

How is that, sir?

A tree bends in proportion as it bears fruit; but a tree without fruit does not bend. Know that so it is.

24.

Children, although a wise man come from a distance, he will appreciate another's acquirements; but a man wanting in wit, though accustomed to associate with him, cannot detect his merits.

How is that, sir?

Though the bee come from a distance, it drinks the honey of the water-lily; but the frog, its neighbour, has not the pleasure of drinking its honey. Know that so it is.

25.

Children, we must not judge, from a person's beauty, that he is a good man, or, from his want of beauty, that he is a bad man.

How is that, sir ?

The arrow, though without crookedness, kills; but the lute, though bent, gives pleasure to the ear. Know that so it is.

26.

Children, if you do a kindness to superiors, they will well reciprocate it; if to the wicked, they will do you harm.

How is that, sir ?

Give food to a cow, and it will give you sweet milk: give milk to a serpent, aud it will give you poison. Know that so it is.

27.

Children, if the great err from the right course, they are without comfort; but if an inferior person stray, he gets over it.

How is that, sir ?

When men and other large creatures fall from a height, they are not likely to survive; but if such little things as the ant fall, they still live. Know that so it is.

28.

Children, a person may be small in figure, and yet possess ability to do rare actions : though another have a large shape, he may be destitute of such power.

How is that, sir ?

Though the seed of the banyan-tree is small, yet,

when grown, it affords a shadow in which many can sit down ; but if the big nut of the palmyra grow into a tree, it will not give shade enough for a single person to sit under. Know that so it is.

29.

Children, though many children be born of one mother, the disposition of one will be different from that of another.

How is that, sir ?

Though the lotus, red lily, white lily, and neythal flower are produced in one pond, yet the nature of one is not that of another. Know that so it is.

30.

Children, good people are few in the world, but bad men are many.

How is that, sir ?

Gems are costly and rare, but other stones are abundant everywhere. Know that so it is.

III.—*Lessons of three Ideas.*

31.

Children, people of the highest class make returns of kindness to those who did them honour in the beginning, and those of the middle sort to such as have done honour to them many times, but the lowest to those only who have humbly served them every day.

How is that, sir ?

The palmyra gives its produce to those who buried

and watered its seed in the beginning, and the cocoa-nut tree to those who have watered it many times, but the betel-nut tree to those only who have poured water on its roots every day. Know that so it is.

32.

Children, a service done to a superior lasts always with profit and lustre; kindness to an ordinary man wears an appearance of brightness; a favour bestowed on a low person is lost directly.

How is that, sir?

The rain-drop, falling into the oyster, becomes a pearl; when it falls on a lotus-leaf, it resembles a pearl; when it falls on the ground, it disappears immediately. Know that so it is.

33.

Children, when superior persons are angry with any one, and leave him, they cool directly, and are friends as before; when common people become estranged, they are reconciled on the mediation of another; when anger separates the low, they can never associate again.

How is that, sir?

Water, cleft, reunites directly as before; and gold when a person melts it together; but a breach in a stone can never be healed.

TALES ABOUT YOUNG PEOPLE.

1. *A Father's Example.*

A rich man poured boiled rice and water for his

father into a potsherd. His child, seeing it, took the
piece of earthenware, and hid it away. Afterwards
the rich man, looking at his father, asked, " Where is
the potsherd ? " and beat him. The boy said, " Father,
do not beat my grandfather. I took and hid the potsherd, because, after I am grown big, I shall not get
another sherd for you." When the rich man heard
that, he was ashamed; and from that day he waited
upon his father with more attention.

2. *A Boy's Plea.*

The king of a city called Sagathilagam, rising early
one day, peeped into the road at the back of his
palace, and saw a little Vēlāla boy picking up the
refuse of stores lying about. Drawing his head in
again, he knocked it against the door-sill; and a little
blood was visible. He said, " From getting up early
to-day, and seeing his face, my head is wounded and
bleeding. As many as thus see his face every day,
what evil will come upon them ! " Therefore, according to the saying that it is not good to place in the
earth an enemy of many people, he sent for the
executioners, and commanded them to catch and slay
the boy. They went and seized the child, and dragged
him along, explaining, " From seeing your face, the
king struck his head on the door-sill, so that blood
could be seen; and therefore he has ordered that you
shall lose your head." On hearing that, the boy
earnestly besought them to let him see the king, and
speak a word to him: afterwards they might cut him
down. They reported his request, and by the monarch's

leave brought him into his presence. The boy looked upon the king, bowed, and said, " O great king, a slight injury has happened to you through getting a sight of my face in the early morning, and you have therefore commanded that I shall be executed. When I awoke, I beheld your sacred face ; and the evil has come to me that I am liable to lose my head. What retribution is there for this ? I came to submit this question, and afterwards to yield my head." Hearing that, the king was startled and ashamed, praised him in his heart, gave him a position in the palace, had him taught all science, and finally appointed him his minister.

3. *The Best Son.*

A priest went to the house of a follower of his, and, in the course of a few words, said, " Disciple, which is the most deserving of your four children ? " He answered, " Look, swamy, the best of them is he who is carrying a bundle on the top of the thatched house." The guru asked, " What sort are the other three ? " He put his finger upon his nose, heaved a great sigh, and said sadly, " Are they such ? "

4. *A Foolish Child.*

A householder said to a son of his who could not learn, " Boy, big as you are, you have no sense. To-day, catch and bring some fish." The lad said, " Good," and went, and cut and opened the pond by four channels ; and the water flowed away. Afterwards, in the middle of the tank, in a place of mud and water, feeling with his hand, he caught seven or eight fishes. These he brought, and laid before his father. The father, somewhat delighted that so much sense had shown itself after such a length of time, said, " Why are you so tired, my son, that, late as it is, you do not come to your meal ? " He answered, " Some of the water of that pond is not yet drawn away." He asked, " What has happened ? " Then he told him of his breaking the dam, and taking the fish. His father, beating him on the head, said, " Have you ruined my family ? " Ruined he was, through his crops not growing that year because of the emptying of the tank. Thus destruction always comes from a child that is a fool.

5. *A Wise Child.*

A person who possessed ten thousand pagodas, perceiving that the time of his death was near, called his two children, and, presenting each of them with five fanams, said, " I will give my property to him who fills the house with this." The elder of them bought straw with the five fanams, and spread it to fill the house. The younger purchased wax candles, and mounted them to shed light everywhere. Beholding the two methods, the father delivered his wealth to him who hung up the light. Thus he who is wise is great.

6. *All but the Tail.*

When a guru was teaching a disciple, the latter saw a rat enter its hole, and could think of nothing else. Directly the guru had finished, he asked,

R

"Disciple, has it all entered?" The disciple answered, "All has entered except the tail." So wisdom fares when it addresses fools.

7. *Plenty of Sugar.*

A merchant from the west country brought ten oxen laden with sugar. One of the beasts, becoming unruly in the way, threw down a bag. Then the merchant called a boy who was there tending cows, and requested him, saying, "My little brother, take hold with me of this bag of sugar, and lift it up on the ox, and afterwards I will give you plenty of sugar." The boy said, "Very well," and so lifted it. Afterwards the trader offered him a ball of sugar. "This is little, give plenty of sugar," said the boy. The merchant gave him a little more. However much he gave, the boy kept on saying, "This is little, give plenty." Then a wayfarer, who came that road, practised a trick. He took in one hand a little more sugar than in the other, and, showing the sugar in his two hands, said, "Say how much this is, and how much this is." The boy said, "That is a little, this is plenty." He answered, "This being plenty, take it, and be off." The youth with confusion took it, and went away without speaking.

8. *Science and Sense.*

Of four brothers who went into a foreign country, three acquired from a teacher all knowledge, but the fourth did not learn well. One day the four took counsel thus together. The first brother said, "We will go by and by to the king over a distant country, and show him our skill, and divide among all four the presents accruing, and then go home." The second brother said, "We must divide among three of us the money that comes from learning gained by labour. The fourth brother is stupid, and has learnt nothing. Therefore to give him a share is out of the question." "True, brothers," said the third, "the youngest is unlearned; but he is smart in worldly affairs. From those who know worldly matters comes advantage to kings, who therefore confer greatness on them. So we will not leave him behind, but let him go with us, and allow him a share." To this they all agreed. When they were travelling in the jungle together, they saw a tiger lying dead. The learned three said, "We will try on this tiger the science of bringing the dead to life." Then the one without learning checked them, saying, "Do not try your power on the tiger. If life come to it, ruin will thence come to us." The third brother said, "We must believe his word." The others answered, "From pride of ignorance, you are also a fool; what?" and they despised them, and began to revive the tiger. Then the objectors, saying, "If you see a cruel person, it is necessary to get to a distance, is it not?" ran, and climbed a high tree. Directly the clever ones had raised the tiger by their incantations, it seized and slew them.

9. *Riches and Learning.*

Two young men, Sumugan and Suviseshan, of Snāttanapuram, in the Malayālam region, thinking it necessary to go into a foreign country, and make some acquisition with which to return, took each of them a thousand pons,[1] and reached the city of Cāsi in the north district. Sumugan, trading with the thousand pons he had brought, acquired great wealth. Suvisē-shan, giving his thousand pons to those who were great in learning, became a mighty pandit accomplished in all the shastras, but was poor, and attached himself to his friend Sumugan to get his living. Sumugan, intending to return to his own country, mounted all his substance on camels, and invited Suvisēshan to go with him. As they went on their way, in a certain jungle, robbers set upon them, and deprived him of all his goods. Afterwards both arrived at their own country poor men. While it was thus, the king who governed that country made it known that he wanted a learned man. At that time Suviseshan went, and displayed the knowledge he had acquired, and attained greatness. Sumugan, thinking of the wealth he had lost, got grief. Thus evil comes to material riches, but there is no destruction to acquired learning.

10. *The Advantage of Learning.*

A man had two sons. The younger of them listened to the advice of his mother and father, and acquired learning. The elder paid no attention to their counsel, and remained ignorant. One day they went into the forest to pluck leaves. There the first-born son, seeing an inscription on a stone, but not knowing how to read it, called his younger brother, and said, " Look at this stone." He examined it, and

---

[1] Pon = three shillings and sixpence.

discovered that under it were ten thousand pagodas. He concealed the discovery from his elder brother, telling him something else, and afterwards came without his seeing, and dug up and carried off the treasure, and was a prosperous person. Therefore it is necessary to obtain knowledge as the principal thing.

11. *Civility won by Respectfulness.*

The elder of two brothers was respectful to all, the younger roughly abusive to everybody. One day, when the two were going to a certain town, they encountered four robbers. The younger abused them; and they kicked him over and over, and seized all that was in his hand. The greater spoke with deference; and they did nothing to him, but gave him a smile, and dismissed him with a hundred pagodas.

12. *Curse on the Mischievous removed by the Good-natured.*

A person had two sons. The elder of them was a worthy youth, who committed no wickedness. The younger associated with bad boys, and was always doing mischief. The two went into a forest near the town to pluck leaves. There the younger climbed up into a banian-tree. In the hollow of that tree a hermit did penance, closing his eyes. The boy bent down a branch, and fastened to it his long hair. On its lifting him up, the hermit, opening his eyes and looking, gave him his curse. The greater youth came and released him; and to him he gave the blessing of riches and knowledge, and said, " Do you want anything else ?" He answered, "I wish you to remove the curse from my younger brother." He did so. Mischief should not be wrought.

13. *Borrowed Garments.*

A son-in-law, meeting with a fellow son-in-law, went to the house of his mother-in-law. All his garments were borrowed except his turban. He therefore charged his companion, " Do not tell this in the house of my mother-in-law." When they were seated, the mother-in-law and the father-in-law, looking upon the companion, inquired concerning his health and welfare. He answered, " His turban only is your son-in-law's own; do not ask me about his other garments." The son-in-law was put to shame. Such is the friendship of a fool.

14. *Changing a Name.*

A householder, obtaining a Pariah slave, asked, " What is your name ?" He said, " Sir, my name is Perumāl."[1] The householder, being a Vaishnavan, could not consent to call this Pariah by the name Perumāl, and therefore asked him, " Will you take another name ?" He said, " I will, sir ; but it will cost something." " Say how much it will cost," he answered. " My father," said he, " spent ten pagodas, and ten measures of rice-grain, to feast four Pariah villages, and give me my present name. Now to reject this, and assume another name, the expense will be double." Consenting, the householder gave

[1] Great One, a title of Vishnu.

him twenty pagodas and twenty measures of rice. The Pariah, laying it out in a wholesome way, and supplying food for four months, came back with the name Periya-Perumāl.[1] The Vaishnavan, looking on the slave, asked, " What name have you assumed and brought ? " He replied, " Swamy, the name I now go by is Periya-Perumāl." Hearing that, the master was confused. Thus with vain contrarity the ignorant join vain expenditure.

15. *Pride of new Wealth.*

When a boy was one day tending a flock under a hill, he pushed a stone, and saw beneath it a brass jar full of pagodas. He covered it, thinking nobody would find it afterwards, and was rejoiced in mind and refreshed in body. In the evening, when he led the flock home, the master said, " Boy ! Karuppā ! have you seen that all the sheep have fed well ? " He angrily answered, " It is no use crying Karuppā, and you need not disrespectfully say boy." The master said nothing, thinking in his mind, " What now ? There is a wonder : we shall know." Next day the boy took the sheep to the foot of the mountain, looked on the treasure he had discovered there, and returned with joy. His master asked, " Karuppā, have you cared for the sheep well, and brought them home safely ? " To that the boy said, " Cannot you call me Karuppanā ? " On the following evening the master cried, " Karuppanā ! " Hearing that, he said, " From to-day call me Karuppannāpillay." When accordingly he next day addressed him, saying, " Karuppannā-

[1] Great Great One.

pillay!" the boy complained, "What is that? My food is put in an earthen bowl: cannot it be placed on a plantain-leaf?" So his master put it on a plantain-leaf. Next morning, saying, "We must understand this," he followed him when he led the sheep, without his knowing. The youth opened and looked at the treasure, covered it and sat on it with a complacent smile, and then went beyond. After he had gone, his master went and saw the source of his boldness and pride. He took up the treasure, and carried it home, and provided Karuppan's meal in a respectful style. Next day Karuppan, not seeing the treasure, languished, and knew not what to do; and he went back with the sheep sorrowfully in the evening, and lay down in weariness and grief. His master called most politely, saying, "O Karuppannā-pillayyavargal, to-day is placed a silver bowl; come to eat." Then said the shepherd boy, "The old Karuppan is the Karuppan: the old earth-bowl is the bowl." Hence this proverb.

THE ACCOMPLISHED JUDGE.

THE English found India a continent of political volcanoes, earthquakes, and storms. Caprice and vice ruled in every region. The tyranny of one district was unlike that of another. In the same petty kingdom the succession of a rajah was a violent introduction of new measures. Iniquity was religion, and morality a dream in many places. The criminal was as often on the bench as in the dock. A bribe was necessary to open the judge's eyes; and he used torture to bring accused persons to his way of thinking. Prosecutors were liars, and witnesses actors. There was often no standard of law. If a man had property, his head sat loose on his shoulders. Jewels were not safe, even when buried underground. There were treatises on short and easy methods of burglary and slaughter.

By nothing has India been more benefited than our impartial administration of justice. The high do not now trample upon the low; and the rights of rich and poor are equally sacred. Venality is a crime, as well as perjury; and the wretch who dares to employ torture is as guilty as the worst transgressor to whom it can be applied. Not particular districts only are brightened and healed: the blessing is diffused like the sunshine, and pervasive as the air. The land that was all in pieces has been joined together.

Ere England's power to govern and heal was felt, proof often occurred that " there is a spirit in man, and the inspiration of the Almighty giveth them understanding." As the rainbow paints the cloud, and as stars shine in the night, now and then a genius arose whose face shone with God's image, and in whose hands were the tables of His law. Reason, conscience, and common sense spread their gifts in his proceedings; and there was protection for the people till the lofty tree was laid low. " For they saw that the wisdom of God was in him, to do judgment." When he fell, it was like the withdrawal of divine favour, and the exposed country sighed and smarted.

The following Tamil history gives a glimpse of such a native hero. It is a specimen of the tales current among our Eastern fellow-subjects, being, with the exception that a story unfit for our language has been omitted, a faithful translation of one out of many such works issued from the Hindu press. As far as possible, the indelicate expressions characteristic of Indian publications have been rejected. The liberty has also been taken of dressing prose in rhyme. Not free from fiction, yet the narrative is most likely founded upon fact.

It exemplifies the old despotic practice of elevating persons with no special training, and on the impulse of an hour, to the highest offices. One day Rāman had the applause of children with whom he played; the next he was the man whom the king delighted to honour. This record of cases in which he is said to have given judgment exhibits the disposition of the Hindu to cheat and lie, and his opinion that falsehood

is pardonable if only clever, and shows how service-
able to a shrewd magistrate is circumstantial evidence.
The wisdom of the East speaks in proverbs. When
any striking event is witnessed or related, it is usual
to quote as the moral of it some common saying. It
will be observed that each of the following stories
illustrates a popular adage cited at its close.

Our hero belonged to the Velāla or agriculturist
caste, and was therefore of respectable origin. He
was a native of the *Country of Chōla*, spoken of in
previous pages. The ancient capital of Chōla-mandalam,
or, as modern geography has it, Coromandel, was
Urayūr ; but the kings more recently resided at
Tanjore, one of the chief seats of learning and religion
in Southern India. Chōlan, the dynastic appellation
of those monarchs, was a proud title. By cutting
canals from the river Cāvery, they made their territory
most fertile. Eastern exaggeration says that ghee was
to be drawn from a reservoir in its metropolis like
water from a well.

If any part of India was an exception to the general
corruption and misrule, it was this land flowing with
milk and honey. Its kings prided themselves on their
justice. A common Tamil saying for governing so
that no one shall have cause to complain is, " Governing so that not even the tongue of the bell shall move."
This saying originated in the use made of the familiar
instrument by a Coromandel rajah. He had a bell
hung up at his palace gate, that by means of it such
as failed to obtain redress from his subordinates might
attract his royal notice. Alas ! even in ghee-abound-
ing Chōla the tongue was not still for any length of

time. Our history introduces itself with a case in which a woman who had been unjustly directed to restore a vessel of brass, if she did not ring the bell, wrung her hands, and, instead of His Majesty's clapper, made good use of her own.

Some of the traditional anecdotes of the Southern Carnatic are met with in various forms. For instance, the following version of the opening tale in Mariyāthay-Rāman's history is found in *Kathāmanjari* :—

When four persons were journeying in a certain district together, they saw a bundle of money in the way, and took possession of it. A dispute arising among them about its division, they talked a long time, but could not come to a decision. So they said to a dealer in the place whom they saw opening his shop, " Lo, O merchant, we are going to this tank you know of, and will come back after eating the rice we possess. If we four come again, and ask for this, give it." Having deposited with him the bundle of money with a mark upon it, they proceeded to the tank, and bathed themselves thoroughly; and then they made their meal. Immediately afterwards they sat down, and rested on the shore of the tank in the shade of a banian-tree. Then they sent one of their party, saying to him, " Go and purchase betel, areca, and tobacco of the shopkeeper whom we saw and talked with." " So be it," said he, and went, and requested the tradesman to yield him the bundle of money. The merchant replied, " I will not give without those." He said, " But I speak for them, see ; " and from where he was, looking towards them, he shouted, " The merchant says he will not give it without your concurrence ;

what say you?" They shouted back, "Give, give, without uttering any objection." The trader therefore took the bundle, and delivered it into the man's hand. Receiving it, he made off, without any one knowing. When twenty-four minutes had passed without his coming, those three came to the merchant, and asked, "Where is he?" He answered, "He then received the bundle, and left." They exclaimed, "O ho, merchant, you have made a mistake. We said, if we four come and ask for it. As we have not done so, you must produce the bundle." They seized him by the girdle, and dragged him to the magistrate in that town, and told him what had happened. When the magistrate had heard it all, he answered, "Very good: if, as you said, the four come and ask, the merchant will give up the bundle." Hearing that, they went shame-faced away.

Who can tell how many webs of light literature in the languages of Europe have been spun from Oriental story? Some version of this tale seems to have been the origin of a garnished narrative by an English writer, of which we may present the outline. Three men left a bag of gold in the care of a widow who kept an inn, to be delivered only when applied for by all three. One of them returned to put his seal on it, as the other two had done, and, when the innkeeper was called to a customer, disappeared with the treasure. The innocent woman was on the point of being sentenced as a thief, when a young lawyer saved her by pleading the condition that the bag was to be surrendered, not to one or two, but all the three.[1]

[1] *Casquet of Literature.*

It is not pretended that such accounts as those which follow are peculiar to India. Similar anecdotes and traditions circulate, no doubt, in Arabia, Abyssinia, Egypt, and other transitional countries, fallen from civilisation, or not risen to it, in which justice is administered according to the law of a judge's sagacity or a ruler's ready wit. An apposite anecdote of a former Bey of Tunis reveals an aspect of judicial resource and dealing to be improved upon by Frenchmen.

"A certain Moor lost his purse one day, containing sundry gold pieces or sequins. Desirous of recovering it, he proclaimed his mishap by means of the good offices of the town-crier. The person who had found it was an upright man, conspicuous for his probity; and the moment he discovered to whom it belonged, he made haste to restore it to its rightful owner; but the latter, finding that he had to do with a rich man, thought it a good opportunity for a little illicit gain at the expense of him who had so conscientiously restored it. He therefore maintained that there were eighty sequins missing out of the purse in question, and violently insisted on their restitution. The quarrel became uproarious, and of course was referred to the decision of the Bey. One man declared that the purse originally contained a hundred sequins, whilst his adversary affirmed with many oaths that he had given it back just as he found it. As both assertions bore the same aspect of probability, the Bey was for a moment embarrassed as to his decision. He asked, however, to see the purse, and, having examined it attentively, withdrew from it the money it contained, ordering, at the same time, that another hundred sequins be brought from his own treasury. He tried to put them into the purse, which, however, would only contain about fifty. Then, emptying it afresh, he invited the prosecutor to try his hand at it, and fill it with the hundred sequins which he had sworn it originally to enclose. Of course he was unable to do so; and the Bey, handing the purse and the sequins to the defendant, said, 'You had better take possession of it, as it does not answer the description given of it.' The false accuser received two hundred blows from the bastinado." [1]

MĀRIYĀTHAY-RĀMAN.

I. *One of four thieves*
The rest deceives.

Four lodgers with an ancient dame
Received contentedly what came,
Were gainers by what others lost,
And boarded at the public cost.
Now coins and jewels music yield,
Within a brazen vessel sealed;
But they must keep the common prey
To charm them on a safer day.
"Ho! bury this beneath the floor,
Till call'd for, mother, by all four,"
They said, and still their lodgings kept,
And ate and drank, and watch'd and slept.

---

[1] *Under the Palms in Algeria and Tunis.* By the Hon. Lewis Wingfield. 1868.

One weary day, as o'er the way
In a verandah's shade they lay,
And of the common good conversed,
The friendly four were dry with thirst.
" Who'll go to the old dame, and say
That we must have a pot of whey ? " [1]
Was ask'd ; and, flying like a shot,
One said to her, " Produce the pot."
Pledged not the treasure to restore
Without an order from all four,
Across the road the woman went,
And ask'd if for the pot they'd sent.
" Yes, give it him, and don't be slow."
So, turning back, an iron crow
She lent her lodger, and revealed
The place where she'd the jar concealed.
" With this you'll turn it up with ease,"
She said ; and he was on his knees.
The metal in his hands he feels,
And tries the mettle in his heels ;

[1] Buttermilk, esteemed none the worse for being sour, is a favourite drink in India for quenching thirst. It is usual to take it early in the morning ; and no doubt the parched souls had passed a feverish night. With the exception of the messenger, they had now allowed their wits to go to sleep. The direction they gave him, *Tondi yeduttuk kondu va,* was ambiguous ; one of its words, *tondi,* being either a verbal participle or a noun. The noun means *a small earthen vessel ;* the participle, *having dug in the ground.* The words therefore not only signify, " Bring a small jar," but equally, " Dig up, and bring." The intended meaning was evident from the addition, " to get some whey ; " but that addition the rogue suppressed, it not being true always that there is honour among thieves.

Through the back door he bears the prize,
And like a thief of thieves he flies.
Minutes twice twelve the thirsty three
Had waited, wondering not to see
Their partner with a pot supplied,
When all got up and went inside.
The cheat perceived, the dame they cursed ;
And vengeance now was all their thirst.
They haled her to the judgment bar,
And swore she'd stolen their brazen jar.
The Lord Chief Justice weighed the case,
Look'd the poor woman in the face,
And said he could not let it pass,
She must restore the pot of brass.
" O dear ! what shall I do ? " she cries,
And tears are streaming from her eyes.
As bright a youth as e'er you'll meet
Was in the middle of the street,
With playmates busy at the game
Of pitch and toss : [1] he ask'd the dame,
" Good grandmother, why all these tears ? "
She with her story fill'd his ears.
Then, turning to his play anew,
As from his hands the nuts he threw,
Exclaim'd the grieved precocious soul,
" May these as surely find the hole
As earth his mouth shall quickly choke
Who this unrighteous sentence spoke ! " [2]

---

[1] *Ketcheyk-kay*, something like a game of marbles ; instead of marbles, areca-nuts being used. The aim in it is, from a fixed distance, to pitch the nuts into one or more of two or three holes scooped in the ground.

[2] The allusion is to the situation of a buried corpse, uncoffined,

S

Some busybodies to the throne
Made Rāman's daring comment known.
The youth was to the monarch led,
And thus the awful Chōlan said,
" Who thinks the sentence so unjust,
Himself the case may try, and must."
The child of Menu, unappalled,
The prisoner and the plaintiffs called,
The matter sifted, set her free,
And thus address'd the baffled three :—
" She will, as pledged, the jar restore,
When told to do so by all four."
Grief goes the way that treasures go,[1]
They say : the lady found it so.
The king with joy the tidings heard,
The title of " The Just " conferred
On Rāman, made the bench his own,
Sent gifts of honour from the throne,
With special countenance caressed,
And held him a familiar guest.

II. *How one denied*
Infanticide.

When made aware of what was done,
The father, trembling for his son,

with the face turned up ; and the wish conveyed the opinion that
the gods would not allow so unrighteous a judge to live very long.
The prophecy was fulfilled. The mouth of the unfortunate
magistrate was soon filled with dirt. He was as good as dead.

[1] Wealth in possession is grief, in the anxiety it occasions.
This grief ceases, when the wealth disappears. When property
is stolen, the greater affliction is with the stealer. The unfortunate lover is less unhappy than the miserable thief.

And for himself, with anger said,
" O Rāman, have you lost your head ?
By subtilties of justice vexed,
The very gods are oft perplexed ;
And who to master them are you ?
From one mistake will scores ensue.
This office full of fear decline,
And show not where you cannot shine."
Rāman the Just made answer, " Sire,
There's small occasion for your ire,
Since God will be my faultless Guide,
And aid me wisely to decide.
Pray let the king my station choose,
And do not force me to refuse.
When fortune's goddess deigns to pay
A visit, kick her not away."
" Do as you like," he then replied,
Unable to say aught beside,
And home again his footsteps bent,
Reflecting as he thither went,
" If here I stay, more than I dare,
His slips and troubles I must share.
Attempting, he but tempts the law.
I must to other lands withdraw." [1]

His purpose hidden from his son,
Forthwith his journey was begun.
Night reach'd, he at a dwelling lay
Whose lord had gone from home that day,

---

[1] It is not in all instances good to have a friend at court. The highest in the king's favour is the nearest to his frown, and may carry his kindred with him in suddenly falling to the lowest place.

Leaving his wives, the childless first,
And second who an infant nursed.
The elder woman went to rest.
No sleep the careful man refreshed,
Who on the seat outside the door
Lay turning his misfortunes o'er.
　　Believing both in slumber sound,
And that her wish'd for chance was found,
The second wife at midnight made
The signal her gallant obeyed.
The startled infant at her side
Inopportunely woke and cried.
Exposure dreading more than death,
She grasp'd it, to restrain its breath,
A lasting lesson soon conveyed,
And by the first its body laid.
　　With night she let her lover go.
With daylight she took up her woe,
Beginning loudly to complain
Her rival had the baby slain.
The village heard, the proofs rehearsed,
The envious murderess fiercely cursed,
And when the mother sought relief
In Rāman's court, display'd their grief.
　　By all he'd chanced to see surprised,
The fugitive soliloquized,
" If right he do in this dispute,
I'll trust my son in any suit."
In studious disguise he dressed,
And near the seat of justice pressed.
　　The new-made judge, with thoughtful look
The woman's deposition took ;

Was quick his officers to send
The elder wife to apprehend;
And, when they'd brought her, ask'd her why
She'd caused the little child to die.
" This hell-deserving sin," said she,
" God knows, was never done by me."
" O base and artful woman!" cried
The younger wife, and said she lied.
Perplex'd, his lordship would be told
If any did the deed behold.
" My eyes beheld," the accuser cried,
" The deed was seen by none beside."
The judge first turned to God his mind,
Then ponder'd how the truth to find.
" In scanty dress befitting vice,
You both the court must compass thrice,"
He said.   Agreed the younger wife.
" I will not, though it cost my life,"
The other thought; then spoke, ashamed,
" I'm willing rather to be blamed
And punish'd in a murderer's place;
O drive me not to this disgrace."
Observing carefully the two,
Rāman the vile dissembler knew,
By stripes constrained her to confess,
And hanged the actual murderess.
The ancient saying was fulfilled,—
She one thing, God another willed.
    The father then, with boundless joy,
Approach'd and bless'd his wondrous boy.
" Your title and exploit agree:
Rāman the Just my son shall be.

Such wisdom none but God could give.
In health and wealth long may you live ! "
And, happy man, he stay'd at home :
What need had he abroad to roam ?

III. *Going to law*
O'er pussy's paw.

Four partners in the cotton trade,
That rats might not their stores invade,
Procured a cat, and made a law
That each of them should own a paw.
Then each a leg adorn'd with rings
And ankle-chains and beaded strings,
Till, tortured by the glittering load,
A wounded foot grimalkin showed.
A strip of cloth the owner found,
And dipp'd in oil, and wrapp'd it round.
The kindly embers pussy sought ;
The lurking fire the bandage caught ;
The flying cat the flame convey'd,
And burnt up all the stock in trade.
  The three, who all the ruin saw,
Resolved to get redress in law ;
Their partner before Rāman brought,
And utmost compensation sought.
What they had lost he should provide
The oily dressing who'd applied.
The judge the claim unrighteous thought
No wilful damage had been wrought.
He must the prisoner set free,
And turn his sentence on the three.

" The bandaged foot was lame, and so
Could not assist the cat to go ;
Its going caused what you lament ;
By means of your three legs it went ;
And you must, be it understood,
To the accused his loss make good."
   They only added to their woes,
As with its own proboscis throws
The elephant, in baffled tread,
The blinding dust upon its head.
The man accused from lowest grief
In highest joy found quick relief,
Proving, like sailor tempest-toss'd,
Escaping when confused and lost,
Himself not knowing east from west,
'Tis God who succours the distressed.

IV. *No pearls were e'er*
Placed in his care !

A man who own'd two pearls of cost,
Determin'd they should not be lost,
When starting on a journey, thought
He'd leave them in safe hands, and sought
A trusty neighbour.   " If you please,
Till I return take care of these,"
He said, and left his wealth behind,
Departing with an easy mind.
   In time, his journey at an end,
He call'd to thank his honest friend,
Who, to his sore amaze, denied,
" No pearls to me did you confide."

Forthwith he to the judge complained;
And Rāman the accused arraigned,
And read his guilt upon his face;
But, wanting proof to seal the case,
Heard what each party had to say,
And coolly sent them both away.

He saw, ere many suns had shone,
The loser of the pearls alone,
And ask'd, with cautious scrutiny,
What sort and size the pearls might be.
Then took he from his casket straight
Of such-like pearls just *ninety-eight*,
And strung them on some rotten thread,
And sent for the accused, and said,
" An honest face like yours I'll trust.
So take these *hundred* pearls you must,
And bring them newly strung; for see,
This cord's as rotten as't can be."

The joyful rogue went home, and there
He strung the pearls with cunning care,
Then counted them,—again,—again,
And search'd about the floor in vain.
Two pearls he'd lost! so with the rest
He strung the two that he possessed,
And then, presenting all, proclaimed
Himself the thief he had been named.

The fowl among the hemp that dares
To scratch with greed its feet ensnares.
The owner had his pearls returned,
The thief the punishment he'd earned.

V. *The iron fed*
The rats, one said.

Ten pigs [1] of iron having bought,
A man a likely neighbour sought,
And left them in his careful hands,
While he should visit foreign lands.
  Some years ere his return transpired,
When for the iron he inquired.
The saucy keeper shook his head,
And, " Rats have eaten it," he said.
  Indignantly the owner strode
To Rāman, and his grievance showed.
The judge upon a measure hit
By which the biter should be bit.
The plaintiff saw the promis'd fun,
And undertook it should be done ;
In seeming friendship learn'd to smile,
As taught the saw concerning guile,—
The fondness of a kinsman show,
Your foeman's house to overthrow.
  He fetched one day his neighbour's boy
To share a homely feast of joy.
The willing child the threshold crossed,
And in a room was lock'd and lost.
Next morning, when his father cried,
" Where is my child ? " the host replied,
" A kite has pounced on him at play,
And borne the darling boy away."
  The parent Rāman's presence sought,
To whom the kidnapper was brought.

___

[1] 10 params = 5000 lbs.

The judge demanded, " Can you say
A kite convey'd his son away ? "
" I placed," he answer'd, " in his care
Ten pigs of iron : ask him where
They are, and hear if he'll repeat
That rats did all my iron eat."
The judge severely eyed the twain,
And, frowning, said in angry vein,
" The trick each on the other tries
Is covering a whole gourd with rice.
The father must the iron yield ;
The boy no longer be conccaled."

VI. *Never to me*
Lent she the ghee.

Two cows a woman kept ; but o'er
The way another own'd a score,
Who, midst her plenty, ask'd if she
Would lend her a few pounds of ghee,
And, when the time for payment came,
Denied that she'd received the same.
  The former therefore found the face
Of Rāman, and explained the case.
When summon'd, and with questions tried,
The guilty borrower replied,
" I've twenty cows, and she's but two ;
'Tis envy makes her falsely sue."
In doubt the judge sent them away,
To come again the following day.
  Ere they arrived, where they must tread
He had the ground with mire o'erspread.

With muddy feet the women stood
Before him in bewilder'd mood.
His lordship, at their plight appalled,
For brazen jars of water called,
And to the bearers gave command
To each an equal jar to hand.
The poorer woman made her clean,
And yet half-full her jar was seen.
An empty jar the other placed,
Yet half the filth her feet disgraced.
Then could the judge unerring see
Which dairy-dame had wanted ghee.
Her faculty of management
Proved that the poorer one had lent.
The wasteful owner of the score
Was more than sentenced to restore.
The ancient proverb came to mind,
The lowest place will water find.

VII. *Give what you choose,*
You'll meet my views.

A loving father, near his end,
Handed a tried and valued friend
Ten thousand pagods, that the same
Might be disposed of in his name.
" Give what you like," his will so ran,
" To my dear son when grown a man."
The friend devoted saw him die,
Took home the gold, and put it by.
When in due time the boy up-grown
Applied to him to have his own,—

" What I should like, your father told,
Must be your portion of the gold ;
Now this is what I like," said he,
And let him but a thousand see.
The youth exclaim'd, " That will not do,"
And angry to the court-house flew.

The guardian's plea his lordship heard,
And judged him after his own word :—
· " The thousands nine you like, 'tis plain,
Since they are what you would retain :
The thousands nine you must let go,
To give him what you like, you know :
What you don't like so much enjoy,
The tithe you offer'd to the boy."[1]

Nothing was gain'd by greed of gold,
According to the saying old,—
With demon swiftness though he fly,
Who'll catch his neighbour's property ?

[1] Hindus are not alone in covetous grasp of little wit. A minister "had been preaching on the golden rule. His host said to him, 'I do not quite see your point. You say, " Whatsoever ye would that men should do unto you, do ye even so to them." Well, I should very much like you to give me a thousand pounds.' ' O,' replied the minister, 'your duty is perfectly clear : you must please hand *me* a thousand pounds ; for, " Whatsoever *ye* would," etc.' " (*The Thorough Business Man.* By the Rev. Dr. Gregory.) A mother reproved her little boy for having struck a companion. " He hit me first," was the reply ; "and you tell me I am to do to others as they do to me." " No, as you would like them to do to you," the lady answered.

VIII. *He found it hard,*
Who'd robb'd the bard.

A lonely bard, his wandering o'er,
Returning with his gather'd store,
Drew near the town with weary feet,
When it was his mischance to meet
A man who seized his bag, and swore,
" 'Tis mine," and home the bundle bore.
There yet was hope, the poet saw,
While Rāman minister'd the law.
Inclined to give the bard relief,
He question'd the audacious thief,
Who answer'd, with astonish'd face,
" I nothing know about the case."
Then Rāman form'd his careful plan,
And home dismiss'd the perjured man.
He had not reach'd his house before
Two spies were lurking by the door.
As in he went, his wife's first word,
" How did your business end ? " they heard.
" I baffled them, and got scot free,
By feigning ignorance," said he.
Their hiding-place the spies forsook,
And their report to Rāman took.
He had the rogue put in arrest.
To scourging all would be confessed ;
As ancient sages truly spoke,
The grindstone yields to stroke on stroke.
And when he'd been examin'd well,
And tortured all his guilt to tell,

And back his bag the bard had gained,
He suffer'd as the law ordained.

IX. *He would not own*
He held the stone.

One who a sardius possessed,
To have his anxious mind at rest,
Committed to a merchant's hand
The priceless gem, with this command,
" Take care of this while I'm away ;
I go abroad, some time to stay."
    Returning when four years had flown,
He ask'd the trader for the stone,
Who said persistently, " You know
You had it back some time ago."
Than cash more ready with a lie,
Three customers for rice stood by,
A washer, black who white could make,
A potter, skill'd the mould to take,
A barber, who could closely shave ;
And all would witness for the knave.
They heard his lips the word declare,
And sold themselves the same to swear.
    Observing this, the injured man
To Rāman the unerring ran,
The stealing of the gem explained,
And how false swearers were retained.
    The secret whisper'd in his ear,
The judge commanded to appear
The merchant who had done the wrong,
And bring his witnesses along ;

And having heard what each could say,
He order'd all the five away.
Confined in silence, each alone
Must shape in clay the precious stone.
  With ease th' accuser and accused
Fac-similes apart produced;
But vainly every witness tried
To show what he had never eyed.
The barber's gem was like a hone;
The washerman's, a washing-stone;
The potter's, that he deftly holds
When the revolving earth he moulds.
  Remarking how these disagreed,
The judge from all his doubts was freed.
The gem its owner repossessed:
Due punishment o'erwhelm'd the rest.
The flame the pois'nous nightshade earns
The cotton-tree contiguous burns.
Who sided with the lying thief,
Together with him came to grief.

X. *One claim'd with strife*
Another's wife.

A wife, obedient to a word,
The country tramp'd, behind her lord.
Across their path a river ran:
They forded it, he in the van.
A stranger unperceived drew near,
And silent waded in their rear.
Her dress the woman lifted high,
Amid the stream, to keep it dry.

The wretch who follow'd her could see
A fish-like mole behind her knee.
The woman was his wife, he swore,
When they had reach'd the farther shore,
And let her lawful husband know
She should no longer with him go.
    The men, not settling it alone,
To Rāman made their quarrel known.
The angry husband said, " My spouse
Is his, this lying scoundrel vows."
The question'd rival stoutly cried,
" She is my wife; I have not lied."
Then ask'd the judge, " Which, let me know,
Brings witnesses, the truth to show ? "
The traveller said, " In this strange land
We have no witnesses at hand."
Too vile the foulest sin to fear,
The other answer'd, " I've none here ;
But, if I must, I'll give a sign
To prove the precious woman mine :
If female searchers look, they'll find
A fish-like mole her knee behind."
    When they reported such the case,
The judge said, looking in her face,
" Which is your husband, on your word ? "
She pointed to her lawful lord.
The puzzle to unravel, he
Gave her to female custody,
And sent the claimants both away
In proper charge till break of day.
    At dawn he call'd both to his feet,
The executioner to meet,

Whom he commanded, " Be not slow,
For well the criminal you know ;
I've told you which affirm'd the lie ;
Proceed, and let the villain die."
The sword was drawn, and, starting, one
Cried, " Do not kill me, wrong I've done ;
And, trembling, to the court made known
Whence all the fierce dispute had grown.
The happy husband thanks outpoured
To have his grateful wife restored.
The alien, punish'd for his crime,
Fulfill'd the saying of old time,—
What can't be borne if any do,
What can't be borne must suffer too.[1]

    XI. *An equal lot*
       Share brute and pot.

A gay procession's drawing near :
The newly-married pair appear.
In trappings proud, a yāney[2] strong
Majestically steps along,
By Moslem owner lent on hire
To the Velālan bridegroom's sire.

---

[1] The story has a different turn in *Kathāmanjari.* The king, before whom the case was brought, decided in favour of the complainant, and dismissed the unhappy husband with upbraiding. The claimant, satisfied with his success, was not content with the woman. He said to the king, "I am a jester, and, coming to see you, and earn a gift, thought I would show my cleverness, and acted thus to make it evident." Hearing the explanation, the king was ashamed of the sentence he had spoken, and made amends to the lawful husband before he sent him away.

[2] Elephant.

T

But sudden fate can strength surprise :
The elephant falls down, and dies.
   Without delay the father ran,
And thus address'd the Mussulman :
" By God's decree your yāney's dead ;
I'll pay, or find one in its stead."
" Neither its price nor substitute,"
He said, " I'll have my living brute."
   With this impossible demand
Before the judge he dared to stand.
Wise Rāman the Velālan heard
Relate the facts as they occurred,
And said that he was free from blame ;
From God the visitation came ;
The Moor must take, for what he'd lost,
Another yāney, or its cost.
But nothing could the fool persuade
To hear the just proposal made.
He swore by the Almighty's name,
" I'll have no other, but the same ;
Neither its price nor substitute,
Bring me again my living brute."
Troubled the honest borrower stood,
And Rāman sate in thoughtful mood.
At length he said, " You'll both go home,
And both again to-morrow come."
   He then, by secret message brought,
In private the Velālan taught :
" You need not, as appointed, meet
The Moslem at the judgment-seat.
Have your house door, not fasten'd, mind,
But insecurely closed ; behind

Old pāneys[1] in the entrance pile.
The Moorman shall be caught with guile.
Before me duly he'll appear :
I'll say, ' Your enemy's not here,
Fetch him.'   He'll push your door with haste,
And smash the pots behind it placed.
Then let your lamentations flow,
And weeping to your neighbours go :
' My pāneys, old as old can be,
From ancestors come down to me,
This man has broken,' loudly cry ;
And in whatever way he try
To heal your simulated woe,
' I'll have those pāneys,' let him know."

 All happening as the judge foresaw,
Both reach'd again the court of law.
" This man," the self-defender swore,
" Has smash'd my pāneys, made of yore.
I'll have them back, a precious lot,
A priceless heirloom, every pot."
The judge fix'd on the Moor his eye,
And said, " To this what's your reply ? "
He answer'd, " Nobody's to blame :
Yāney and pāney fare the same."
How true the saw, in him was shown,
Wise fools will lose what wealth they own.

XII. *The chit is torn,*
The debt forsworn.

A citizen, for money lent,
A note of promise did present.

---

[1] Earthen pots.

The lender, when some days had flown,
Demanded payment of the loan.
" I shall," the gentleman replied,
" Be on the hill, the town outside,
To-morrow; bring the note I signed,
And all, with interest, you'll find."
He went: the note the debtor took,
And eyed it o'er with searching look.
A fire with fuel fresh supplied
Was burning ready at his side.
He tore, and cast it in the flame,
And said, " Be off, you have no claim."
The merchant sought the judge's face,
And sorrowfully told his case.
The summon'd rogue heard the demand,
" Why did you tear the note of hand ? "
" No note have I destroyed," said he,
" This fellow nothing lent to me."
Its size the judge inquired aside.
" A span," the creditor replied.
" Say two, when I in public ask,"
Urged Rāman, and resumed his task.
Then from the bench, on his return,
He, with judicial aspect stern,
Inform'd the lender 't must be learnt
How long the bond was that was burnt.
He solemnly a cubit[1] named.
The knowing citizen exclaimed,
" He lies, your lordship, in his throat,
Calling a span a cubit-note ;

[1] Two spans.

If here such glaring lies he'll dare,
How many won't he tell elsewhere ? "
" Ah," said the judge, " my clever man,
How could you know it was a span,
If not by your own fingers made,
And by you to your friend conveyed ? "
    Then not alone the perjurer's due,
As law imposed, the offender knew ;
But all for which the note he'd signed
With heavy interest resigned.
He show'd how well the saying fits,
A man in haste outruns his wits.

XIII. *One orders rice*
    A lime in size.

To all who'd purchase, young or old,
A Brahmani refreshments sold.
A traveller beforehand paid
His money, and politely said,
" I'm very hungry, in a trice
Bring me a lime in bulk of rice." [1]
    Upon a leaf she placed no more,
And set it down her guest before.
He look'd at her, and said, " This rice
For four fanāms will not suffice.
Speaking genteelly, it is true,
I said a lime in size would do.
And thus a gentleman you treat !
Call this a bellyful of meat !"

---

[1] The word may apply to a grain or a quantity. When people
ask for a crumb or drop, or thimbleful, they mean more.

She answer'd, " That's the quantity
You order'd, and no more you'll see."
 He went to Rāman, and implored
His four fanāms might be restored.
Before the righteous judge the dame,
Obedient to his summons, came.
He said, " Did you this person tell
Some rice a lime in size you'd sell ? "
" Yes," answer'd she, " as he desired."
" But have you done so ? " he required.
" I have," she said, " as you shall know :
 The untouch'd lump of rice I'll show :
I'll fetch it on the plantain-leaf :
In vain he tries to bring me grief."
 No sooner said, than off she flew,
And brought the very dish to view.
" O ho ! " said Rāman, " it is clear
No grain a lime in bulk is here.
The price restore, or feast his eyes
With rice each grain a lime in size."
 Alarm'd she gave, with nought to say,
The money back, and went away.
The cash its owner found, you see,
As fruit will fall beside its tree.

   XIV. *'Twas no such thing !*
    He'd had no ring !

A dandy to a wedding went,
Sporting a ring that one had lent.
So proud the jewel to display,
He wore it after, day by day,

Until its owner saw it shine,
And said, " Return that ring of mine."
" Your ring! how can you breathe the lie?
'Tis mine: be off!" was the reply.
The lender, full of fear and grief,
Of Mariyāthay sought relief.
Each claim'd the ring as his on oath;
And without witnesses were both.
A goldsmith should the truth decide,
Who had no interest either side.
The skilful man was quickly brought,
Whom first in whispers Rāman taught;
" A golden ring to you they'll show;
The touchstone let it roughly know;
And then its quality and weight
Emphatically underrate."
His lordship, handing soon the gold,
An officer his duty told;
" With plaintiff and defendant go;
This jewel to yon goldsmith show,
That he its value may declare,
And each obtain an equal share."
When he the test severe applied,
" Gently!" the troubled owner cried.
When he asserted 'twas impure,
" Not so," he said; " you're wrong, I'm sure."
Its worth pronounced, " My property
Unjustly you appraise," cried he.
The lender's tongue the assembly heard:
The borrower did not say a word.
The watching judge himself expressed
In favour of the man distressed.

Again the honest had his own.
This saying in the cheat was shown,
Who handles gold by means not fair,
To see it tested feels no care.

XV. *The mouth did hide,*
And then denied.

Before they will their guilt reveal,
There are who swallow what they steal.
A woman sinn'd this double sin,
Whose next door neighbour's fowl stepp'd in.
Its owner saw the visit paid,
But did not see an exit made.
"My fowl," she was compell'd to say,
"Enter'd your house: which is it, pray?"
"If so," the woman made reply,
"It has escaped my watchful eye."
The owner told the judge her grief,
Who question'd soon the summon'd thief.
She swore the hen she never saw;
And, as no witness help'd the law,
The learned judge, with puzzled face,
Pretended to dismiss the case.
But when they'd gone a little way,
The startled woman heard him say,
What he intended her to hear,
Address'd to people standing near,
"She cooks the bird she dared to steal,
And, having made her guilty meal,
Is not afraid, you see, to wear
Some of its feathers in her hair;

And impudence enough has left
Before us to deny the theft."
   Raising her hand with sudden care,
She gently felt her knot of hair.
The judge the conscious movement saw,
And call'd her back to aid the law,
Herself to witness to her shame,
With her own mouth her guilt proclaim,
And, with an added fine, to pay
A fowl for that she took away.
She proved the ancient saying sooth,
Shall falsehood fight and conquer truth ?

     XVI. *The peas revealed*
       What they concealed.

About to go on pilgrimage,
What cares the Brahman's thoughts engage !
His money, by alms-begging got,
He places in a metal pot,
And to the brim, his mind to ease,
Fills it with closely shaken peas.
Then to a dear and trusty friend
He and his wife their footsteps bend,
And say, " Deposit, if you please,
In a safe place this jar of peas ;
There let it, till we come, remain ;
And mind you never touch a grain."
The smiling merchant gave consent,
And on their pilgrimage they went.
   It happened on a certain day,
When they had been some time away,

An evening party to supply
Of many guests already nigh,
No peas could anywhere be got
Save those within the Brahman's pot.
Then to his wife the trader spake,
" The peas the Brahman left we'll take,
And afterwards, when we can buy,
With other peas their place supply."
She brought the jar, the peas outpoured,
And then they saw the pilgrim's hoard.
The peas that had been up were down ;
The thousand pagods form'd the crown,
Till man and wife, with high delight,
Agreed to put them out of sight.
Next day more peas they chanced to obtain,
And fill'd the heavy jar again.

The pious pair, when months were passed,
From pilgrimage return'd at last ;
Took home, without a thought of theft,
The jar that look'd as it was left ;
Made haste its contents to outpour,
And count again their golden store ;
With changing face the peas search'd through ;
And not a pagod came to view.

The priest, exceedingly distress'd,
Regain'd the merchant's house ; expressed
How very much obliged he was
To him and to his wife, because
They'd kindly done as he'd desired ;
And softly for the cash inquired.
" You nothing placed with us beside
The pot of peas," they quick replied.

Before the judge, to end the feud,
The merchant and his wife were sued.
But Rāman could no light obtain,
His questioning was all in vain.
He might as soon the matter clear
As give an idol ears to hear.
He had a hollow image cut,
And a detective in it shut.
The merchant and his lady both
Must take the image, and their oath,
And bear the god the temple round,
If innocent they would be found.
They wash'd their heads, and so they swore,
And then their weight of conscience bore.
When they had lifted it half-way,
The panting man found breath to say,
" What have we done ? what will it cost ?
To perjured persons hope is lost."
The tickled auditor within
Caught this confession of their sin,
And, when released, told every word
That in the idol's ears he'd heard.
The angry judge in threats was strong,
And made the couple own the wrong.
The thousand pagods they returned,
And had the punishment they'd earned.
They found the proverb true indeed,
God things inscrutable can read.

XVII. *One sells his rice*
At any price.

A paddy[1]-buyer, purse in hand,
Comes to a store, and to a stand.
" I want to buy some rice," says he ;
" A sample of it let me see."
The paddy-seller is not slow
A little measureful to show.
The buyer asks, " Have you no more ? "
The seller says, " This is the store :
Pagodas one or ten will buy
No other rice than now you spy."
The neighbour pays pagodas ten,
And says he'll soon be here again.

And back he comes, with bullock strong,
To fetch his purchase before long,
And, like a man of means and mirth,
Demands his ten pagodas' worth.
The dealer brings his measure small,
And says, " Pour out, and take it all."
" This all for ten pagodas ! " cries
The purchaser. The cheat replies,
" For one or ten, I said before,
This is the rice, and there's no more.
Agreeing, ten you chose to pay ;
So take your bargain, and away."

The jest no joke the good man feels,
And to the judge the trick reveals,
To whom the storekeeper is bold
To say he's done as he was told.

[1] Rice in the husk.

Rāman ordains, " A month must glide,
Ere I this matter can decide.
Be it till then your equal doom
To eat your meals in the same room.
You, plaintiff, the boil'd grain receive,
And just a half to this man give."
　　Then privately he shows his plan :
" You take a bellyful, my man ;
But break a grain of rice in two,
And give him half of it to chew."
　　Two meals of half a grain suffice
The hungry seller of the rice
So far that loudly he complains,
And access to the judge obtains.
Rāman the other calls, and, " Why,"
He asks, " your messmate's food deny ? "
Says he, " I duly dealt the meat,
One half the grain : he would not eat."
The storekeeper begins to explain :
" He pinches off just half one grain,
And tells me all my dinner's there :
How can I live upon such fare ? "
The buyer, " Tit for tat," replies ;
" He in a basket show'd some rice ;
‘ Whatever price you pay,' said he,
‘ This is the article you see ; '
I ten pagodas paid ; behold,
'Twas but the sample that he sold !
So I the letter keep, and deal
With him by contract at each meal."
　　The judge now to the culprit turns,
Who with long face his sentence learns.

" According to the country-price,
His ten pagodas' worth of rice
Supply to him, or be agreed
A month on his half-rice to feed."
　　Complying, as compell'd by law,
The seller verifies the saw,
By meanness meanness is made void,
And trick by counter-trick destroyed.

　　　XVIII. *The case made clear*
　　　　　From ear to ear.

Rejoiced a choultry's shade to find,
Two travellers face to face reclined.
One slept, who on his right side lay :
The other took the ring away
His left ear uppermost that graced,
And in his own right ear it placed.
　　" Why take my ring ? " the loser cried,
When he his eyes had open'd wide.
His bedfellow was quick to whine,
" Your earring ! you have stolen mine."
The injured man to Rāman went,
Who for the accused directly sent.
　　With right ear jewell'd, ringless left,
As each the other charged with theft,
The judge the travellers thus addressed,
" Tell me your postures when at rest."
　　Then to the thief, " The case is clear :
You lay, you own, on your left ear :
How could he take a ring from you ?
His left ear was exposed to view.

The ring immediately restore,
And, ringless as you were before,
Receive two dozen stripes, and dwell
Six months within the prison cell."
    Half-witted are the wiles of crime.
The rogue forgot the knowing rhyme,—
If lies you ever choose to tell,
Let them at least be plausible.

    XIX. *The cows conveyed*
        Their thief betrayed.

Thus one who many beasts possessed
His neighbour, who'd but ten, addressed:
"Your cows with mine, in field and stall,
May mix, if you will tend them all
Whenever I'm from home." One day,
When business had call'd him away,
His neighbour left in charge was glad
To carry out a plan he had.
Three heifers from the herd he led,
And left three sorry calves instead.
    A murrain pass'd the country through,
And all the farmer's cattle slew,
But spared the stolen cows full-grown,
A calf each suckling of its own.
    The owner of the emptied stall
For cup of milk was fain to call.
'Twas brought from one of the young kine.
"The cow you have just milk'd is mine,"
When he had tasted, he averred,
To Rāman hasted, and was heard.

The judge inquired, with darkening brow,
" Why did you steal your neighbour's cow ? "
" 'Tis false," the man said, " let him bid
His witnesses, to prove I did."
" True," Rāman answer'd, " show me now
How you can tell it is your cow."
The farmer said, with tongue not slow,
" The taste of my cow's milk I know."
The judge replied, " The case to weigh
Will take a fortnight and a day :
Both go, and wait."   Three plots of ground
With vegetables set he found ;
Applied, to make his judgment sure,
To each a different manure ;
And, when the plants were ripe at last,
The herdsmen bade to a repast.
From every bed a share he drew,
Then all the three together threw ;
And with the mass three sorts of curd,
The sheep's, cow's, buffalo's, were stirred.
The dish was served in fashion neat,
And each was urged to take and eat.
It was not long before the thief
With seeming relish cleared his leaf.
Ask'd if he had been satisfied,
" 'Twas admirable ! " he replied.
The other stopp'd to taste and taste,
And to the end would make no haste.
Ask'd his opinion, thus 'twas shown :
" I tasted vegetables grown
In three manures, nor fail'd to find
Three several sorts of curds combined."

In wisdom knowing now the case, ·
The judge look'd in the culprit's face,
And said, " At once the truth reveal,
If punishment you would not feel."
He then confess'd, " Three cows I led
Away, and put three calves instead."
The clever farmer gained his cause,
And left the court 'mid high applause.
Deny the proverb no one can,
There's nothing hard to a wise man.

XX.[1] *A god disguised*
Because despised.

When one a country girl had wed,
And to his house the lady led,
Her mother on an early day
Appear'd, to take the bride away,
Engaging, " Grant ten days with me,
And back again my child you'll see."
A weary month he for her mourned,
And still his wife had not returned.
Then went he to her mother's house,
And press'd her to send back his spouse.
She, fondly aiming to dissuade,
With pious tongue this answer made :
" 'Tis now the Ninth Day from the moon,
And, says the Brahman, 'tis too soon
To travel o'er the country wide."
Her son-in-law with scorn replied,

---

[1] This is XXI. in the Tamil book. The omitted tale is unfit for translation.

"What's the Ninth Day, I'd like to know,
That with my wife I may not go?"
And taking her in anger strode:
But trouble caught him on the road.
    Beneath a tree she had her seat
While in a tank he cool'd his feet.
His shape the god of the Ninth Day
Assumed, and led his wife away.
Surprised on his return to see
That she had left the sheltering tree,
He look'd about, and then he ran,
For she was following a man!
"What's this? Who're you?" he shouted, "stay:
Why, fellow, take my wife away?"
At one the beauty look'd, and then
The other, so alike the men
Her husband she could not declare,
Could nothing do but stand and stare.
When both in vain dispute had spent
Much time, to Rāman's court they went.
Amazed two gentlemen to view
Alike in figure, feature, hue,
The judge required the puzzled dame
Her husband to point out and claim.
She said, "Does not your lordship see
That they are like as like can be?
How can I tell him? you must show
Which is the man, and let us go."
Then Rāman bade them come next day,
And hear what he might have to say.
His wisdom did not fail to see
It was a sacred mystery.

Having in meditative thought
His wonted god's assistance sought,
He told a potter to essay
In kettle-shape a vase of clay,
With spout his little finger's size.
'Twas made, and brought to Rāman wise.
   The following morn the bench he graced:
The trio were before him placed.
He look'd on them, and said, " Who both
This woman claim upon your oath,
I thus decide: the husband's he
Who, entering the pot you see,
Shall come from it triumphant out,
Before all present, at its spout."
One hung his head.   " I quite agree,"
The other said, " with your decree ; "
Enter'd the kettle's mouth ; came out,
As was appointed, at the spout ;
And like a solid statue stood.
As quickly as for awe he could,
The judge descended from his seat ;
In worship true, with trembling feet,
Went on the right the victor round,
And thus to question boldness found:
" Reveal, what deity art thou ?
Before what great one do I bow ? "
" I am the god of the Ninth Day,"
He answer'd: " this man strode away,
Exclaiming, ' What, I'd like to know,
Is the Ninth Day to me ?   I'll go,'
Although my Brahman priest had said
The journey must not yet be made.

To punish his offence I came,
And vindicate my injured name.
You've caused my greatness to be known,
And, doing so, your merit shown.
For this world joy to you is given,
And in the next you'll dwell in heaven."
His blessing having thus bestowed,
To whence he came he found the road.
 Then Rāman to the husband spake:
" Impiety and sin forsake.
This trouble came on you because
You spurn'd and broke religion's laws,
Walk'd obstinately on, and chose
The counsel of the great to oppose."
So having kindly deign'd to say,
He sent him and his wife away.
 'Tis proved the proverb is not vain,
The day of blessing and of bane
Does for a man what, good and true,
His nearest kindred could not do.

OTHER JUDICIAL CASES.

1. *The Mother.*

 The judgments of Mariyāthay-Rāman will have reminded the reader of the famous decision of Solomon,
and stratagems adopted, in cases of litigation, by
Claudius, Ariopharnes, and others whom commentators
mention.[1] It is impossible to say how old a particular

[1] 1 Kings iii. 16–28.

Tamil tale is, or from what source it is derived. Most will see the wise King of Israel in the following story.

After the death of a certain person, a babe was born to each of his two wives. Ere long, one of the infants died. Both women nourished the surviving child in the same way. At length hatred came to them, and each said, "It is the child I bore, I bore the child." After quarrelling greatly, they went to the judge. Not gathering from their statements which of them was the parent, he practised a stratagem. Looking upon them, he said, "I cut this child in two, and give it to you both." One consented, saying, "Good." Weeping and trembling, the other said, "Sir, do not slay the babe. I do not want that child. Let it be hers." The judge decided, saying, "The child belongs to her," and punished the woman who told the lie.

2. *Both Sides of a Question.*

A hanging-nest bird, having built its dwelling from the branch of a tree on the bank of a river, laid its eggs, and hatched its young ones. One day, when the wind blew and heavy rain fell, it saw a monkey at the foot of the tree beaten and distressed by the weather, and said, "O monkey, whatever the state of things, having prepared my nest without hurt from wind and rain, I am safe with my young ones, am I not? You not only have feet and hands, as men have, but a tail; and yet, for a time of severity like this, you are not capable of making a place that will help you." Anger coming to the monkey, it answered, "Is it you who give me advice?" and, mounting the tree, pulled away the bird's nest, and cast its young ones into the water to perish. Then the bird, sorely troubled, said, " Are you to do what is wrong, when I say what is right ? " and went and spoke with the judge of the country. He, having heard, said, " It is necessary to punish the monkey that has acted so unjustly," and sent for the offender. In the way, as it came greatly afraid, it tore off a jack-fruit, and brought and placed it behind the judge ; and then it went in front of him, and bowed respectfully. On seeing it, the royal dispenser of justice, red in his eyes, and gnashing his teeth, exclaimed with anger, " Wicked monkey, you saw the affliction caused by the rain, and yet, when that gentle hanging-nest bird spoke to you politely, you killed its young ones, and spoilt its nest. Is it not so ? Stand, and I will slash your flesh." The monkey appealed to the judge, bending humbly, and saying, " My lord, you should look before and behind when speaking." His lordship, wondering what he meant, looked behind out of the corner of his eye, and saw a jack-fruit lying like a pot of gold. Afterwards, chuckling, he was like one considering a little ; and then he looked again at the plaintiff-bird, and said, " Insignificant creature, how enormous your presumption in offering advice to a monkey of mountain-like greatness ! Henceforth leave off this evil giving of counsel, and live reverently with great and small according to their merits. I forgive you this time, and you may go." Afterwards he turned to the monkey, and said, " Bear patiently the offence which the mean creature committed," and spoke to him pleasant words, commending him, and sending him away.

3. *A Dumb Witness.*

A wayfaring man, going from one district to another, tied his horse to a lonely tree by the side of a tank, and sat down on the shore to eat his boiled rice. A conceited traveller coming up, dismounted, and proceeded to tie his horse to the same tree. The Tamil shouted, "Mine is a very vicious horse: do not fasten yours there, do not fasten it there." "I will," said the proud man; and, having done so, he sat down on the bank to take his meal. Then the two horses began to fight; and, when their masters ran to stop them, the Tamil's horse kicked, and bit, and killed the other. The gentleman, saying he would have damages, seized the Tamil by his dress, and dragged him before the magistrate. Looking upon the Tamil, the magistrate asked him many times, "What do you say?" But he was like a dumb man. Then the judge turned to the complainant, and asked, "What can I do to this mute?" "Sir," said the gentleman, "he is dissembling: he said to me before at the tree, 'Do not tie the horse, do not tie it.'" Hearing this, the magistrate laughed, and dismissed him, saying, "Then, go away: he has no need to pay for your horse."

4. *Tearing the Bond.*

A merchant went to a householder who had owed him a hundred and ten pagodas for ten years, and demanded payment. They quarrelled, and said, "We will tell it to the judge;" and both started towards the town in which he lived. In the middle of the way the householder, speaking blandly to the merchant, said deceitfully, " Sir, where is the note obliging me to pay ?   I would see how many years have passed. Show me the agreement." The trader took it from his girdle, and gave it to him, saying, " Look, here it is." Then the householder, pretending to examine it, tore it up immediately, and threw it into a well that was there.   As soon as he did this, the merchant seized him by his girdle, and dragged him along, and told the affair to the judge.   On the judge saying to the householder, " Did you tear up the bond ? speak the truth," he answered, " I neither borrowed money, nor have I torn a bill."   Afterwards the judge sent the merchant, saying, " Go and collect the fragments, if they are in the place where he tore the writing up, and bring them : we shall see."   A little time after, when the householder was beginning to rejoice in the hope that he had been forgotten, the judge asked him, " Will the merchant have got to the place by this time ? "   He replied, " He cannot have reached it yet : it is a long way off."   The justice, hearing that, had him bound and beaten, got the pagodas from him, and gave them into the hand of the merchant, whom he then dismissed.

5. *The Size of the Gem.*

A merchant, receiving a gem for which he paid a great price, entrusted it to a servant to deliver into the hand of his wife. The servant did not hand it to her. When the trader asked his wife if such an one had given her a gem he had sent, she answered, " No." On his asking the recipient if he had done as he had been told, he replied, "I gave and left it." The merchant acquainted the king with the deceitful trick. The king summoned the offender, who answered, "I gave and left it." "Are there witnesses?" he asked. He said, "There are two." Next day he placed the defendant, the merchant, and the merchant's wife each alone, so that they could not speak to one another. He first called and questioned the dealer's wife. She said, "He did not give it into my hand." On his asking the trader, "What size is the gem you gave?" he answered, "The size of a grape." On his afterwards asking the accused, he also said it was that size. When he asked the witnesses separately, one said, "It is as large as a lemon;" the other, "It is as big as a mango." Knowing from the difference in their answers that they were telling lies, he chastised them; and then they confessed, "He instructed us to give false witness: we do not know." The defendant, fearing, restored the gem to the merchant.

6. *Dispute about a Ring.*

Two youths went to the north country, and were returning home. One of them wore an earring. The other said, "As a mark of friendship, let me have your ring a little while. I will try it in my ear, and give it you again." Receiving it, he put it in his ear. Two days having passed without his restoring it, the owner of it said, "Give me my ring." He answered, "What ring is yours? This is my ring." Thus quarrelling, they both applied to the magistrate. As there was no witness in the case, nothing was clear to him ; and he said, " You may go home." Without their knowledge, he sent a man after each of them, to hear and report what should be said in their houses. They departed. Directly the boy entered to whom the ring belonged, his father said, " Son, where is your ring ? " The father of the other asked, " Son, where did you get that ring ? " Having heard these things, the judge secured the ring, and gave it into the hand of its owner.

7. *Theft by Scissors.*

A merchant who was travelling lay down in a rest-house, and slept in the night. Others were lying there, and one of them stole a jewel tied in the merchant's cloth. When the merchant awoke, and missed the jewel, he thought, " I will feel and notice the breasts of those reposing. His who took it will beat with fear, and so I shall detect the thief." When he did so, the chest of only one throbbed; and he cut off that man's tuft of hair, and lay down again. The rogue, who had pretended to be asleep, then got up, and cut off with his scissors every sleeper's tuft. He trimmed his own docked hair to match the rest, and then again reclined. Not aware of this, the merchant rose before break of day, and spoke with the super-intendent of the rest-house. " As a sign," said he, " by which to distinguish the thief, I cut away his tuft of hair. Mark him, and lay hold of him ; and get possession of my property, and restore it to me." Accordingly the keeper made those who were recumbent get up, and examined their heads. The tufts of all having been removed, he was unable to find out the guilty person. He therefore took all of. them into custody, and going with them to the judge, reported what had happened. " From their hair being clipped in the same style," thought the judge, " the thief must be either a tailor or a barber." Afterwards he inquired into the caste of those concerned. Discovering the tailor, he seized and punished him, and recovered the jewel, which he gave to the merchant, sending him away.

8. *A Witness for two Parties.*

A district chief stole the horse of a village ruler, and, having got it away, and cut off its tail, placed it in his own premises. The village ruler traced the footsteps, and went to the king, and made complaint. The king said, " Is there any witness that it is yours ? " He referred to a shopkeeper in his village. When the king called the poligar, and made the inquiry, he affirmed that the accuser's witness was the very man who would testify that the horse belonged to him. The king sent for the shopkeeper and the horse, and asked the tradesman if it was the village headman's or the district chief's. Reflecting for a little time that if he stated the fact that it was the village ruler's his house would be sacked, and that if he said it was the district magnate's he would not only have to run away from the village, but to suffer punishment if the falsehood should be found out, the shopkeeper hit upon an expedient by which he might seem to be favourable to both parties, and yet make the truth apparent. He answered the king, " Swamy, if you view the horse before, it looks like the villager's: if you regard it aft, it seems to be the poligar's." The shrewd king perceived the meaning of the cunning trader's evidence. Before meant before the thief came, and in front of the horse's face which was unaltered; and aft meant after the coming of the thief, and behind the tail trimmed in a new style. He praised the witness for his wisdom, and gave judgment in favour of the village headman.

9. *Guru Noodle.*

A Hindu magistrate is pictured in the history of Guru Noodle, a compilation of tales by Beschi.[1]

It became necessary for the guru and his disciples to make a long journey. As they could not go such a distance on foot, they hired a hornless ox, agreeing to pay for it three fanams a day. After occupying a watch of four hours in attending to many needful things, they started. It being a severely hot season, the excessive heat struck them as they went on, and they were caught in an open plain, where they could find neither tree nor bush, neither hiding-place nor shade. As they proceeded, the guru, like a drooping plant, could no longer bear the intense heat, and was on the point of falling under the ox. The disciples, seeing that, took him down, and, in the absence of any other shelter, detained the ox, and placing him in its shadow, fanned him with a cloth. After he had been thus greatly refreshed, a cool breeze springing

[1] *Paramatta-guru-Kathay.* Strangely diluted by Alfred Crowquill in *Strange Surprising Adventures of the Venerable Gooroo Simple.*

up, he remounted, and resumed the journey in silence. He reached a small village before sunset, and there alighted. Having entered a humble rest-house, they presented three fanams to the owner of the ox. " It is not enough," said he. They spoke up, saying, " What ? is not this the daily hire we agreed upon with you ? " He objected, crying out, " Certainly this is the price agreed upon for the help of the ox as a conveyance ; but is no pay due for its assistance in the way afterwards as a covering from the heat ? " They angrily contradicted, and insisted that the demand was unjust. The whole of the villagers knew from the excessive noise that there was a great quarrel going on, and men and women all gathered in a crowd.

As the affair proceeded, a guardian of the peace, having stilled the noise, and heard the dispute on both sides, asked, " Will you take the decision I pronounce?" Obtaining their consent, he said, " Once I myself, when I went into a village, stayed for the night in a large lodging-place, where they provided those who came, not only with room, but, on payment, with all that they wanted to eat. Having no means to bear the expense, I said, 'I do not require anything.' For those who had arrived that day, they fixed a great haunch of goat on an iron spit, and roasted it, turning it over the fire. As it smoked from the heat, the smell emitted was very pleasant. Thinking it would be nice, amid this fragrant steam, to eat the boiled rice I had brought tied in a bundle, I asked leave to turn the spit for a little while. Disposing the rice in the savoury smoke, I turned the spit with one hand, and ate with the other. Afterwards, when I wanted to depart, the lodging-keeper demanded payment for my having smelled the sweet odour. 'This is injustice,' I said; and we both went to make complaint to the chief authority of the village. A man of much knowledge, clever, skilful, righteous, he gave this sentence: 'The price of eating the curry is money; the price of smelling the odour of the curry is the odour of money: this is the decision.' Then, calling the lodging-keeper close to him, he pressed and rubbed the bag full of money on his nose, till he cried out, 'My nose, alas! is going! that is sufficient pay.'

"Do you hear?" continued the wise man. "This is right, this is justice, is it not? It is the judgment for you. The price for riding on the ox is money, and a sufficient price for being in the shadow of the ox is the shadow of money; but, as the sun has set, accept the sound of money for the price of the ox's shadow." So saying, he took hold of the fellow suddenly, and, smiting his ear again and again with the bag of money, asked, "Do you hear it?" "Yes, sir," he replied. "O yes, sir, I hear, I hear it plainly: my ear is smarting. The price is sufficient: it is sufficient, father!" Then the guru said, "I have had enough of your ox, too. I cannot do with trouble of this sort. Take your ox, and go. For the short time of the remaining journey, I will walk gently, gently." So saying, he sent him away; and, praising the justice who had settled the dispute so well, he dismissed him with his blessing.

10. *Rain in the Night.*

Generally the stories current show the administrators of justice to advantage; but, as in the following tale from *Kathāmanjari*, they are sometimes represented as being outwitted.

A villager fattened a sheep. The village watchman set his eyes on it, and stole it; and his wife and he killed and cooked it in secret. When it was ready, he looked at his wife, and said, "My dear, we two will eat as much of this curry as we can, and bury what remains out of sight." She replied, "What talk are you talking? do you think you will cheat the child? Go along." Her husband said, "The boy is now asleep in the doorway. Sprinkle him with water, and say it is raining fast, and he must get up; and bring him, and let him have some of the curry." She did so. Next day the owner of the sheep, having his suspicion, went to the watchman's child as he was playing, and asked, "My little fellow, what curry was in your house last night?" "Mutton," he answered. With this evidence, he made complaint to the magistrate, who directed the watchman and his wife to be brought before him, and asked them, "Were you cooking mutton in the night?" "No," they said. He answered, "But your child says you were." They replied, "Can he know what we eat?" The judge asked the little boy, "When did you eat?" "Sir," said he, "it rained in the night: then it was." The judge dismissed them, saying, "It did not rain in the night. Does the little child always eat when it rains? He says as much. The statement that curry was made in the night is not true." So thieves escape by artfulness.

KINGS AND MINISTERS.

I T will have been observed that the poets lay their good advice at the feet of kings. In doing so they define, not only the duties of monarchs, but those incumbent on all. Rulers are regarded, or taught to regard themselves, as the exemplars of their people; and what is law for them is to be considered, as far as applicable, the code for subjects.

Rājās, for their own sake, and the good of those whom they rule over, must be careful with whom they associate. Discretion is especially needful in selecting ministers of state. The duties of the prime minister are as minutely prescribed as those of the king. The monarch's conduct and safety, and the prosperity and happiness of the kingdom, are measured by the premier's loyalty, astuteness, and virtue. He replenishes and guards the royal purse, and directs the conscience of his master.

As in the *Arabian Nights' Entertainments*, so in Tamil story, kings and their viziers are seen in close intimacy. Homeliness and stateliness keep company. The minister goes forth with the sovereign to resolve his perplexities as they arise, share his adventures, and keep him within bounds. They laugh together at the expense of those whom they meet, lose their equilibrium by turns, sometimes unite in redressing wrong, and occasionally seem to forget all virtue. If

320

the minister cannot always prevent the king from falling into mischief or danger, it is his business and pride to extricate him from his difficulties. Stories about them throw not a little satire on anointed and official heads.

The *Kathā-sinthāmany*, or *Gem of Stories*, a collection in which Mariyāthay-Rāman's history is included, contains tales concerning Irāyar and Appāji. Some of them are too coarse for translation; but those selected will serve to illustrate the Tamil character. The title Irāyar, meaning emperor or king, is used as a proper name. He flourished when the Great Mogul, or, as the stories call him, the Pāchā of Delhi, was firmly established on his throne; and he was a thorn in the usurper's side. The grasping ambition of the intolerant Mohammedans comes to view; but they found it impossible to defeat Irāyar, or make him pay tribute, because of the tact and wisdom of his prime minister Appāji.

The hero of these brief popular narratives is more the servant than the master. It is impossible to account for the antipathy of Irāyar's consort towards Appāji; for, besides being merry and wise, he was, as described in one of the tales which we do not venture to translate, so handsome a man, that a princess in a neighbouring kingdom fell in love with him at first sight, and straightway persuaded her royal father to procure him to be her husband. Not a pattern of moral excellence, he was a prompt adviser, and self-governed and faithful agent, who could relieve the anxiety of State-craft with droll trickery and effective humour.

The scene of the following stories is Tondamandalam, corrupted into Tondiman's Country, a division of the Southern Carnatic. Its capital was Vēlūr (Vellore). Like the contiguous principality of Tanjore, it boasts of never having been subdued by the Mohammedans. It early accepted the English alliance, and has, to its own great advantage, been remarkably faithful to the connection.

IRAYAR AND APPAJI.

1. Conferring on Appāji the Dignity of Prime Minister.

In the time when Irāyar reigned, he commanded all the subordinate kings to come to him. All presented themselves but one, in whose stead his minister made his appearance. When they had all waited upon Irāyar, he saw each separately, and transacted affairs with him alone. Last of all, the representative entered his presence. " What is your name ? " the king asked. He answered, " My name is Appāji. I am come in place of my master." Wroth that the prince had not come himself, but sent his man, yet Irāyar did not show his anger. He simply commanded, " Summon your lord." Appāji did so, but stopped him in a village outside, distant about four miles. One day, while the case stood thus, Irāyar went out with his attendants to the market. Directly he saw a butcher tying and flaying a sheep, he said to Appāji, " Call your master quickly." Because he gave the command in such circumstances, it seemed to Appāji that he meditated treating his chief like the sheep. He therefore speedily acquainted his lord with what had taken place, and counselled him to depart into his country. The advice was taken. When a few days had passed, Irāyar, while in a merry mood, regarding Appāji, asked, "Has your master arrived?" "Not yet," he replied. He inquired the cause of the delay. "Sire," said he, "only give me your word that you will spare my lord, and I will tell you." "As you wish, I have given it: say." He proceeded, "My master had reached the neighbourhood, but, when I saw you were angry, I wrote him word to go to his country." "How did you know that anger had come to me?" "When you were going near the shambles, immediately on your witnessing the flaying of a sheep, you ordered me to despatch the summons; and therefore it appeared to my mind that you meant to treat my master like the sheep." Hearing that, Irāyar was much astonished, and appointed Appāji his minister; and he did no harm to his chief. Thus nothing is without good to the clever.

2. *The Constitution is according to the Occupation.*

Once it rained without ceasing all night. At break of day, after the rain had ended, Irāyar and Appāji went forth to look at the state of the flood in the open plain outside the town. A herdsman was there asleep, near his cattle, having placed a stone under his head, another under his haunches, and another under his feet, and covered himself with a plank; and his hair was waving in the flood that ran below. Irāyar, observing him, asked in astonishment, "Is he alive?"

Appāji answered, "He is not dead, but fast asleep." Hearing that, he asked, "Will one snatch sleep, with the hair of his head floating in a rain-torrent like this as it rushes beneath him, and stones hurting his body?" Appāji replied, "Health is suited to occupation." To test that, Irāyar sent for the herdsman to his palace, gave him a superior employment, and kept him supplied day by day with food, dress, jewels, vehicles, and other comforts, and protected from glare, wind, rain, dew, and such-like. After that, he caused moist plantain-leaves to be spread on his door-sill. When he walked across, and went in, he was immediately afflicted with influenza and fever. Irāyar exclaimed, "What Appāji said was right," and was glad, with the help of a physician, to restore the man to health.

3. *This Woman also has a Husband.*

One evening, when Irāyar and Appāji were going along a street, they saw reclining on a raised seat a woman repulsive in form and not attractive in fragrance. The king asked, "Will any one consort with such a female?" Appāji said, "Even she no doubt possesses a husband." "I wonder," replied the king, "what sort of a man he is; I would like to see him." They went on a little, when one who wore a good cloth, a turban, a jacket, and a scarf, and was manipulating betel-leaf and areca-nut for mastication, took up in his hand without any sign of disgust filthy water from the ground to moisten the dry lime he held for the mixture. Seeing that, Appāji said, "Swamy, this man himself is her husband." To find out they turned, and came a little behind him. He went with a brisk step to the woman, sat down by her side, gave her some of the areca and betel to chew, and behaved caressingly towards her. The raja greatly applauded his minister's discernment.

4. *Give a Kiss to the Mouth that drivelled, and an Ornament with Bells to the Foot that kicked.*

One day Irāyar's wife introduced and recommended another man in Appāji's place. The king asked, " Has he Appāji's ability? " She said, " I think he is much more able." " But we must try," said he, and commanded the candidate to withdraw. Afterwards one night Irāyar's infant slavered on his breast and face, and kicked him with its feet in play. After sunrise Irāyar summoned the applicant for the minister's office, and said to him, " One came in the night, and spat on my face and breast, and kicked me with his foot: what shall be done to him? " He answered, " Pour molten lead into the mouth of him who has done this contempt to you who are the head of all the world, and cut off his feet." Telling him to go outside, he sent for Appāji, and asked him the same question. Appāji said, " Whatever foot kicked you, put on it a ring with golden bells; whatever mouth slabbered on you, give it a kiss." After that Irāyar asked, " You recommended the man as more competent than Appāji: have you seen the different genius of the two? " She replied, " How can you be certain from one experiment only? "

5. *What Sounds like Insolence may be Praise.*

Three dancing-women, skilful in acting and singing, came one day from the south, and displayed their art in Irāyar's court. He watched them, and rewarded them handsomely. Of the three, one remarked, " The disposition of this great king is root and stick." Another, " It is prickly and rough." The third, " It is stony and hard." Irāyar called the man whom his wife had recommended, and demanded, " What ought I to do for the things these women have said ? " He answered, " Because they have spoken thus contemptuously of you, the king of kings, let them be shaven bald, and beaten, and driven away." Appāji, sent for and asked, replied, " Swamy, their words were not spoken in scorn. Saying root and stick, is comparing your temper with the sweet sugar-cane. Saying prickly and rough, is likening it to the delicious jack-fruit. Saying stony and hard, is that it resembles sugar-candy. You ought greatly to reward them for speaking thus in commendation of your real disposition." Irāyar was delighted, and made known to his wife what the two ministers said. She answered, " Unless you make one more experiment, my doubt will not be satisfied."

6. *Giving Hair and Ashes to other Kings.*

One day Irāyar, setting his wife within hearing in a place outside, gave one of two bags containing hair and ashes into the hand of him whom she had recommended, and sent him, saying, " Put this into the hand

of the king of the Cannada country, observe, and
return." Giving the other bag into the hand of
Appāji, he commissioned him in the same form, saying,
"Give this into the hand of the king of the Telungu
region, observe, and return." The man whom the
queen had recommended went, and gave it into the
hand of the king named, saying, "Irāyar commanded
me to bring this to you." The king, opening and
inspecting it, asked, "What is this?" He said, "It looks
as if our sovereign had sent it to you to signify that it
would be well if you were to cease opposing your
kingship to his, and get a living by handling ashes
and plucking hair." So soon as the Cannada king
heard that word, his eyes flamed with anger, and he
assembled his hosts, and marched to war. Appāji,
having opened the bag and seen what was in it, put it
into a golden casket set with gems, spread a silk
covering over it, placed it on a palanquin, carried it in
a procession with singing and music, and addressing
the king of the Telungu country, said, "Irāyar has
been making a great sacrifice, and sends you, with
greeting and goodwill, some of the consecrated ashes,
and of the hair of the sacrificial beast." The king was
rejoiced to receive the gift, made all sorts of presents
to the ambassador, intrusted him with many for his
royal master, and collected a force of soldiers with
elephants, instructing them to accompany him to
Irāyar. Before Appāji got back, the army of the king
of the Cannada country arrived, encompassed the fort,
and made ready for war. In this extremity, when
Irāyar was thinking, "Appāji is not," he made his
appearance. Joining with his own the army that had

come with him, Irāyar engaged in battle, and routed the king of the Cannada country. Hearing of the things that had happened, the queen was ashamed, and looking on Irāyar, besought him with much reverence, saying, " Bear patiently my blunder in recommending a fool."

7. *Examining the Images.*

The Pāchā of Delhi, to test the ability of Appāji, sent Irāyar three images of one sort, with a letter requesting to know, in answers to be written upon them, which was like the superior man, which like the ordinary, and which like the inferior. Irāyar, having read the letter, showed the images to all his court, and directed that their distinctive properties should be ascertained. The three being in appearance exactly alike, the courtiers were perplexed, and failed to detect any difference. Appāji, carefully examining all the parts of each separately, observed that there were little holes in the ears. Into those apertures he introduced a fine wire, and noticed how it proceeded. In one of the images it went out at the mouth, and in another at the opposite ear; but out of the third it found no exit. Deciding that the highest man is he who keeps in himself what news he hears, like the penetrating instrument staying inside ; that he is the midmost who lets what he takes in at one ear pass out at the other, like its going out at the ear opposite ; and that he is the lowest who publishes things without reserve, like its issuing from the mouth,—he advised that the images should be returned with these solutions inscribed on them respectively. The king was much delighted, and sent them so to the Pāchā.

8. *Defeating the Pāchā's Minister.*

A rude Mohammedan servant, because of the rain, came and sat down on the raised seat under the verandah of a house. A man in consumption took shelter by his side, and coughed. The Mussulman said, " Do not cough here." He coughed again. Then the ruffian, in a rage, drew his dagger, and with one stroke killed the sick man. All who were near and saw this together seized him, and delivered him to Irāyar. The king asked, " Why did you slay him ? " He replied, " I said, Do not cough. Rejecting my speech, he coughed. That is why I slew him." Hearing that foolish defence, Irāyar laughed, and, looking on Appāji, who was near him, said, " What punishment shall we inflict on this man ? " He answered, " Do nothing to him, but put him in prison, and make him fat by feeding him daily on two sērs [1] of flesh and one of ghee, with fitting accompaniments. Then, at some good opportunity, he will be of service." One day, during the time he was being so treated, the Pāchā, looking on his ministers, said, " Irāyar is not subjected to us, and pays us no tribute, because of the ability of sagacious Appāji. Say, if any one is able to conquer him." One of them answered, " I will overcome him." He assembled large forces for the volunteer, and sent them with him to subjugate Irāyar. The minister-general descended upon the

[1] One sēr equal to eight ounces.

neighbourhood of the royal city, and by messengers made his arrival known to Irāyar. Looking on Appāji, who was in attendance, the king said, "A most cruel man, and a famous strategist, he is come, like a giant, with large forces. Never was there such a misfortune. What is to be done?" Appāji, sending for the rough Mussulman who had been kept and well fed, caused to be written a pacific letter from Irāyar, to this effect, "Will you thus bring armies, and wage war upon this poor beggar, and expect us to spend treasure in paying tribute for him?" This despatch he gave into the hand of the savage, sending him with it to the Pāchā's minister. The rude Mussulman snatched the letter of peace, took it, and delivered it into the minister's hand. The minister, having received and read it, repeated, "The amount for which we have come to wage war against this prowess-lacking pauper!" and retched and spat down in contempt of Irāyar. Thinking he so acted in contempt towards himself, the Mohammedan brute slew him with two thrusts of his knife; and they who were at his side killed the assassin. The minister being dead, the forces broke up and fled. Irāyar greatly praised Appāji's cunning.

9. *Appāji releasing Irāyar.*

The Pāchā thought, "So long as Appāji helps Irāyar, it is impossible to conquer him in war: we must therefore vanquish him by practising deceit." With a thousand valuable horses he sent a thousand soldiers, who were to conceal their weapons, and, pretending to

be horse-dealers, seize and bring the king. Taking
the animals, and dismounting at a distance of an
Indian league [1] from Irāyar's city, they made known
to him the news of their arrival. One day, in the
eventide, Irāyar took some persons skilled in judging
horses, and looked at those understood to be for sale.
"What is the price of these horses?" he inquired.
They answered, "A thousand pagodas each. All have
the same pace, and they are therefore all one price.
Try them. Mount one of them, and ride forth; and
we will come with all the rest at the same pace. See."
So, while all the other horsemen mounted each his
own steed, he mounted one, and set forward. After
they had gone four miles, they put Irāyar into a
palanquin, and conducted him to the Pāchā. Appāji,
hearing of the abduction, was sorely troubled, and said
within himself, "What is to be done in this matter?"
Devising a plan, he disguised himself as a madman,
and went into the Pāchā's city, saying, so that all
might hear, "I am Appāji, and have brought my
Irāyar to seize and carry off the Pāchā." Then crying
"Oho!" he got up, and leaped, and began to wander
round about. One day when he was thus wandering,
and speaking in the presence of the imperial court,
before the citadel, in the promenades, in front of the
houses of ministers and others, and in many more
places, the Pāchā said, "We must ascertain whether
this man is really out of his wits, or a disguised
robber." He sent some officers, saying, "Where does
he eat? Without his knowledge, follow him, find out,
and bring me word." When the night was more than

[1] Ten miles.

four hours advanced, the pretended lunatic took the rice he had begged, and his bowl, and went to the burning-ground. There he laid a fire, kindled it with a brand from the corpse-burning, and cooked his food. He had sense to know, while doing this, that the spies were come to watch him. Having called out in the usual manner, he broke his rice-plate, and ran off. On the officers returning, and reporting these things to the Pāchā, he decided that he was certainly mad. Afterwards Appāji sent a letter to his people, directing them to embark some precious jewels in a large vessel, and bring them as if for sale. They who came in the boat with the jewels, took a few specimens, and carried them for inspection to the Pāchā. Demanding a higher price for the jewels than his experts set on them, they said, "Is any one more competent than Irāyar to determine the value of such jewels?" The Pāchā, hearing that, commanded, "Bring all the jewels you have besides." They replied, "We have brought so large a quantity, that you will do best to come and see them, and take such as you want." "Let it be so," said his majesty; and, with Irāyar and some appraisers, he proceeded to the vessel. The madman joined them, keeping behind the Pāchā, and speaking according to his custom; and, going on board with the rest, he cried out again in the same manner. In that moment the boatmen weighed anchor, and spread sail; and the vessel gained Irāyar's country. The king took the Pāchā to his fort, paid him great respect, and detained him a few days. Then the Pāchā, knowing the artifice that had been practised upon him, applauded Appāji's wit, promised the king, "Henceforth I will not intrude into your affairs," and took his departure. Irāyar embraced and praised Appāji, saying, " You are my tutelary god."

10. *Mental Worry reduces Strength.*

A youth in Irāyar's city, nourished by his mother without stint, and free from every care, was in the habit of seizing with his hands the tusks of elephants that came in his way, and thrusting them back to a distance. The king, taking an airing one day, saw him push away an elephant, and asked Appāji, " What is the cause of his doing thus ? how is there so much strength in this little lad ? " The answer given was, " He possesses strength in proportion to his exemption from domestic care." Afterwards they called together on the boy's mother, and said, " Does your son manage no sort of family affairs ? " She replied, " He is my only son, and I therefore bring him up without any care to himself." They advised her, " It is not good to do so. It will be a cause of trouble hereafter. You should let him have a little to occupy his mind. To-day, when you set his food, say, ' There is no salt for to-morrow, get a little.' " She said so to her son ; and from that time he was full of concern, wondering, " How shall I procure this ? " Next day,. when he went into the street, he laid hold of an elephant's tusk to make it pass before him ; but it lifted him up with its trunk, and left him. Besides showing that to the king, Appāji sent for the mother, explained the things that had happened, and made known that mental anxiety occasions loss of strength. Irāyar marvelled at his wisdom.

11. *What One has, the World has: what One has not, the World has not.*

Irāyar asked a barber who was shaving him, "Are all in this city well off?" He answered, "There are none among them, however poor, who have not gold the size of a lemon." The king looked at Appāji, who was by. After thinking the matter over a little, the minister managed to inspect the barber's bag. Thence he took gold the size of a lemon, and showed it to Irāyar, explaining, "From this he thought what he had the world had, and what he had not the world had not." They kept the gold. "On another occasion ask him," said the minister, "what you have asked now, and mark what he says." The next time the barber was sent for, he said, "Nobody possesses gold the size of a lemon except the highest kings." Afterwards Irāyar, looking on Appāji, praised him, saying, "It were hard in any country to get so shrewd a minister as you." He restored the barber his gold.

12. *Similitudes explained.*

One day, when Irāyar went hunting, and was sitting on the shore of a lake to relieve the weariness occasioned by the heat and glare, one of three women who were journeying said in their conversation, "Foot and branch are one;" another, "Feather and leaf are one;" and the third, "Mouth and fruit are one." The king heard what the three said, and tried for a long time to make out their meaning; but the sense did not appear to him. When he regained his palace,

there was not one in all the assembly who could give
the explanation. So he sent for Appāji, and asked
him the import of those words. He meditated for a
little while, and then made the sense known, saying,
" Those women would be talking of a parrot seen by
them in a banyan-tree. Saying that foot and branch
were one, was speaking of the foot of the bird and the
bark of the tree. Saying that feather and leaf were
one, was speaking of the parrot's plumage and the
tree's foliage. Saying that mouth and fruit were one,
was saying that the bird's beak and the tree's fruit
resembled each other." Irāyar, having heard, exclaimed, " Right ! " and was much gratified.

13. *Penetrating the Disguise.*

The Pāchā of Delhi sent a request to Irāyar that he
would allow Appāji to pay him a visit. The king
accordingly sent the premier. Before Appāji saw him,
the Pāchā had devised a stratagem. He put on
another his royal robes, and made him sit upon his
throne; and he disguised himself as a minister of
State, and sat in the row of the ministers. Afterwards he commanded that Appāji should be shown in.
Appāji looked, stood before the Pāchā in the ministers'
rank, presented his offerings to him, and did reverence.
The Pāchā, regarding Appāji, said, " How did you
know me ? " He replied, "Your majesty, I knew from
the eyes of all in the assembly falling upon you."
Hearing that, the emperor was delighted, and dismissed
him with presents. Subsequently, he spoke with his
Council, saying, " It is because Irāyar has such a

minister that he neither pays us tribute nor regards us with fear."

More Tales of Rulers and Premiers.

1. *An Utter Sinner becoming Virtuous.*

A great person said to a man guilty of every kind of vice, "Forsake these sins, which lead to hell." He answered, "I will not give them up." The great one said, "Only leave off lying." "Very well," replied the man guilty of the five capital transgressions;[1] and from that day he ceased from falsehood. On a certain night he went to the king's house to steal. Coming disguised to inspect the city, his majesty saw the thief, and asked, "Where are you going?" Unable to tell a lie, he said, "I am going to rob the king's house." "May I come with you?" asked the surprised monarch. "Come," said he. Setting the king outside to watch, he took the iron crow, entered the palace, and opened a box in which were three jewels. Thinking, "We must not spoil the shares," he left one, and carried two away. He gave one of these to the king, and kept the other. Going in afterwards, the rājāh was glad to see a jewel left. He sent for his minister, and said, "A robber seems to have entered the palace in the night; go and see what is stolen." The minister, having looked into the box, appropriated the jewel it contained, and reported, "There are three jewels gone." Directly the ruler heard that, he dismissed the minister as an unworthy person, and gave his office to the

[1] Murder, theft, drunkenness, lust, and lying.

burglar, believing him to be trustworthy. Thus, if there be only truth, it dispels many vices.

2. *The Responsibilities of a King.*

Rājā-Kēsari ruled like a father to his people, without fail of justice, so that they were like a cow and a tiger drinking from the same river. When he perceived that old age was come upon him, setting his mind on the heavenly world, he concluded that he was no longer equal to the duties of his royal line. He therefore sent for his son without delay, embraced him tenderly, caused him to sit near him, and regarding him with a cheerful face, said, " My dear child, old age having come upon me, I feel that I must put off from my shoulder the great burden of this kingdom, and lay it on yours, and have rest. This you will understand ; but you may profit me in the heavenly world, and I beg you to render me so great a help." Happy to discover signs that the prince would not reject his father's word, he further said, " My son, governing is not easy. Always wakefully keep your mind upon the affairs of the kingdom. Get to know all news by well-chosen and faithful messengers, and walk according to their report. Make glad the commander of the army, and others who pay respect to one another. Know especially that many ministers are wanted to counsel kings. Beware of doing anything that would pain and distress the poor. If they weep, do not think that the tears they shed are water, but that they are a sharp weapon to cut up the kingdom by the root. Conduct yourself in the belief that the sceptre·

Y

is the weapon that gives victory to kings." When he had taught the prince many such righteous rules, he anointed him, and withdrew to his work of penance.

3. *The Advantage of a Standing Army.*

When a king saw that there was no money in his treasury, he turned to his minister, and said, " I have conquered all enemies, and subdued their countries, and kings without exception pay me tribute. So I have no adversaries, not even one. Why, then, make the useless expense of keeping up all these armies ? Disband them, and you replenish the treasury." The minister answered, " This counsel is not wise. If we dissolve the armies, opponents will arise. Our enemies will see their opportunity, and come to war. It is not well, therefore, to dismiss the armies." The king said, " There could be an army when wanted. If there were only money, everything could be had and maintained." The minister replied, " Not even by expending money, can you raise armies when they are needed. To collect flies, you may heap up molasses in the night-time, and you may beseech the flies, but will they then swarm in the place ? Keep the armies together, and your foes will fear, and remain quiet." " This is true," said the king ; and he walked according to the word of his minister.

4. *Prosperous Government.*

A king's son, as soon as his father was dead, caused himself to be crowned, and was eager to go to expense on useless things. The result of his excesses was a deficiency in the treasury. Calling his minister, he said, "Because those who dwell in my country pay their yearly dues to me little by little, my coffers are not full a single day. As a beginning, I want to fill the treasury by increasing the taxes on their articles of merchandise, and on their rice-fields, fallow ground, houses, and groves. I would punish those who do not pay, and would confiscate their goods; and I would collect the salt-tax for twenty years all at once. What is your opinion?" The minister answered, "Great king, graciously hear my suggestion without being angry, and afterwards do as you please. To the poor inhabitants who are without the means of cultivating their ground, advance money, to be returned a little at a time, with a tax on their produce. Should you pursue this course, both the inhabitants and their king will profit. If, instead of supplying a cow with fodder, and milking her regularly, you cut off her udder, saying you will have all at once as much as she gives in a month, will you get any milk? He who makes his subjects happy wins the name of king. He who protects men acquires the title of preserver." The minister used other arguments, until the young king, turning as a horse to the bridle, conducted the government according to his word.

5. *The King's Eye.*

From lust of goods, a king cruelly oppressed his subjects, laying excessive taxes on ploughed and pasture land, and even on dried-up crops, and barren bushes and trees. Therefore his starved and ragged subjects abhorred him, and set their desire on the ruler of another country. The minister, knowing this, reflected, " Evil is coming to our king, and it is the part of a minister to acquaint him with the threatening evil." He therefore said to him, " Sir, an object placed on a rolling ball cannot stay. Neither can a crown on the head of a king whose subjects are without repose. You will presently lose this kingdom, through your government affording no peace to the people. It is necessary to throw up a bank before the tank bursts. Before evil comes to you, it is needful to take care." " But," said the king, " how will authority over the people come to me ? " He answered, " You will have sway and profit, if you preserve the poor people, giving loans to them, and receiving fair taxes for their produce, and ceasing to burden the weak as if they were strong. Does not the gardener enjoy good gain afterwards, if he first manure, weed, water, work, and watch ? " The king, having heard all these things, was aware that they were true, and began to act accordingly. Thus a monarch without a good minister is like a traveller without an eye.

6. *Emigration.*

A gardener approached a sovereign who exacted undue tribute from his subjects, and begged him, saying, " Sir, I am a very poor man, and cannot pay all the taxes you have imposed. Be gracious, and remit some of them." The king answered, without the least pity, " You must pay them all." He said, " Sir, I have not the means." The king said, " You

are not worthy to stay in my country." The gardener
answered, " Then, where shall I go ? " " You may go
where you like," said the king. Thereupon he replied,
" You yourself name the place, and if it be suitable
for me, I will go there." Then the king said, " Go to
Sīrangapatam." The gardener said, " I will not go
there : if you ask why, your elder brother rules that
country." The king said, " Go to Tanjore." He said,
" Neither will I go there, for there is your younger
brother." The king said, " Go to Panthar." The
gardener said, " There your uncle governs ; so I have
no mind to go there." Anger coming to the king, he
looked on the gardener, and said with a loud voice,
" Then go to hell, you devil." To that the gardener,
in a high tone, responded, " Sir, I cannot go there.
Would you know why ? Your deceased father is there
established." Then the king was much ashamed, and
forgave him all the taxes.

TENNĀLU-RĀMAN.

1. *Becoming a Jester, and joining Irāyar.*

IN a north country town called Tennālu, was born a
Brahman, who was named Rāman. A sanniyāsi
who saw him one day, marking his fine figure and
brave spirit, taught him an incantation, and said, " If
you go into the temple of Cāli, and in one night
repeat this mantra thrice ten million times, Cāli will
appear to you with a thousand faces. Do not be
afraid when you see her, and you shall have what
gifts you desire." Selecting a favourable opportunity,
Rāman went into the temple of Cāli outside his town,
and repeated the incantation according to instruction.
Pattira-Cāli, assuming a great shape, appeared with a
thousand faces and two hands. Beholding her dreadful form, Rāman, who was very courageous, laughed
without fear. Cāli demanded, "How dare you laugh?"
" Mother," he answered, " though we have two hands
to one nose, it is hard work blowing it when we catch
cold. If, with a thousand faces, you should chance
to take cold, how will you blow these thousand noses
with only two hands?" Pattira-Cāli said, " Naughty
boy, because you have made fun on seeing me, go and
be a jester from this day forward." He said, " Ah!
you have bestowed on me a pretty gift! If I look so,
a merriman! if thus, a buffoon!" On hearing that,
she took pity, and said, " The royal court will appreciate

your service: so be a jester." Then she vanished;
and he, becoming skilled in making sport, went and
joined himself to Irāyar, and gained a living.

2. *Escaping the Punishment of having his Head trundled by the Foot of an Elephant.*

One day, for blame incurred by Tennālu-Rāman's
tricks, Irāyar was angry, and commanded that he
should have his head rolled off by the foot of an
elephant. The officers took him, and, having dug a
pit in an open plain outside the town, and buried him
all except his head, went to fetch an elephant. At
the critical moment, a crook-backed washer of clothes
going that way inquired, "Why are you buried, sir?"
Tennālu-Rāman answered, "I was hump-backed for a
long time, and a physician buried me here to make
my back straight. My crookedness is quite cured:
dig me out, and see." The washerman did so, and,
on examination, perceiving that he was without any
bend in the back, said, "I must be buried too, that
my crookedness may be made straight." Tennālu-
Rāman put him in the pit, and buried him up to the
neck, and taking up his bundle, carried it away, and
saw Irāyar. He asked, "How is this? I directed
that your head should be knocked off by an elephant's
foot? How have you avoided the punishment and
come?" He said, "Using diligence, to let a washerman be executed instead of me, I received his
bundle, and have brought it." When the king heard
that, he laughed, and forgave the fault.

3. *Avoiding Decapitation.*

Another day Tennālu-Rāman committed so serious a fault by his trickishness that Irāyar, witnessing it, was exceedingly angry, and, calling two officers, gave him into their custody, saying, "Do not let him escape, but take him, and cut off his head." They conducted him to a distance, and were on the point of despatching him, when he said a nice word to them, and continued, "In any case you will kill me. That I may obtain a good birth, let me descend into a tank, and meditate on God for a suitable time up to the breast in water. When I say *Now*, will be the propitious moment. Then you two, being on both sides of me, strike off my head with one blow." They agreed; and he accordingly went down into a tank, and after a while said "Now," in a jocular vein, and sank in the water. Because the executioners struck with swift force, the sword of each fell on the other, and both were slain. Tennālu-Rāman rushed off, and went and stood before Irāyar. The king asked, "How have you escaped and come?" He answered, "Making the soldiers kill each other, I got away." On that day also he bore with his fault.

4. *Going about hiding his Head.*

Tennālu-Rāman having been guilty of a very bad fault, Irāyar sent for him, and said, "If from to-day, going about, you hide your head, and never show it in my presence, you may live; but if you do not hide it, you shall lose it." Hearing that, Tennālu-Rāman inverted a jar,[1] and put it over his head, and so went about in public. Irāyar seeing, summoned him, and asked, " Why do you indulge in this unbecoming behaviour ? " " Lord," he answered, " I go thus about with my head hid because you graciously commanded me to do so." Irāyar was amused, and had patience with him on that occasion also.

5. *Causing the Keepers to be beaten.*

History players came one day from the Telungu country. Irāyar, commanding them to perform, charged two sentries not to let Tennālu-Rāman come to the place. At the time for the entertainment, Tennālu-Rāman approached the first custodian, and said, " Only let me go, and I give you half of what comes to me," and obtained his consent. He spoke to the second with the same effect. Going in, with a churning-stick which he had brought concealed, he hit a man who was acting Crishna. The actor, weeping, cried out, " O ! alas ! " The intruder remonstrated, " Fie ! only this ? Crishna was beaten many times by the sticks of many shepherdesses, and you cannot bear one stroke from the stick of one person ! " Irāyar saw, and asked, " How did he get inside ? " and commanded, " Give him twenty-four strokes." When they were proceeding to inflict the sentence upon him, he addressed the second watchman, saying, " You agreed to receive half of what should come to me, did you not ? " " True," he said. So he had him beaten,

---

[1] Having made two holes in it for his eyes to look through, adds the *Kathā-manjari.*

saying, "Take half of the twenty-four strokes I have gained." He caused the remaining twelve to be given to the first keeper in the same way. Thus he escaped himself without one stroke.

6. *Branding the Brahmans.*

When Irāyar's mother was dying, she said she would like a mango-fruit to eat. Before he could procure and present it, she passed away. It grieved him that she had gone without her wish being gratified, and he sent for some Brahmans, and said to them, " My mother set her heart upon a mango-fruit, but died before I could get it for her. What can be done to satisfy the departed soul ? " They answered, " If you make some mangos of gold, and give them to as many Brahmans on the anniversary of her death, there will be relief to her soul." Irāyar, believing what they said, bestowed the gifts accordingly. Tennālu-Rāman fetched all the Brahmans who had received the present to his house, saying it was his mother's anniversary ; and, having heated the handle of a ladle, he branded each of them twice. They all wept, and told Irāyar. He called Tennālu-Rāman, and asked, " May you commit such wickedness as this ? " The offender replied, " When my mother was dying, she was seized with numbness and contraction of the hands and feet, and therefore asked that a brand might be applied. Before the spoon-handle could be made hot, she died ; and I have done this from a wish to give satisfaction to the soul." After hearing the explanation, Irāyar laughed a long time.

7. Rearing a Horse.

Irāyar, sending for some young horses, gave one to every house in his city, commanding, "Take nine pagodas each for the grass, gram, and medicaments needed, and so bring up the colts that I may have them soon in good condition." Receiving them, all tended them with great care, except Tennālu-Rāman. He erected a wall on the four sides, enclosing the foal, and made a door in the wall, and a pit within. Every morning and evening he carried a handful of grass, and gave it in at the door; and by the same opening he poured water into the pit. The pagodas he appropriated. After three years, Irāyar commanded to bring all the young horses; and all except Tennālu-Rāman brought them leaping and prancing. Irāyar, calling him, asked, "Why have you not brought the young horse?" He said, "Nobody can take hold of the horse I have. If you will send one of your clever grooms, I will bring it." So he sent a horsekeeper who had a beard a cubit long. Rāman took him, and told him to stand at the door, and peep in, and look at the animal. The groom did so; and the horse seized his beard, supposing it to be grass. The horse-man cried out, and was in great fear. Tennālu-Rāman went quickly to Irāyar, and reported, "The horse has laid hold of the groom, and will not let him go." Irāyar called Appāji, and they went to see what was the matter. He found the horse retaining the beard, and the man in a state of exhaustion. Ordering the wall to be knocked down, he seized the horse, and released the beard; but the creature had only strength to walk slowly. Addressing Tennālu-Rāman, the king asked, "How is it the horse is so feeble?" He replied, "I had carefully given it the proper quantity of food, when it seized the groom's beard. Can anybody lay hold of a horse when it is overfed?" Irāyar so laughed at his misbehaviour, that his whole body shook.

8. *Bringing up a Kitten.*

One day Irāyar gave a kitten and a cow to each house, ordering that the cow's milk should be poured out to feed the kitten. Tennālu-Rāman, like the rest, received and took away a kitten and a cow. Every one else, milking the cow, continued to pour out the milk to nourish puss. He, the first day, having drawn the milk, made it boiling hot; and then he set it for the kitten to drink. Coming quickly, it put its mouth in, and as far as it dipped its mouth was scalded. From that day, if it saw milk, it ran to a distance. He drank the milk himself. When six months were gone, Irāyar ordered all the householders to bring each his cat. Observing that Rāman's only was as if it would decline and die, he asked, "Tennālu-Rāman, why is this cat wasting thus?" He answered, "If it sees milk, it runs. What can I do?" Irāyar at once ordered milk to be brought; and directly the cat saw it, it was afraid, and cried and ran. The king told them to catch, and bring it back. When he examined it, half its mouth was a burn. Discovering that, by giving it boiling milk, and scalding its mouth, he had

made it fear and run whenever it saw milk, according
to the proverb, " A burnt cat will not go near the fire,"
Irāyar fell into a fit of laughter.

9. *Causing Robbers to draw Water.*

One day six robbers got into Tennālu-Rāman's
premises from behind. Knowing from signs that they
were watching their opportunity, he entered the house,
and carefully put away all his money, jewels, silk
garments, and other valuables. Then he called his
wife, and, so that the thieves could hear, said, " As
there is much distress in the town on account of
robbers, if we put into a large box all the treasure in
our house, we can take it out again when the trouble
of the robbers is over." Then he put into a box stones
and clods, and his wife and boy and himself lifted it
up, and carried it to a well, and threw it in. The
robbers, having heard the aforesaid speech, and the
noise of the splash at the well, said, " We will not go
into the house together, but into the garden, and take
up and away what is in the well." With eager delight
they told one of their number to go down into it, and
see how matters stood. He descended and examined,
and said, " If we draw water without stopping, we
shall be able to carry it off." " Right," said they, and
began to work the two machines on the spot for raising
water. Tennālu-Rāman came secretly, and turned the
channels to all the plantain, lime, orange, citron, betel,
cocoa-nut, and other trees in the garden. They drew
and drew without ceasing till day dawned, and Tennālu-
Rāman had watered all the garden. Then he cried

clearly, "Stop the drawing." Directly the robbers heard that, they said, "If we give over at once, we have done enough," and made their exit.

10. *Driving away a Pandit learned in all the Shastras.*

There came one day to Irāyar's assembly a pandit acquainted with all the shastras, who bore the name Vittiyāsakkārar. All the learned men belonging to Irāyar were afraid of him, and took counsel with Tennālu-Rāman, saying, "Whatever our ability, it is unequal to his. If he conquer, contempt will be to us all. Irāyar, too, will despise us. What is to be done?" Tennālu-Rāman said, "You need not fear. I will practise a fit device, and win the victory." On a certain day Vittiyāsakkārar came to Irāyar's court to engage in discourse. Then Tennālu-Rāman, having laid flat pieces of oil-wood together in the form of a book, tied them with string such as is used for tying buffaloes, and wrapped a cloth round it, took it up, and went and sat opposite the pandit. The master of all the shastras looked, and asked, "What book is that?" He answered, "It is *Tila-kashda-magishda-panthanam.*" On hearing that, the pandit was taken by surprise, and after reflection said, "Though I have read all the shastras, yet I have never met with this book. I never heard its name." Tennālu-Rāman, addressing him, said, "You have the fame of being learned in all the shastras, and have you not seen this great work hitherto?" The pandit said, "I will answer to-morrow," and went to the place where he was staying. After much consideration, he concluded, "I cannot get

any way at the meaning of the title of the book.
What it is about, I do not know. If I stay here, I
incur shame." He therefore departed at dawn of day.
Irāyar, informed that the pandit who knew all the
standard writings had run away without saying a
word, sent for Tennālu-Rāman, and asked, "How did
you vanquish the learned man?" He said, "With
this book, *Tila-kashda-magishda-panthanam.*" "Loose
it," said he. Undoing the covering, he showed it.
Irāyar, seeing the tying of the oil-wood with buffalo-
cord, said, "*Tilam* is the name for oil, *kashdam* for
wood, *magishdam* for buffalo, and *panthanam* for string.
Have you overcome by this deceptive trick?" And
he laughed.

11. *Baffling an Athlete.*

A wrestler called Athysūran, who had conquered all
the wrestlers in numerous royal courts, came to that of
Irāyar with many memorials of conquest. Tennālu-
Rāman, seeing all the king's wrestlers alarmed and
perplexed, asked, "What is the matter?" They said,
"Hitherto we have made an honourable living at the
great king's. Now there is a wrestler come who will
bring disgrace and want to us. What shall we do?"
Tennālu-Rāman directed them, saying, "Do not fear.
Lend me all the trophies you have gained, and make
me your master, and all of you follow me." He put
on all the memorials entrusted to him, and under the
name of Vīra-Kēsari (Brave Lion) summoned his
followers, and erected a tent opposite that of Athisūran.
The fencer, thinking, "It looks as if he were an
opponent, and I may as well go and find out his

qualifications," sent him word that he was coming to him. Tennālu-Rāman answered, "There is no need for him to come here. To-morrow, before the great king, he will be made to know all particulars." Hearing that, and learning his name, Athisūran was confused, and wondered what sort of a man his adversary was. Irāyar came next day, and commanded that Athisūran and Vīra-Kēsari should engage in combat. Vīra-Kēsari asked Athisūran, "What code do you fight by?" He replied, "By the treatise on fencing." Vīra-Kēsari said, "I will mention a few manual rules. If you can show me which and which of them are correct according to the shaster, the conflict can afterwards go on." "Be it so," said Athisūran. Then Vīra-Kēsari, standing in front of him, pointed with his forefinger to himself and to him, joined his three middle fingers and struck with them his own breast, and went through other symbolic gesticulations. The fencer, comprehending none of the things he saw, and lost in endeavouring to recollect the few rules he had learnt, stood without any power to speak. Tennālu-Rāman, snatching the prizes, drove him off, beat the drum of victory, and went to his tent. Next day Irāyar asked him, "What were the rules of hand you showed yesterday?" Repeating them, Tennālu-Rāman explained that so he said to Athisūran, "If I come to you, you will stab me with your sword in my breast, and then I shall fall on my back, and who will take care of my wife and my child?" Irāyar was amused.

12. *Making a black Dog white.*

Irāyar slept one morning till an hour and a half after sunrise. As it was his day for being shaved, the barber came, and having gently operated while he lay in bed, without disturbing his sleep, went away. After awaking and rising, the king looked into the upright mirror, and saw how nicely he had been shaven. Greatly delighted, he called for the barber, and asked, " What is there that you wish ? " He said, " Swamy, I would like to be made a Brahman." Irāyar assembled the Brahmans, and promised them exemption from taxes if in six months they should receive the barber into their order. Exceedingly distressed, they subjected him to various ablutions and ceremonies. When the six months were over, Irāyar determined to go to their village, and see the barber sit and eat in their ranks. They went weeping to Tennālu-Rāman. He said, " You have no need to fear ; I will do a trick, and get you off." He tied a rope round the neck of a black dog, dragged it along after him, made a sacrificial pit on the bank of a tank near the village, and employed four Brahmans to perform the needful rites. He then dipped the dog he had brought, and it barked repeatedly. Then he drew it round the pit he had dug, bathed it once more, and made it again circumambulate. Irāyar coming while he was acting thus, demanded, " Why do you treat the dog in this way ? " Tennālu-Rāman said, " I am going to make this black dog white." Irāyar replied, "Madcap, how can a black dog become white ? it is impossible." Tennālu-Rāman said, " When a barber can be made a Brahman, is

z

turning a black dog white a wonder?" So soon as he heard that, the king reflected, "Right! I spoke without deliberation." He did not go to the neighbourhood of the Brahmans, but returned to his palace, and summoning the barber, pacified him in another way, and sent him home. Hearing the news, all the Brahmans were delighted.

13. *Painting and arranging Pictures.*

Irāyar, having built a beautiful terraced house, sent for an artist, and commanded him to paint some handsome pictures. As soon as the painter had finished, he let the king know. When Irāyar went with his ministers and others, and looked at the work, he was rejoiced. Tennālu-Rāman, examining one of the pictures before him, said, "Great king, to this there are only the limbs of one side: where is the other half?" The king laughed at him, and replied, "Do not you know they are supposed to be on that side?" "Now I understand," he said. On a certain day, after some months had passed, addressing the king, Tennālu-Rāman told him, "Since that day I have been practising the art of painting, and at length I have perfected my hand in it: you must see the style of my work." "So indeed?" exclaimed the king, and was greatly pleased. The pictures in his palace being a little old, he said, "Wipe out all these, and draw worthy pictures;" and meanwhile he removed to the other residence. Tennālu-Rāman, washing out the beautiful pictures that were there before, filled the royal dwelling with his performances, in one situation a nail, on one side a finger, in another place a hand, and so every separate member, spoiling the appearance of the house. Afterwards he went to the king, and said, "The pictures are all finished, and wait for your approval." When, believing it true, the king, with many persons, entered and looked, he said, "Tennālu-Rāman, what is this? there is only one member!" He replied, "Have you now forgotten the fancy of all the rest being on that side?" "O ho!" spoke the king, and said, "I am deceived, you have done great mischief." And he hung down his head, and went away in anger.

14. *Providing for the Family.*

One day Irāyar, perceiving that Tennālu-Rāman was much distressed, asked, "What are you sorrowing for? Of what are you in want?" Then Tennālu-Rāman said, "Sir, the astrologers tell me I shall die in one or two months. But I have not thought anything about death; and, after my time, who will take care of my family as I do? There is no one; and that is why I am afflicted." Irāyar answered, in a way to inspire trust, "Do not fear in the least about that. I can protect your family ten times better than you can. Is that a great thing to me?" From that time Tennālu-Rāman pretended to be sick, and getting worse and worse; and one day he carried out a scheme to make all believe he was dead. Depositing elsewhere the money, jewels, and vessels that were in his box, he entered it himself. Directly Irāyar heard the news of his death, having been informed that

Tennālu-Rāman was very rich, he commanded some officers to go to his house, and fetch the box quickly. They brought it to his apartment. When with greediness he opened it and looked in, he saw Tennālu-Rāman, and said, "Oh! oh! they said you were dead." He replied, "Am I going to confide in you, and die? Will you be yourself the protector of my family?" The king left ashamed and speechless.

SINGERS.

1. *An Ass brought to Mind.*

A SINGER, ignorant of his faults, thinking he would earn a reward by singing to the ruler of another country, came and lodged in a house in that city. Next day he got up at dawn, and practised singing. A washerwoman in the neighbouring house wept, making a great noise. Directly he gave over singing, she also ceased from weeping. Thus it went on for a week. Therefore the singer sent for the washerwoman, and asked her, "Why do you cry whenever I sing?" "Sir, when I hear your golden voice, the thought comes of a donkey I had, which died last month. Therefore I cry," she answered, bursting into tears. So put to shame, the singer returned to his own country, without seeing the king. The simpleton who goes about not knowing his own failing will be despised in the world.

2. *Loss of Dignity.*

Travelling through a jungle, a singer saw a shepherd there with his flock, and thought, "If I sing him a song, I can ask for some milk, and get it and go." Attending to the song, the shepherd wept a stream of tears. The singer looked at him, and asked, "What cause have you to weep?" He answered, "You are neither old nor lame, but a young and handsome man. Tell me what misfortune has befallen you, and I will tell you my tale." The singer said, " There is no need to hesitate : tell me your story." " I weep," said he, " because yesterday a sheep made a noise exactly in the same way from morning watch to sunrise, and then died with a swollen head. You have been making the noise for an hour and a half, and in an hour and a half more will swell in the head and die." The singer was confounded, and went away without saying anything, reflecting, " We have seen an illustration of the proverb, if you go to one who does not know a rare accomplishment, your dignity is diminished."

3. *A dying Sheep.*

A singer sitting on a raised seat in the street, moving his head, sang a hymn. Many people were listening. Then a shepherd, going in the way, stopped, looked on for a little, and then, sobbing and sobbing, wept without ceasing. Those present, supposing that he wept for joy, said, " What are you crying about ? Do not cry." He answered, " Alas ! this disease came to a sheep in my flock. Bending and bending, it fetched up. Nothing cured it. It died. I weep because that affliction has come to this young man. But if you immediately apply to him a burning brand, perhaps he will live." They scolded the shepherd, and chased him away.

4. *Branding the Bard.*

A cowherd, having acquired a lac of rupees, became

a prosperous man. An accomplished singer went to him, and sang songs. While singing, he moved hand, head, and eyes, according to the sound. Seeing that, and thinking he was seized with convulsions, the herdsman went inside, and heated a brand-iron, and, coming out, called to him. The singer went, supposing he called him to give him a present. The herdsman, making two persons hold him, applied the brand. The singer was frightened, and cried out, wept, and went home. Healed by a surgeon, he decided that it would not be well for him to go professionally to any one again. While this was the case, a man learned in the sciences, with whom he had long been acquainted, said to him, "When you are so skilful in song, why bring poverty on yourself? A noble-minded king is friendly to me. I will give you an introduction to him. Come along." So calling him, he took and presented him, and told him to sing. The king heard with great pleasure, and, purposing to give him an ample reward, got up, and went within, to direct it to be brought. Then doubt was born to the singer, and he ran off, suspecting, every moment he lingered, that this also was a time of preparing to brand him. Though ever so many persons called after him in civil language, he went home without turning to see. The king came, and asked the learned professor, "Where is the singer? What has frightened him away?" Grieved at his being so afraid of him, he caused many presents to be conveyed, and went to the singer's house, and bestowed them with much politeness, greatly cheering him, and inquired, "Why did you run away?" He told of the branding inflicted on him before, and said, " I ran off, thinking it would happen so this time." The king was astonished at the explanation, and remarked, " If fortune come to fools, they neither know what to do nor what to shun."

THIEVES.

1. *Hand in Hand.*

A N intimate friend came one night to a merchant.
The man of business was emptying his money-
bag, and counting, when the lamp went out. Suspecting that his visitor was going to take the money, the
merchant laid hold of his two hands, and said, " I ask
a word. You have hitherto been a most trusty friend
to me, and I want you to be so while your life shall
last. In order to that, lo! a light is coming. Strike
hands and swear in the presence of that light." He
told his wife to bring a light quickly, retaining the
hands till she brought it; and directly it came, striking hands so that the light should witness, he released
his friend.

2. *Climbing a Cocoa-nut Tree.*

A thief climbed a cocoa-nut tree that was in a
man's garden, wishing to steal the fruit. The owner
of the tree, knowing the noise, ran out of his house in
a temper; and on his appearance the robber came
down from the tree. The owner said, " You fellow,
why do you mount my tree?" "Elder brother," he
answered, "I went up to pluck grass for a calf." "Indeed!" he replied, "is there grass on a cocoa-nut tree?"
"Because there is not, I have come down : do not you
know this?" he said mockingly, and went away.

3. *Saving a Brass Pot.*

A trader, knowing that some robbers were watching close by, to steal a brass water-jar that he carried, said. as if speaking to himself, but so that they might hear, " O, I have come without that necklace ; I will fetch it." The thieves waited idly, supposing that he would return ; but he got off with his brass pot, and, reporting the affair in the village, caused them to be apprehended. A prudent man will escape in the time of danger.

4. *Great Thoughts.*

When a king was grieving about the death of his fine horse, his minister said, " Sire, if you commission me, I will go to Arabia, and fetch you a good one." He gave him the needful money, and sent him. Going to that country, he bought for ten thousand rupees a swifter and better-tempered steed than the king had before. As he was returning with his face to his own land, he stayed for a night in a rest-house in the middle of the way, at a place where there was a fear of robbers. So, looking on the horsekeeper, he said, "Because there is a fear of robbers, you must not sleep, but keep awake. In order to that, think on any great subject : then sleep will not come." Having told him this device, he went and lay down. In the second watch the king's treasurer woke, and said, " Horse-keeper, are you awake ? How is it ? " " Yes, sir," he answered. " What are you thinking about ? " " I am thinking who made and set so many stars in the sky." " Good ! so keep awake," he said, and went asleep. In the third watch, calling the horsekeeper in the same way, he asked, "What are you thinking of now?" The man replied, "Sir, I am meditating who dug out this sea, and where he put the displaced earth." "Good! be watchful," said he, and lay down. Then for a little time the horsekeeper slept soundly; and, ere he woke, a robber took away the horse. Afterwards, the master woke again, and said, "Horsekeeper, what are you thinking about?" The horsekeeper said, "Sir, the horse has stolen itself. I am thinking whether you will take and bring, or whether I must carry, the saddle and other harness belonging." The treasurer said, "Alas! has the horse gone?" and ran, and saw. Then he said, "I am deceived," and went sorrowing to the king.

5. *Playing with Water.*

One night a robber was hiding in the bean-shed of a merchant's house. Going to wash his hands, the householder detected his presence, and told his wife to bring a large pot full of water. When she brought and gave it, he, receiving it, spilt it gurgling, gurgling upon the thief. When all the water was used, again he told her to bring a pot of water, and then poured it gurgling, gurgling out. Whereupon his wife asked, "Why thus vainly do you pour away with a gurgling sound?" He then bubbled it forth four times upon herself. She concluded that a madness was come on her husband, and, afraid, ran into the street, and collected many persons with her cries, and went in with them. Approaching the tradesman, they asked,

" What folly has seized you ? Why do you spout the water on your wife ? " To that he said, " I married her when five years old, have placed in her possession a thousand pagodas, and have cherished her in comfort hitherto; and now, when I give her four jets of water, she does not bear it, but comes and tells you. I never did a kindness to the man who is under the bean-shed, and never made his acquaintance. On him, in gurgling jets, I have poured all the water of two pots, and he has borne it. If you want to know whether this is true or false, ask him in the course of your investigation." Thereupon they seized the robber, perceiving that the stratagem had been adopted to secure his apprehension.

6. *Naming a Child.*

One night a robber sneaked up into the loft made of planks under the roof of a merchant's house. When the merchant and his wife retired to rest, he saw signs of a thief being up in the loft, and devised a plan. Addressing his wife, he said, „ If a daughter be born, what will you do ? " She said, " I will call her Sīthay, have a boy in the house, give her in marriage, and endow her with all my goods." Having heard that, he said, " It cannot happen as you think. A boy will be born. I shall call him Rāman, and endow him with all I possess. I shall put him to school to learn ; and if he should not come home at dinnertime, I shall call him, shouting thus, ' Rāmā ! Rāmā ! ' " Rāman was the name of the chief watchman, who lived in the next house ; and he got up, collected and brought ten persons, and asked the trader, "Why did you call?" "I did not call you," he answered, and told him of the conversation between himself and his wife, assuring him that there was no unpleasantness between them. "If perchance you doubt, there is one in the loft yonder who will decide the matter." So saying, he showed him the man on the planks. Whereupon they, knowing that he was a robber, laid hold of him, and caused him to be suitably punished.

7. *Bite of a Scorpion.*

A robber was squatting upon his legs one night on the loft of a merchant's house. The merchant went to lie down in the house. Perceiving signs of the intruder's presence, he devised and carried out a scheme. Like one looking to see if all the boxes were fastened, he kept touching them, till, as if a scorpion had stung him in the hand, he wept and cried aloud, "Alas! alas! a scorpion has stung me; what shall I do?" Hearing the great noise of weeping which he made, all the neighbouring householders came and saw, and inquired, "In response to incantations, has the poison gone down?" He answered, "The poison is gone down, only that good man has not yet got down from the loft;" and he showed them the stranger on the boards. They seized the thief, and admired the merchant's clever device.

8. *A faithful Dog.*

A Mohammedan kept a dog, which was useful for hunting and other purposes. To meet a difficulty, he put it in pledge for a hundred pagodas, and went to his own town. While it was so, one night, a robber descended from the top of the pawnbroker's house, seized four purses of money, and went out by the door. The dog, which was there, flew upon him, bit and killed him, and then barked, and awoke the master. He came, and was happy to discover the benefit the dog had done. Early next day, he tied to the dog's neck a lawful receipt, acknowledging that he had been paid the hundred pagodas with interest, and an ola describing the good exploit of the dog, and sent it, saying, "Go to your master." Off it ran with eagerness; and when it was coming near his house, the Mohammedan, seeing it, said, "O ho! it has inflicted an injury on the man, and runs to bring the blame of it on me." Roused to anger, before the dog got close to him, in his excitement, looking neither before nor behind, he struck it on the skull a single stroke with a cudgel. The dog dropped its head, and died. Afterwards the Mohammedan said, "What is the letter on its neck?" and opened it. Having ascertained the contents, he exclaimed, "Can the sinner live who has killed such a dog?" and he broke his own skull, and died. Thus let him die who does not consider the merits of a case.

9. *Minding your own Business.*

A washerman, who made white the clothes of a large village, procured a donkey to carry the clothes, and a dog to guard his house. While thus it was, one night in the deep darkness six burglars came to break into his house. Then the dog that was there remained still, without barking. The donkey said, "O dog, why are you lazy? Robbers are come and lurking to rob our master's house. If all the costly garments go that are in our premises, the master will be reduced in circumstances." To that the dog replied, "O ass, these persons have come many times thus to steal. Then I barked and barked, and woke the master. The robbers ran away. You know it yourself. The master had not the sense to distinguish the benefit. Therefore, if they enter and steal, let them do so. It is no affair to us." The ass said, "But this time I will call and rouse the master," and began to bray like thunder. The robbers were lying in wait on that side. The washerman, not having patience to bear the noise, rose and ran, exclaiming, "O fat donkey!" and, upbraiding it, beat it severely on the loins with a stick, and then with anger lay down. The robbers came back, broke in, and collected, tied up and carried away all the clothes and valuables. The dog that saw it, looking on the donkey, said, "Though I told you, you would not hear. Did the master perceive the good you did? This is what has come from your doing work that belongs to me. Every one must do his own business. If one does another's business, it turns out thus."

10. *Consorting with Simpletons.*

A simpleton went behind a merchant on a journey through the country. In the course of their journey, in a very dark night, he laid himself down in the road in an open place, while the trader reclined in a retired spot close by in the jungle. In this state of affairs, the simpleton's foot was struck by the feet of robbers going along the way. One of them said, " What is this ? It is like a log of wood." In a paroxysm of anger, the blockhead exclaimed, " Go, go ; will five fanams be tied up carefully in the loins of a piece of house timber ? " The robbers seized him, and as they deprived him of the money, said, " Will it pass or not ? " He responded, " Ah ! is my money of that sort ? If you want to know whether or not it will pass, see, there is a merchant, show it." And he pointed them to the merchant. They took by force a hundred pagodas which the trader had, and went off. Ruin inevitably comes from alliance with fools.

1. *Choice of Friends.*

YOGASITTAN, who ruled in the city Santhanataru, governed with a view to every one in his dominions doing good and no evil. One day when Mathiyūgi and Athiyūgi paid the king a visit, he asked them, " With whom may we be friends? and with whom. may we not be friends?" To that Mathiyūgi said, " An honest man who lived in the village of Attūr kept a dog, which never left him. One day he went to the tank to bathe. The dog, running before, and seeing a crocodile in the water, barked, and turned back running, and put itself in the way of him by whom it was kept, and remained near him without going away. When he pushed it aside, and went to descend into the water, it snatched at his dress, and pulled him, and stayed by him. Kicking the dog away with his foot, he went down into the water. Thinking that, if the crocodile in this water should seize and devour its keeper and feeder, there would be no one to give it food, and that therefore it must befriend and take care of him, it went and fell before him into the water. The crocodile seized and dragged the dog; and seeing that, the man was distressed, and said, ' For my sake this dog has given its body, and resigned its life.' Therefore, it is well to be friends with one like a dog." Athiyūgi said, "A king appointed a good driver to take charge of his elephant. That elephant-driver daily washed it in the river, and supplied the fodder it needed. One day he hid a meal. The elephant, thinking he had stolen its food, and forgetting that he provided for it every day, killed him. Therefore it is not well to accept the friendship of one like the elephant." The king was much pleased with what he heard, and paid them respect. A person's disposition ought to be tested before accepting his friendship.

2. *Help to the Cruel.*

When a tiger was pursuing a hunter, he ran and climbed a tree. The tiger, sitting beneath the tree, looking at a monkey there was in it, said, " Throw him down. He is a hunter. Therefore he is a killer of us all. He is a bad one." The monkey answered, "Though he be an evil one, I will not do harm to one who has come to me in fear. Depart." The tiger waited below. Afterwards the monkey, because the hunter was hungry, went to fetch fruits for him. Then the tiger, looking at the hunter, said, " The monkey's young one is there. Throw it down, and I will leave you, and take it and go away." So the hunter threw down the monkey's young one. Directly the monkey that had gone for fruit returned, the tiger said, " O monkey, the hunter to whom you did such kindness has thrown your offspring down. Therefore he is a bad one. Throw him down, and I will leave your young one, and go." The monkey refused to push him away. "If you do kindness to a cruel one, ruin will come to you from it," responded the tiger, and, without eating the young one, withdrew. The hunter, having devoured the fruits the monkey had brought, said, " Wife and children have no meat," and slew it as it hung in repose, and carried it off. So will it come to pass, if you give help to the cruel.

3. *The Good of Kindness.*

At the season when the sugar-canes, plantains, and rice-corn, which the inhabitants of the village of Nelvilayyūr in the country of Nalvalanādu had planted and sown, became ripe, the elephants and rats of the mountain and jungle near the place came by night, and ate, and destroyed, and departed before daybreak. After their arrival one night, the rain fell, and the river was flooded. When on that occasion, as usual, the elephants and rats were going away after eating the sugar-cane, plantains, and rice-corn, the rats, from their inability to cross the river-flood, said respectfully, " O elephants, if you will carry us over to that side of the swollen river, whatever service we can render shall be done you at any time." The elephants all, saying, " Can there be any service to us from these diminutive beings ? " went away with laughter and scorn. Among them there was one elephant only that, without de- spising, took those rats upon his back, and carried them to the farther side of the river. Afterwards one day all the inhabitants of that place combined, con- cluding, " It is necessary to capture the elephants that destroy all our crops," and dug and concealed pitfalls in the way the elephants came. The elephants, coming according to their custom in the night, all fell into those pitfalls. The rats going that way, seeing the elephant that had done them the kindness, commiserated it, and went and pushed into that pit the earth which had been thrown on its four sides. The elephant trod down the earth, raised the ground, came out, greatly praised the rats, and afterwards kept from the pits other elephants its kindred. Coming evil will leave the relatives also of those who render assistance.

4. *A narrow Escape.*

When a Brahman came alone by the way of a forest, a tiger that was caught there in a trap, and had been without food for two days, beholding him, called him with fair words, and besought him, saying, " Sir, if you will open this, and let me out, it will be great virtue to you." The Brahman said, " You are a wild beast: therefore, if I let you out, you will kill me." The tiger answered, " Shall I kill one who will have done me a kindness ? I will not." This it spoke in such a way as to produce confidence : and the Brahman, believing its word, immediately opened the trap. No sooner had he done so than the tiger, looking at him, said, " You must be food to me ; I will kill you." He remonstrated, " Will it be right to kill one who has done you a favour ? " The tiger said, " Killing men and other animals is the work of our race : it is therefore right to slay you." The Brahman replied, " We will tell this affair to some person, and act as he shall say." Afterwards they consulted a jackal that came there. The jackal said, "I cannot understand, if you only speak to me. If you actually show me, so that I can see, how the tiger was caught in the trap, and in what way you opened it, I shall know what is right, and will decide the case for you." "Good," said the tiger, and entered the trap. Directly it did so, the trap closed. The jackal, turning to the Brahman, said, "Foolish Brahman, will you do kindness to a savage? Now you are wise after experience. Thus you have settled this affair. Run away." The rescued Brahman departed.

5. *A Donkey making Love like a Dog.*

In a man's house, an ass, which carried burdens about, thinking one day that, whatever its efforts to please, its master still beat and hurt it, reflected, "What is the reason of this? There is a dog in this house. Though it does no work, yet the master places it by him very fondly, and nourishes it, even with food when he himself eats. Whatever I do, he only gives me a little straw, hard to digest. If I consider why there is this difference, I observe that the young dog is in the habit of caressing the master, mistress, and children. It places two feet on their hands or bosoms, and kisses them. Thus it is that it gains their affection: and if I do the same, they will be kind to me. This is a good plan." One day, when the owner of the house was lying asleep, the ass went and lay down upon his breast, lifted two feet, and put them on his head, and pressed its face to his, and gave him a kiss. The master, getting up in a rage, took a stick, thrashed it severely, and drove it away. He who does what is intolerable, shall suffer what cannot be borne.

6. *A Jackal courting a Crow.*

A young jackal, coveting the morsel which a crow had carried in its beak to a high tree, told it that men must be born blind to say it was black like coal, when its soft wings were as white as snow, and pretended to be in love with it, and to wish it could hear its sweet voice in a song; and the foolish crow accepted the flattery, and opened its mouth to sing, so dropping the morsel, with which the now mocking jackal ran away.

7. *Shutting the Hatchet in the Box.*

The wife of a silly fellow laid down a fish which she had got with a cash.[1] A cat ate it. When the dolt saw it, he took to shutting up his hatchet in the box. His wife asked him, " Why do you shut up the hatchet in the box every day ? " He said, " If the cat that ate the one-cash fish should eat the four-fanams axe, what shall we do ? "

8. *The Company of Fools.*

A poor man who lived in a mud village, knowing that his brother-in-law resided in a city at a great distance, went to his house, and made himself known, saying that he was such an one. That night, when he sat down and ate with him, seeing the lamp burning

---

[1] Eighty cash = one fanam.

in the niche to light up the whole house, he was astonished, and looking at his brother-in-law who was at his side, said, "What is this thing that makes such a light? I have not seen such a thing before." He answered in sport, "This is a little one of the sun. It comes here by ship from distant islands." "So?" replied he, and was silent in simplicity. Afterwards, seeing the men of the house go out for a while, he, meaning to steal the sun's little one, and convey it to his own country, took it quickly, and hid it in the eaves of the house, and without speaking left it there. It was a house thatched with straw, and therefore caught fire directly. So soon as it was burnt down, and the fire abated, while the other men stirred with a stick, and took out the goods that lay hidden, the blockhead from the inland country occupied himself in a similar way. They asked, "What are you seeking?" He answered, "I hid the sun's little one here; that is what I am looking for." "O ho! is it you who have done this mischief?" they said, and beat and kicked him, and drove him away. Such is companionship with fools.

9. *High Example.*

A revenue surveyor called the village watchman, and said, "I say, our infant wants some fresh rice. In the course of the night, pluck and bring some." "Very well, my master," said the watchman; and he brought and presented some that night. Taking the hint, from that day he gathered from four to six pans from each division of the rice-ground, and took them to his own house. When harvest-time had come, the surveyor went to look at the yield. Observing in two or three of the divisions that rice had been taken, he looked at the watchman, and said, "How do you account for this stealing?" The watchman answered, "It is the secret permission you gave that day," and so he replied when the question was repeated all over the rice-ground. The surveyor said nothing. Thus it will happen when any make known base practices to subordinates.

10. *The Potter caught.*

A villager made his living by moulding, baking, and selling pots and pans. Officers of the king's court often caused him trouble, telling him to give them pots and pans, and carrying them off without paying for them. While things were so, one day, seeing an officer coming, the potter went and hid in a grove of palmyra-trees. The officer, having gone and inspected the house, said that as the potter was absent he would come next day, and went by way of the palmyra-grove. Seeing him, the potter was afraid, and got up and stood, and was as one examining a palmyra-tree. "Which tree are you looking at?" said the officer, not knowing who he was. He answered, "I am seeing if this palmyra-tree will do for a plough." The officer replied, "Why, you have the look of a potter : will a palmyra-tree do for a plough?" "Who told you I was here?" asked the potter. "Yourself, potter; come along," said he, taking hold of him, and leading him off. He made him lift pots and pans on his head, without giving him the price, and went away. Fools standing in the midst of a flood have not water enough to allay their thirst.

11. *Helping the Needy.*

A king was wont daily to bestow gifts on mendicants. One day there came begging to him two Brahmans, one learned, and the other illiterate. He gave them a pagoda a day. Afterwards the learned one said, " I am very learned, and lead a worthy life. Not so that Brahman. Moreover, he keeps two concubines. Will you give the same to him and me ? There is a proverb which says, Knowing the family, give the daughter; knowing the begging-bowl, give alms." That accomplished king gave afterwards two pagodas to the illiterate man. The envious one asked, " Why have you done so ? " He said, " I do not inquire as to learning and conduct, but render help according to the family. Such being the case, in agreement with your statement that this man's family is the larger, I give him twice as much." He went away confused.

12. *Feeding the Outside.*

When a learned man went to a city, he heard of one in the place who was very liberal in entertaining travellers. Whereupon he went and waited upon him in his ordinary dress. The generous man not only gave him no assistance, but did not even offer him a seat. So the man of letters went away troubled. Next day he borrowed and wore an elegant dress, and repeated the visit. Directly the gentleman saw him, he treated him courteously, made him sit near him, and engaged with him in conversation. Afterwards he partook of food with his guest. Then the learned man took a mouthful, and put it on his dress. The head of the house, seeing that, asked, " Why have you done so ? " He explained, " When I came yesterday in my old clothes, I could get nothing to eat. Now, because I have come well dressed, lo ! elegant food is obtained. Therefore, shall I appropriate this food to myself, and not devote it to my dress ? " Then the master of the house, ashamed within himself, made excuses.

13. *A lucky Sight.*

A person heard that to him who should see a pair of crows before getting up at break of day there would be good luck that day. Afterwards, calling his servant-man, he said, " Boy, when you see a couple of crows at daybreak, come and call me." So the servant, seeing a pair of crows, came and awoke his master. When the master got up, and went and saw, one crow had flown away, and the other was alone. Then the master was angry, saying, " You did not awake me before one was gone," and beat and kicked the servant. The servant said, " Lo ! Sir, have you not seen the luck which is come to me from seeing two crows ? " Hearing that, the master was ashamed.

14. *Training and selling a Parrot.*

A merchant, bringing up a parrot, taught it, what-ever he should ask, to say in reply, " No doubt of it." Every day he buried a hundred pagodas he possessed in a certain place, and, so that others should know, asked, "Parrot, is there treasure buried in this place ? " It answered, " No doubt of it." Hearing it so speak, he dug the pagodas up. Seeing that, one coveted it, saying, " If I had this parrot, I should be a Cupēran;"[1] and he bargained, gave a thousand pagodas, and took it home. When he asked in four or five places, " Is there treasure buried here ? " it replied, " No doubt of it." Believing what it said, he dug and looked. Finding nothing, he grieved, saying, " We are taken in," and asked, " Parrot, have you put dirt in my mouth ? " As usual, it answered, " No doubt of it." Hearing its word, he laughed, and formed plans to dispose of it.

15. *Showing the House to a Friend.*

A prosperous man spent a great amount of money, and built eight houses one behind another. Meaning himself always to live in the eighth house, he adorned it with mirrors, pictures, and other handsome objects. A friend of his in another town was in great distress, and sent his son to him, saying, " Beg and bring what you can towards the cost of food." The boy arrived hungry and weary. Without asking about his welfare, the rich man took him, and showed him one after another the houses he had built, and his own dwelling last. When the boy saw it, restraining his anger, he said, " Sir, you have settled in' this last residence. If you should die, it would be a trouble to decline among these houses." The proprietor thought it an evil speech, but kept his displeasure in his mind, and told him to go and send his father. The boy did so ; and deaf to his son's complaints, the friend came. Without

---

[1] A god of riches, a Plutus.

asking him if he had eaten as much as he wanted, he showed him also all the houses, and then remarked, " When I thus showed them to your son, he spoke an evil word ; " and he told him what he had said. Hearing that, the wealthy man's friend, looking at him, answered, " He is a little boy, and therefore spoke without thought. It is unnecessary to take the least notice of what he said. If you should so die in this mansion, its outer walls will also be overthrown." When the rich man heard that, he was much troubled, and said to himself, " Of death to me only the boy spoke : this man thinks of destruction to the house." Meditating a little while, he perceived the instability of the body and of wealth, gave his friend what he required, and speaking courteously, sent him away.

16. *Wearing unwonted Possessions.*

In the order of events, one of three poor people put on a gold ring, another a silver girdle, and the third a pearl earring. When they were sitting with complacency in a public place, a person coming there said, " Have you seen my calf ? " He who wore the ring, that it might be known, got up, stretched his hand out, counted his fingers, and answered, " We have not seen it for about four naligays,[1] have we ? " He who wore the girdle got up, that it might be evident, and put his hand to his waist, saying, " It was this height, was it not ? " He who wore the earring, to make it known, got up and nodded his head, saying, " It went so, it went this way." The interrogator departed, mocking

---

[1] A naligay is twenty-four minutes.

them, with the thought, "They are mean fellows, and fancy that acquiring this property is obtaining supreme bliss."

17. *The Honey-drop Disturbance.*

When a Mohammedan went and procured honey in the market of a great town, a drop of it fell down. Upon that drop a fly settled. A lizard seized the fly. The tradesman's cat laid hold of the lizard. The Mohammedan's dog bit the cat. The shopkeeper hit and killed the dog. The Mohammedan cut down the shopkeeper. The other market-sellers slew the Mohammedan. Mohammedans came and surrounded those market dealers. Observing the gathering of Mohammedans, many people assembled on behalf of the bazaar-traders. Those and these mixed, and engaged in a hand-to-hand fight. On that side a hundred persons, and a hundred on this died. The whole city, fearing and troubled, left their homes like a wave of the sea. Then a man asked, "Who began this disturbance?" One who had come to the bazaar replied, "It is a row caused by a honey-drop." Hence the proverbial use of these words.

18. *A Story without an End.*

Narēnthiran, the ruler of a certain country, asked no question of the learned men who came to his court but, "Do you know a story?" On their telling in reply all the tales they knew, he, having heard, said contemptuously, "Do you know no more than these? you may go." When a learned man, aware that the king thus scornfully dismissed all comers, went to him

the king asked, " What is your name ? "   " Kathayk-
kadal,"[1] he answered.   " But," said he, "how many
stories are known to you ? "   He replied, " It is
because there is no limit to the tales known to me,
that I have my name."   " Tell me a tale now," said the
king.   He proceeded, " In a royal lake, four thousand
yōsanays[2] broad and six thousand long, there grew
lotus flowers, upon which a hundred billions of gold-
winged swans alighted.   At a time when wind and
rain began to beat together, those birds in their pain
entered a mountain-cavern which was sheltered from
the gale."   " What next ? " said he.   " One of them
went forth," he said.   " What next ? " said he.
" Another went forth," he said.   Every time the king
asked, he answered in the same manner.   " Another
went forth, another went forth."   The king, put to
shame, said, " There is no conquering this man," and
treated him civilly, made him a present, and sent him
away.

[1] Sea of Stories.   [2] A yōsanay is 130 miles.

INDEX.

383

MORRISON AND GIBB, EDINBURGH,
PRINTERS TO HER MAJESTY'S STATIONERY OFFICE.

Standard & Popular Works

PUBLISHED BY

T. WOOLMER, 2, CASTLE STREET, CITY ROAD, E.C.

PRICE SIX SHILLINGS.

The Light of the World: Lessons from the Life of Our Lord for Children. By the Rev. RICHARD NEWTON, DD., Author of *Rays from the Sun of Righteousness*, etc., etc., etc. Fcap. 4to. Numerous Illusts.

'A most attractive and deeply interesting Sunday book for children.'

PRICE FIVE SHILLINGS.

Sermons by the Rev. W. MORLEY PUNSHON, LL.D. With a Preface by the Rev. W. ARTHUR, M.A. These Sermons contain the latest Corrections of the Author. Two Volumes. Crown 8vo. 5/- each.

'Here we have found, in rare combination, pure and elevated diction, conscience-searching appeal, withering exposure of sin, fearless advocacy of duty, forceful putting of truth,' etc., etc.—*London Quarterly Review.*

Lectures by the Rev. W. MORLEY PUNSHON, LL.D. Crown 8vo.

' One and all of the Lectures are couched in the powerful and popular style which distinguished the great preacher, and they are worthy of a permanent place in any library.'—*Daily Chronicle.*

Toward the Sunrise: being Sketches of Travel in Europe and the East. To which is added a Memorial Sketch (with Portrait) of the Rev. W. MORLEY PUNSHON, LL.D. By HUGH JOHNSTON, M.A., B.D. Crown 8vo. Numerous Illustrations.

Fiji and the Fijians; and Missionary Labours among the Cannibals. Sixth Thousand. Revised and Supplemented with Index. By Rev. JAMES CALVERT; and a Preface by C. F. GORDON CUMMING, Author of *At Home in Fiji*, etc. Crown 8vo, with Portrait of Thakombau, a Map, and numerous Illustrations.

PRICE FOUR SHILLINGS.

Our Indian Empire: its Rise and Growth. By the Rev. J. SHAW BANKS. Imperial 16mo. Thirty-five Illustrations and Map.

' The imagination of the young will be fired by its stirring stories of English victories, and it will do much to make history popular.'—*Daily Chronicle.*

' A well condensed and sensibly written popular narrative of Anglo-Indian History.'—*Daily News.*

Zoology of the Bible. By HARLAND COULTAS. Preface by the Rev. W. F. MOULTON, D.D. Imperial 16mo. 126 Illustrations.

' We have in a most convenient form all that is worth knowing of the discoveries of modern science which have any reference to the animals mentioned in Scripture.'—*Preacher's Budget.*

Missionary Anecdotes, Sketches, Facts, and Incidents. By the Rev. WILLIAM MOISTER. Imperial 16mo. Eight Page Illustrations.

' The narratives are many of them very charming.'—*Sword and Trowel.*

12-84.

Northern Lights; or, Pen and Pencil Sketches of Nineteen
Modern Scottish Worthies. By the Rev. J. MARRAT. Crown 8vo. Portraits
and Illustrations.

'It is a charming book in every sense.'—*Irish Evangelist.*

The Brotherhood of Men ; or, Christian Sociology. By Rev.
W. UNSWORTH.

PRICE THREE SHILLINGS AND SIXPENCE.

Sabbath Chimes : A Meditation in Verse for the Sundays of a
Year. By Dr. PUNSHON. Crown 8vo, gilt edges.

Uncle Jonathan's Walks in and Around London. Foolscap
4to. Profusely Illustrated.

Our Sea-Girt Isle : English Scenes and Scenery Delineated.
By the Rev. J. MARRAT. Imperial 16mo. Map and 153 Illustrations.

'An unusually readable and attractive book.'—*Christian World.*

Rambles in Bible Lands. By the Rev. RICHARD NEWTON,
D.D. Imperial 16mo. Seventy Illustrations.

'From the juvenile stand-point, we can speak in hearty commendation of
it.'—*Literary World.*

' Land of the Mountain and the Flood ' : Scottish Scenes
and Scenery Delineated. By the Rev. JABEZ MARRAT. Imperial 16mo.
Map and Seventy-six Illustrations.

'Described with taste, judgment, and accuracy of detail.'—*Scotsman.*

Popery and Patronage. Biographical Illustrations of Scotch
Church History. By the Rev. J. MARRAT. Imperial 16mo. Ten Illustrations.

'Most instructive biographical narratives.'—*Derbyshire Courier.*

Wycliffe to Wesley : Heroes and Martyrs of the Church in
Britain. Imperial 16mo. Twenty-four Portraits and Forty other Illustrations.

'We give a hearty welcome to this handsomely got up and interesting
volume.'—*Literary World.*

John Lyon ; or, From the Depths. By RUTH ELLIOTT.
Crown 8vo. Five Full-page Illustrations.

'Earnest and eloquent, dramatic in treatment, and thoroughly healthy in
spirit.'—*Birmingham Daily Gazette.*

The Thorough Business Man : Memoir of Walter Powell,
Merchant. By Rev. B. GREGORY. Seventh Edition. Crn. 8vo, with Portrait.

The Life of Gideon Ouseley. By the Rev. WILLIAM
ARTHUR, M.A. Eighth Thousand. Crown 8vo, with Portrait.

The Aggressive Character of Christianity. By Rev. W.
UNSWORTH.

Garton Rowley; or, Leaves from the Log of a Master
Mariner. By J. JACKSON WRAY. Crown 8vo.

Honest John Stallibrass. By J. JACKSON WRAY. Crown 8vo.

A Man Every Inch of Him. By J. JACKSON WRAY. Crn. 8vo.

Paul Meggitt's Delusion. By J. JACKSON WRAY. Crown 8vo.

Nestleton Magna. A Story of Yorkshire Methodism. By J.
JACKSON WRAY. Crown 8vo.

Chronicles of Capstan Cabin ; or, the Children's Hour. By
J. JACKSON WRAY. Imperial 16mo. Twenty-eight Illustrations.

Missionary Stories, Narratives, Scenes, and Incidents.
By the Rev. W. MOISTER. Crown 8vo. Eight Page Illustrations.
'Intensely interesting.'—*Methodist New Connexion Magazine.*

Scenes and Adventures in Great Namaqualand. By the
Rev. B. RIDSDALE. Crown 8vo, with Portrait.

Melissa's Victory. By ASHTON NEILL. Crown 8vo, gilt
edges. Illustrations by GUNSTON.

Two Saxon Maidens. By ELIZA KERR. Crown 8vo, gilt
edges. Illustrations by GUHSTON.

Gems Reset; or, the Wesleyan Catechisms Illustrated by
Imagery and Narrative. Crown 8vo. By Rev. B. SMITH.

Vice-Royalty; or, a Royal Domain held for the King, and
enriched by the King. Crown 8vo. Twelve page Illustns. By Rev. B. SMITH.

Sunshine in the Kitchen; or, Chapters for Maid Servants.
Fourth Thousand. Crown 8vo. Numerous Illustrations. By Rev. B. SMITH.

Way-Marks : Placed by Royal Authority on the King's
Highway. Being One Hundred Scripture Proverbs, Enforced and Illustrated.
Crown 8vo. Eight Page Engravings. By Rev. B. SMITH.

The Great Army of London Poor. Sketches of Life and
Character in a Thames-side District. By the River-side Visitor. Third
Edition. Crown 8vo. 540 pp. Eight Illustrations.
'Admirably told. The author has clearly lived and mingled with the
people he writes about.'—*Guardian.*

PRICE TWO SHILLINGS AND SIXPENCE.

Elias Power, of Ease-in-Zion. By Rev. JOHN M. BAMFORD.
Fourth Thousand. Crown 8vo. Seventeen Illustrations. Gilt edges.

Life of John Wicklif. By Rev. W. L. WATKINSON. Portrait
and Eleven Illustrations. Crown 8vo.

Good News for Children; or, God's Love to the Little
Ones. By JOHN COLWELL, Crown 8vo, gilt edges. Fourteen Illustrations.

Pleasant Talks about Jesus. By JOHN COLWELL. Crown 8vo.

Little Abe ; or, the Bishop of Berry Brow. Being the Life of
Abraham Lockwood, a quaint and popular Local Preacher. By F. JEWELL.
Crown 8vo, gilt edges. With Portrait.
'The racy, earnest, vernacular speech of *Little Abe*, and his quaint
illustrations and home-thrusts, are humorous indeed. . . . Cannot fail to be
a favourite.'—*Christian Age.*

Cecily : a Tale of the English Reformation. By EMMA LESLIE.
Crown 8vo. Five full-page Illustrations.
'This is an interesting and attractive little book. . . . It is lively and
healthy in tone.'—*Literary World.*

Glimpses of India and Mission Life. By Mrs. HUTCHEON.
Crown 8vo. Eight Page Illustrations.
'A well-written account of Indian life in its social aspects, by the wife of
an Indian missionary.'—*British Quarterly.*

The Beloved Prince : a Memoir of His Royal Highness, the
Prince Consort. By WILLIAM NICHOLS. Crown 8vo. With Portrait and
Nineteen Illustrations. Cloth, gilt edges.
'An admirable condensation of a noble life.'—*Derbyshire Courier.*

Glenwood: a Story of School Life. By JULIA K. BLOOM-
FIELD. Crown 8vo. Seven Illustrations.

'A useful book for school-girls who think more of beauty and dress than of brains and grace.'—*Sword and Trowel.*

Undeceived: Roman or Anglican? A Story of English
Ritualism. By RUTH ELLIOTT. Crown 8vo.

'In the creation and description of character the work belongs to the highest class of imaginative art.'—*Free Church of England Magazine.*

Self-Culture and Self-Reliance, under God the Means of
Self-Elevation. By the Rev. W. UNSWORTH. Crown 8vo.

'An earnest, thoughtful, eloquent book on an important subject.'—
Folkestone News.

A Pledge that Redeemed Itself. By SARSON, Author of
'Blind Olive,' etc. Crown 8vo. Numerous Illustrations. Gilt edges.

'We are informed in the preface that it is "an etching from life," and we can well believe it, for it bears all the marks of a genuine study of living men and women.'—*Literary World.*

Old Daniel; or, Memoirs of a Converted Hindu. By the Rev.
T. HODSON. Crown 8vo, gilt edges. Coloured Illustrations.

The Story of a Peninsular Veteran: Sergeant in the 43rd
Light Infantry during the Peninsular War. Crown 8vo. 13 Illustrations.

'Full of adventure, told in a religious spirit. We recommend this narrative to boys and young men.'—*Hastings and St. Leonard's News.*

Rays from the Sun of Righteousness. By the Rev. RICHARD
NEWTON, D.D. Crown 8vo. Eleven Illustrations. Gilt edges.

In the Tropics; or, Scenes and Incidents of West Indian Life.
By the Rev. JABEZ MARRAT. Crown 8vo, gilt edges, Illustrations, etc.

'A vivid description of scenes and incidents, . . . with an interesting record of the progress of mission work.'—*Sheffield Post.*

Climbing: a Manual for the Young who Desire to Rise in
Both Worlds. By the Rev. BENJAMIN SMITH. Crown 8vo. Sixth Edition.

Our Visit to Rome, with Notes by the Way. By the
Rev. JOHN RHODES. Royal 16mo. Forty-five Illustrations.

The Lancasters and their Friends. A Tale of Methodist
Life. By S. J. F. Crown 8vo.

Those Boys. By FAYE HUNTINGTON. Crown 8vo. Illustrated.

Leaves from my Log of Twenty-five years' Christian
Work in the Port of London. Crown 8vo. Eight Illustrations.

East End Pictures; or, More Leaves from My Log
of Twenty-five Years' Christian Work. By T. C. GARLAND. Crown 8vo.
Portrait and Five Illustrations.

The Willow Pattern: A Story Illustrative of Chinese Social
Life. By the Rev. HILDERIC FRIEND. Crown 8vo, gilt edges. Numerous
Illustrations.

Passages from the Diary of an Early Methodist. By
RICHARD ROWE.

Orphans of the Forest; or, His Little Jonathan. By A. E.
COURTENAY. Foolscap 8vo. Four Illustrations.

MARK GUY ·PEARSE'S WORKS.

Nine Volumes, Crown 8vo, Cloth, Gilt Edges. Price 2s. 6d. each.

1.—Daniel Quorm, and his Religious Notions. FIRST SERIES. 70,000.

2.—Daniel Quorm, and his Religious Notions. SECOND SERIES. 22,000.

3.—Sermons for Children. 19,000.

4.—Mister Horn and his Friends; or, Givers and Giving. 21,000.

5.—Short Stories, and other Papers. 8000.

6.—'Good Will": a Collection of Christmas Stories. 9000.

7.—Simon Jasper. 11,000.

8.—Cornish Stories. 6000.

9.—Homely Talks. 11,000.

'Scarcely any living writer can construct a parable better, more quaintly, simply, and congruously. His stories are equally clever and telling. . . . One secret of their spell is that they are brimful of heart. . . . His books should be in every school library.'—*British Quarterly Review.*

Thoughts on Holiness. By MARK GUY PEARSE. Eleventh Thousand. Royal 16mo. Cloth, red edges.

PRICE TWO SHILLINGS.

Punchi Nona : À Story of Female Education and Village Life in Ceylon. By the Rev. SAMUEL LANGDON. Crown 8vo. Numerous Illustrations.

Friends and Neighbours: A Story for Young Children. Crown 8vo. Illustrated.

The Oakhurst Chronicles : A Tale of the Times of Wesley. By ANNIE E. KEELING. Crown 8vo. Four Illustrations. 'This beautiful story.'—*Sheffield Independent*. 'A fascinating story.'—*Christian Age*.

Poet Toilers in Many Fields. By Mrs. R. A. WATSON. Crown 8vo. Thirteen Illustrations.

The 'Good Luck' of the Maitlands: a Family Chronicle. By Mrs. R. A. WATSON. Five Illustrations. Crown 8vo.

Valeria, the Martyr of the Catacombs. A Tale of Early Christian Life in Rome. By the Rev. W. H. WITHROW, D.D. Crown 8vo. Illustrations.

Tina and Beth; or, the Night Pilgrims. By ANNIE E. COURTENAY. Crown 8vo. Frontispiece.

Wilfred Hedley ; or, How Teetotalism Came to Ellensmere. By S. J. FITZGERALD. Crown 8vo. Frontispiece.

Equally Yoked: and other Stories. By S. J. FITZGERALD. Frontispiece.

Master and Man. By S. J. FITZGERALD. Frontispiece.

Coals and Colliers ; or, How we Get the Fuel for our Fires. By S. J. FITZGERALD. Crown 8vo. Illustrations. 'An interesting description of how we get the fuel for our fires, illustrated by tales of miners' families.'—*Christian World*.

James Daryll ; or, From Honest Doubt to Christian Faith.
By RUTH ELLIOTT. Crown 8vo.
' We have seldom read a more beautiful story than this.'—*The Echo.*

The King's Messenger : a Story of Canadian Life. By the
Rev. W. H. WITHROW, M.A. Crown 8vo.

Illustrations of Fulfilled Prophecy. By the Rev. J. ROBINSON
GREGORY. Crown 8vo. Numerous Illustrations.

The Basket of Flowers. Illustrated. Crown 8vo, gilt edges.

The Great Apostle ; or, Pictures from the Life of St. Paul.
By the Rev. JABEZ MARRAT. Foolscap 8vo. 28 Illustrations and Map.
' A charming little book. . . . Written in a style that must commend itself
to young people.'—*Sunday-School Times.*

Martin Luther, the Prophet of Germany. By the Rev. J.
SHAW BANKS. Foolscap 8vo. 13 Illustrations.
' Mr. Banks has succeeded in packing a great deal of matter into a small
space, and yet has told his story in a very attractive style.'—*London
Quarterly Review.*

Sir Walter Raleigh : Pioneer of Anglo-American Colonisation.
By CHARLES K. TRUE, D.D. Foolscap 8vo. 16 Illustrations.
' We have here a book which we strongly recommend to our young readers.
It will do boys good to read it.'—*The Methodist.*

Homes and Home Life in Bible Lands. By J. R. S.
CLIFFORD. Foolscap 8vo. Eighty Illustrations.
' A useful little volume respecting the manners and customs of Eastern
nations. It brings together, in a small compass, much that will be of service
to the young student of the Bible.'—*Watchman.*

Hid Treasures, and the Search for Them : Lectures to
Bible Classes. By the Rev. J. HARTLEY. Foolscap 8vo. With Frontispiece.

Youthful Obligations. Illustrated by a large number of Appro-
priate Facts and Anecdotes. Foolscap 8vo. With Illustrations.

Eminent Christian Philanthropists : Brief Biographical
Sketches, designed especially as Studies for the Young. By the Rev.
GEORGE MAUNDER. Fcap. 8vo. Nine Illustrations.

The Tower, the Temple, and the Minster : Historical and
Biographical Associations of the Tower of London, St. Paul's Cathedral,
and Westminster Abbey. By the Rev. J. W. THOMAS. Second Edition.
Foolscap 8vo. 14 Illustrations.

Peter Pengelly ; or, ' True as the Clock.' By J. J. WRAY.
Crown 8vo. Forty Illustrations.
' A famous book for boys.'—*The Christian.*

The Stolen Children. By Rev. H. BLEBY. Foolscap 8vo.
Six Illustrations.

My Coloured Schoolmaster : and other Stories. By the Rev.
H. BLEBY. Foolscap 8vo. Five Illustrations.
' The narratives are given in a lively, pleasant manner that is well suited to
gain and keep alive the attention of juvenile readers.'—*The Friend.*

Female Heroism and Tales of the Western World. By
the Rev. H. BLEBY. Foolscap 8vo. Four Illustrations.

Capture of the Pirates : with other Stories of the Western Seas.
By the Rev. HENRY BLEBY. Foolscap 8vo. Four Illustrations.
' The stories are graphically told, and will inform on some phases of
Western life.'—*Warrington Guardian.*

The Prisoner's Friend: The Life of Mr. JAMES BUNDY, of Bristol. By his Grandson, the Rev. W. R. WILLIAMS. Foolscap 8vo.

Kilkee. By ELIZA KERR, author of *Slieve Bloom.*

Adelaide's Treasure, and How the Thief came Unawares. By SARSON, Author of 'A Pledge that Redeemed Itself,' etc. Four Illustrations.
  'This graphic story forms an episode in the history of Wesleyan Missions in Newfoundland.'—*Christian Age.*

Two Snowy Christmas Eves. By ELIZA KERR. Royal 16mo. Gilt edges. Six Illustrations.

PRICE EIGHTEENPENCE.

'Little Ray' Series. Royal 16mo.

Little Ray and her Friends. By RUTH ELLIOTT. Five Illustrations.

The Breakfast Half-Hour: Addresses on Religious and Moral Topics. By the Rev. H. R. BURTON. Twenty-five Illustrations.
  'Practical, earnest, and forcible.'—*Literary World.*

Gleanings in Natural History for Young People. Profusely Illustrated.

Broken Purposes; or, the Good Time Coming. By LILLIE MONTFORT. Five Page Illustrations. Gilt edges.

The History of the Tea-Cup: with a Descriptive Account of the Potter's Art. By the Rev. G. R. WEDGWOOD. Profusely Illustrated.

The Cliftons and their Play-Hours. By Mrs. COSSLETT. Seven Page Illustrations.

The Lilyvale Club and its Doings. By EDWIN A. JOHNSON, D.D. Seven Page Illustrations.
  'The "doings" of the club decidedly deserve a careful perusal.'—*Literary World.*

The Bears' Den. By E. H. MILLER. Six Page Illustrations.
  'A capital story for boys.'—*Christian Age.*

Ned's Motto; or, Little by Little. By the author of 'Faithful and True,' 'Tony Starr's Legacy.' Six Page Illustrations.
  'The story of a boy's struggles to do right, and his influence over other boys. The book is well and forcibly written.'—*The Christian.*

A Year at Riverside Farm. By E. H. MILLER. Royal 16mo. Six Page Illustrations.
  'A book of more than common interest and power.'—*Christian Age.*

The Royal Road to Riches. By E. H. MILLER. Fifteen Illustrations.

Maude Linden; or, Working for Jesus. By LILLIE MONTFORT. Four Illustrations.
  'Intended to enforce the value of personal religion, especially in Christian work. . . . Brightly and thoughtfully written.'—*Liverpool Daily Post.*

Oscar's Boyhood; or, the Sailor's Son. By DANIEL WISE, D.D. Six Illustrations.
  'A healthy story for boys, written in a fresh and vigorous style, and plainly teaching many important lessons.'—*Christian Miscellany.*

Summer Days at Kirkwood. By E. H. MILLER. Four
Illustrations.

> 'Capital story; conveying lessons of the highest moral import.'—*Sheffield Post.*

Slieve Bloom. By ELIZA KERR, Author of *The Golden City.*
Three Illustrations.

> 'The style of the book is graphic, and of considerable literary merit.'—*Literary World.*
> 'A real children's story, well told, with many beautiful touches of an artist's hand, and the evidences of a true woman's heart.'—*Christian Age.*

Holy-days and Holidays; or, Memories of the Calendar for
Young People. By J. R. S. CLIFFORD. Numerous Illustrations.

> 'Instruction and amusement are blended in this little volume.—*The Christian.*

Talks with the Bairns about Bairns. By RUTH ELLIOTT.
Illustrated.

> 'Pleasantly written, bright, and in all respects attractive.'—*Leeds Mercury.*

My First Class : and other Stories. By RUTH ELLIOTT.
Illustrated.

> 'The stories are full of interest, well printed, nicely illustrated, and taste-fully bound. It is a volume which will be a favourite in any family of children.'—*Derbyshire Courier.*

Luther Miller's Ambition. By LILLIE MONTFORT. Gilt
edges. Illustrated by GUNSTON.

'Wee Donald' Series.' Royal 16mo.

An Old Sailor's Yarn : and other Sketches from Daily Life.

The Stony Road : a Tale of Humble Life.

Stories for Willing Ears. For Boys. By T. S. E.

Stories for Willing Ears. For Girls. By T. S. E.

Thirty Thousand Pounds : and other Sketches from Daily Life.

'Wee Donald' : Sequel to 'Stony Road.'

PRICE EIGHTEENPENCE. *Foolscap 8vo Series.*

Two Standard Bearers in the East : Sketches of Dr. DUFF
and Dr. WILSON. By Rev. J. MARRAT. Eight Illustrations.

Three Indian Heroes : the Missionary; the Soldier; the
Statesman. By the Rev. J. SHAW BANKS. Numerous Illustrations.

David Livingstone, Missionary and Discoverer. By the
Rev. J. MARRAT. Fifteen Page Illustrations.

> 'The story is told in a way which is likely to interest young people, and to quicken their sympathy with missionary work.'—*Literary World.*

Columbus; or, the Discovery of America. By GEORGE
CUBITT. Seventeen Illustrations.

Cortes; or, the Discovery and Conquest of Mexico. By
GEORGE CUBITT. Nine Illustrations.

Pizarro; or, the Discovery and Conquest of Peru. By GEORGE
CUBITT. Nine Illustrations.

Granada; or, the Expulsion of the Moors from Spain. By
GEORGE CUBITT. Seven Illustrations.

James Montgomery, Christian Poet and Philanthropist.
By the Rev. J. MARRAT. Eleven Illustrations.
'The book is a welcome and tasteful addition to our biographical knowledge.'—*Warrington Guardian.*

The Father of Methodism: the Life and Labours of the Rev.
John Wesley, A.M. By Mrs. COSSLETT. Forty-five Illustrations.
'Presents a clear outline of the life of the founder of Methodism, and is calculated to create a desire for larger works upon the subject. The illustrations are numerous and effective,—quite a pictorial history in themselves.'

Old Truths in New Lights: Illustrations of Scripture Truth
for the Young. By W. H. S. Illustrated.

Chequer Alley: a Story of Successful Christian Work. By
the Rev. F. W. BRIGGS, M.A.

The Englishman's Bible: How he Got it, and Why he Keeps
It. By the Rev. JOHN BOVES, M.A. Thirteen Illustrations.

Home: and the Way to Make Home Happy. By the Rev.
DAVID HAY. With Frontispiece.

Helen Leslie; or, Truth and Error. By ADELINE. Frontispiece.

Building her House. By Mrs. R. A. WATSON. Five Illustns.
'A charmingly written tale, illustrative of the power of Christian meekness.'
—*Christian World.*

Crabtree Fold: a Tale of the Lancashire Moors. By Mrs. R.
A. WATSON. Five Illustrations.

Davy's Friend: and other Stories. By JENNIE PERRETT.
'Excellent, attractive, and instructive.'—*The Christian.*

Arthur Hunter's First Shilling. By Mrs. CROWE.

Hill Side Farm. By ANNA J. BUCKLAND.

The Boy who Wondered; or, Jack and Minnchen. By Mrs.
GEORGE GLADSTONE.

Kitty; or, The Wonderful Love. By A. E. COURTENAY.
Illustrated.

The River Singers. By W. ROBSON.

PRICE EIGHTEENPENCE. *Crown 8vo Series.*

Patty Thorne's Adventures. By Mrs. H. B. PAULL. Illustrated.

Fighting to Victory. By EZEKIEL ROGERS. Second Edition.

The Dairyman's Daughter. By the Rev. LEGH RICHMOND,
M.A. A New Edition, with Additions, giving an Authentic Account of her Conversion, and of her connection with the Wesleyan Methodists.

Footsteps in the Snow. By ANNIE E. COURTENAY, Author
of *Tina and Beth*, etc., etc. Illustrated.
'Every page is genial, warm, and bright.'—*Irish Christian Advocate.*

The Beloved Prince: A Memoir of His Royal Highness
the Prince Consort. By WILLIAM NICHOLS. Nineteen Illustrations.

Drierstock: A Tale of Mission Work on the American Frontier.
Three Illustrations.

Go Work: A Book for Girls. By ANNIE FRANCES PERRAM.

Picture Truths. Practical Lessons on the Formation of Character, from Bible Emblems and Proverbs. By JOHN TAYLOR. Thirty Illustrations.

Those Watchful Eyes; or, Jemmy and his Friends. By EMILIE SEARCHFIELD. Frontispiece.

The Basket of Flowers. Four Illustrations.

Auriel, and other Stories. By RUTH ELLIOTT. Frontispiece.

A Voice from the Sea; or, The Wreck of the Eglantine. By RUTH ELLIOTT.

Rays from the Sun of Righteousness. By the Rev. R. NEWTON. Eleven Illustrations.

A Pledge that Redeemed Itself. By SARSON.
'A clever, sparkling, delightful story.'—*Sheffield Independent.*

In the Tropics; or, Scenes and Incidents of West Indian Life. By the Rev. J. MARRAT. Illustrations and Map.

Old Daniel; or, Memoirs of a Converted Hindu. By Rev. T. HODSON. Twelve Illustrations.

Little Abe; or, The Bishop of Berry Brow. Being the Life of Abraham Lockwood.

CHEAP EDITION OF MARK GUY PEARSE'S BOOKS.

Foolscap 8vo.   Price Eighteenpence each.

1. Daniel Quorm, and his Religious Notions.   1ST SERIES.
2. Daniel Quorm, and his Religious Notions.   2ND SERIES.
3. Sermons for Children.
4. Mister Horn and his Friends; or, Givers and Giving.
5. Short Stories: and other Papers.
6. 'Good Will': a Collection of Christmas Stories.

PRICE ONE SHILLING. *Imperial 32mo.   Cloth, gilt lettered.*

Abbott's Histories for the Young.
Vol. 1. Alexander the Great. Vol. 2. Alfred the Great. Vol. 3. Julius Cæsar.

PRICE ONE SHILLING. *Royal 16mo.   Cloth, gilt lettered.*

Ancient Egypt: Its Monuments, Worship, and People. By the Rev. EDWARD LIGHTWOOD. Twenty-six Illustrations.

Vignettes from English History. From the Norman Conqueror to Henry IV. Twenty-three Illustrations.

Margery's Christmas Box. By RUTH ELLIOTT. Seven Illusts.

No Gains without Pains: a True Life for the Boys. By H. C. KNIGHT. Six Illustrations.

Peeps into the Far North: Chapters on Iceland, Lapland, and Greenland. By S. E. SCHOLES. Twenty-four Illustrations.

Lessons from Noble Lives, and other Stories. 31 Illustrations.

Stories of Love and Duty. For Boys and Girls. 31 Illusts.

The Railway Pioneers; or, the Story of the Stephensons, Father and Son. By H.C. KNIGHT. Fifteen Illustrations.

The Royal Disciple: Louisa, Queen of Prussia. By C.R. HURST. Six Illustrations.

Tiny Tim: a Story of London Life. Founded on Fact. By F. HORNER. Twenty-two Illustrations.

John Tregenoweth. His Mark. By MARK GUY PEARSE. Twenty-five Illustrations.

'I'll Try'; or, How the Farmer's Son became a Captain. Ten Illustrations.

The Giants, and How to Fight Them. By Dr. RICHARD NEWTON. Fifteen Illustrations.

The Meadow Daisy. By LILLIE MONTFORT. Numerous Illustrations.

Robert Dawson; or, the Brave Spirit. Four Page Illustrations.

The Tarnside Evangel. By M. A. H. Eight Illustrations.

Rob Rat: a Story of Barge Life. By MARK GUY PEARSE. Numerous Illustrations.

The Unwelcome Baby, with other Stories of Noble Lives early Consecrated. By S. ELLEN GREGORY. Nine Illustrations.

Jane Hudson, the American Girl. Four Page Illustrations.

The Babes in the Basket; or, Daph and her Charge. Four Page Illustrations.

Insect Lights and Sounds. By J. R. S. CLIFFORD. Illustrns.
'A valuable little book for children, pleasantly illustrated.'—*The Friend.*

The Jew and his Tenants. By A. D. WALKER. Illustrated.
'A pleasant little story of the results of genuine Christian influence.'— *Christian Age.*

The History of Joseph: for the Young. By the Rev. T. CHAMPNESS. Twelve Illustrations.
'Good, interesting, and profitable.'—*Wesleyan Methodist Magazine.*

The Old Miller and his Mill. By MARK GUY PEARSE. Twelve Illustrations.

The First Year of my Life: a True Story for Young People. By ROSE CATHAY FRIEND.
'It is a most fascinating story.'—*Sunday School Times.*

Fiji and the Friendly Isles: Sketches of their Scenery and People. By S. E. SCHOLES. Fifteen Illustrations.
'We warmly recommend this little volume to readers of every sort.'— *Hastings and St. Leonard's News.*

The Story of a Pillow. Told for Children. Four Illustrations.
'Simply and gracefully told.'—*Bradford Observer.*
'Little folks are sure to be interested in this wonderful pillow.'—*Literary World.*

UNCLE DICK'S LIBRARY OF SHILLING BOOKS.
Foolscap 8vo.   128 pp.   Cloth.

Uncle Dick's Legacy. By E. H. MILLER, Author of 'Royal Road to Riches,' etc., etc.   Illustrated.
'A first-rate story . . . full of fun and adventure, but thoroughly good and healthy.'—*Christian Miscellany.*

Beatrice and Brian. By HELEN BRISTON.   Three Illustrns.
'A very prettily told story about a wayward little lady and a large mastiff dog, specially adapted for girls.'—*Derbyshire Advertiser.*

Becky and Reubie; or, the Little Street Singers. By MINA E. GOULDING.   Three Illustrations.
'A clever, pleasing, well-written story.'—*Leeds Mercury.*

Gilbert Guestling; or, the Story of a Hymn Book. Illustrated.
'It is a charmingly told story.'—*Nottingham Daily Express.*

Guy Sylvester's Golden Year. Three Illustrations.
'A very pleasantly written story.'—*Derbyshire Courier.*

Left to Take Care of Themselves. By A. RYLANDS. Three Illustrations.

Tom Fletcher's Fortunes. By Mrs. H. B. PAULL.   Three Illustrations.
'A capital book for boys.'—*Sheffield and Rotherham Independent.*

The Young Bankrupt, and other Stories. By Rev. JOHN COLWELL.   Three Illustrations.

The Basket of Flowers. Four Illustrations.

Mattie and Bessie; or, Climbing the Hill. By A. E. COURTENAY.

Tom: A Woman's Work for Christ. By Rev. J. W. KEY-WORTH.   Six Illustrations.

The Little Disciple: The Story of his Life Told for Young Children.   Six Illustrations.

Afterwards. By EMILIE SEARCHFIELD.   Three Page Illustns.

Mischievous Foxes; or, the Little Sins that mar the Christian Character. By JOHN COLWELL.   Price 1s.
'An amazing amount of sensible talk and sound advice.'—*The Christian.*

Joel Bulu: The Autobiography of a Native Minister in the South Seas. New Edition, with an account of his Last Days.   Edited by the Rev. G. S. ROWE.   Foolscap 8vo, cloth.   Price 1s.

Robert Moffat, the African Missionary. By Rev. J. MARRAT. Foolscap 8vo, Illustrated.   Price 1s.

The Dairyman's Daughter. By the Rev. LEGH RICHMOND, M.A.   A New Edition, with Additions, giving an Authentic Account of her Conversion, and of her connection with the Wesleyan Methodists.

Polished Stones from a Rough Quarry. By Mrs. HUTCHEON. Price 1s.
'A Scotch story of touching and pathetic interest.   It illustrates the power of Christian sympathy.'—*Irish Evangelist.*

Recollections of Methodist Worthies. Fcap 8vo.   Price 1s.
'Deserves to be perused by members of all Christian communities.'— *Sword and Trowel.*

PRICE NINEPENCE. *Imperial 32mo. Cloth, Illuminated.*

1. The Wonderful Lamp: and other Stories. By RUTH ELLIOTT. Five Illustrations.
2. Dick's Troubles: and How He Met Them. By RUTH ELLIOTT. Six Illustrations.
3. The Chat in the Meadow: and other Stories. By LILLIE MONTFORT. Six Illustrations.
4. John's Teachers: and other Stories. By LILLIE MONT-FORT. Six Illustrations.
5. Nora Grayson's Dream: and other Stories. By LILLIE MONTFORT. Seven Illustrations.
6. Rosa's Christmas Invitations: and other Stories. By LILLIE MONTFORT. Six Illustrations.
7. Ragged Jim's Last Song: and other Ballads. By EDWARD BAILEY. Eight Illustrations.
8. Pictures from Memory. By ADELINE. Nine Illustrations.
9. The Story of the Wreck of the 'Maria' Mail Boat: with a Memoir of Mrs. Hincksman, the only Survivor. Illustrated.
10. Passages from the Life of Heinrich Stilling. Five Page Illustrations.
11. Little and Wise: The Ants, The Conies, The Locusts, and the Spiders. Twelve Illustrations.
12. Spoiling the Vines, and Fortune Telling. Eight Illusts.
13. The Kingly Breaker, Concerning Play, and Sowing the Seed.
14. The Fatherly Guide, Rhoda, and Fire in the Soul.
15. Short Sermons for Little People. By the Rev. T. CHAMPNESS.
16. Sketches from my Schoolroom. Four Illustrations.
17. Mary Ashton: A True Story of Eighty Years Ago. 4 Illusts.
18. The Little Prisoner: or, the Story of the Dauphin of France. Five Illustrations.
19. The Story of an Apprenticeship. By the Rev. A. LANGLEY. Frontispiece.
20. Mona Bell: or, Faithful in Little Things. By EDITH M. EDWARDS. Four Illustrations.
21. Minnie Neilson's Summer Holidays, and What Came of Them. By M. CAMBWELL. Four Illustrations.
22. After Many Days; or, The Turning Point in James Power's Life. Three Illustrations.
23. Alfred May. By R. RYLANDS. Two coloured Illustrations.
24. Dots and Gwinnie: a Story of Two Friendships. By R. RYLANDS. Three Illustrations.
25. Little Sally. By MINA E. GOULDING. Six Illustrations.
26. Joe Webster's Mistake. By EMILIE SEARCHFIELD. Three Illustrations.
27. Muriel; or, The Sister Mother.
28. Nature's Whispers.
29. Johnny's Work and How he did it. Five Illustrations.
30. Pages from a Little Girl's Life. By A. F. PERRAM. Five Illustrations.
31. The Wrens' Nest at Wrenthorpe. By A. E. KEELING. Five Illustrations.

ᵥ.
PRICE EIGHTPENCE. *Imperial* 32*mo. Cloth, gilt edges.*

The whole of the Ninepenny Series are also sold in Limp Cloth at Eightpence.

Ancass, the Slave Preacher. By the Kev. HENRY BUNTING.
Bernard Palissy, the Huguenot Potter. By A. E. KEELING.
Brief Description of the Principal Places mentioned in Holy Scripture.
Bulmer's History of Joseph.
Bulmer's History of Moses.
Christianity Compared with Popery : A Lecture.
Death of the Eldest Son (The). By CÆSAR MALAN.
Emily's Lessons ; Chapters in the Life of a Young Christian.
Fragments for Young People.
Freddie Cleminson.
Janie : A Flower from South Africa.
Jesus (History of). For Children. By W. MASON.
Little Nan's Victory. By A. E. COURTENAY.

Martin Luther (The Story of).
Precious Seed, and Little Sowers.
Recollections of Methodist Worthies. Foolscap 8vo, limp cloth.
Sailor's (A) Struggles for Eternal Life.
Saville (Jonathan), Memoirs of. By the Rev. F. A. WEST.
Soon and Safe : A Short Life well Spent.
Sunday Scholar's Guide (The). By the Rev. J. T. BARR.
The Wreck, Rescue, and Massacre : an Account of the Loss of the *Thomas King.*
Will Brown ; or, Saved at the Eleventh Hour. By the Rev. H. BUNTING.
Youthful Sufferer Glorified : A Memorial of Sarah Sands Hay.
Youthful Victor Crowned : A Sketch of Mr. C. JONES.

THE CROWN SERIES. 16*mo. Cloth, gilt lettered. Coloured Frontispiece.* PRICE SIXPENCE.

1. A Kiss for a Blow : true Stories about Peace and War for Children.
2. Louis Henrie ; or, The Sister's Promise.
3. The Giants, and How to Fight Them.
4. Robert Dawson ; or, the Brave Spirit.
5. Jane Hudson, the American Girl.
6. The Jewish Twins. By Aunt FRIENDLY.
7. The Book of Beasts. 35 Illust.
8. The Book of Birds. 40 Illust.
9. Proud in Spirit.
10. Althea Norton.
11. Gertrude's Bible Lesson.
12. The Rose in the Desert.
13. The Little Black Hen.
14. Martha's Hymn.
15. Nettie Mathieson.
16. The Prince in Disguise.
17. The Children on the Plains.
18. The Babes in the Basket.

19. Richard Harvey ; or, Taking a Stand.
20. Kitty King : Lessons for Little Girls.
21. Nettie's Mission.
22. Little Margery.
23. Margery's City Home.
24. The Crossing Sweeper.
25. Rosy Conroy's Lessons.
26. Ned Dolan's Garret.
27. Little Henry and his Bearer.
28. The Little Woodman and his Dog.
29. Johnny : Lessons for Little Boys.
30. Pictures and Stories for the Little Ones.
31. A Story of the Sea : and other Incidents.
32. Aunt Lizzie's Talks about Remarkable Fishes. 40 Illusts.
33. Three Little Folks who Mind their own Business ; or, The Bee, the Ant, and the Spider. 25 Illustrations.

The whole of the above thirty-three Sixpenny books are also sold at Fourpence, in Enamelled Covers.

PRICE SIXPENCE. *18mo. Cloth, gilt lettered.*

African Girls; or, Leaves from the Journal of a Missionary's Widow.

Bunyan (John). The Story of his Life and Work told to Children. By E. M. C.

Celestine; or, the Blind Woman of the Pastures.

Christ in Passion Week; or, Our Lord's last Public Visit to Jerusslem.

Crown with Gems (The). A Call to Christian Usefulness.

Fifth of November; Romish Plotting for Popish Ascendency.

Flower from Feejee. A Memoir of Mary Calvert.

Good Sea Captain (The). Life of Captain Robert Steward.

Grace the Preparation for Glory: Memoir of A. Hill. By Rev. J. RATTENBURY.

Joseph Peters, the Negro Slave.

Hattie and Nancy; or, the Everlasting Love. A Book for Girls.

Held Down; or, Why James did Not Prosper.

Matt Stubbs' Dream : A Christmas Story. By M. G. PEARSE.

Michael Faraday. A Book for Boys.

Our Lord's Public Ministry.

Risen Saviour (The).

St. Paul (Life of).

Seed for Waste Corners. By Rev. B. SMITH.

Sorrow on the Sea; or, the Loss of the *Amazon*.

Street (A) I've Lived in. A Sabbath Morning Scene.

Three Naturalists: Stories of Linnæus, Cuvier, and Buffon.

Young Maid-Servants (A Book for). Gilt Edges.

PRICE FOURPENCE. *Enamelled Covers.*

Precious Seed, and Little Sowers.

Spoiling the Vines.

Rhoda, and Fire in the Soul.

The Fatherly Guide, and Fortune Telling.

Will Brown; or, Saved at the Eleventh Hour.

Ancass, the Slave Preacher. By the Rev. H. BUNTING.

Bernard Palissy, the Huguenot Potter.

The Story of Martin Luther. By Rev. J. B. NORTON.

Little Nan's Victory.

The whole of the thirty-three books in the Crown Series at Sixpence are sold in Enamelled Covers at FOURPENCE each.

PRICE THREEPENCE. *Enamelled Covers.*

'The Ants' and 'The Conies.'

Concerning Play.

'The Kingly Breaker' and 'Sowing the Seed.'

'The Locusts' and 'The Spiders.'

Hattie and Nancy.

Michael Faraday.

John Bunyan. By E. M. C.

Three Naturalists: Stories of Linnæus, Cuvier, and Buffon.

Celestine; or, the Blind Woman of the Pastures.

Held Down; or, Why James didn't Prosper. By Rev. B. SMITH.

The Good Sea Captain. Life of Captain Robert Steward.

PRICE TWOPENCE. *Enamelled Covers.*

1. The Sun of Righteousness.
2. The Light of the World.
3. The Bright and Morning Star.
4. Jesus the Saviour.
5. Jesus the Way.
6. Jesus the Truth.
7. Jesus the Life.
8. Jesus the Vine.
9. The Plant of Renown.
10. Jesus the Shield.
11. Being and Doing Good. By the Rev. J. COLWELL.
12. Jessie Allen's Question.
13. Uncle John's Christmas Story.
14. The Pastor and the Schoolmaster.
15. Laura Gaywood.

The above Twopenny Books are also sold in Packets.

Packet No. 1, containing Nos. 1 to 6, Price 1/-
Packet No. 2, containing Nos. 7 to 12, Price 1/-

PRICE ONE PENNY. *New Series. Royal 32mo. With Illustrations.*

1. The Woodman's Daughter. By LILLIE M.
2. The Young Pilgrim : the Story of Louis Jaulmes.
3. Isaac Watkin Lewis : a Life for the Little Ones. By MARK GUY PEARSE.
4. The History of a Green Silk Dress.
5. The Dutch Orphan : Story of John Harmsen.
6. Children Coming to Jesus. By Dr. CROOK.
7. Jesus Blessing the Children. By Dr. CROOK.
8. 'Under Her Wings.' By the Rev. T. CHAMPNESS.
9. 'The Scattered and Peeled Nation ': a Word to the Young about the Jews.
10. Jessie Morecambe and Her Playmates.
11. The City of Beautiful People.
12. Ethel and Lily's School Treat. By R. R.

The above twelve books are also sold in a Packet, price 1/-

NEW SERIES OF HALFPENNY BOOKS.

By MARK GUY PEARSE, LILLIE MONTFORT, RUTH ELLIOTT, and others. *Imperial 32mo. 16 pages. With Frontispiece.*

1. The New Scholar.
2. Is it beneath You?
3. James Elliott ; or, the Father's House.
4. Rosa's Christmas Invitations.
5. A Woman's Ornaments.
6. 'Things Seen and Things not Seen.'
7. Will you be the Last?
8. 'After That?'
9. Christmas; or, the Birthday of Jesus.
10. The School Festival.
11. John's Teachers.
12. Whose Yoke do You Wear?
13. The Sweet Name of Jesus.
14. My Name ; or, How shall I Know?
15. Annie's Conversion.
16. The Covenant Service.
17. The Chat in the Meadow.
18. The Wedding Garment.
19. 'Love Covereth all Sins.'
20. Is Lucy V—— Sincere?
21. He Saves the Lost.
22. The One Way.
23. Nora Grayson's Dream.
24. The Scripture Tickets.
25. 'Almost a Christian.'
26. 'Taken to Jesus.'
27. The New Year ; or, Where shall I Begin?
28. The Book of Remembrance.
29. 'Shall we Meet Beyond the River ?'
30. Found after Many Days.
31. Hugh Coventry's Thanksgiving.
32. Our Easter Hymn.
33. 'Eva's New Year's Gift.'
34. Noble Impulses.
35. Old Rosie. By MARK GUY PEARSE.
36. Nellie's Text Book.
37. How Dick Fell out of the Nest.
38. Dick's Kitten.
39. Why Dick Fell into the River.
40. What Dick Did with his Cake.
41. Dick's First Theft.
42. Dick's Revenge.
43. Alone on the Sea.
44. The Wonderful Lamp.
45. Not too Young to Understand.
46. Being a Missionary.
47. Willie Rowland's Decision.
48. 'Can it Mean Me?'
49. A Little Cake.
50. A Little Coat.
51. A Little Cloud.
52. The Two Brothers : Story of a Lie. By MARK GUY PEARSE.

The above Series are also sold in Packets.

Packet No. 1 contains Nos. 1 to 24. Price 1/-
Packet No. 2 contains Nos. 25 to 48. Price 1/-

LONDON:
T. WOOLMER, 2, CASTLE STREET, CITY ROAD, E.C.